CALL TO VALOR

GARY BECK

Excerpts from *Call to Valor* have appeared in these magazines:
The Smoking Poet, Atlantean Publications, Green Silk Journal, Underground Voices, Events Quarterly, Sugar Mule, Combat, The Moon Magazine, Pens on Fire, Blue Fog Journal, Coffee Cramp, and *Type AB+*

Cover design copyright © 2024 by Niki Lenhart
nikilen-designs.com

Published by Paper Angel Press
paperangelpress.com

ISBN 978-1-962538-87-9 (Trade Paperback)

FIRST EDITION

10 9 8 7 6 5 4 3 2 1

To Robert,
whose efforts and intelligence have helped sustain me.

CALL TO VALOR

1

D OCTOR WILLIAM TECUMSEH CARVER, Carv to his friends, didn't completely conceal the annoyance he was feeling with his senior staff. At 6'6" and 235 pounds, he was still close to his playing weight in college, where he had wisely used his basketball ability on scholarship to develop a more important ability. He was very black, very big and could be intimidating in the confines of the conference room.

"Ladies and gentlemen. I shouldn't have to remind you that United Nations Day next Monday will be a major celebration for the Euro-Arab coalition. Since it falls toward the end of October, it's right after the beginning of Ramadan. When our foreign guests, particularly those of the Arab persuasion, visit us in Bellevue Enclave, you will all maintain correct decorum, no matter what the provocation."

"Chief?"

"Yes, Doctor Yi?"

The petite woman's huge, dark eyes fastened on him accusingly. "You told the female doctors that they didn't have to attend, which would spare them the sexual abuse they get from the Arabs."

"That's right. I did. But the Enclave Manager insisted that all staff physicians must be present."

There were murmurs of discontent from the female doctors, who made up more than a third of the medical staff.

"Shouldn't we be allowed to say no to their sexual aggressiveness?" Doctor Yi asked.

A helpless look flashed momentarily across Doctor Carver's normally stoic face. "I wish we could, Mei, but it's not my call. All the other department heads agreed with the manager that there will be no complaints, and cardiology has to go along. I got a letter of rebuke from the Deputy U.N. Undersecretary for American Affairs, warning us not to repeat last year's insults, even though I wasn't in charge then. He complained that most of you wore old rags on your heads, which outraged the Arabs. He threatened to revoke our accreditation if there were any more incidents. Do I make myself clear?"

There was a general response of, "Yes, Chief."

"Good. It's time for some of you to accept the fact that we don't have certain rights anymore, except those allowed by the U.N. If they didn't need our medical expertise, we'd probably all be in a poverty zone."

There was a tense silence as the doctors digested his harsh warning.

"How long can we go on like this?" Doctor Yi asked. "This makes me yearn for the tyranny of the HMO's."

"I don't know, Mei," Carver answered. "But we don't have much choice."

"I heard a rumor that the Army is secretly recruiting again, somewhere in Wyoming or the Dakotas, and they'll support a government that will protect its people," one of the doctors announced.

"I heard that the Saudi ambassador pinched President Beaumont's breast at a state dinner, and she didn't do anything," another chimed in.

"What could she have done?" Carver demanded.

"She could have knocked his hand away, or poisoned his camel, or at least done something."

"She's as powerless as we are," Carver replied.

"It's her fault we're in such a mess," the same doctor retorted bitterly. "If she didn't back down everywhere, we might still have a country that could defend us."

"This is neither the time nor the place for political discussions," Carver said with finality, ending the conversation. "It's time for rounds."

Dr. Carver led the staff that now included residents, interns and nurses to the wards. They started with the veterans they had accepted when the U.N. evicted most of the patients from the Veteran's Administration Hospital on First Avenue, except the Marines. As per U.N. instructions, these patients received minimal attention, which galled Carver. They went on to the lower-level dependants of Enclave personnel. Then they worked their way up to the higher ranks of celebrities and important Americans. They saved foreign dignitaries for last, since the foreigners generally condescended to the very people who were saving their lives.

When they finished, Carver led them to the Veteran's Hospital to examine the Arab veterans and Saudi exiles. Carver paused as they reached the door of the private ward that some staffers deridingly called the 'pasha pit'. It was named for the twenty odd princes of the former ruling house of Saud, who were avoiding extradition by pretending to be ill. The doctors silently suffered the indignity of electronic search by the Saudi guards, who paid special attention to the female doctors, who were forced to submit to the intrusions on their persons and mask their resentment.

As they waited for admission, Carver recalled the events that led to the sudden fall of the House of Saud. After years of the royals paying Islamic fundamentalists to practice terrorism anywhere but in Saudi Arabia, the oil wells started to run dry, and they couldn't afford to buy the extremists off anymore. With incredible swiftness and efficiency, which indicated long term preparation, terrorists bombed the remaining producing wells. This led to the immediate loss of funds to pay the soldiers of the National Guard, the bulwark of the House of Saud, who disappeared overnight. American troops tried to save the kingdom, but the leadership faltered, then abruptly fled, leaving everyone else to their fate. Thousands of princes, spoiled by years of huge allowances and worldly indulgences, were captured before they could escape. After a sham trial, they were beheaded in the Riyadh soccer stadium in the biggest public execution spectacle in the history of Islam, shown live and in color all over the world, courtesy of Al Jazeera TV.

The ward door opened, ending Carver's musing. His entourage followed him into the luxurious penthouse quarters, and he proceeded with the pro forma examination of one of the few groups of princes who escaped the bloodbath of Riyadh. He didn't understand how they managed to get sanctuary from the great Satan that they had tried so hard to undermine. He assumed that it was another instance of convoluted U.N. policy that was so often slanted against America, but it didn't stop them from taking advantage of the republic's generosity. He greeted the princes courteously, never forgetting to maintain a professional attitude with his pseudo-patients, no matter how much he disliked them. The prince who had been selected for this day's token examination carried on a monologue in Arabic, while Carver applied his stethoscope. There was no doubt that he was insulting the doctor, judging by the smirks from his fellow princes.

Carver ignored the rudeness, thinking instead about his recent appointment as head of the cardiology department. The unexpected elevation, which he wasn't allowed to refuse, compelled him to be a politician and severely limited his time for his duties to his patients. He consoled himself with the thought that he was at least able to practice his profession.

He still had a modicum of freedom, unlike lawyers, who had been banned from holding government office and were mostly restricted to clerical jobs. This was the result of strong public reaction after their endless lawsuits significantly contributed to the collapse of the American economy. Despite all the novels glorifying lawyers as heroes, the public finally realized that they were being leeched by greedy parasites. Like many doctors, he blamed the lawyers for the outrageous malpractice suits that had disrupted the medical profession.

He finished his distasteful chore, nodded to the haughty princes and gestured to his staff that they were leaving. They went back to the cardiology department's main conference room and reviewed the results of morning rounds.

After the last case was presented, Carver addressed the group. "My recent appointment as department head came as a surprise to some of you. I know we haven't had much time to get to know each other in these new circumstances, so let's keep things simple for the moment. Perform your duties properly and give me your loyalty, and I'll look out for you to the best of my ability. There should be no doubt that my appointment was political.

"When the New York University medical division agreed to join the Bellevue Enclave one of the stipulations was that they would be the senior medical partners. The municipal hospital doctors, regardless of where they studied and trained, would be junior. Being an N.Y.U.'er is one of the main reasons for my appointment, but I assure you that I'll treat all of you fairly. As you know, our proximity to the U.N. makes us their medical service station, so we must satisfy their needs, regardless of our personal feelings. I hope we understand each other … By the way. All senior physicians are invited to a Kobe steak dinner Wednesday night at my house." Then he grinned disarmingly. "Attendance is compulsory."

After the meeting, Carver walked the short distance to the townhouse on east 37th street that was one of the perks of being a department head. His fifteen-year-old daughter, Mavis, was watching Al Jazeera when he walked into the living room. As usual, he couldn't help feeling amazed at her uncanny resemblance to her deceased mother, who died in the great flu epidemic of 2013, along with their two other daughters, when the country ran out of vaccine and the U.N. refused to approve vaccine donations. Mavis was as dark-skinned as her father, an athletic 5'11", and distinctly sexually developed. She even sounded like her mother.

"What are you doing home so early, Dad? Playing hooky?"

"Very funny. I just wanted to see if the place was presentable. The doctors on my staff are joining us for a Kobe steak dinner Wednesday night."

"I'm glad you didn't wait until the last minute to tell me," she said, hands on hips, with that look of exasperation that daughters reserve especially for fathers.

"Sorry, Mav."

"That's alright, Dad," she said matter of factly. "How many?"

"Fourteen."

She thought quickly. "I'll call the commissary for what we'll need and arrange for more help in the kitchen and for serving."

"Thanks, Mav. We'll go into details later."

When they finished lunch Carver walked back to the hospital, confident that Mavis would be a capable hostess. He wondered for a moment if he was letting too many responsibilities fall on her young shoulders, then dismissed the thought, reassured by her competence.

He went to his office, summoned his secretary, Ms. Bellini, and Ronnie, his personal assistant, and reviewed the preparations for U.N. Day. They made a priority list for what still had to be done and set goals for what they hoped to accomplish for their political agenda during the various ceremonies and meetings. His assistant reminded him that the Enclave manager had stressed the need to lobby the U.N. Energy Commissioner for an increase in their power allocation.

"How do I do that, Ronnie?" he asked plaintively. "I don't know anything about power needs."

"Don't worry, Chief. Just tell him that the new MRI equipment requires more power," she explained. "And that is the equipment that will help save our U.N. patient's lives."

He shook his head in frustration, knowing how awkward he generally was in social situations, especially when there were important consequences at stake. Social skills were not crucial at the Bellevue Enclave, which had run from east 25th street to east 30th street, and from First Avenue to Second Avenue. When N.Y.U. joined the Enclave, it was expanded from 23rd street to 40th street, and from First Avenue to Fifth Avenue. This made them direct neighbors of the U.N.

They were now the closest American service center to the U.N., with new obligations and responsibilities. His appointment as a department head signaled other changes. At N.Y.U.'s insistence, a company of Marines was requested to back up the private guard force that provided security in the Enclave. This created ongoing tensions between the two groups. The employees of Guardwell were poorly paid and resented the well-disciplined Marines, who in turn despised the barely trained rental cops. This was one more complication for Carver in running his high-profile office, which required him to be a tightrope walker, always feeling on the verge of falling.

He shook off his doubts and resumed the review of preparations for U.N. Day. First there would be a morning ceremony in Madison Square Park, honoring the Euro-Arab freedom fighter volunteers who gave their lives to free Saudi Arabia from the American aggressors. Then there would be a visit by heads of state to the Veterans Hospital on First Avenue, to decorate the crippled Arab soldiers who helped drive out the American crusaders. The formal luncheon given by the victorious Arab nations would take place at the former Armenian church on east 34th street, that had been ceded to the U.N. and converted to a mosque. Then there would be the Parade of Nations, with troops and delegations from the victorious nations that had defeated the United States, marching from 23rd street up Fifth Avenue, to 42nd street, then east to the U.N. Events of the day would conclude with a Nations for Peace rally, designed to remind Americans how much they had offended the world. He could just imagine the anti-American venom that would pour out, but attendance was mandatory.

2

"TEN … HUT," Gunnery Sergeant Hanson ordered in a firm, confident voice. He ran his eyes over the starting-to-fray full-dress uniforms of the honor guard platoon. One Marine, an upstate New York redneck, hadn't snapped to attention as smartly as the others and his uniform wasn't neatly pressed. "Wilkins. Why are you once again the only Marine who isn't properly turned out?" Hanson asked, with a tinge of exasperation.

"By the time it was my turn to use the iron, Gunny, we had another brownout," Wilkins whined.

"Do you always have to be last? "

"It's not my fault, Gunny. It just works out that way."

"Then you're assigned outside rear-door duty."

"Aw, Gunny. It's cold out there."

"Next time be prepared."

"Aw, Gunny. What difference does it make? The docs and them U.N. bigwigs'll never notice us, and I'll be dead before things get better."

"United Nations Day is going to be a big event," Hanson said, "whether we like it or not. When the troubles are over, we'll have our own holidays again …"

"The snail'll even be late for his own funeral, Gunny," someone in the formation yelled, and the men and women cracked up with laughter.

"Silence in the ranks," Hanson ordered, with a hint of a smile. "Don't forget that Bellevue Enclave is a good duty station. Now, squad leaders take over. Dismissed."

Hanson watched them move out to change into camis, the uniform of the day, before going to their posts. Staff Sergeant Jed Davis joined him. Davis was a tall, powerfully built, light-skinned African-American from Georgia, who chose the Marines over primitive cotton farming by hand. He became one of Hanson's most trusted enlisted members of his battalion during the bloody retreat from Riyadh, in 2014.

"Why do you tolerate that clown, Sam?"

Hanson, a lean, taut-muscled six footer, with black hair, cold blue eyes that had already seen it all and a controlled expression on his sharply chiseled face, smiled warmly.

"He's a fighter when the time comes, and he keeps the boys and girls diverted from some of their troubles. If he crosses the line, I'll remind him gently."

They grinned at each other in appreciation of the understatement. A troubled look crossed his friend's face.

"What if he's right, Sam? What if things get worse?"

"We survived the desert, Jed. It can't get worse than that. I'll see you later. I've got to report to Captain Beasley."

"Him."

"Yes, him."

"Is he still brown-nosing the docs?"

"Later, Jed."

Hanson went to Captain Beasley's office and his clerk, a young, bright looking Sergeant named Danowski, announced him. He heard the click of a bottle being put away, then a high-pitched voice called, "Enter."

He stood in front of his commanding officer's desk without showing a hint of the contempt he felt. Beasley was a short, over-age, well-fed officer who bulged out of places in his uniform that were not intended by design. He always had a sly, sneering expression on his small, chipmunk-featured face, except with his superiors.

"Is everything ready for U.N. Day, Hanson?"

"Yes, sir."

"Well?"

"Well, what, sir?"

"Details, man. Details."

"What would the captain like to know?"

"Don't give me that high and mighty attitude. Just because you were an officer once, doesn't mean you can forget your place now. I know about your being reduced to the ranks for disobeying orders."

"Yes, sir."

"Is that all you have to say?"

"Yes, sir."

"Well in that case, since I have a few moments, I'd like to hear your side of the story."

"I'd rather not, sir."

"That's an order, Sergeant."

Hanson suppressed the urge to smack his over-stuffed face. He knew that Beasley ached to get him dismissed from the service and striking a superior officer would give him an excuse. Beasley belied the adage, 'Every Marine a rifleman'. He had deeply embedded himself in food services and had always managed to avoid discomfort, until he was assigned to command the Bellevue Enclave detachment. He resented Hanson's confidence and competence and hated him because he was dependent on the ex-officer.

"Speak," Beasley ordered.

Hanson ignored the tone of the degrading command and reluctantly started.

"When President Beaumont signed the truce of Amman, she ordered all the troops in the field to surrender." Memories of that shameful time flooded his mind as he remembered the predicament their orders had forced on them. "We knew the Arabs were butchering and beheading our men and raping and mutilating our women, but the Army obeyed, even though she was condemning them to torture and death."

Beasley smirked at him. "So, you chose to disobey a presidential order."

The words poured out of Hanson. "She should have been tried and shot for abandoning our troops."

Beasley shook his head smugly. "All our allies had deserted us. We were retreating everywhere. Korea, Europe, Afghanistan, Columbia. The economy was a shambles. We didn't have the funds, equipment or supplies to resist anymore."

"I know that. But she had an obligation to the troops to bring them home safely," Hanson insisted.

"She made a political decision," Beasley said admiringly. "That took guts."

Hanson stared at him in amazement. "She betrayed us. Marines aren't sheep to be slaughtered like dumb beasts."

"So, you led your battalion into the desert. Who did you think you were, Moses?"

Hanson ignored the sarcasm. "I knew the Arabs wouldn't honor the Geneva Convention and I wasn't about to let my good men and women get massacred. So we fought our way across the Au Nafud desert, until we finally reached the Red Sea. We commandeered a small freighter and sailed to Eritrea. When we disembarked at Asmera there were three hundred and forty-five survivors left, out of a battalion of six hundred, but we brought our dead and wounded with us. If we had obeyed the president, we'd all be dead."

Beasley stared at him resentfully. "I guess you thought you were some kind of hero?"

"No. I was fulfilling my obligation to the men and women in my command."

The intercom buzzed and Beasley snapped at his clerk for interrupting, then switched to the unctuous voice reserved for his superiors.

"Captain Beasley here, Doctor." He listened respectfully, then said, "Yes, sir," and hung up.

"I have to see Doctor Carver immediately," he announced pompously. "We'll continue this discussion another time. Dismissed."

Hanson turned and left without revealing the rage he was feeling. It took him a few minutes to calm down, but then he consoled himself that Beasley would get his comeuppance someday, either because of his gross incompetence, or for not licking Carver's boots sufficiently. He had to smile when he pictured Beasley fawning over the doctor, or any other authority figure, trying to ingratiate himself so his complete lack of ability would remain undiscovered. The thought of Beasley roasting on a spit while Carver took his temperature rectally partially restored his good spirits.

Hanson did a quick swing around the hospital complex to make sure the guardposts were properly manned. When he was satisfied that even Wilkins was alert, he walked across First Avenue to the apartment building where he had his quarters. The private security guard, Greg, nodded politely and opened the door.

When Hanson first moved in with his sixteen-year-old son, Kyle, the guard had been really unpleasant. He was resentful that Hanson had a spacious apartment, nastily remarking that the three-bedroom apartment was supposed to be for a large family. Hanson didn't know that the Guardwell security men and their families were quartered in small apartments, in buildings that were once public housing. He tried to explain that the apartment was assigned to him, but it didn't make a difference. He finally ran out of patience and took him aside and offered to rearrange certain body parts gratis. After that, Greg was on his best behavior, even with Kyle.

Other non-commissioned officers from Hanson's company lived in the building and Hanson was seriously considering having Marines guard the premises instead of the private security force, who were less than diligent in carrying out their duties. The only problem was Captain Beasley, who would automatically oppose any request of Hanson's. Hanson decided to make friends with Dr. Carver. Once that was accomplished, he would have him suggest to Beasley that a Marine detail guard their building. Until then, he regularly took the building security staff to the PX for bargain shopping. In return they kept an eye on Kyle. Except for Jed and his other close friend, Staff Sergeant Alexandra Kent, no one knew how much he loved his son and how much he worried about him.

Ever since Hanson's wife, Celia, and his older son, Warren, died in the great flu epidemic of 2013, Kyle started showing a wild streak. If an incident came to the attention of Beasley, always alert for a chance to get Hanson, he would send for the boy and give him an insulting lecture, hoping to provoke his father.

Kyle had been a bright, outgoing boy, until the death of his mother and brother. The closing of the United States military academies, as stipulated in the Treaty of Tehran in 2015, dashed Kyle's hope of going to Annapolis and becoming a Marine officer. He became morose and lost interest in school and other activities.

Hanson wasn't sure how he felt about Kyle's desire to be a Marine, especially in this time of degradation of America's military, but he respected his right to choose. In desperation, after a year went by without much improvement, Hanson asked Jed to start a karate class and get Kyle to participate. It had worked out well so far. Kyle was going to the class three or four nights a week and showed a renewed interest in his schoolwork. He even rejoined the Marine soccer team that played on Saturday mornings and seemed to be enjoying himself.

Hanson's military duties frequently compelled him to be on call around the clock, so he snatched any opportunity to spend a few extra minutes with his son.

"Hi, Kyle."

"Hi, Dad."

Hanson noticed that Kyle quickly blanked the screen of his computer.

"What was on the screen, son?"

"Just an old video game, Dad," Kyle responded vaguely.

"You know we're not allowed to have computer or video war games anymore," Hanson remarked. "According to the Congress of Tehran, war games stimulate American aggression and are therefore banned."

"I know, Dad, but I'm not online. No one can monitor what I'm doing."

"Don't be so sure. The occupying powers have sophisticated monitoring capabilities, especially this close to the U.N. They hate the Marines more than anyone else and they'd love to use you to get at me and the company."

Kyle stiffened in anger. "How long are they going to regulate everything we do?"

"Until we can change things. You have to be patient, son."

"I know, Dad … I was just studying an urban warfare tape that's really instructive. You know I still want to be a Marine officer."

"I know, son. We just have to be careful."

"Do you think they'll let us open Annapolis again?"

"I hope so. In the meantime, you might want to consider becoming a doctor. These days they seem to be the only ones with any privileges."

"I want to be a Marine," Kyle insisted.

"Even if you can't be an officer?"

A bitter look flitted across Kyle's face, but he answered resolutely, "Yes, Dad."

Hanson impulsively hugged his son. "We'll see what we can do. In the meantime, meet me for dinner at the mess hall at 1800 hours."

"Aye, aye, sir."

"You don't call N.C.O.'s sir."

"I know, sir."

They smiled at each other for a special moment, then Hanson nodded goodbye and left for the hospital complex.

3

CAPTAIN BEASLEY WAITED in Dr. Carver's outer office, shifting nervously under the disapproving gaze of his secretary, Ms. Bellini. She reminded him of his high school principal, Ms. Digney, who had seemed pleased when she informed him that he wasn't college material. When no other options had presented themselves, he obtained admission to Brooklyn College by joining the Reserve Officers Training Corps. The Army, Air Force and Navy quotas were filled, so he joined the Marine R.O.T.C. He knew he wasn't a warrior, but the recruiter assured him that there were alternatives to combat roles and suggested a career in transportation or supply services.

Beasley graduated college with the lowest grade point average that passed. He barely made it through Officer's Basic school but found his niche in food services and was happy, until he was assigned to command a line company in the Bellevue Enclave. He was still bewildered as to why he had been selected, considering his complete lack of qualifications, and was terrified of failure to carry out his assignment.

"You can go in now," Ms. Bellini said, breaking his reverie.

Beasley went in and stood at attention, while Carver looked at him doubtfully. In the short time that Carver had been chief of cardiology, he already realized that Hanson was responsible for the efficient functioning of the Marine force. He hadn't figured out yet how to bypass Beasley and deal directly with Hanson.

"I want to review our plans for U.N. Day. Before we begin, are there any problems I should be aware of?"

"No, sir. Everything is under control."

"Good. I'm particularly concerned with the luncheon arrangements. I understand you have a food services background?"

"Yes, sir."

"In that case, I'd like you to liaison with the U.N. staff. Do you have someone who can take charge of security in your absence?"

Beasley thought quickly but couldn't find an acceptable alternative.

"Yes, sir. Gunnery Sergeant Hanson."

"Have him call my secretary and make an appointment for this afternoon."

"Yes, sir. Will there be anything else?"

"No. Thanks for coming."

"You're welcome, sir."

Beasley fumed all the way back to his office. He only calmed down after a second drink from the bottle of rye he kept in his desk. He gruffly ordered his clerk to locate Hanson and have him report to his office immediately. He wallowed in self-pity for a few minutes, wondering how he was expected to run a Marine company without any officers. He knew that the Treaty of Damascus had reduced the United States officer corps by ninety percent but couldn't help thinking how unfair it was to be burdened with Hanson, even though he realized he would be helpless without him.

He knew he didn't have a future in civilian life, so he had to make a go of it in the Corps. His fantasy of eventually owning his own restaurant in sunny southern California had evaporated with the collapse of the American hegemony. Like every paranoid American, he heard the rumors that Mexico was plotting to repossess part of California, along with whatever slices of Texas, New Mexico and Arizona could be snatched. He shook his head, dismissing the threat to dismember a good portion of America as being secondary to his own problems.

His clerk buzzed on the intercom, bringing him back to the problem at hand.

"Gunnery Sergeant Hanson is here, sir," Danowski announced.

"Send him in."

Hanson entered and stood at ease, without waiting for the order. Beasley suppressed his irritation with the casualness.

"I've decided to put you in charge of security for U.N. Day. You'll review arrangements with Dr. Carver. Call his secretary and make an appointment for this afternoon. Dismissed."

Hanson walked out without saying a word. On the way back to his office he considered how to better get to know Carver. He didn't know the man at all, so he decided to wait and see how things developed. He couldn't help smiling about the coincidence of being able to meet him so soon after he decided that Carver was an important part of his plans.

Hanson made an appointment to see Carver at 1300 hours, then went to the mess hall for lunch. Afterwards, he stopped at the enlisted personnel's barracks, on the second floor of the leaky, dilapidated old brick monstrosity on First Avenue and 30th street, that was the Marine headquarters, and looked like a prison, or public school. Rumor had it that the building, once a psychiatric hospital, used to house the homeless, until they and the rest of the local poverty population were evicted from the Bellevue Enclave. The only remaining undesirables still in the Enclave were the hard-core homeless who lived in the closed east side subway like tunnel rats, or as migrants in the sewer system, nicknamed prairie dogs, for the way they suddenly popped up unexpectedly, P Dogs for short.

When the Marines first took charge of security in the Enclave, the manager ordered them to eliminate the P Dogs and tunnel rats. Beasley was about to accept the mission, when Hanson pointed out that they didn't have the personnel to do underground sweeps and maintain Enclave security. This didn't add to his popularity. The assignment was given to the Guardwell security force, who gleefully set out like they were going on a scavenger hunt but came back with smelly uniforms and scraped shins.

As usual, the barracks were as clean as Marines could make them. One of the Marines, a former roofer's assistant, realized that it was way beyond their meager resources to fix the leaky roof. He scrounged plastic drop cloths and lined the top floor of the building with the plastic sheeting to keep the water from coming downstairs. Then he cleverly rigged a drain system with some discarded plumbing pipes to let the water run off outside the building.

Fortunately, they had a portable generator that provided air conditioning or heat, as well as removing the excess moisture in the air. This was one of the many benefits of Enclave duty. All things considered, the barracks were reasonably comfortable for the unmarried personnel, who were a lot better off than most of the remaining Corps troops, who were still housed in tents, in hard duty stations.

Staff Sergeant Alexandra Kent, another veteran of the Riyadh retreat, and Iraq and Afghanistan before that, was 5'9", 145 lbs, blonde, blue-eyed, with features that seemed plain, until looked at closely. Then she became an attractive woman, besides being a tough, no-nonsense Marine. Among the many debts she owed Hanson, foremost was his saving her life in an insurgent ambush in Falluja, another was for getting her a one-bedroom apartment in the N.C.O. family building, even though she was single. She was leading a weapons-cleaning exercise when Hanson greeted her.

"Hi, Al."

"Hi, Major. How are you?"

"It's Gunnery Sergeant."

"Yes, sir."

Like many of the vets who had been through three battle zones with him, she continued to call him by his previous rank. Despite all Hanson's efforts to stop the practice, which infuriated Beasley when he heard it, some of the old hands continued to address him that way in front of others. Hanson observed the stripping of the M 16's and their reassembly without comment. He admired the way Al handled her platoon. She never got angry or impatient and always stressed the need for constant alertness. She had learned its necessity so painfully in the streets of Falluja in 2004, where the Marines mastered the dangerous craft of urban warfare, hard-earned knowledge paid for with the blood of many good Marines.

When the exercise concluded he took her aside.

"I've been put in charge of security for U.N. Day. I'm meeting with Dr. Carver for official confirmation at 1300. I should be finished by 1400, when I want to inspect the perimeter of the Enclave with you and Jed. I'll call you if I'm running late."

"Yes, sir."

"Don't call me sir, Al."

She looked around and made sure no one else could hear her. "We respect the man, Sam, not the rank."

He put his hand jokingly on his holster. "Don't make me shoot you for insubordination."

"I doubt that you could hit me," she teased. "When was the last time you fired that club, Sam?"

He grinned triumphantly. "Three nights ago. I won twenty euros off a would-be hotshot on the Guardwell force."

She shook her head disbelievingly. "That's not what I heard."

He didn't take the bait. "Catch you later, Al."

•   •   •

Ms. Bellini ushered him into Dr. Carver's office as soon as he arrived. Carver greeted him with an outstretched hand.

"I've been looking forward to meeting you, Mister Hanson."

"The same here, sir. And it's Gunnery Sergeant Hanson."

"I've read your file and talked to General Griffin about you. He told me you were one of the most outstanding officers in the Corps. He said you were on the fast promotion list for Lieutenant Colonel when the incident at Riyadh occurred. He confided that the Commandant wanted to promote you and award you the Medal of Honor, but President Beaumont wanted you court-martialed and dismissed from the service. A lot of influential people went to bat for you and arranged a compromise. How do you feel about that? Are you bitter?"

"No, sir. I'm still alive. I'm still in the Corps, and hopefully I'll be able to contribute something to the rebuilding of our country."

Carver stared at him appraisingly and liked what he saw. "I didn't have a lot of confidence in Captain Beasley, so I arranged to put you in charge of security for U.N. Day." He paused for a moment, then asked suddenly, "How do you feel about Captain Beasley's qualifications for command?"

"He's my commanding officer. It would be inappropriate for me to discuss him. It's my duty to assist him to the best of my ability."

"So you're loyal?"

"It's the way I was brought up. The Corps only reinforced it."

Carver nodded. "I like that. I was brought up the same way. Now that I'm a department head it's all political and things have changed. How do you maintain your loyalties?"

Hanson looked at him fiercely. "I took an oath to support the Constitution of the United States, not individuals. I deal with everything else as best I can."

Carver sighed. "You're my kind of man. It's too bad that the current political climate will prevent us from getting to know each other socially. I've been requested to maintain my distance from enlisted Marine personnel. Maybe someday."

They were silent for a few moments, then Carver handed him a piece of paper.

"That's the agenda for U.N. Day. You know a lot more about security than I do. Review it, then get back to me with your recommendations."

"I'll have a plan for you by 0900 hours tomorrow."

"That's nine a.m. my time, right?"

They smiled companionably at each other.

"There are several items I'd like to bring up, sir."

"What are they?"

"There should be a decision about whether the Marines or Guardwell should be in charge of security, otherwise there might be disputes over authority."

"Do you think Guardwell is qualified to take charge?"

"No, sir."

"Neither do I. I'll have the manager and the other department heads inform them that you're in command."

"Yes, sir. The same situation applies to the police and National Guard."

"You're in charge. What's the other item?"

"I'd like to officially assign Marines to guard the non-commissioned officer's building."

"Did Captain Beasley suggest this?"

"No, sir."

"Why don't you go to him?"

"He may have other priorities."

Carver got the hint. "I see. I'll send him a memo of request. Anything else?"

"No, sir."

"Then I'll see you at 0900."

4

H ANSON WALKED to the barracks, picked up Al and Jed, then they went to his office. He outlined some of their responsibilities for the events of U.N. Day.

"The morning ceremony in Madison Square Park will require a security check of the buildings surrounding the park. We wouldn't want snipers to interrupt our former enemies while they're busy reviling us. Monitoring the crowd will be difficult, but the police will be a big help. The Veteran's Hospital visit will be easy. Just make sure your troops stay cool when the Arabs insult them.

"The lunch at the mosque should be a snap. Tell your troops to stay alert for Armenian suicide bombers who want to blow up the mosque that was once their church. The only event I'm worried about is the parade. I'll assign the police to check all the buildings on the route and they'll have National Guard troops with them for insurance. Once the parade passes 40th street, it's no longer our jurisdiction, although if anything happens, I'm sure we'll be blamed."

Al looked at Jed and winked. "What do you think will happen if some of the Arab bigwigs get snuffed during a counter demonstration?"

Hanson pretended to consider the question. "I guess we'll have a court martial for the platoon leaders, then shoot them for dereliction of duty."

"That's not fair," Jed protested. "The company commander should be the only one who gets shot."

"Seriously, folks. Let's make sure nobody gets shot on our watch. Now I'd like to inspect the entire perimeter of the Enclave, then check the sites of the event. We'll look over the parade route last. We'll take my Hummer and have plenty of time to discuss things as we go. Take notes and make sketches when necessary and feel free to speak up if you see anything that'll give us a problem. This is the first time in a while that the Arabs will be seeing their old friends, the Marines. Let's make sure the day goes off without a hitch. Questions?"

"Full combat loads?" Al asked.

"Yes. Just make sure no one gets trigger happy. Now let's go."

It took more than three hours to inspect the entire Enclave perimeter. They started at 23rd street and the East River, where Hanson made a note to check on the yacht basin and the seaplane base. Jed pointed out the outdoor swimming pool in Asser Levy Park. "Maybe we can swim there in the spring, when the weather gets warm, huh, Sam?"

"That's a long way off," Hanson replied.

"I bet Al would look great in a thong," Jed murmured suggestively.

"In your dreams," she teased.

"Alright, kiddies. Knock it off. Now list every building that has to be secured."

"That's a lot of buildings, Sam," Jed commented. "We don't have the personnel to cover a fraction of them."

"We'll have the police and the National Guard. I know we should have at least a battalion, but we'll have to make do with what we have."

"Sure we will," Al said. "As long as there's no trouble."

They slowly drove west on 23rd street, until they got to Fifth Avenue. Virtually every building they passed was put on the list to be inspected and secured. They instantly saw that Madison Square Park was potentially a major problem. As well as the buildings on three sides of the park in the Enclave's jurisdiction, dozens of commercial loft buildings looked down on the park from the other side of Fifth Avenue. Hanson made a note to review the adjacent area with Carver and get whatever permission and assistance would be necessary to protect the event.

At Fifth Avenue and 40th street they turned east and went to the river, then came back to First Avenue and the hospital complex. He assigned Jed's platoon the vital task of securing subway entrances and exits in the Enclave. He assigned Al's platoon to secure the midtown tunnel openings and any outlets for the Pennsylvania Railroad Tunnel along 32nd and 33rd streets.

Hanson outlined a plan where two platoons would be stationed on the parade route, one on 23rd street, the other just outside Madison Square Park. As Jed and Al's platoons finished their tasks, they would detach squads and send them to the park.

"You're right about our needing at least a battalion to secure the Enclave," Al offered.

Hanson nodded. "A regiment, more likely. We'll have to rely extensively on police, National Guard, and Guardwell cooperation. I'll resolve that with Dr. Carver in the morning. Jed. Make sure our two remaining Strykers are operational. Al. Let me know how many SMAWs your platoon has."

"Are we expecting armor, Sam?".

"No. But shoulder held missiles'll be real useful if we have to take out a sniper in a window. Tomorrow we'll drive up and down every street in the Enclave and make sure we've covered everything. That's all for now. I'll see you later at the mess hall, where I intend to have dinner with my son."

•   •   •

Kyle's best friend, Tyrone, Jed's son, was seventeen, a year older than him, but they were in the same class in their senior year of high school. Tyrone was as light-skinned as his father and already almost as big. His handsome face had lost the innocence it once showed to the world after his mother and two older brothers died in the flu epidemic of 2014. Kyle and Tyrone had been friends since they first met at Camp Pendleton in 2003, when their fathers shipped out for the invasion of Iraq. They became closer when they shared the worry about their fathers during the retreat from Riyadh. The mutual loss of their mothers and siblings forged an inseparable bond that was never discussed, but deeply felt.

Tyrone knocked loudly on Kyle's door and yelled, "This is the cyberpolice. Open up."

Kyle couldn't help smiling as he shut off his computer. He grabbed his jacket and opened the door. "I hope you don't say that anywhere else. You might give the bluefish ideas."

"Is that how you refer to the fair and neutral U.N. Peacekeepers?" Tyrone teased.

"Neutral my ass. They're always against us."

"Let's get going," Tyrone urged. "I'm starving. We can discuss the bluefish after chow. Did you run this morning?"

"No."

"How about we run halfspeed up Second Avenue to 40th street, then down First Avenue to the mess hall?"

"Sounds good, Ty. Do you want to go to karate tonight?"

"Right on. I heard that some new honeys signed up for the beginner's class. We can check them out."

"Is that all you think about lately?"

Tyrone's face got the serious look that Kyle had gotten to know well. "I think about certain Arabs we know who I'd like to kill, but that's not practical right now."

•   •   •

The mess hall was cheerful and bustling after the dark and somber streets. Two factors combined to make the mess hall a bright spot in the tense lives of the Marines. First was the opening of the mess hall to family members during a time of shortages and uncertainty. Second was the absence of officers, since Captain Beasley ate in his office, which created a democratic illusion, even though Hanson was still treated with the utmost respect by military and civilian personnel alike.

The boys took trays, joined the line and moved from service station to station, until their trays were almost overflowing with tasty, nourishing food, another benefit of Enclave duty. They made their way to the senior N.C.O. table where they were warmly greeted by their fathers and friends. They both jostled for the empty chair next to Al, who they both had a crush on, and Tyrone grinned triumphantly when he outmaneuvered Kyle.

The conversation that had been going on paused for a few moments, then resumed with added intensity. "How do we deal with the bluefish if they threaten us?" Al asked. "I heard they pushed a lot of people around last year."

"We have to avoid an incident, no matter what the provocation," Hanson answered.

"What if they hit us?" Jed asked.

"Don't let it get to that point. I'm counting on the senior leadership to make sure there's no trouble. A lot of people will be watching us and most of them are not our friends. We can't allow any kind of disturbance to disrupt the day's events. Some of the guests will be Al Qaeda, or Iranians and you know how much they hate us. They'd love to have us moved out of the Enclave to an internment camp. Don't let anyone give them an excuse."

The meal concluded in silence as they digested the implications of what they would have to deal with in a few days. They finished eating, dumped their trays and left the mess hall in a group.

"What are you two mischief makers up to tonight?" Hanson asked.

"We're going to karate, Dad. I'll be home by 2200. Will you be there?"

"I'll try, son. If not, I'll see you in the morning and we can have breakfast together … By the way. Ask around at your dojo if there've been any P Dog sightings."

"Sure, Dad. See you later."

The two boys walked off and as soon as they were alone Tyrone turned to his friend. "So. Have you decided yet? Are you going to the doctor's Halloween Ball, or are you going to desert me and let me go alone?"

"I'd like to go, Ty, but I don't want to cause any problems for my dad."

"We'll be in costumes. We'll wear masks. Nobody'll know who we are. Trust me. It'll be dope. And there'll be lots of honeys. Maybe you'll get your M16 off at last."

Kyle laughed. "Alright. You convinced me."

●　　　●　　　●

Hanson, Jed, and Al went back to his office and discussed perimeter staffing for U.N. Day, and Hanson outlined his preliminary plan.

"Guardwell personnel will man the checkpoints on the East River Drive at 23rd street and 40th street with police back-up. They'll stop and inspect all traffic. They'll man the entire U.N. border on 40th street. Police will man the 40th street posts with the Guardwells, and we'll post two of our squads nearby for a rapid reaction force. Police and National Guard will line the parade route from start to finish. Al. Your platoon will be at Madison Avenue and 24th street, so you can monitor the park and cover 23rd street if necessary. Jed. Your platoon will be at Park Avenue and 34th street, so you'll cover the thirties. I'll command the honor guard …"

"No way, Sam," Jed interrupted, "That would give some Arab a chance to waste you while the others are shooting in the air."

"Alright," Hanson conceded, "I'll lead your platoon until you rejoin."

That settled, Hanson continued, "The honor guard will present the colors during the ceremony at Madison Square Park, then return to barracks, change into camis, and remain there as our ready reserve."

Al and Jed looked at Hanson in astonishment. "Aren't you going to send the honor guard to the Veteran's Hospital and the luncheon?" Al blurted.

"No, Al. I'm not going to let those Al Qaeda pigs abuse our men and women."

"That's inviting trouble," Jed remarked.

"No, Jed," Hanson explained patiently. "It's avoiding two flashpoints where there might be a confrontation. The park ceremony will be so public that the Arabs probably wouldn't start anything there. But we'd be too close to them at the V.A. Hospital, or the luncheon. That's where we'd have trouble with them. Now you two are the only ones who know the security arrangements. Don't say anything about this to anyone."

"Sure, Sam," Al replied.

"What about Beasley?" Jed asked.

"What about him? If he don't ask, I don't tell. He'll be too involved with the luncheon to know what's going on. Now can you think of anything I've overlooked?"

Al and Jed both said, "No."

"Then I'm out of here. We'll continue this in the morning, after I see Dr. Carver."

5

KYLE AND TYRONE FINISHED their workouts, showered, and at Tyrone's insistence, hung around until the beginner's class was over. Their attempts to flirt with the new 'honeys' met with a complete rebuff. The two girls they had targeted both turned out to be seventeen years old and the louder girl, Angie, condescendingly explained, "You boys are much too young for us. I'm dating a college senior and he's twenty-two. Tamika's boyfriend is a radiology technician and he's twenty-three. You better stick to fourteen-year-olds. You can take them for a ride on your skateboards."

The girls flounced off, laughing derisively at the boys, who they had effortlessly reduced to clumsy teenagers.

Tyrone turned to Kyle self-consciously. "Now don't say I told you so."

"Are you kidding?" Kyle responded. "So what if we got shot down. I admire your nerve and confidence. We'll try some other girls at the next class."

Tyrone beamed. "That's why you're my main man." He looked at his watch. "If we hurry, we can beat the 2200 curfew."

•   •   •

Mavis and her new best friend, Jennifer Van Meer, had finished their calculus homework and temporarily exhausted the topic of their costumes for the Halloween Ball and the exciting young men who would swarm them. They were relaxing for a few minutes before Jennifer had to go home.

Mavis remembered how they recently met at the introductory dinner for Dr. Carver, given by the other department heads to welcome his official appointment as head of cardiology. Mavis was used to important social functions, but she had never been to such a high-powered event. Medical department heads in the distressed condition of America now ranked even higher than the former heavy hitters of the military-industrial complex and politicians. Although she didn't understand all the nuances of her dad's new position, Mavis knew enough to realize that he was now a man of importance. She also knew that her behavior would reflect on him, so she was very careful to behave properly.

She had bowed to everyone she met, according to rank and station. Dozens of faces set in formal expressions blurred during the ritual of bow and smile, except Jennifer's. Her mischievous look was fleeting, but her wink was unmistakable. Mavis had to fight for self-control, or she might have burst into laughter, which would have profoundly offended Jennifer's father, Doctor Van Meer, the influential head of virology. He had an air of self-importance that hinted he wouldn't appreciate Mavis's frivolity.

Later, Mavis had a moment alone with Jennifer and took her to task.

"What did you think you were doing, girl? I almost laughed in your father's face."

"But you didn't. I wanted to find out right away if you were the right kind of material."

"What do you mean?"

"I needed to know if you were an upwardly mobile, capable American woman. I don't have time for ward scrubbers."

One part of Mavis verged on anger at Jennifer's blunt, elitist attitude, but the other part liked her refreshing directness and that part won out.

The two girls became as close as sisters, confiding almost all their secrets to each other. They quickly built an alliance that strengthened them in the lofty political world their fathers moved in. Jennifer was sixteen, only a year older than Mavis, but seemed more mature. She had bright red hair, green eyes, and a deceptively plain face that was lit up by the energy of her dynamic character. She was tall and slim, with a runner's body.

She was quite bright, although not as smart as Mavis, but unlike Mavis, she had a life plan. She was going to be a doctor, predetermined by her roots and training. She had already decided to be a radiologist since she would be able to control her work schedule. This would allow her time to fulfill her agenda of acquiring a suitable doctor husband and conceiving two doctor-to-be children. She was appalled by Mavis' casual attitude to the future.

"You have to get with it, kid," she urged Mavis. "This isn't the old days, when there was time to find yourself. The world's a difficult place for Americans now and I want the best life I can get. I strenuously suggest that you should want the same good things for yourself. We could become very important people some day and help each other."

Mavis didn't really disagree with Jennifer's way of thinking, she just resisted out of stubbornness. When she confessed that she still harbored fantasies of being a modern ballet dancer, Jennifer tried to give her a quick dose of reality.

"That would have been fine in the nineties, kid, when everybody wanted to be some kind of artist. These days, the arts don't play a very prominent role in America. The only work you'd probably get would be at one of those strip clubs, where you'd have to suck off the customers."

"Ooky … Have you ever been to one of those places?"

"No, silly. But I've heard some of the interns describe them. Believe me, it's not for you."

"But I love to dance. I can't give that up."

"Fine. Take class whenever you can, but don't forget your priorities. You can't let dance interfere with your preparations for medical school. Once your career is on track, you can give small performances for a select audience, if you feel like it."

"You're so sensible, Jen. I really appreciate that."

"Among your many fine qualities, kid, you're smart. You just have to grow up faster than you'd like."

•   •   •

It was after 2300 when Hanson got home, and a light was still on in Kyle's room. Hanson knocked on his door quietly, in case he was asleep.

"Kyle. Are you awake?" he whispered.

"Yes, Dad. Come in. I was just reading The Small Wars Manual, the one that was revised in '05."

"You know that's forbidden. Why can't you look at porn like normal teenagers? Where did you get it?"

"Some of the Marine kids in school who are seniors are interested in the military and circulate books and videos to guys they trust."

"You can get us into serious trouble if you're caught with contraband learning materials."

"Don't worry, Dad. We're very careful."

"Is Tyrone in this with you?"

"Is this just between us?"

"Yes, son."

"Then he is."

"Did he get you into it?"

"No, Dad. I got him involved."

Hanson shook his head. "I wish you'd think about becoming a doctor. That's the only secure future these days."

"That's not for me, Dad. You know what I want."

"There might not be a Marine Corps in the future."

Kyle was horrified. "Don't say that. There'll always be a Corps."

"I hope so. I've got to get some sleep. I love you, son."

"I love you, Dad."

•   •   •

Hanson was at the mess hall by 0630 and the senior mess sergeant, Carstairs, was pleased to cook bacon and eggs for him. Then he went to his office and finalized the security plan for U.N. Day. He got to Dr. Carver's office at 0855 and Carver didn't keep him waiting.

"Good morning, Major."

"Good morning, sir. And it's Gunnery Sergeant."

"We'll have to see what can be done about restoring your rank, once we get through the November elections."

"Then the rumor is true? The elections won't be canceled?"

"That's what we've been told. All medical department heads received a memo that said registered voters will be given bio sheets at the polls about the independent parties, from which they'll select their candidates."

"That doesn't give them much time to decide if they don't want to vote for a mainstream candidate," Hanson remarked.

"Do you think we can do worse than the last election?" Carver retorted.

Hanson grinned in response. "I may be personally prejudiced against her, but anyone could do a better job than Beaumont."

"I hope so. There'll be more than twenty candidates to choose from. But we'll talk about Election Day after U.N. Day. Right now, that's my priority."

Hanson unfolded a map of the Enclave and explained the security plan, step by step. He was pleasantly surprised by Carver's grasp of the situation.

"I think I picked the right man for the job," Carver said. "I had no idea how many potential problems there were."

"I'm glad you understand how complicated this could be. If everything goes according to plan, we should be able to successfully bring off all the events."

Carver frowned. "What could go wrong?"

"The police and National Guard could miss a sniper hiding out in one of the buildings. A suicider could drive into the park or the parade and detonate his car bomb ..."

"Holy shit," Carver exclaimed. "Is that possible?"

"I hope not. We're begging, borrowing, or stealing every security barrier we can find. I just don't know if we'll have enough to cover everywhere."

"How will you deal with that?"

"Top priority will be to barricade all access to Madison Square Park. After that, 23rd street, then Fifth Avenue, from 27th to 40th street."

They studied the map in silence for a few minutes, then Carver said, "I'm almost afraid to hear the other threats."

"The truth of the matter is we have very limited resources to do a difficult job," Hanson stated. "But we'll do our best with what we have."

"That's very reassuring. I'm sorry to add to your worries with a rumor."

"What is it, sir?"

"One of the ward nurses at the V.A. hospital told her supervisor she overheard the vets talking about making some kind of demonstration at the park. One of the vets noticed she was listening, and they stopped talking. She wasn't sure if they were serious but reported it anyway."

"I seem to remember that all of those guys are in wheelchairs," Hanson said, "but I'll alert everyone to keep a special eye out for them. My biggest worry is that some of those primitive Arabs will fire their Kalashnikovs in the air during the park ceremony. They never learn that whatever goes up, comes down."

"How do we prevent that?"

"You and the other department heads will have to discuss it with the U.N. liaison, but I don't think it'll do any good."

The thought of dozens of people being killed or wounded from indiscriminate shooting in the air by careless Arabs, dampened any feeling of satisfaction they might have gotten from their preparations. After they thoroughly covered everything on their agenda they arranged to meet on Friday, for a final review before the big day on Monday. Just before Hanson left, Carver again mentioned that he would look into getting Hanson's rank restored.

"That's very thoughtful of you, sir, but I don't think it will be practical. A lot of Arabs I once fought against are now in powerful positions at the U.N. They'll never forget what I did in Iraq and Saudi Arabia. To them I'm a symbol of American hegemony. The Euro-trash who turned against us wanted to try me in the World Court as a war criminal. I was lucky to escape indictment. Now that I'm in the Bellevue Enclave, I'm right next door to a lot of people who hate me. I think it's better if I keep a low profile. But I want you to know that I appreciate your good will. I'll see you Friday morning at 0900, sir."

Hanson returned to his usual duties. At lunchtime he let all of his platoon leaders know that there would be a surprise inspection in the morning. He knew the quality of his people, so he assumed that everything would be up to standard. He briefly thought about scheduling some special exercises that could fit possible scenarios they might confront on U.N. Day. After careful consideration, he realized that his people were experienced enough to deal with most urban situations. He knew that if he tried to prepare them for every eventuality the odds were probable that they'd miss the obvious. He did make a mental note to review all possible threats with his platoon leaders, no matter how far-fetched. They were tough and smart enough to come up with good ideas. At various times during the day, he couldn't help thinking about Carver's interest in restoring his rank. By now he was cynical enough to realize that it would benefit Carver somehow, but the possibility of being an officer again was unsettling. He dismissed it as fantasy, but the tantalizing thought kept creeping back into his mind, despite all his efforts to reject it.

6

H ANSON SPENT WEDNESDAY with Jed and Al, going up and down every street in the Enclave, investigating all possible danger spots. On Thursday, he toured the Enclave with the police precinct captain, Mike Lonigan, the senior Guardwell supervisor, Grant Browning, and the Colonel commanding the 69th regiment of the National Guard, Oliver Warrington. He expected some resistance to his authority from Captain Lonigan and Colonel Warrington, but it turned out that they both were familiar with his reputation. Guardwell's supervisor, Grant Browning, ex-paper pusher from the FBI, without any military or real law experience, turned out to be an obnoxious know-it-all, who kept challenging Hanson's decisions. Hanson was on the verge of losing his temper, when Captain Lonigan, a grizzled bear of a man who had seen New York City become at risk of resembling neo-Baghdad, glared at Browning.

"Will you please shut up. If you have any constructive suggestions, make them now. Otherwise, I don't want to hear from you."

They completed the inspection without further incidents and Hanson was careful to treat each of them with equal courtesy. Just before they got back to where they started from, Hanson told them bluntly,

"We need to set up a joint communications system, so we can stay in touch throughout the day and exchange information and instructions."

Captain Lonigan offered police radios and Colonel Warrington suggested walkie-talkies. Browning was still sulking and volunteered nothing. The three active participants decided that the police radios were the most practical choice for their needs. Captain Lonigan recommended that they wait until Monday morning to distribute the radios and assign the frequencies, in the best interests of security. Hanson and Colonel Warrington quickly agreed. When Colonel Warrington offered a room at the Armory for a communications center, Hanson and Lonigan promptly accepted. Hanson mentioned that he had designated a rapid reaction platoon for the day, in case of emergency and Colonel Warrington offered them the use of the Armory.

"I think the days of dogface and jarhead rivalry are over," Warrington said wistfully.

Hanson brought them back to where they left their vehicles at First Avenue and 31st street. As they got out of his hummer, he said goodbye to Captain Lonigan and Colonel Warrington with the feeling that they understood each other and were on the way to becoming friends. He also knew that he had a cooperation issue to resolve with the Guardwell man.

"I'd like to talk to you alone for a minute," he told him.

"What is it?" Browning snapped. "Are you going to threaten me like you threatened Greg?"

"No, sir," Hanson answered in surprise. "I just want to resolve any tension between us that might interfere with our responsibilities on Monday."

"I'm listening," Browning said frigidly.

Hanson ignored his hostility. "The Enclave Manager and the docs want to avoid anything on U.N. Day that could cause trouble for the Enclave. They put me in charge of security. If you have a problem with that, take it up with them. In the meantime, it's in Guardwell's best interests to cooperate. You don't want to jeopardize our efforts because of personal issues."

Browning nodded sulkily, then abruptly stalked off. Hanson filed him away in the slot of future problems to be dealt with, then proceeded to the barracks for the previously announced surprise inspection.

Despite the decayed condition of the building, the barracks were up to Marine standards. The weapons and personal equipment were immaculate. The camis were beginning to show some wear and tear, but there wasn't much they could do about replacements. The uniforms were manufactured in China, and since the Congress of Tehran, the Chinese communist leadership refused to ship anything to America, except consumer goods at a huge profit.

Hanson mused that an even bigger problem for the diminished and ill-equipped American military was China's lawsuit in the World Court for the lion's share of the United States Strategic Petroleum Reserve as part of the debt the U.S. owed them. If the court decided against the U.S., this would create dangerous shortages for the military, as well as inflicting tremendous cuts in heating oil and gasoline for the civilian population. To add abuse to injury, the Euro-Arab coalition was demanding that President Beaumont give them their share of the Strategic Petroleum Reserve as a war indemnity before she left office. Hanson shook his head to drive away the disturbing distractions that he was powerless to control. He dismissed the company after commending their good turnout.

Hanson met with his platoon leaders after lunch and informed them of the arrangements with the police and National Guard.

"I didn't hear you mention Guardwell," Al said.

"They don't like us, Al, because we've got women who are better looking than they are," Jed explained.

"That sounds like a sexist remark to me," Al responded. "Seriously, Sam," she continued, "What are we going to do about them?"

"I'll ask Captain Lonigan to assign cops to every Guardwell station and have them communicate with us if there are any problems. I'll also ask Colonel Warrington to prepare his troops to be extra alert. There's no doubt that Guardwell doesn't like the Marines, but we have to make sure there are no incidents between their personnel and ours. A lot of eyes will be on us Monday, looking for any pretext to get us shipped out of the Enclave. We're better off here than anywhere else right now, so don't let anything go wrong."

The only thing that marred Hanson's day was an unexpected run in with Captain Beasley. He hadn't encountered his annoying superior for a few days, but just as he was leaving his office early for a change, he bumped into him in the corridor.

"Well. If it isn't our self-proclaimed security expert," Beasley blared loudly.

Hanson ignored the slur. "Good evening, sir," and turned to go.

"Just a minute, Sergeant. I want an update on our security plan."

"Now, sir?"

"Yes. Some of us are still working, Sergeant."

"I've been putting in twelve to fourteen hours a day. I'm not on a 9-5 schedule."

"We'll discuss your ability to carry out your duties another time. For now, give me your report."

Hanson refused to get angry at the deliberate provocation. "Sir. This isn't the place for a discussion of security. If you really want an update, let's go to your office, or mine."

"I only have a moment, Hanson. Stop wasting my time."

"Sir, I respectfully remind you that security arrangements are confidential. We're in a public space. It's inappropriate to talk about it here."

"Are you implying that our Marines can't be trusted?"

"No, sir. I'm trying to make you understand that this should only be discussed in private."

"Well, I don't have time right now to listen to your quibbling." He sailed out like a decrepit motorboat, oblivious to the pathetic spectacle to the nautically knowledgeable.

Hanson took a few moments to disperse the irritation that Beasley left him with. He knew that Kyle was having dinner with Tyrone at Jed's house and would be spending the night there, so for the first time in months he had the entire night to himself, but without the faintest idea what to do. It had been quite a while since he had sex, and the thought of a visit to one of the U.N. pleasure houses flitted through his mind. All he had to do was change into civvies and walk in confidently. His French was good enough to fool the brothel staff and he could easily act as dumb and arrogant as a Frenchman.

It was tempting, but he quickly rejected the idea because he didn't want to add to the degradation of the American women who had chosen prostitution over malnutrition. An image of Al in a thong popped into his mind, but he instantly dismissed it. Even if she was willing, any relations with her would violate regulations and his own code of professional behavior.

Feeling a little less buoyant than he did a few hours earlier, Hanson ate dinner at the mess hall, then went to see a movie at the cine complex on Second Avenue and 31st street. The films offered that evening were in Japanese or Hindi, with English subtitles. They were made by the two biggest Hollywood studio owners, Japan and India.

He definitely wasn't in the mood for the standard thriller about the American drug dealer, a former soldier, who abducts a beautiful Japanese or Hindu girl, to extort money from her father. As usual, the Japanese or Hindu girl resolutely resists the sexual advances of the depraved American. The climax would be a violent, bloody shootout, with the American's gang getting exterminated. Then the Japanese or Hindu girl would kill the American, after a desperate battle in which she demonstrates her moral and physical superiority. He sat through the only alternative, an old Walt Disney film, 'Bambi', and went home without any idea why that particular film was officially approved by the U.N. He went to bed early, exhausted after his hot night on the town.

•   •   •

Mavis spent the night at Jennifer's house. After the restrained atmosphere at the dinner table with Jennifer's father, the two girls retired to Jennifer's room, where they lay down on her bed and indulged in real conversation.

"Alright, kid," Jennifer demanded. "I want a detailed description of last night's dinner party. Were the docs formally dressed? How did the younger ones look? Did you want to have sex with any of them?"

"Slow down, girl," Mavis admonished, torn between laughter and embarrassment. "I was my dad's hostess. I didn't have time to waste on fantasies."

"Don't give me that. I've been a hostess for two years. It's just another chore. I take advantage of the situation to consider eligible men for sex partners."

"You don't," Mavis gasped.

"Don't be such a child. I'm too young to get married, so what I look for is a suitable man who will be discreet. I can't afford any kind of scandal that would interfere with my plans."

Mavis shook her head in wonder at her friend's determination to accomplish her purpose. "You always sound so sure of everything, Jen. It's different for me. I don't know what I want, or even what I want to do."

"Listen to me, kid. We're at the top of the heap now. The only way to go is down. That's not for me. It doesn't matter if you don't know what you want. Make a decision that seems right for your future and follow through on it."

"What if I pick something that doesn't make me happy?"

"Blog happiness. Your father's position shelters you and it provides you with comforts and security. Do you want to end up marrying some Guardwell clod, or crude hospital maintenance man and live in the projects?"

"There are worse things," Mavis said defensively.

"Name one," Jennifer challenged. Mavis stared at her friend indignantly, then burst into laughter at Jen's mock-pitying expression. After a moment, Jennifer laughed with her, then reached over, pulled her close and looked into her eyes.

"There are things you have to do that may be unpleasant, but there are other ways to find happiness."

She kissed Mavis on the mouth and after a moment's hesitation, Mavis responded. Jennifer slowly ran her hands down Mavis' body, and she felt the heat rise between them. She rolled Mavis on her back while continuing to kiss her, sliding her tongue in and out of her mouth. She gently squeezed Mavis' breast and her nipple popped erect. She slid her hand down Mavis's stomach, unbuttoned her jeans, then stroked her through her panties. Mavis moaned and Jennifer suddenly pulled down her panties and rubbed her clitoris hard, until she came with a gasp.

She let Mavis lie there for a minute, then she undressed her, brushing away her feeble resistance. Mavis lay there, torn between pleasure and self-consciousness, and watched Jennifer undress with mounting excitement. Jennifer's' sleek body moved against her, sending little thrills of excitement through her. She started to kiss and touch Jennifer, who licked her way down between her legs and licked and sucked her. Mavis pulled her around so they could lick each other, until they both came at the same time with deep spasms of pleasure.

They shifted positions and lay next to each other, gently touching and caressing.

"That was wild, girl," Mavis whispered.

Jennifer ran her hand down her back, lingering on her buttocks, sending shivers through her. "You're a delectable child."

"I'm not a child," Mavis protested.

"You didn't object to being delectable," Jennifer said with a grin.

Mavis grinned back. "So are you."

"Before I have to have you again," Jennifer said throatily, "let's discuss how you'll lose your virginity."

"Didn't I just lose it?" Jennifer giggled.

"I mean with a man. We'll pick some clean, vigorous intern at the Halloween Ball, who'll appreciate the gift of your as yet unpenetrated body."

"You're horrible, Jen … Why an intern?"

"Because we can make sure he's not diseased, and he'll know enough about the body to perform satisfactorily."

"You make it sound so business like," Mavis protested.

Jennifer shrugged. "It's a necessary chore that has to be done properly. Now come here and we'll do something that isn't business like."

7

HANSON GOT AN UNPLEASANT SURPRISE when he arrived at Dr. Carver's office Friday morning, at 0855. Captain Beasley was sitting in the waiting room, under the faintly disapproving gaze of Ms. Bellini. He immediately asserted his authority when he saw Hanson. "Good morning, Sergeant."

Hanson didn't bother to correct his improper form of address, that should have been Gunnery Sergeant. "Good morning," he replied.

"Sir," Beasley admonished.

"Sir."

"I thought it would be useful to meet with you and Dr. Carver for a final review of security arrangements for Monday," Beasley explained loftily. "I also have some orders and instructions for you from headquarters."

"What are they?"

"Sir," Beasley again reminded smugly.

"Sir."

"I'll inform you when we're with Dr. Carver."

"Don't you think we should discuss military orders privately, sir?"

Beasley frowned. "I'll decide who should or should not be informed."

Before it could become another source of tension between them, Ms. Bellini said, "You can go in now."

Beasley jostled Hanson as he rushed to enter first. Ms. Bellini caught Hanson's eye and gave him an encouraging smile, which he didn't acknowledge.

"Good morning, Dr. Carver," Beasley gushed. "We're here to finalize security arrangements for Monday."

Dr. Carver was obviously not expecting Beasley, but greeted him politely, although not as warmly as Hanson.

"Thank you for coming, gentlemen. Why don't you update me on the luncheon preparations, Captain Beasley?"

"I thought I'd save my report for last, sir. When we're alone."

"I have limited time, Captain. Proceed."

Beasley instantly wiped the scowl of annoyance from his face. "Yes, sir. I've had to deal with all kinds of problems from the Arabs who are hosting the luncheon, but I managed to solve most of them, and everything is on schedule. I don't think you'll be disappointed."

Carver looked at him appraisingly. "Is that all?"

"Well, we still have to finalize seating and the Arabs are insisting that no Marines be allowed in or near the mosque. I tried to make them understand that I was a supply officer, not a combat Marine, but they said that I was included in the ban. I reminded them of my efforts to make the event special, but they laughed at me. You'll be glad to know that I didn't allow their insults to affect my attitude."

Hanson stared at Beasley in amazement, appalled that he was wearing the same uniform as the men and women who died for their country. Carver noticed Hanson's anger and before he could say something rash that would challenge Beasley's authority, he said smoothly, "Thank you for coming, Captain. I know you have other important duties. I'll try to get you invited to the luncheon. Good morning."

Beasley was shocked at the abrupt dismissal. "But we haven't reviewed security yet."

"I'll do that with Mr. Hanson."

"But I have orders for him."

"See him alone. Good morning."

"Yes, sir. Report to my office at 1000, Sergeant," and he slunk out, deflated.

They were silent for a few moments, then Carver remarked,

"I hope my sending him away like that won't cause you any trouble."

"I can deal with Captain Beasley."

"I'm sure you can. Now bring me up to speed on security."

"We've prepared as best we can with our resources. The police and National Guard have been completely cooperative, which will improve the safety factor considerably."

"What about Guardwell?"

"They resent the Marines, but I've posted police officers with their men to ensure that we'll have good coverage."

"Is there anything more you can do?"

"Not really. Our biggest concern is still Arabs shooting in the air."

"I'm working on it, Mr. Hanson, but I don't expect the U.N. liason to be supportive. What about the rumors of a demonstration by the vets?"

"All personnel will be alert to them, as well as P Dogs, or any other possible disruption. If you have the time, I'll show you our personnel positions on the map."

"Please do."

Hanson went over the events of the day from beginning to end, and once again he was impressed with Carver's grasp of details way out of his specialty.

"You've done an excellent job so far, Mr. Hanson."

"Thank you, sir."

"Now tell me what can go wrong."

Hanson laughed bitterly. "Do you have all day?"

This alarmed Carver. "I thought everything was under control? You said you were fully prepared."

"That's right, sir. Within the limitations of our resources. We'd need ten times more troops to secure the Enclave. To the best of my ability, I've concentrated our assets where they're most needed. We'll deal with any unexpected eventualities as best we can."

"How do you propose to do that?"

Hanson grinned. "The traditional Marine way; improvise, adjust, overcome."

"Will that be enough?"

"We'll probably know by Monday night, sir."

Carver laughed. "I like your style. So tell me what to worry about."

"My staff and I considered just about every type of scenario. Let us do the worrying."

"Alright, Mr. Hanson. Should we meet again before Monday?"

"No need. I'll call you, if necessary, or you call me."

"Then have a good day."

"You too, sir."

•　　　•　　　•

The meeting with Beasley was quite unpleasant and verged on getting out of hand. Beasley poured out all his resentments, frustrations, and humiliations on Hanson, who took it all with stoic indifference.

"Just because I allowed you to deal with some of the security problems, Sergeant, that doesn't mean you can forget who's in command. Your attempt to ingratiate yourself with Dr. Carver is inappropriate and I'll note it in your file. How dare you exclude me from vital information? Don't you know your place?"

Hanson didn't reply, which irked Beasley further.

"Well?"

"Well, what, sir?"

"Explain yourself, man."

"I have nothing to say, sir. You put me in charge of security and that's what I've been taking care of."

Beasley sputtered with rage. "You're supposed to report to me."

"When should I report? Every time I tried to talk to you, you were too busy."

Beasley began to realize that the meeting was becoming even more aggravating, and with an exertion of will he calmed himself.

"Alright. We'll continue this particular discussion another time. Right now, I have some orders for you from headquarters. I have been instructed to tell you that the honor guard are not to wear ribbons or medals on their dress uniforms on Monday. I agree with the order. We shouldn't flaunt our aggression." Beasley waited for the eruption.

"Are you serious?"

"Sir."

"Sir."

"Those are the orders, Sergeant. You are expected to carry them out without question."

"Don't be ridiculous. We're in the Marines, not the Russian army."

"What did you say?" Beasley demanded indignantly.

"You heard me. Our men and women paid for those decorations with their blood and the lives of their comrades. Even you should understand that."

Beasley was furious, but he knew he couldn't afford to lose Hanson at present. "You will carry out your orders, Sergeant. Dismissed."

Hanson left without another word. He called his platoon leaders and told them to meet him at his office. They were outraged when they heard the order; no ribbons or medals.

"Is this some kind of bad joke, Sam?" Jed asked.

"I'm afraid not. It's obvious that the Arabs and the U.N. are out to put it to us again."

"Our Marines won't like this, Sam," Al cautioned.

"There's nothing we can do about it. You will instruct the troops that there are to be no complaints about it to anyone."

"Not even to their squad mates?" Jed asked with a straight face.

Hanson finally smiled. "Just tell them to be discreet. No gripe sessions outside of the barracks."

"Yes, Sam," they both said in unison.

"May I make a suggestion, Sam?" Al asked.

"Sure. What is it?"

"Give everyone but the guard detail a 24-hour pass."

"I'd love to, Al, except for one problem."

"What?"

"As you know, we're not allowed to leave the Enclave without special permission. Besides, the Enclave will be crawling with Arabs this weekend and we can't afford an incident."

"I see," she said.

"Tell you what," Hanson said. "Tell your troops that if Monday goes off without a hitch, I'll arrange furloughs for everyone. That's all for now. I'll see you at the mess hall for lunch."

When everyone left, Hanson sat at his desk staring blankly at the wall. Thoughts about the order banning medals flashed through his mind. He reluctantly accepted that it was one more degradation inflicted on the elite service of the beleagured superpower. He remembered his meeting with General Griffin after the remnants of his battalion were repatriated from Eritrea. U.N. peacekeepers met them at Kennedy airport and supervised every step of the disembarkation of the troops from Airbus A 380's provided by the Euro-Union. The bluefish escorted all the returnees to health stations set up on the tarmac for typhoid and polio shots. Hanson objected vigorously, until General Griffin ordered him to be silent.

"But, General," Hanson protested, "we don't need those shots."

Griffin took him aside. "There's nothing we can do about it, Sam. I've been ordered to obey all U.N. mandates without resistance, and so will you."

The deprocessing of the troops took hours, with each Marine being interrogated by U.N. officers, who asked the most intrusive questions, ranging from war crimes to personal sexual activities. If a Marine objected, or refused to answer, there was an instant threat of jail.

One female Marine punched a bluefish for touching her breasts, and his colleagues immediately beat her into unconsciousness. Her squadmates heard her screams and rushed to her aid, but were confronted by heavily armed peacekeepers, who were eager for a chance to shoot Marines. They had been disarmed before boarding the planes, so there was nothing they could do. Hanson tried to intercede, but the peacekeepers shoved him away with rifle butts. He protested to their commanding officer, an arrogant Swede, who sneered at him.

"It is a different foot you're on now, imperialist mercenary."

Hanson instantly reached for his sidearm, momentarily forgetting that it had been confiscated at the Asmera airport. General Griffin drew him away.

"Take it easy, Sam. We can't afford an incident."

Later, when they were finally alone, Hanson was near to bursting with questions, but Griffin put him off.

"Another time, Sam. Right now, we've got to deal with two problems. What we'll do with your troops and how to prevent your court martial."

"What do you mean a court martial?"

"You disobeyed a presidential order, Sam."

"I saved my troops. They all deserve medals. In fact, I'm putting some of them in for the Medal of Honor."

"No you're not. There've been some big changes that have taken place that you're unaware of. All our military has been withdrawn to the continental United States under the supervision of the U.N. Our former friends and enemies are trampling each other in the stampede to grab our overseas possessions. We'll be lucky if I can keep you from a war crimes tribunal. I'm afraid there won't be any medals …"

Hanson came back to the present with a sigh, and for the dozenth time opened the map of the Enclave and stared at it intently, looking for possible threats.

The rest of the weekend sped by with Hanson perfunctorily carrying out his regular duties and concentrating most of his efforts on last minute preparations for U.N. Day. He invited Jed and Al to dinner on Sunday and included Tyrone at Jed's request.

Throughout the meal, Kyle and Tyrone vied for Al's attention, waiting on her hand and foot, to the amusement of their fathers. Later, when it was time to get to the business of final planning and review, Hanson sent the boys to the movies because they had been distracting, cavorting like puppies around Al. Just before he said goodnight to them, Hanson looked at his trusted comrades.

"I don't want any unexpected surprises tomorrow, so make sure your troops are on the ball."

"You got it, Sam," Al replied.

"Sure, Sam," Jed said.

"Then I'll see you at company formation at 0600."

8

I T WAS A VERY SATISFACTORY inspection of the formation behind the barracks on a clear, cool Monday morning, with even Wilkins looking smart. Hanson was about to dismiss the company at 0625, when Captain Beasley ambled out.

"Company. Attention," Hanson ordered. He turned and saluted Beasley. "All present and accounted for, sir."

Beasley slowly studied the formation. "Well. It's good to see the troops turned out so nicely for a change."

Hanson suppressed his irritation at the unfair criticism.

"Thank you, sir. I was about to dismiss them for breakfast, before they report to their duty stations."

"I'd like to inspect them first. Just to be sure everything's in order, Sergeant."

A murmur of protest rose from the nearby ranks at the insult and Jed ordered sternly, "Steady."

"I've already inspected them, sir. If we don't dismiss now," Hanson cautioned, "they won't have time for a good meal and it's liable to be a long day."

Beasley leaned close to him. "You're always thwarting me, Sergeant. I'll deal with you later. Dismiss the company," and he abruptly turned and stomped off.

Jed and Al walked to the mess hall with Hanson.

"How did he ever become a Marine, let alone an officer?" Al wondered.

"Knock it off, Al," Hanson insisted, without anger. "He's our C.O. and we're managing. We have bigger problems to be concerned about today. I've got a strange feeling that we're overlooking something."

"Is that a hunch, or just general worry?" Jed asked.

"I wish I knew. We've prepared as thoroughly as possible and I can't put my finger on anything, but it's been going too smoothly. There are too many potential trouble spots with the Arabs, Russians and the bluefish."

"Our men and women are ready, Sam," Al reassured him. "They're not kids anymore. Not after the snafu'd Nafud."

Hanson nodded sadly, as a wisp of memory of the agonizing desert retreat flitted through his mind. "Alright. Let's eat, then go to work."

•   •   •

The first official event of U.N. Day was at Madison Square Park at the World War I Memorial, an obvious act of triumphalism over weakened America. Fifth Avenue was closed, and loudspeakers were set up for the crowd. The ceremony for Euro-Arab freedom fighter volunteers who died fighting Americans in Saudi Arabia featured the expected.

Speaker after speaker mounted the platform, starting with the president of Russia, Alexander Rostov, followed by the Russian president-elect, Ivan Schedrin, who praised the fallen heroes. The Russian sneers at the defeated American aggressors were followed by representatives of the Arab nations, who heaped invectives and threats on the American infidels, while the Russian infidels applauded enthusiastically. The crowd stirred and the Arabs cheered frantically and fired their Kalashnikovs in the air when Mohammed el-Islam Bin Laden appeared, accompanied by his pet tiger. The nephew of the former Al Qaeda leader, was now the absolute ruler of Saudi Arabia, accepted worldwide, despite his crushing the hopes of the Arab Spring. He joined his fellow Arabs in cursing America.

When the bullets inevitably plummeted back to earth, three people were killed and fourteen were wounded. Despite the chaos when ambulances rushed in to remove the casualties, the procession of Arab ranters continued, each one more rabid than his predecessor. A great hush fell on the crowd when Khaled Meshal stood up to speak. He was once the most hated leader of Hamas, responsible for the deaths of many Israelis and Westerners, with a ten-million-dollar bounty on his head, dead or alive, that was never collected. Now he was the Ayatollah of Jordan, appointed by the Grand Ayatollah of Saudi Arabia, Mohammed bin Laden, after the slaughter of King Abdullah and all his relatives of the Hashemite dynasty.

Some of the Marine honor guard who had endured the Arab stream of abuse without reaction, now rumbled angrily and muttered curses when they saw him. They knew he had sent Palestinian volunteers to Saudi Arabia to kill Americans. Jed instantly commanded, "Steady. Not another sound."

Some of the Arabs were watching the Marines, hoping for a pretext to attack them, but loud yelling from another direction distracted them. A group of vets in wheelchairs, carrying anti-Arab and anti-U.N. banners, chanting, "No, No. Arabs go," tried to enter the park from Madison Avenue. The Marines were able to turn them away before the Arabs could respond, but not without the vets spitting on them and calling them traitors.

The police escorted the vets back to the hospital and left them simmering in frustration. The rest of the ceremony took place without disruption and the final activity set the crowd into a frenzy. President Rostov awarded the Hero of the Russian Federation, posthumously, to all the Russian volunteers who died fighting the Americans in Saudi Arabia. This sparked another round of shooting in the air by the Arabs and the notables rapidly departed. The crowd quickly dispersed, and this time left only one dead and nine wounded.

As the Marines marched back to the barracks, Wilkins announced loudly, "I sure wish I could have shot that Meshal raghead."

"Thinking about the ten mil, snail?" a voice in the back of the column yelled.

"I wouldn't turn it down, but if I had to pick the money or the shot, I'd take the shot."

"Right on, snail."

•　　　•　　　•

Hanson watched the disorderly end of the ceremony through his binoculars, as the heavily guarded motorcade of the notables sped off to their next destination, the Veterans Hospital. He focused for a minute on the video crews from Al Jazeera, Al Manar and CNN International, which was broadcasting on all other stations. He knew without a doubt that they wouldn't air footage of the dead and wounded unless they blamed it on the Marines.

They would show the President of Russia, the most faithful Arab ally, albeit a temporary infidel one, awarding honors to fallen Arab heroes, and the Arab leaders flaunting their triumphs over the great Satan. He made a mental note not to watch TV this weekend. Then, after a final scan of the park, he signaled Tico, the driver of his hummer, and they headed for a vantage point on 25th street, where he could observe the Veterans Hospital.

The Bellevue Enclave doctors and bigwigs were lined up on First Avenue to greet the prominent visitors, who poured out of their armored limos and brushed past the welcoming committee, who forlornly trailed after them. Hanson didn't know what transpired inside, but the rapid reappearance of the visitors indicated that they didn't pause to speak to the maimed, blind or paralyzed wrecks of the mujadaheen, who had sacrificed their bodies when they answered the call to jihad.

The visitors quickly reentered their vehicles and the motorcade sped up First Avenue, turned on 35th street and pulled up in front of the former Armenian Cathedral of Saint Vartan, now the Mosque of bin Laden. Turkish pressure in the U.N. had influenced the Secretariat to expropriate the church for the use of Islam. Captain Beasley and the Enclave manager were waiting in front of the entrance and wagged eagerly, but the visitors ignored them and rushed inside, leaving Beasley and the manager to follow them.

Hanson had Tico park across the street from the mosque and he settled down to await the emergence of the visitors, who would then join the parade, already forming a few blocks away on First Avenue. A group of Armenian-American demonstrators tried to storm their defiled church in the vain hope of reclaiming it. The police, although not unsympathetic, hustled them away with unusual forbearance and no injuries. The bluefish were eager to crack American heads, Armenian or other, but the prompt response of the police forestalled them.

Hanson made a mental note to praise the efficiency of the police to Captain Lonigan, whose men had prevented an incident that could have caused casualties, without changing anything. He watched the police escort the demonstrators up 34th street, until they were out of sight. He shook his head with discouragement at another profound insult inflicted on the American people, whose generosity to the needy of the world was always conveniently forgotten.

Hanson waited patiently and snacked on a packet of meals-ready-to-eat, while inside the former church, his former enemies feasted. The Arabs and their guests took their time dining, certain that the parade wouldn't begin without them. It started to rain, which would add a further element of discomfort for the marchers. More than two hours went by, which meant that some groups had been waiting in place for two to three hours. The Arabs finally finished their leisurely lunch, sauntered out and chatted on the sidewalk, before slowly getting into their limos and driving to the starting point of the parade. Captain Beasley and the Enclave manager emerged, and Beasley peremptorily signaled Hanson to join him.

Hanson told Tico to pull up in front of the former church. He felt a sense of apprehension at Beasley's summons, without any idea what he wanted. "Good afternoon, Captain."

"Sergeant. Now that my lunch duties are over, I'll take charge of security for the rest of the day."

"Sir?"

"You heard me. The Arabs are very unhappy about the presence of police, National Guard and Marines. They requested that they be removed and replaced with U.N. Peacekeepers."

"That's not a good idea, sir. The bluefish aren't trained for security."

"I don't like that name for them, Sergeant, and I expect you to change personnel before the parade starts."

"It's a mistake to change the arrangements. There isn't time to do it properly."

"This is not open for discussion, Sergeant. Make the change. That's an order."

Hanson turned to the manager in desperation. "We shouldn't do this, sir."

The manager shrugged. "It's not my call, Sergeant."

"I'll do it under protest, sir, and only with a written order."

Beasley frowned, but took out his notebook, wrote an order and handed it to Hanson. "Will that do?"

Hanson read it quickly. "Yes, sir. But I still insist this is a mistake."

Beasley glared at him. "I'll deal with you tomorrow. Now carry out your orders."

Captain Beasley walked off with the manager without another word. Hanson tried to think of some way to get the order canceled but couldn't come up with anything. He briefly considered talking to Dr. Carver, then rejected that idea as impractical.

Reluctantly, he called Captain Lonigan and told him to withdraw his police officers. Lonigan's irate cursing could have been heard at the U.N., then he calmed down.

"Are you out of your mind?" he demanded. "Who the hell will provide security, the leprechauns?"

"The U.N. Peacekeepers."

"The bluefish? That's crazy."

"Captain Beasley has taken charge of security at the request of the Arabs and ordered the police, National Guard and Marines replaced by Peacekeepers."

"Do you want us in reserve somewhere?" Lonigan asked.

Hanson was tempted but didn't want to risk exposing the police to bluefish aggression. "No, Captain. You better resume normal routine and avoid the parade route."

Lonigan cursed a bit more, then signed off.

The call to Colonel Warrington was just as frustrating, but not as profane as the one to Lonigan.

"What idiot decided that?" Warrington asked.

"It was at the request of the Arabs, sir. I recommend you recall your troops to the Armory and avoid any confrontation with the Peacekeepers."

Warrington muttered something about the imbecile who issued the order, then said, "Let's get together when this is over. I'll call you."

"I'll look forward to it," Hanson replied.

The calls to his Marine platoons weren't any easier. He talked to Jed at length, because he knew he would be particularly agitated and require soothing.

"Take it easy, Jed. Those are our orders."

"It was Beasley, wasn't it? It sounds like that asshole."

"Knock it off, Jed. Take our people back to the barracks. I'll see you there."

Hanson knew that Jed stomped off angrily and had to admit to himself that he felt the same way.

9

KYLE AND TYRONE had ignored their fathers' instructions not to attend the parade. They staked out a spot on the Fifth Avenue side of Madison Square Park and sat on the rail fence. The boys sat there for more than an hour, with no sign of the parade getting underway. Kyle was the first one to notice the withdrawal of the American security forces.

"Hey. Look at that, Ty. The police and National Guard are leaving."

Tyrone looked around and said, "So are the Marines. I wonder what's up?"

Kyle pointed. "That's Al's platoon. Let's ask her." They ran towards the Marines and Kyle called, "Al. Al. What's happening?"

She signaled one of her squad leaders to take over and turned to the boys. "Weren't you told not to be here?"

"Yes," Kyle admitted. "But we wanted to see what was happening. Where are you going?"

"We've been ordered back to barracks."

"What about the police and Guard?" Tyrone asked.

"They've been withdrawn," Al answered.

"I bet it was that asshole, Captain Beasley," Kyle muttered.

Al glared at him. "I've got to go. You two better get out of here. There's liable to be trouble."

Al trotted off after her platoon and the boys looked at each other.

"What do you think, K? Do we stay or go?"

"What if we move halfway into the park? We can stand on a bench and watch the parade and be able to take off if there's trouble."

"Sounds good to me … Hey. I've got an idea. Let's sit on top of the statue of Chester Arthur. We can see better from there."

They found a comfortable perch on the bronze statue of a former president, more used to hosting pigeons, that gave them a good view of Fifth Avenue. A few minutes later they heard the squalling, grating music of an Arab band that signaled the parade was finally underway. Various Arab military units marched by at quick pace, arms swinging more in Nazi style than British. Elderly Russian armored vehicles trundled by, flaunting their non-battle victory over the Americans.

Some of the American veterans in wheelchairs rolled through the park, heading for Fifth Avenue. Unlike their raucous demonstration in the morning, this time they were silent, grim, and determined. The boys watched them pass and respectfully saluted. One of the vets noticed and nodded acknowledgement. The boys instinctively knew that these men weren't going to be spectators.

"Should we alert someone?" Tyrone asked.

"Who? The bluefish? I wouldn't tell them anything," Kyle replied. "That asshole Beasley pulled back the people who would handle the vets the right way," Kyle explained. "You know what the Arabs or bluefish would do to them."

Tyrone nodded. "I guess you're right. But the vets are up to something. I could tell."

"Me too. Whatever it is, I hope they won't get hurt," Kyle said.

Tyrone shrugged. "Let all the shit happen to the Arabs."

The boys lost sight of the vets as they rolled into the crowd, and they watched as a company of Russian Special Forces marched by at the slow, controlled pace that hinted of their ferocity. They were followed by the Russian President and President-elect, and the crowd cheered wildly for them.

The crowd fell silent and there was an expectant hush. Then a murmur started. 'Meshal'. 'Meshal'. A company of mujahadeen, wrapped in white from head to toe, carrying Kalashnikovs, preceded a limousine with Meshal and Moktada al-Sadr, the Grand Ayatollah of Iraq. Suddenly a vet in a wheelchair rolled into the mujadaheen formation and doused himself in gasoline. All eyes turned to him as he lit a flare, yelled, "Gung ho," and ignited himself.

There was a shocked silence and while everyone stared at the incendiary man, another vet rolled up to Meshal and al-Sadr's limo. He tore off his fatigue jacket, which revealed a harness of C-4 plastic explosives, yelled, "Semper Fi," and detonated himself. The tremendous explosion ripped the limousine apart and practically vaporized the occupants. The crowd was stunned for a minute, then the mujadaheen began to wail and fire their weapons wildly, which sent everyone ducking for cover, except the television crews who kept their cameras recording the spectacle. Tyrone turned to Kyle.

"Holy shit. Did you see that?"

"Yes. I wonder how the Arabs like a dose of their own medicine?"

Kyle and Tyrone watched in horror from their distant perch as the parade broke up in a swirl of chaos. The notables and their bodyguards zoomed off up Fifth Avenue, running down anyone luckless enough to be in the way.

"It's time to get out of here," Kyle said, "before the Arabs start shooting at any Americans."

"I'm with you. Let's split."

The boys scrambled down from the statue, ran east on 25th street and didn't slow down until they crossed Park Avenue South. Kyle took out his phone, which had the same secure encryption as all the Marine's phones, but without the multiple channels, and called his dad. When Hanson answered, Kyle said breathlessly,

"Dad. It's me. Tyrone and I just came from the park. A vet torched himself and while everyone was watching, another vet blew up the limousine with Khaled Meshal and Moktada al Sadr. The Arabs went wild and started firing at the crowd."

"Where are you?" Hanson demanded.

"We're heading east on 25th street. We're going home."

"Don't go home. Come to the barracks. There may be reprisals, or some other kind of violence. I'll feel a lot better knowing you're safe. So will Jed."

"Alright, Dad. What happened to the cops and the Guard? I bet that asshole Beasley ordered them out."

"Knock it off, Kyle. He's my C.O."

"It was him," Kyle insisted.

"Just get here right away."

"Yes, Dad."

Hanson called Captain Lonigan, Colonel Warrington and Dr. Carver and they discussed how to deal with the latest crisis. They all agreed that they had to keep a low profile, if possible, and that the police should put extra patrols on the street.

"Whatever happens," Dr. Carver ordered, "avoid any confrontation with the Arabs or U.N. personnel." Everyone acknowledged the order and Dr. Carver asked, "Why did you pull our security forces back, Mister Hanson?"

"Captain Beasley ordered it, sir."

"Didn't you object?"

"Yes, sir. I told him it was a mistake, but he wouldn't listen. I even appealed to the Enclave manager, but he said it wasn't his call. I insisted on a written order, assuming that Captain Beasley would refuse and give me a reason to disobey, but he wrote the order."

Dr. Carver sighed. "Do you have it?"

"Yes, sir."

"Well, when this business is resolved, we'll use it to get rid of him."

"Yes, sir."

Hanson suggested to Captain Lonigan that he have the police officers advise all Americans in the Enclave to stay at home until things settled down. Then Dr. Carver requested the participants to meet in his office at 9:00 a.m. to review the situation.

"I'll ask several department heads and the Enclave manager to attend. I'll order Captain Beasley to be there. If there's nothing else at the moment, I'll see you in the morning. If anything significant happens between now and then, call me immediately. Thank you for your efforts, gentlemen."

"I'm going to keep two of my platoons on alert, in case of emergency," Hanson told the others.

"That's a good idea," Colonel Warrington responded. "I'll keep two platoons on alert also."

"Captain Lonigan, if your officers see or hear anything unusual, let us know," Hanson requested. Lonigan agreed, then they said goodbye.

When Kyle and Tyrone got to the barracks Hanson asked them to tell him what they saw. He let any of the Marines listen in if they were interested. It was one more reason why he was so admired by his troops. He let them know what was happening, except if it was restricted information.

"We were sitting on the fence on the Fifth Avenue side of the park and decided to move back into the park and stand on a bench so we could see better," Kyle said.

This elicited a glare from Hanson, which meant a discussion later about disobedience to orders.

"I suggested to Kyle that we should sit on top of the statue of Chester Arthur," Tyrone added.

Kyle nodded, then resumed. "We were watching from there when some vets rolled by. They looked intent on serious business. There were no Marines around and we didn't know what to do. A few minutes later one of the vets burned himself alive. While everyone was watching him burn, another vet blew himself up along with the limo with Meshal and al Sadr. The Arabs started shooting and we took off. You know the rest."

There was a long silence while they digested the news, then Wilkins yelled,

"Hey, gunny. Those vets should get the ten million reward. They earned it."

"I don't think so, snail," Hanson replied softly. "Marines shouldn't be suicide bombers. That's not our way."

An argument started between two groups of Marines, one approving the bombing, the other against.

"Who's Chester Arthur, gunny?" Wilkins asked.

"He was a president of the United States, snail," Hanson answered, then sent the two boys to the mess hall and said he'd join them there in a while for dinner. He told the platoon leaders to come to his office, where he updated them on security conditions and put Jed's and Al's platoons on ready alert.

"What do you think will happen?" Al asked.

"I'm hoping the Arabs will go to the U.N. and complain," Hanson answered. "Then there'll be a chance to talk, and cooler heads will calm things down. But you never know. If the Arabs start anything in the Enclave and the police can't handle it, we'll have to stop them."

They looked at each other solemnly, aware of the potential dangers they might face.

"Do we return fire if the rags fire at us?" Jed asked.

"If it's a real attack, yes. If they're just trying to scare you by shooting in the air, avoid a fight. If anything at all happens, call me immediately. I'm going to double the guard at the hospital complex and the barracks, and I want a detail stationed at the N.C.O.s building for the next few days."

"Thanks, boss," Jed said. "The troops will feel a lot better knowing their families are safe."

"What about Beasley?" Al asked. "That man is a danger to us all. I wouldn't be surprised if he sold us out to the Arabs."

Hanson started to rebuke her, but reluctantly accepted that he felt the same way. "I'll call General Griffin and discuss it with him. I think we're finished for the moment. You know what to do. See to your troops. I'll see you in the mess hall."

10

E VERYONE WITH ANY SENSE had vacated the streets after the explosion, so the Arabs didn't have ready targets for their anger. They proceeded up the parade route on Fifth Avenue in a disorganized mass, and some of them fired Kalashnikovs at the Empire State Building as they went by. They didn't do real damage but felt better shooting at a symbol of Yankee imperialism. The nearby police officers were smart enough not to intervene, thereby avoiding a shoot-out with a better armed, fanatic opposition.

The Arabs turned east on 42nd street and gathered in front of the U.N., where they called for vengeance. This situation was more volatile than the previously scheduled hate America rally, and U.N. officials and notables could barely control the angry Arabs.

Russian President Rostov finally pacified the crowd by promising an immediate investigation of the incident and pledged to bring to justice anyone else involved in the attack besides the suiciders. The official ceremony was canceled, and the Arabs dispersed, pausing to loot several stores on 42nd street, then they headed for Arab town around Atlantic Avenue, in Brooklyn.

Most of the stores had wisely closed for the day, so damages were confined to the Arab-owned fast food stores and delis that had remained open for parade business. There were no fatalities and calm finally prevailed in the recently chaotic streets. President Rostov officially requested Secretary-General Mohamed ElBaradei to appoint a committee to formally investigate the attack by American veterans.

A funereal silence reigned in the Bellevue Enclave, where no one ventured out unless it was an emergency. Extra police patrols in cars and on foot blanketed the neighborhood, displaying a reassuring presence that partially relieved the worried residents. The Guardwell private security men complained vehemently to the police that they would be blamed for the actions of a few crazy vets. This outraged many of the officers who happened to be vets, but their supervisors were able to prevent any confrontations.

The police were as divided about what the vets did as the Marines were, but they presented a unified front to the Guardwell men, almost none of whom had served in the military. For the rest of the afternoon, Captain Lonigan frequently called Hanson and Colonel Warrington, keeping them up to speed on local conditions, that fortunately were quiet.

Captain Beasley hadn't been seen or heard from since the explosion. When Hanson couldn't reach him, he called General Griffin to advise him of the situation.

"Why didn't you call me when Beasley ordered you to withdraw our personnel?" the general demanded.

"It would have meant an argument in front of the Enclave manager who was with Captain Beasley. I told the captain it was a mistake, but he insisted that I obey. I requested the order in writing, and he actually did it. I really thought he'd back down when I asked for the order in writing."

"This isn't like you, Sam. You knew the order was wrong."

"Yes, sir. But the last time I disobeyed a wrong order I got hung out to dry. This time the situation didn't seem as consequential, so I hoped for the best."

"Well, I'm not going to second guess you, Sam. Send me a copy of the written order. In the meantime, I'm relieving Captain Beasley of command. I'll get back to you when I reach him, then you'll take over."

"Yes, sir."

Hanson made copies of Beasley's order and locked the original in his secure drawer. He went to the mess hall, got his dinner and joined his son and staff at the N.C.O. table. He discreetly gave Jed and Al copies of Beasley's order and asked them not to show them to anyone and put them in a safe place.

"Why, Major," Al teased. "You sound like you don't trust the system."

Everyone chuckled, and Hanson replied, "I trust the Marine leadership, not necessarily the civilian politicians who control them. But no more about that. I've got news. General Griffin informed me that he was going to relieve Beasley of command and appoint me in his place."

"That's great news, Sam," Jed enthused. "Will he restore your rank?"

"That's a wait and see."

"Congratulations, sir," Al said. "We need a real commander."

Hanson looked at the men and women who had served with him in victory and defeat and felt a warm surge of pride in them.

"Thanks for your support. You've been good friends and good Marines in difficult times. Things will get worse before they get better. I'm counting on your help."

"You've got it, Sam," Jed responded.

"Just ask, Major," Al added.

Just then a thought occurred to Hanson, and he pulled out his phone and called General Griffin. "Sir. The Russians are sure to demand a U.N. investigation. We should have the police, the FBI, the Army and the appropriate Marine authority investigate the incident immediately. With your approval, I can start the process with the police through Captain Lonigan, and the Army through Colonel Warrington. You should take care of the Marines and the FBI"

"Good idea, Sam. Get to it."

"Yes, sir. I'll keep you posted."

Jed and Al had politely pretended not to be listening but were intently considering the implications of what they heard.

"This means big trouble," Jed muttered. "Those poor vets are going to be in the shit."

Hanson nodded agreement.

"Did anyone else hear Beasley issue the withdrawal order, Major?" Al asked.

"Captain Beasley," Hanson corrected automatically. He thought for a moment. "The Enclave manager and my driver … You are a very suspicious individual, Al."

"She's right, Sam. You've been screwed by the system before," Jed reminded.

"They would have to suborn the manager and my driver, Lance Corporal Gonzales," Hanson said.

"It's possible," Al insisted.

"Tico's a good Marine. He wouldn't lie," Hanson asserted.

"Nevertheless, I'll make sure Tico remembers every word correctly," Jed insisted, then added, "You should make sure of the manager."

"I'll have to think about that one," Hanson replied.

Kyle had been following the conversation carefully. "What about the vets?" he asked. "What's going to happen to them?"

Hanson looked at him in surprise, then felt a stab of annoyance that he hadn't thought of them. "I don't know yet, son. The investigation will probably determine that. We don't know who else was involved and where they got the C-4. Off the top of my head, I'd guess this was a well-planned action by a determined group that goes beyond the wheelchair brigade."

"They're our people, Dad."

"I know, son," Hanson replied sadly, "but they didn't consult us. They decided to launch a terror attack and now they'll have to face the consequences."

"But they have some real grievances," Kyle protested.

"I know, son, but that wasn't the way to do it."

"What else could they have done? They were deprived of services in their hospital and abandoned. It's not fair."

"You're right," Hanson admitted, "but I have other things to do now. We'll talk about it tonight."

"Alright, Dad."

After a quick word with Jed, Hanson told Kyle and Tyrone that they should spend the night at the barracks. "Probably nothing will happen, but we want to be sure that you boys are safe, in case there's trouble tonight."

"Aw, Dad," Tyrone grumbled. "We'll be alright at home."

"I'm glad to get the benefit of your security expertise," Jed growled, "but you'll sleep in the barracks. Besides, it'll give you some firsthand experience for when you become a Marine."

"Maybe I'll go to medical school instead," Tyrone muttered.

"What's that?" Jed demanded.

"Nothing, Dad."

"You boys can hang out in the lounge until you turn in," Hanson ordered.

"Yes, Dad."

"Yes, sir."

"I'll have someone check on them if we're not here," Jed offered.

"Aw, Dad," Tyrone whined. "Don't you trust me?"

"I'd trust you with my life, but not to stay out of mischief. Now get going."

"Yes, Dad."

Once the boys left the table, Hanson turned to Jed and Al. "We're probably ready for anything short of all-out war. Now it's time to find Captain Beasley."

"Can we give him to the Arabs?" Jed quipped.

"Let's not have any more insulting of our C.O.," Hanson ordered. "It sets a bad example for our men and women, and I expect you to jump all over anyone who mouths off."

"Yes, sir," Jed replied.

"Al. Check his quarters and his office."

"Yes, sir."

"Jed. Check the medical complex. I'll check with the police and meet you back in my office in an hour. If you find him, call me immediately."

"What if we find him and he orders us to do something, or not reveal his location?" Al asked.

"You will inform him that you are carrying out orders issued by General Griffin to Gunnery Sergeant Hanson, then call me. Understand?"

"Yes, sir," Jed and Al replied.

"Good. Get cracking."

Jed and Al met Hanson an hour later and reported they could find no sign of Captain Beasley.

"Does he have any friends in the Enclave?" Hanson asked.

"Not that I know of, sir," Al answered.

"Where the devil is he hiding out?" Hanson asked, more to himself than the others. Then it came to him in a flash. "I bet he's hiding out with the Enclave manager." He dialed the manager's number and when someone answered, asked, "May I speak to Captain Beasley, please?" A few moments later he heard the familiar voice.

"Captain Beasley, here."

"This is Gunnery Sergeant Hanson, sir. I'd like you to join me in my office to review the current situation."

"I'm in a very important meeting with the Enclave manager. I'll call you later," Beasley replied, and disconnected before Hanson could say anything else.

Hanson shook his head, foreseeing trouble, then called General Griffin. "We've located Captain Beasley, sir. He's at the Enclave manager's office and he won't meet with me. With your permission, sir, I'd like to send a detail to escort him back to our headquarters."

"I don't know if I want him arrested yet, Sam."

"We'll only arrest him if he refuses to accompany the escort, sir."

"Do it, Sam."

"Yes, sir." Hanson turned to Al. "Pick two Marines and go get him. Avoid a scene."

"Yes, sir."

"Can I lead the detail, Sam?" Jed asked. "I'd love to see his face when I slap the cuffs on him."

"That's why I'm sending Al. We don't want any trouble and he'll only be arrested if he won't cooperate." Hanson laughed at Jed. "You sound as mature as Tyrone."

Jed shrugged self-consciously, then grinned winningly. "Tell me you wouldn't enjoy busting him."

Hanson tried to keep a straight face, then grinned. "Well … You have your orders, Al."

"Aye, aye, sir."

11

C APTAIN BEASLEY WAS LIVID by the time the escort delivered him to Hanson's office.

"What's the meaning of this, Hanson? I could have you brought up on charges for exceeding your authority in dealing with a superior officer."

"Sir. It's very important that we deal with the bombing situation that resulted from your ordering the withdrawal of our security forces."

"How dare you! Who do you think you are?" Beasley screamed. "I'll have you put under arrest and court-martialed." He turned to Al, who was standing at ease with her detail. "Sergeant. Arrest this man."

Before Al could refuse the order, Hanson cautioned Beasley. "Captain. I'm acting on orders from General Griffin. Either you cooperate with me, or I'll have to put you under arrest."

Beasley instantly realized he couldn't intimidate Hanson and switched gears.

"Dismiss the detail and we'll discuss things."

Hanson shook his head. "Sergeant Kent will remain here as a witness, sir."

Hanson dismissed the other two Marines and waited until they left, then turned to Beasley.

"We may have a real problem on our hands, sir. I suggest you give me the names of the Arabs, or anyone else who requested that our security personnel be withdrawn."

"Why do you want those names?"

"Their negligence or evil intentions makes them directly responsible for the suicide attack. I would prefer to think that you made a mistake in judgment, rather than you were part of a conspiracy."

"What do you mean?" Beasley asked, this time in a much more subdued tone.

"The Marines would have stopped the vets and prevented the attack. They never should have been withdrawn. Besides, you don't change security measures at the last moment, except in response to an emergency. There will be all kinds of investigations and you don't want to take all the blame."

"What if I say you gave the order?"

Hanson grinned at the puny ploy. "I have your written order, as well as witnesses, sir. If you're thinking about accusing me, I suggest you get a lawyer."

Beasley sat there stunned. He started to speak several times, then stopped. Suddenly he started sobbing and repeated over and over, "What'll I do? What'll I do?"

Al looked at him in disgust, then shook her head and gestured to Hanson, who ignored her.

"Get hold of yourself, sir. They're not going to shoot you. Give me the names and I'm sure that will be taken into account at the inquiry."

"Inquiry? What inquiry?"

"The Marine investigation. I don't think they'll turn you over to the U.N., or the Arabs."

"But they're the ones who told me to do it," Beasley moaned.

"If you would like some advice, sir …"

"Yes?"

"Tell them the truth. The Marines look out for their own, even in a case like this."

"But it'll ruin my career. What if they kick me out of the Corps? What'll I do then?"

"I don't know, sir. Right now, I suggest you go to your office and call General Griffin."

Hanson and Al watched Beasley slowly shuffle out of the room, a crushed man.

"What do you think will happen, Sam?" Al asked softly.

"If he's lucky, they'll transfer him back to supply as quietly as possible. The Corps has enough trouble without an officer being in the spotlight as the cause of this foul-up. If he wasn't foolish enough to write the order, they'd probably blame me. I'd be the ideal scapegoat," Hanson added bitterly.

"The Corps would support you, Sam."

"I wouldn't count on it. If the Arabs could blame me for the order, they'd be howling for my blood. I don't know if our leadership would stand by me."

"I'm sure they would, Sam." But he could hear the uncertainty in her voice.

Just then Captain Lonigan called and told Hanson what happened near U.N. headquarters in the aftermath when the parade broke up. "The Arabs looted a few stores, but there wasn't much damage and no injuries were reported. The Arabs dispersed and it looks like we'll have a quiet night, but I'll keep my cops on the street, just in case."

"Thanks for the update," Hanson said. "I'll talk to you in the morning."

Hanson called Colonel Warrington and after a brief consultation they decided that their ready platoons could stand down for the night. Hanson disconnected and told Al to inform Jed and dismiss their platoons.

"Yes, sir. Question?"

Hanson nodded.

"What do we do if Beasley issues any orders?"

"Call me immediately. It shouldn't be a problem, but I'll call General Griffin now and request clarification."

"Yes, sir."

She threw him a snappy salute, about-faced and left.

General Griffin was quite blunt about his conversation with Beasley. "I relieved him of command and ordered him to report to my headquarters immediately. I'll be sending you a fax in a few minutes placing you in command and appointing you temporary brevet Major. I'm assigning another company to you, just in case of possible threats, if I can figure out a way to get them to you without attracting attention."

"If I may make a suggestion, sir. Transport them to Staten Island, then send them by waterferry to east 34th street. I'll meet them there."

"Outstanding. I'll call you later, Major."

"Thank you, sir."

Hanson went over a list of what had to be done and concluded he covered everything but a final update for Dr. Carver, who he called. "This is Major Hanson, Dr. Carver. I'd like to fill you in on current conditions."

"Go ahead, Major. Is the rank official?"

"I just got confirmation from General Griffin."

"Congratulations."

"Thank you, sir. We don't expect any trouble tonight, but Captain Lonigan has extra patrols throughout the Enclave and we've advised residents to stay off the streets. The Arabs demanded a U.N. investigation of the incident and I recommended to General Griffin that we have our own investigation by the FBI and some of our other agencies. Captain Beasley has been relieved and I'm in command. I suggest we meet tomorrow afternoon and review the situation."

"So you think we're safe tonight?"

"Yes, sir. I just don't want to take any chances."

"Agreed. One o'clock?"

"Yes, sir. Have a good night."

"You too, Major."

• • •

Carver went to Mavis' room and knocked on the door.

"Who is it?" Mavis asked playfully.

"It's me."

"Come in, Dad. What's up?"

Mavis and Jennifer were hunched over the computer monitor and Mavis quickly switched screens, which Carver pretended to ignore. "There was some trouble today at the U.N. parade. Did you hear about it?"

"Of course, Dad. Some of those Arab terrorists finally got a taste of their own medicine. No pun intended."

He smiled at her affectionately. "Things are pretty quiet now, but we've been advised to stay off the streets. I think it would be a good idea for Jennifer to spend the night here, unless her father wants her home. Would that be a problem?"

"No, Dad."

"Do you want me to call your father?"

"No, Dr. Carver. I'll call him. He'll be glad that you're looking out for me."

"Alright. Dinner at 7:30. I'll see you then, girls."

As soon as Dr. Carver shut the door behind him, Jennifer turned to Mavis and said in a deep, throaty voice, "At last we are alone," which sent them into a fit of giggling.

"What are your intentions, Miss?" Mavis teased.

"Not honorable, I assure you," Jennifer replied with a wicked grin. "I had planned to stay overnight, before the Arabs obliged me by getting blown up."

"What do you think about the suicide attack, Jen?"

"I can understand what those vets did. The Arabs took away the last of their security and dignity."

"I don't know if I could be a suicide bomber," Mavis mused.

"Let's hope you never have to be."

"What'll happen next?"

"Hopefully they'll just drone on at the U.N. But enough of politics for now. I want to show you some implements for use at bedtime."

"What kind of implements?" Mavis squeaked.

"You'll see."

•   •   •

Kyle and Tyrone played pool in the recreation room for a while, then got restless.

"Do you feel like a karate workout?" Tyrone suggested.

"Sure. Let's borrow some sweats and go behind the barracks."

A few minutes later they started their forms and some of the Marines drifted out and joined them. Kyle was surprised that with one exception, a staff sergeant, he was more advanced than the others. By unspoken consent, the sergeant led the group through beginner forms, then segued into more advanced forms, until only Kyle and Tyrone were following him. When they finished, the sergeant nodded approvingly at the boys, then turned to the watching Marines.

"You snuffies better get off your asses and shape up, before some old ladies mug you."

Then he walked off, shaking his head pityingly at the low skills of the troops.

Kyle and Tyrone showered and went back to the rec room, where they alternated watching CNN and Al Jazeera. CNN was less smug in its anti-Americanism than it used to be, but more specific in its disapproval of American policies. The newscaster, a former Hollywood glamour girl, condemned the American suicide bombers as fanatic extremists.

"Yeah. Right," Tyrone growled. "You don't ever see that bitch sticking up for her country."

"Maybe she doesn't want to provoke anyone," Kyle offered.

"She'll sing a different tune when the Arabs kidnap her and rape her," Tyrone retorted.

Al Jazeera was much more excitable. A bearded mullah ranted and raved and there was no doubt who he was yelling about. A translation zipper barely toned down the torrent of hate he launched on the infidel, imperialist dogs who cowardly murdered the Arab heroes who fought for Islam. The mullah was replaced by news clips that showed rioting and violent street protests in Muslim countries around the world, especially in France.

The boys discussed the vets' suicide bombing at some length. They both agreed that the vets' extreme action could be justified by what happened to them. Tyrone's position was that they had nothing more to lose, so they took some enemies of America with them.

"I've been thinking about what my dad said," Kyle mused, "that Marines shouldn't be suiciders. I know if Marines are surrounded by hostiles who will butcher them if they surrender, they should fight to the death. I think the vets felt something like that. I just hope it doesn't cause trouble for all of us."

"Would you have done it?" Tyrone asked softly.

"I don't know. Maybe. If I was desperate enough."

"Do you think they were desperate enough?"

Kyle nodded. "I guess so."

●　　　●　　　●

Hanson made one last phone call to Captain Lonigan, who assured him that all was quiet in the Enclave. Then he decided to indulge himself in a rare treat and spend some time with his son.

He found the boys in the rec room, playing 'Capture the Canal', a banned computer game featuring an attack on the Suez Canal, to free it from control by the Islamic Fundamentalists who currently ruled Egypt. The boys were battling two Marines who had refused to be 'rags'. They were in a state of shock from the boys rapid repelling of a poorly organized assault that resulted in the capture of many of the invaders, and the retreat of the rest. Hanson watched for a few moments and concluded that the battle was over.

"I'm sorry to interrupt you, but I need to speak to my son."

"That's alright, gunny," one of the Marines said. "They whipped our asses. Maybe we'll get revenge on Tyrone."

"Fat chance, snuffies," he quipped.

"Don't let anyone outside of the company see you playing that game," Hanson admonished.

"Don't worry, gunny, the sergeant of the guard will alert us if we get visitors."

Hanson led Kyle to one of the empty N.C.O.'s rooms that he occasionally used when he stayed overnight at the barracks. "What's up, Dad?"

"I know how much you were upset by what the vets did today and I wanted to talk to you about it."

"I hope you're not sore at me for mouthing off like that."

"Not at all. In fact, you reminded me that I had neglected them."

"What would you have done in their place, Dad?"

"Just between us?"

"Sure."

"Truthfully, I don't know. I wouldn't encourage Americans to be suiciders unless there was no other way. I believe suicide is morally wrong."

"What options did the vets have?"

"I don't know, Kyle. I'm ashamed to say I didn't think about their situation."

"It really bothers you, doesn't it?"

"Of course. They paid their dues and we abandoned them."

"What could you have done about it?"

"I don't know. I keep saying that, don't I?"

They sat quietly for a few moments, thinking how they were both familiar with being abandoned.

"What's going to happen tomorrow, Dad?"

Hanson snapped back from the remembrance of being disarmed by U.N. peacekeepers at the Asmera airport. "Hopefully there'll be the usual tantrums and screaming at the U.N. and it'll blow over in a few days."

"And if it doesn't?"

"We'll be in for some trouble."

"What'll happen to you?"

"Well General Griffin has relieved Captain Beasley …"

"Yay. It's about time."

"If I may continue."

"Sorry, Dad."

"I've been promoted to the temporary rank of brevet Major and placed in command."

"That's great, Dad."

"I hope so."

"What do you mean? Isn't that what we wanted?"

"Yes. Unless I'm being set up to take the fall for the vets' attack."

"General Griffin wouldn't do that to you."

"No. But others who outrank him might."

"That sucks. What can we do?"

"Nothing right now. Maybe I'm being too paranoid … I need to get some sleep. Tomorrow's likely to be a busy day. You can bunk in here, if you like."

"Thanks, Dad. I told Tyrone I'd bunk with him."

Kyle leaned over and hugged his father, then kissed him on the cheek. The first time in a long time.

"Goodnight, son."

12

HANSON WAS ABOUT to shoot a U.N. peacekeeper who didn't want to let the wounded Marines on the plane, when a loud noise yanked him out of sleep and his recurring nightmare of Asmera airport.

"Wake up, gunny. It's me. Wilkins."

The repeated knocking snapped him wide awake. He looked at the clock that read 0545 and opened the door. "What is it, snail?"

"There's some FBI and N.I.S. dudes at the barracks entrance flashing badges and they're mighty pissed that I made them wait for a superior officer."

Hanson couldn't help grinning at what he knew would be their indignant reaction.

"You didn't shoot them, did you?"

"No, gunny. Not without your order."

They smiled at each other in a moment of camaraderie.

"Tell them I'll be with them in a few minutes and escort them into the day room."

"Yes, gunny."

"Snail."

"Yes, gunny?"

"Be polite, but don't let them wander around."

"Can I butt-stroke them if they won't listen?"

"No, snail. Dismissed."

Wilkins walked off, muttering something about 'no fun around here'.

Hanson decided to wear his Gunnery Sergeant rank and not appear to be the brightest of bulbs. The good sense of his decision was confirmed a few minutes later when he was confronted by the obviously hostile investigators.

"I'm Special Agent-in-Charge Royce. This is Special Agent Madison. The two gentlemen from Naval Investigative Service are Captain Evans and Commander Hooper."

"May I see your identification, please," Hanson requested formally.

While they showed their credentials, Hanson discreetly looked them over. Royce was a large, fleshy, pink-skinned man, already weighed down by food and drink. It was clear that he resented being selected for this career threatening investigation. Madison was a tall, athletic black woman, who looked like a sprinter and was probably a showpiece for the FBI Evans and Hooper weren't line officers and possibly came closest to sea duty in their bathtubs. They were cops.

"What can I do for you, gentlemen, ma'am?"

"You know why we're here, Hanson," Royce barked.

"Gunnery Sergeant Hanson, sir. Am I being accused of anything?"

"That's what we're here to determine," Royce snarled.

"How can I help you, sir?"

"Why did you remove the security detail for the parade?" Royce demanded harshly.

"I was ordered to do so by my commanding officer, Captain Beasley."

"Can anyone confirm that?" Agent Madison asked.

"Yes, ma'am."

"Why did he give you that order?" Captain Evans asked.

"I was in temporary command of the security force, sir."

"That's not what I meant, Sergeant. What was the reason?"

"I don't know, sir."

"Didn't you ask?"

"No, sir. I advised Captain Beasley that we shouldn't withdraw security at the last minute, but he ordered me to do it."

Commander Hooper seemed to have a personal grudge against Hanson and asked belligerently, "Did you disagree with the order, Sergeant?"

"Yes, sir."

"But you obeyed it?"

"Yes, sir."

"Is that all you have to say?" Captain Evans asked.

"Yes, sir."

The investigators had a whispered conference that indicated a difference of opinion between the FBI and the Navy.

"What do you think Captain Beasley would say about this incident?" Royce demanded.

"You'll have to ask him, sir."

"You're not being very responsive, Sergeant," Royce accused.

"What would you like me to say, sir?"

"What if Beasley denies giving you that order?" Royce smirked. "It's your word against his."

Royce was invoking the old threat of officer versus enlisted man.

"It's Captain Beasley, sir. And he gave me the order in writing."

The sudden disclosure took Royce aback and, for the moment left him speechless.

"I'd like to see that order, Sergeant," Captain Evans requested.

"Yes, sir. I'll go get it and be right back."

Hanson walked out, smiling to himself at the consternation he had caused. He understood that everyone involved would be looking for a scapegoat and he was determined that it wouldn't be him.

Hanson went to his office, got a copy of the order, leisurely smoked a cigarette, then went back to the dayroom. The revelation of a written order had firmly divided the FBI from the Navy, an organization that placed a premium on written orders. Hanson handed the copy to Captain Evans, who inspected it and passed it on.

"This is a copy," Evans observed.

"Yes, sir."

"Where is the original?"

"On file, sir."

Evans stared at Hanson and almost imperceptibly nodded in recognition of an old Navy tradition, cover your ass.

"We'll need the original," Royce said, in a less aggressive manner. "It'll have to be checked for authenticity."

"I'm sure it will be available at the appropriate time, sir," Hanson replied.

Royce realized that they were at an impasse and decided to end the session.

"That's all for now, Sergeant. We'll be interviewing you again."

"Thank you, sir. Your escort will see you out."

"That's not necessary, Sergeant," Royce said. "We can find our own way out."

"We're under Condition Green, sir. You'll require an escort."

Royce stomped out angrily, followed by the others. Commander Hooper glared at Hanson, recognizing bullshit, but Hanson looked at him imperturbably.

Jed and Al had been hovering nearby during the interview and rushed in as soon as the investigators left.

"How'd it go, Sam?" Jed asked.

"Tell us," Al implored.

"They're probably not going to hang me from a yardarm," Hanson teased.

"Aw. C'mon, Sam. Don't make us beg," Jed replied.

"They hinted that I could take the rap if it was my word against Captain Beasley's …"

"Stop teasing us," Al said. "What happened next?"

"I told them I had a written order and that took the wind out of their sails. They blustered a little longer, decided they had enough information from me, then said goodbye, almost politely."

"Politely," Al mimicked. "So you're off the hook?"

"It seems so."

"That's a relief," Jed muttered. "Sam?"

"Yes, Jed?"

"What's a yardarm?"

"Something that holds the sails, I think."

"Does the navy still use sails?" Al asked.

Hanson laughed. "Let's meet in an hour and set the schedule for the day. Now beat it, you two."

•   •   •

Hanson took out his map of the Enclave and looked at all the places where they were vulnerable to attack. He assumed that there wouldn't be a full-scale invasion sponsored by the U.N., so he considered where an angry mob of Arabs could be a threat. He decided that the East River Drive, 23rd street, Fifth Avenue, and 40th street should be manned by police and Guardwell personnel, with National Guard and Marine back-up.

He called Captain Lonigan and requested that he reinforce the perimeter of the Enclave, while his remaining officers got some rest. Colonel Warrington approved the plan and said he'd assign platoons to the key areas. Only Grant Browning of Guardwell, as usual, gave him a hard time, until he finally got tough.

"Listen, Browning. I'm not running a debate society. Either you cooperate, or we go to Dr. Carver and let him settle it once and for all."

Browning sulkily agreed to take orders.

Hanson reviewed his plan with Jed and Al, then called General Griffin and brought him up to date on recent developments.

"How's Beasley taking it?" the general asked.

"I don't know, sir. I've been too busy to check, but I think N.I.S. has him in their sights."

"It'll settle a lot of problems if they blame him. Then I can send him to peel potatoes in Idaho, or somewhere he won't cause problems."

"I'll look in on him before lunch."

"How are the streets?"

"Quiet, sir."

"Well, I hope they stay that way."

"Me too, sir."

"The rioting in Europe and the Mideast is winding down and the worst may be over."

"I hope so, sir."

"I've got a weapons company en route to you, led by Captain Muzzetti."

"I don't know him personally, sir, but I heard he's a good man."

"That's why I picked him. They should be on Staten Island sometime late tomorrow afternoon. I'll call you when they get there."

"Thank you, sir. I suggest they disembark at 23rd street, rather than 34th. There's less chance of being observed from the U.N."

"Good idea, Sam. Goodbye."

"Goodbye, sir."

Hanson called Captain Lonigan, who reported all was quiet. They decided to talk hourly and anytime there was a problem. Just before they disconnected Lonigan asked,

"What's your first name?"

"Sam."

"I'm Mike. Let's have a drink together when things calm down."

"You got it."

Hanson mused for a moment on the weird way friendships were sometimes formed in an emergency, when you found out what people were made of. He came back to his chores, looked through his inbox for anything urgent and shoved all the usual request forms and bureaucratic correspondence back in the box. He briefly ran over his mental check list to be sure he wasn't forgetting anything important and made a note to check on the boys, who were at school, later in the day.

Hanson told his clerk that he was going to Captain Beasley's office and to forward any calls. He bumped into the FBI and N.I.S. people in the hall, who had returned to interview Beasley. He nodded and started to go by them, but Royce confronted him.

"We went to Captain Beasley's office. He didn't answer and the lights were out," he announced indignantly.

"I'm surprised you didn't do a B and E," Hanson quipped, adding before Royce had a conniption fit, "Was his clerk there?"

"No," Royce snarled.

Hanson called the sergeant of the guard.

"Did Captain Beasley leave the building, Sergeant Jefferson?"

"I'll check, sir." He was back a moment later. "No, sir."

"Thanks, Jeff."

"Let's go back to his office," Hanson told them.

"We have other things to do, Sergeant, besides chasing after Beasley," Royce grumbled.

"Suit yourself," Hanson replied, "but I've got to check on him."

They followed Hanson to Beasley's office, where he knocked loudly, then called,

"Captain Beasley. It's Hanson. Are you there?"

There was no answer and the door was locked. He called Jefferson again.

"Jeff. Where's Danowski?"

"I'll check, sir … He's in the mess hall, sir."

"Thanks, Jeff. Tell him to report to Captain Beasley's office on the double."

"Yes, sir."

Less than a minute later they heard footsteps running quickly and Danowski rushed to them, panting heavily.

"Where's the Captain, Danowski?" Hanson asked.

"He was in his office last time I saw him."

"When was that, soldier?" Royce demanded.

"About twenty minutes ago, when he sent me to the mess hall. And I'm not a soldier, sir. I'm a Marine."

"Whatever," Royce muttered. "Open the door."

As Danowski fumbled with his keys, Hanson had a presentment about what they'd find.

Danowski opened the door, put on the light, then went to Beasley's door, followed by the others. He knocked on the door and said, "Captain Beasley. There are some people here to see you."

There was no answer and he unlocked the door, put on the light and they saw Beasley hanging from a ceiling pipe by his belt. The stench from his voided bowels filled their nostrils and Royce gagged.

"Oh, shit," Danowski said, while the others stared in fascination.

"Get him down," Hanson ordered.

"Don't touch him," Royce countermanded, "until we get a forensics team in here. Wait in your office," he ordered Danowski, who looked at Hanson, who nodded.

When Danowski walked out, Royce turned to the others.

"This could be a convenient solution."

"Not for Captain Beasley," Hanson said bitterly, which elicited a glare from Royce.

"If he wasn't guilty, why did he hang himself?" Royce asked accusingly.

"The only thing he was guilty of was a stupid mistake," Hanson replied.

Royce looked at him in surprise. "I was under the impression that you didn't think much of him, Sergeant."

"He was still a Marine."

13

C IRCUMSTANCES HAD CHANGED so rapidly that the investigating team let Hanson stay in the room during their discussion. Royce studiously turned his back on Beasley, whose purple face and bloody neck indicated a last-minute desperate struggle for life that was a disturbing sight.

"Well, I think this could conclude our investigation, assuming forensics finds no trace of foul play," Royce announced.

The other investigators nodded sagely, obviously relieved to have a simple solution for a volatile problem. No one said anything for a moment, which gave Hanson a chance to decide whether to get involved, or to let these less than dedicated cops off the hook.

"I'm certain you'll find no trace of, how did you put it, Mr. Royce, 'foul play'," Hanson said.

"Why are you so sure?" Royce challenged.

"This is a Marine installation. No one could have done that to him in such a short time, without being discovered."

The investigators looked at each other, then Royce replied, "Assuming you're right. That means he was responsible for allowing the bombing and we can present that as an official finding."

Royce's smugness prompted Hanson's disagreeing response.

"You're forgetting several things. Where did the C-4 come from? Who else is involved besides the vets? Are they planning anything else? It's simple enough to blame Beasley, but some of the U.N. folk aren't so stupid that they won't suspect a group of plotters."

Royce was horrified. "Are you suggesting an anti-Arab conspiracy?"

"I'm not suggesting anything, Royce. I'm merely mentioning questions that would occur to anyone of intelligence who was investigating the incident."

Royce's face didn't quite turn as purple as Beasley's. "Are you questioning our intelligence?" Royce demanded.

"I'm reminding you that the U.N. might not be satisfied by just blaming poor Beasley," Hanson replied, ignoring the outraged tone.

The investigators whispered together for a moment, then Royce turned to Hanson.

"Wait outside, Sergeant. We'll call you in a minute."

Danowski raised an eyebrow when Hanson walked out, hoping for some info for the N.C.O.'s grapevine, that processed almost as fast as the Internet. Hanson ignored him, thinking to himself, 'Well you got involved. Now how far do you go?' He knew that other vets had to be in on the plot. The real questions were where did they get the explosives and was this a one-shot deal. He was speculating that only army or Marine personnel could have access to C-4 in the Enclave unless the plot went beyond the Enclave.

The inner door opened, and Royce interrupted his musing.

"Come in here, Sergeant."

Hanson walked in slowly and knew when he saw the confusion on their faces that they realized a mere scapegoat was no longer sufficient. He decided that at all costs he would try to protect the Marines, his country and the Enclave, in that order. Royce's false smile alerted him that he still had to be very careful.

"Well, Sergeant. We've decided to let you assist us in our investigation."

"That's not a good idea, sir."

"Why not?"

"I'm in command of the Marine detachment. The Arabs hate me. It would just provoke them unnecessarily if you include me."

"You seem to have a pretty high opinion of yourself, Sergeant," Madison commented.

Before he could reply, Captain Evans answered her. "Gunnery Sergeant Hanson was the man who led the retreat from Saudi Arabia and saved his unit. He was reduced in rank by order of President Beaumont."

"I thought your name sounded familiar," Madison remarked, "but I didn't connect it to a Sergeant. You're a hero."

"Shucks, ma'am. T'werent nothing," Hanson drawled.

Royce had been disapprovingly watching the growing compatibility of Hanson and Madison.

"If you're not going to assist us, Sergeant, you better leave the room."

"Not until you're finished on Marine premises. It's my responsibility as ranking officer to be sure that everything is handled properly."

Royce started to flush with anger, but Hanson defused the budding tirade. "That doesn't mean I'll obstruct you. I just have to look out for my troops. If I may offer a suggestion …"

"Go ahead," Royce said begrudgingly.

"It's vital to prevent another suicide attack, but it's even more important to deflect the media from turning this event into a circus that could lead to a disaster for us."

"He's right, sir," Madison agreed, echoed by Evans and Hooper.

Royce pretended to ponder for a few moments, then went along with the consensus.

"Good idea, Sergeant. What do you propose?"

He was formulating an answer when Sergeant Jefferson called him.

"Sir. There's an angry mob of reporters outside with camera crews. They're clamoring to get in and interview the vets and our C.O."

Hanson thought quickly, then turned to the investigators. "The media are outside. Someone should speak to them. Do you want to do it, Mr. Royce?"

Surprised by the offer to bask in the limelight, Royce inflated a bit, then asked the others with false modesty, "Do you want me to be our spokesperson?"

The Navy wanted no part of publicity and instantly agreed.

"How do you think I should handle it?" he asked.

No one else answered, so Hanson replied, "Tell them that the suicide attack seems to have been an isolated incident, carried out by two disgruntled war veterans. There will be a thorough investigation and our findings will be presented to the appropriate authorities. Don't mention Beasley. If asked, say the C.O. is unavailable due to illness."

Royce considered the implications of the statement, then nodded approval. He sailed out, a clumsy brigantine, to face the press.

"That was deftly handled, Major," Captain Evans remarked.

"Thank you, sir. It comes from good schooling."

Hanson had noticed Evans' academy ring, and his reference was appreciated.

"Why did you call him Major?" Madison asked. "I thought he was a Sergeant."

"It was a temporary condition, Agent Madison. He was recently returned to his rank and I think he's on the promotion list after Election Day," Evans answered.

"I don't understand."

"It's a long story. Maybe Major Hanson will tell you about it when you have time," Evans said with a twinkle in his eye.

Just then the forensics team arrived and asked everyone else to leave.

"Now let's go question the vets and make sure they're not up to anything else," Evans said.

"Thank you for your cooperation, Major."

"You're welcome, sir."

Hanson instructed Danowski to keep an eye on things and call him if there were any problems. He went to his office and called General Griffin.

"I have bad news, sir. Captain Beasley hanged himself."

After his loud cursing subsided, Griffin asked, "Why did the idiot do that?"

"I don't know, sir. He left a note that just said, 'I'm sorry'. I found him with the investigating team."

"What's being done?"

"Forensics is checking the scene. Royce is talking to the media, and Captain Evans told me I was on the promotion list."

Griffin laughed. "I wanted to tell you myself."

"Thank you for all your help, sir."

"It's long overdue, Sam. The Corps will need you down the road."

"That's nice to hear, sir. May I make a request?"

"Shoot."

"I'd like to promote my platoon Sergeants to gunnys. It's long overdue."

Griffin chuckled. "Don't be a smart-ass, Sam."

"Yes, sir. I'd also like to promote Staff Sergeants Kent and Davis to 2nd Lieutenants and arrange O.C.S. for them later."

"How about another star for me while you're at it?"

"I wish I could, Charlie. You deserve it."

There was a long silence.

"You're a good friend, Sam. I'll see what I can do."

There was a knock on his door and a moment later Agent Madison poked her head in.

"Can I talk to you for a moment?"

"Sure. Come in. Where's your boss?"

"He'll be dancing with the media as long as he can. I don't have much time. Can I level with you?"

He stared at her, not sure of her intentions. "That depends."

"On what?"

"What you're after. You don't know me. Why should you want to confide in me?"

She took a deep breath. "We were instructed to localize all elements of the attack and blame it on a Marine who went rogue."

"Me?"

"You. I didn't know who you were before …"

"Does that make a difference?"

"Yes. I was going to join the Marines and become an officer, but my mother became ill and I couldn't leave her for long periods of time. The FBI recruited me and it turned out alright … I followed your retreat from Riyadh and I think it's one of the great military feats of our time …"

He looked at her intently. "Don't confuse desperation with something romantic."

"I'm not. Your actions represented the two qualities I most admire, duty and honor."

"What's your first name?"

"Latisha."

"Sit down, Tish."

She stared at him in surprise. "How did you know that? That's what my mom calls me."

He grinned. "A good guess. What did you want to tell me?"

"Now that Beasley committed suicide, he'll probably be blamed for everything …"

"The poor fool just wanted a better life …"

"That doesn't matter now. Certain people in Washington would like to get you for embarrassing them. If we can't contain this case, they'll be after you."

"I expected that."

"I just wanted to warn you. I've got to get back before Royce comes looking for me."

"Thanks, Tish. Are you based in Washington or New York?"

"Here. Why?"

"Just wondering if you'd have dinner with an old Marine some time?"

"You think I came here to get a date?" she asked indignantly.

"No. But that doesn't mean you can't leave with one."

She glared at him, then burst into laughter. "I'll call you."

A few minutes later the investigators returned to his office and Royce was particularly affable after stroking the media.

"We're going to interview the vets now, Sergeant. Do you want to come with us?"

"I think it's a good idea that you come with us," Captain Evans added. "They'll be reassured by your presence."

"Sure. Be aware, though, that they're angry at everyone in authority who they feel betrayed them, including me."

"They'll have to cooperate, if they know what's good for them," Royce declared.

"You might not want to be confrontational with them," Hanson suggested. "They got a raw deal."

"Whose side are you on?" Royce demanded.

"They're our people, Royce. They sacrificed for us and we let the Arabs, the enemy they defended us against, take away the little that they had left. We should use this as an opportunity to help them."

"I don't think you understand the big picture, Sergeant," Royce said.

Hanson shook his head in disgust. "I understand who the enemy is," he responded, looking at Royce.

Before a real argument broke out, Captain Evans intervened and suggested, "Why don't we discuss this after we talk to the vets."

Royce nodded reluctantly and they went to the Veterans Hospital. When they walked into the vet's ward, the stench that greeted them of unwashed bodies, overflowing toilets and decaying food was enhanced by no ventilation. The sickening odor was complemented by mounds of uncollected trash that cluttered the floor. The visitors gaped in surprise at the dreadful conditions, but only Hanson and Madison seemed to feel any sympathy for the plight of the vets.

"We're here to investigate yesterday's events," Royce announced loudly.

The vets ignored him and he repeated his announcement.

After a long silence, one vet said contemptuously, "Fuck you, lardass."

Royce flushed beet red. "I warn you. If you don't cooperate you'll be in a lot of trouble."

"What'r you gonna do, put us in Leavenworth? It's gotta be better than this," another vet said, gesturing around him.

The tension between the two groups was mounting and Royce didn't seem to realize that he had no leverage over the alienated vets. Hanson tried to soften the impact of Royce's threat.

"We know you have issues …"

"Are you with them now, sir?" one vet asked.

"Some of you know me," Hanson answered, "and I'll tell you frankly that my duty is to the Corps. I think you guys got a raw deal, but there's nothing I can do about it. Right now, we're concerned that your suicide attack will provoke reprisals on innocent civilians."

"What else can we do?" another vet asked bitterly. "We've been thrown away and no one gives a shit if we live or die."

"That doesn't give you the right to carry out suicide attacks," Royce said.

"Who're you?" a vet asked.

"FBI Special Agent-in-Charge Royce."

"Well mister Special Agent-in-Charge Royce, how do we get the help we need?"

"Not by breaking the law," Royce insisted.

The vet turned to his comrades. "Do you believe this asshole? Fuck off, rag lover."

Royce was outraged at their disrespect and was about to explode, when Captain Evans spoke up, "We know you men have a real grievance. If you assure us there'll be no more suicide attacks, we'll see what we can do about getting you the services you need."

"We've heard that bullshit before," a vet responded. "Why should we trust you?"

"I give you my word as an officer and a gentleman," Evans answered.

The vet turned to Hanson. "We don't trust squids. If you give us your word, sir, we'll believe you."

"I don't know if I can do anything to help you, but I'll try."

"Is that good enough, guys?" the vet asked his comrades.

Nods and affirmative grunts indicated their acceptance.

"Do we have your word there'll be no more attacks?" Royce asked.

"We'll give you some time to do something," a vet answered.

"Then I guess we're through here for the time being." Royce said. "We'll be back to talk to you tomorrow."

14

D R. CARVER CALLED HANSON in the early afternoon.
"How are you, Major?"

"Hopeful that we can contain the situation."

"Update me."

"I brought the investigating team to Captain Beasley's office and we found him hanging from a pipe."

There was a long silence, then Carver asked, "Suicide?"

"It's not officially confirmed yet, but it should be soon."

"Why did he do it?"

"The pressure got to him, and he was afraid he'd be dishonorably discharged and end up on the junk heap. The poor fool."

"I feel sorry for him," Carver said.

"You and I are the only ones, sir."

"What else happened?"

"We briefly spoke to the vets and sort of got them to agree not to launch any more attacks, if we try to help them."

"What do you mean, 'sort of'?"

"They feel betrayed and abandoned. They're living in squalor, without help or hope. If we can deliver some services that they need, I think they'll cooperate, but be aware that they expect to be deceived."

Carver didn't say anything for a moment, then said softly, "That sounds like blackmail to me."

"It's entitlement, sir. They paid their dues with their bodies. Then we threw them away and did nothing when the Arabs snatched their medical services."

"What do you suggest?"

"Let's start by giving them basic medical care, then see what else they need."

"We'll do it. Will you come with me tomorrow morning for the initial contact?"

"Yes, sir."

"Good. Nine o'clock?"

"Yes, sir."

"Now tell me what you think will happen in the next few days."

"If the U.N. and the Arabs accept the investigator's findings things should calm down quickly. A lot depends on whether or not the Russians are helpful. If they stir up the Arabs, we'll have trouble. I've prepared our security forces to deal with Arab incursions and another company of Marines will arrive tonight. I'll update you again in the morning."

"Then goodnight, Major."

●   ●   ●

There were no reports of disorder in the Enclave and the extensive police presence had eradicated the usual street crime. The investigators departed without indicating whether or not they'd return. An image of Agent Madison in a thong flitted through Hanson's mind. He grinned at the salacious image, then pushed his paperwork aside and went to lunch. The TV in the mess hall was tuned to CNN, which was following a debate in the U.N. The American ambassador to the U.N., Will Blunt, was just concluding his speech.

"We wish to assure our fellow members of this great international body that the unfortunate attack on U.N. Day was carried out by a few disturbed malcontents and does not represent the sentiments of the American people ..."

Catcalls from several representatives of Arab countries interrupted Blunt for a few moments, then he concluded, "We request your patience until the results of our investigations are presented to you within a few days. Thank you."

There were hisses and boos in the General Assembly, but the French Ambassador calmed everyone, a non-Gallic trait, and replied, "We will await your findings," and they adjourned.

General Griffin called Hanson to let him know that the company of Marines had landed in Staten Island.

"I've arranged for two water ferries to bring the troops. Their vehicles will use the regular ferries, land near Battery Park, then take the East Side Drive to 23rd street. Any questions?"

"No, sir. We'll be ready here and have them quartered so they get a good night's sleep."

"Well done, Sam."

"Thank you, sir."

"Any problem with Royce?"

"He was a little pushy, but we seem to have resolved our differences. I just heard Will Blunt ask the U.N. for time to finish the investigation and the premiere frog agreed. We may be over the hump."

"I hope you're right, Sam, but don't let down your guard."

"No, sir. Any chance of your getting down here in the near future?"

"Maybe. Why?"

"I'd like to talk to you about some policy issues."

"I'll see what I can do. Call me when the troops are settled in."

"Yes, sir. Any decision about promoting my sergeants?"

"Do it, Sam."

"Thank you, sir."

Jed and Al joined him in the mess hall and he made final arrangements for housing the incoming company.

"By the way, Sergeant Davis ..."

"Huh?"

"Your promotion to Lieutenant came through today. You'll be in command when Lieutenant Kent and I meet the new troops."

"What did you say, Sam?" Al asked in a shocked voice.

"You heard me. Both of you get your new rank displayed this afternoon."

"Yes, sir," they answered.

"Congratulations, sir. I mean, ma'am," Jed said. "You deserve it."

"Thank you, Lieutenant," she replied loftily.

"I'm promoting the other platoon leaders to gunny and I'll let them know later today. Down the road, when there's time, we'll send both of you to O.C.S."

"Do you think this will be a problem with the other sergeants, sir?" she asked.

Before Hanson could answer, Jed snapped, "I'll personally reeducate anyone who doesn't immediately recognize officer material."

"Thanks, Jed," Al said.

"Meet me in my office at 1800," Hanson ordered her, "and we'll go greet our new guests."

"Yes, sir."

Then they watched the funerals of Meshal and al Sadr on al Jazeera, the zipper on the bottom of the screen translating the Arab curses and threats to America.

To the relief of all concerned, the rest of the afternoon was crisis free. Hanson ate an early dinner at the mess hall, where the new ranks were the main topic of discussion at the snuffies' tables, albeit quietly. Kyle and Tyrone sat down at the senior table and were delighted when they learned of the promotions.

"Congratulations, Dad, Jed, Al. I mean ma'am," Kyle said.

"It's about time," Tyrone added.

"Thank you, boys. Now that I'm an officer, you'll have to have a crush on someone else," Al said with a straight face, which made Kyle blush and Tyrone fidget.

Jed played along with the teasing. "I don't think there's anything in the regulations that forbids young civilians from yearning for officers, ma'am."

The table erupted into laughter and Hanson thought it was a pleasant change from the depressed atmosphere that had become so normal for the Marines.

When they finished eating Kyle took his father aside.

"Can I talk to you for a minute, Dad?"

"Sure. What's up?"

"Some of the kids are having a costume party for Halloween on Monday night. Do you think things'll be calm enough for me to go?"

"Is Tyrone going?"

"Yes, Dad."

"I don't see why not. I'll let you know if there's a change."

"Thanks, Dad. Can I sleep at home tonight?"

"Yes. I'll see you there later."

Hanson watched him walk away and saw that he was almost a man. It seemed like just yesterday he was giving him piggy-back rides, and now … He shook his head to clear his thoughts.

"Al."

"Yes, sir?"

"Come with me."

"Yes, sir."

As they walked to his office he went over the evening's operation.

"Pick a squad from your platoon to guide the troops to barracks. If anyone asks what's going on, say it's a training exercise. The newcomers won't look any different from our Marines. Send another squad to the East Side Drive and 23rd Street to guide the vehicles."

"Yes, sir."

"By the way, Al."

"Yes, sir?"

"You're my executive officer."

"I'm honored, sir."

"Don't be. You'll do all the crap work I hate."

"Don't I already, sir?" she asked innocently.

He grinned. "Dismissed."

•   •   •

Hanson took Al in his hummer when they left to meet the incoming Marines, with instructions to be as casual as possible on the way back to the barracks. They got to the river early, so he could be sure they would be unobserved. Al and Tico, used to waiting quietly while their leader assessed the situation, were comfortable in the silence. Tico kept rubbing his new sergeant's stripes and flexing his arm, which he could barely move due to his fellow N.C.O.'s punches that initiated the new stripe.

Hanson and Al exchanged grins at his discomfort, both of them familiar with the rough ways of the sergeant's club. She rubbed her arm with sympathy pains, remembering when she got her stripes. Some of the sergeants, still opposed to women having a combat role in the Corps, really hit her hard. She took it without flinching, but she knew who was deliberately mean and put them in her to-be-repaid file. Most of them had been killed in action before she could get payback and it no longer mattered.

There was no traffic on the East River Drive and the Enclave was quiet, so Hanson relaxed for a few minutes. He looked at the dark, impenetrable river flowing to the already overburdened ocean, its refuse and pollution concealed by the night. He briefly wondered if there were any clean rivers left in America. He couldn't understand how his countrymen had allowed such violation of their heritage. It was no consolation that every place else he had been in the world was as bad, or worse.

He lit a cigarette, breaking his one-a-day rule and flicked it into the river half-finished, tracking the flight of the burning coal until it was extinguished. He checked his watch and noted that there was plenty of time until the ferries arrived and leaned against the railing, staring at nothing.

The first ferry arrived at 2000 and the troops disembarked with a minimum of confusion. Captain Muzzetti, followed by another officer, walked up to Hanson and saluted.

"Captain Muzzetti reporting, sir."

"Welcome to the Enclave, Captain."

"Thank you, sir. It's a privilege to serve with you. This is my XO, Lieutenant Nakamura."

Nakamura saluted and Hanson returned it and shook hands.

"This is my XO, Lieutenant Kent."

They exchanged handshakes and Hanson looked the newcomers over. They were quite a contrast. Muzzetti was short, stocky, dark-haired and clean-featured, with a boyish look of innocence that belied ten years of service in the Corps. Nakamura was tall, lean, muscular, dark-haired and exceptionally handsome, with distinctly oriental features. He looked like a capable Marine officer. He probably owed his height to good old American protein, a condition that future generations might look back on with envy.

"Al. You and Nakamura lead the troops to the barracks, then return here. Take my hummer. Captain Muzzetti and I will wait for the next ferry."

Both lieutenants saluted snappily, then went to the waiting troops and got them moving.

Hanson and Muzzetti watched the orderly departure of the troops without getting involved.

"You've got a good XO, sir."

"Yes. How's your man?"

"Good record at the Academy and he's served well since he was commissioned. He only reported in two months ago, but so far, so good.

I've only been with the company for three months and it's my first company command. I'd be grateful for any guidance you can offer, sir."

Hanson chuckled. "We don't say 'keep your powder dry' anymore, but this is a very sensitive posting and you'll have to learn a lot that isn't in the handbook."

"Yes, sir. Exactly what is the situation, sir?"

"I'll brief you, your officers and senior N.C.O.'s when we get back to the barracks. In the meantime, I'd like a few minutes alone, until the next boatload arrives."

"Yes, sir."

Muzzetti watched Hanson walk a few steps away and stare at the river. He regarded with admiration the living legend of the Corps, who had defied the President of the United States to save his troops, and hoped he could meet his standards.

Al and Nakamura returned forty-five minutes later and Al reported to Hanson.

"No one paid attention to us on the way to the barracks, and the new troops are settling in. Your orders, sir?"

"Relax until the next boat pulls in and get acquainted with our new officers."

"Yes, sir."

Al and Nakamura, Naka to his friends, had filled each other in on their service backgrounds on the way to the barracks. Al was pleasantly surprised when her combat experience easily overcame her liabilities to Naka of her not attending the Academy and being a woman.

Naka gushed to Captain Muzzetti, "Muzi. Al was in the retreat from Riyadh with Major Hanson."

Muzzetti tried to be cool, but he was obviously impressed.

"He may be the greatest Marine since Chesty Puller," Muzzetti said.

"We think so," Al replied tersely.

Both officers noted her reference to the rest of Hanson's command and were further determined to have him think well of them.

•　　　•　　　•

The second ferry pulled in a few minutes later and the disembarkation went as smoothly as the first. Hanson sent Muzzetti, Al and Nakamura with the company and rode back alone, his first step to establishing the distance between commander and subordinates, which he knew was necessary to ensure the discipline and obedience of troops who were familiar with him as a noncom, a rank much more accessible to casual contact. He also knew there would be no problems from the old hands, but some of the people in the Enclave, particularly the Guardwell personnel would find it easier to accept his authority as a Major.

The streets were still quiet and there was no indication that the arrival of another company of Marines had been noticed by anyone. He called Lonigan, who reported no disturbances, not even petty street crime, or minor bar altercations. Hanson didn't know whether this was the calm before the storm or a sign of real tranquility, but he decided, as usual, to prepare for the worst.

The briefing was a formal event in the conference room, another step in defining the command structure, and included the officer's and senior N.C.O.'s of both companies. Hanson presented the situation simply.

"I'm sure you've all heard about the suicide bombing by our vets on U.N. Day."

There were murmurs of assent.

"Anyone who needs more information about the incident should speak to my executive officer, Lieutenant Kent. What you newcomers don't know is that Captain Beasley, our former C.O."

This instantly got everyone's attention.

"Hanged himself this morning and will probably be blamed for the incident. If we're lucky, if the U.N. and the Arabs accept the investigation's findings, if the Arabs don't seek revenge … There are a lot of ifs, things may stay calm. Tomorrow Lieutenant Kent will assign the duty roster. Captain Muzzetti. Once your troops are settled in barracks, Lieutenant Davis will conduct the officers and N.C.O.'s to their new quarters. We will make arrangements to house your families as soon as possible. If you have any questions, see Lieutenant Kent. Dismissed."

Everyone snapped to attention when Hanson stood up and he gestured to Muzzetti to join him.

"You'll accompany me tomorrow at 0900 to a meeting with Dr. Carver. He's the medical department head who is our liaison to the civilian authorities in the Enclave. He's been very supportive of our mission."

"Yes, sir."

He made a quick decision that he would stay in his old office for the time being.

"I'll assign Captain Beasley's office to you as soon as the investigators are through with it."

"Yes, sir."

"If the investigators question you, you were on leave and know nothing."

"Yes, sir."

"And Captain Muzzetti?"

"Sir?"

"Don't emulate Captain Beasley's example."

"Is that an order, sir?"

"Just a suggestion," he answered, without indicating whether or not he was kidding.

"I'll take it under advisement, sir."

Hanson grinned as Muzzetti walked away, then started reviewing the many changes that he would have to make now that he was in command. He decided to remain in his apartment for the time being, rather than move to the new quarters he would be entitled to, mostly for Kyle's sake, and went home and actually got a good night's sleep.

15

D R. CARVER WAS JUST ESCORTING his daughter out of his office when Hanson and Muzzetti arrived in the morning.

"The Ball won't be canceled, will it, Dad?" they heard her ask with concern. "I've been looking forward to it for months."

"As long as things are quiet, I don't see why not. I'll confirm it with Major Hanson. This is my daughter, Mavis."

"Hello, Mavis … Dr. Carver. Mavis. This is Captain Muzzetti."

Mavis bowed modestly to the Marines, then said, "See you later, Dad," and rushed off.

"Welcome to the Enclave, Captain Muzzetti. Gentlemen. Let's sit down."

Once they were seated, Carver offered cigars and whiskey, which were declined, then offered coffee, which was accepted.

"A lot has changed since we last met, Major. Bring me up to date."

"Yes, sir. The investigators reached an understanding with the vets and the media, and we may have the situation under control."

"And Beasley?"

"It looks like he's been selected to be the scapegoat."

"You don't like that?"

"No, sir. The Arabs caused this situation by evicting the vets from their hospital, then intimidating Captain Beasley, but there's nothing we can do about it right now."

"I'm glad you realize that, Major."

The three men thought about the situation from their different points of view for a few moments, then Carver sighed.

"Nothing's simple off the battlefield, is it, Major?"

"If it's any consolation, Doctor, nothing's simple on the battlefield," Hanson replied.

Carver nodded.

"This is our reality, gentlemen. We are still a sovereign nation, but a lot of our power has dissipated and most of our friends have abandoned us. Each day we're involved in a struggle to maintain our national rights, and each day the Arabs and their Russian allies eat away at our will to endure. What we don't need are incidents like the suicide attack to give them a pretext to make more demands of us."

"I understand, sir," Hanson said.

"Good. We're desperately dependent on Arab oil and they know it. They need our cash to sustain their economies, so we have a little wiggle room to negotiate, but not much. Even though they hate us, we must preserve the semblance of good relations."

"I understand, sir," Hanson repeated patiently, in response to the simplistic analysis.

Carver didn't have an inkling that Hanson might have a much more sophisticated background than he did in world politics and economics.

"Well, enough of international relations 101. What's going to happen in the next few days?"

"Unless something unexpected occurs," Hanson replied, "things should be quiet for a week or so, until the investigator's findings are presented to the U.N. If the Russians accept the findings and persuade the Arabs to accept them the crisis will be over."

"If they don't?"

"Then it becomes a political and diplomatic problem. We'll be prepared for any limited attempts at reprisal in the Enclave."

"What do you mean by limited?"

"We can handle anywhere from a few dozen to a few hundred disorganized Arabs. If we're invaded by disciplined troops with heavy armor, we're in trouble."

Carver looked horrified.

"Is that possible?"

"I don't think so. I just want you to be aware of our capabilities."

It took Carver a minute to recover from his reaction.

"You gave me a scare, Major."

"That wasn't my intention, sir. I just wanted to assure you that we could deal with anything short of a serious invasion."

"I get the message. We'll sit tight and wait to see what develops."

"Yes, sir."

"What about the Halloween Ball? Is there any reason to cancel it?"

"Tell me about it, sir."

"It's scheduled for Monday night at the cinecomplex on Second Avenue and 31st street. There won't be any movies shown that night and we'll use the lobby, mezzanine and basement for the festivities. Are you familiar with the complex?"

"Yes, sir. I've been there."

"We had just planned on having a few Guardwell men for security, but in light of the current circumstances that might not be sufficient. Distinguished and important guests are invited, and we don't want any disruptions."

Hanson pictured the location and quickly came up with a basic security plan.

"If conditions remain calm, there's no reason to cancel the event. We should replace Guardwell with police, both in uniform and civvies. We can stop traffic on the service road and set up an enclosed entrance to admit a few people at a time through a metal detector. We'll set barricade planters so no cars or trucks can get too close. We should have curtains put up on the glass doors, so no one can see inside. Police should be stationed in the stores nearby, at all the exits to the complex and on the roof. There should be some police inside in costume. I'll have Marines discreetly posted nearby, in communication with the police at all times. I'll draw up a complete plan later and email it to you."

"That was off the top of your head?"

"Yes, sir."

"I'm impressed. By the way, you and your officers are invited as my guests."

"They'll be busy, sir, but I might stop by in my Marine costume."

They laughed comfortably together, then Carver said,

"Let's go see the vets."

The visit to the vets turned out to be painful, because of the deplorable state they were in, but easier to deal with than they expected. Carver was outraged at the squalid conditions they were living in and ordered an immediate clean-up of the ward. The vets, who were used to nothing, were moved to tears by the interest. Carver promised to come back the next morning with a full staff of doctors and nurses and examine each one of them.

"I'm sorry for the neglect you've suffered. The Arabs have been demanding all of our time, but we're going to take care of you."

There were murmurs of 'thank you' and 'it's about time', then Hanson spoke to them.

"The Arabs are going to freak out when they find out you're getting medical services, especially after the suicide bombing ..."

"We had to do something, sir, or we'd all die here," a vet said.

"I understand. But it's created a lot of problems for the rest of us."

"You gotta admit it worked, sir," another vet added.

Carver and Muzzetti stared at Hanson curiously, wondering what he was getting at. Hanson grinned at the vets.

"The media are poking around everywhere looking for a story. If it gets out that you're getting services that the Arabs want there'll be an uproar in the U.N. and they'll demand we prosecute you."

"So what do you suggest, sir?" a vet asked.

"Dr. Carver will send out a press release stating that you're getting psychiatric evaluations."

There was a brief silence, then most of the vets burst into laughter, while a few protested indignantly.

Carver and Muzzetti managed not to laugh when Hanson said, "I know that all of you are ex-Marines, so everyone knows you're crazy ..."

This time they all laughed uproariously.

"I realize that it may not be the most dignified approach, but it'll work."

The vets conferred together for a minute, then one of them said, "You got it, sir. Whatta we gotta do?"

"Just be yourselves," he answered with a straight face.

When the laughter died down, Carver said, "I'll see all of you in the morning," and walked out.

Hanson and Muzzetti followed him.

"That went pretty well," Carver remarked.

"Why shouldn't it?" Hanson asked, a note of bitterness in his voice. "Somebody's finally paying attention to them."

Carver ignored the comment.

"You'll email the security plan for the Halloween Ball to me?"

"Yes, sir."

"Two other potential problems that we should consider are Election Day next Tuesday and Veterans Day, which I believe is November 11th."

"Election Day is easy," Hanson responded. "We'll station an enhanced police presence around the polls and keep Marines deployed nearby for rapid response."

"What about Guardwell?"

"They're not appropriate for these occasions. We should review their role in the Enclave when this crisis is over, sir."

"You don't think much of them, do you?"

"Frankly, no, sir. They might be suitable for low level watchmen, but I'd never rely on them for initiative, or decision making, and I'd never trust them with anything vital. Speaking of Guardwell, sir, I'd like to officially replace them with Marine guards at our officers and N.C.O.'s residential building."

"Approved."

"Thank you, sir."

When Carver reached his office, he turned to the officers.

"Thank you for your assistance, gentlemen."

"You're welcome, sir," they responded.

"We didn't discuss Veterans Day," Carver pointed out. "It was canceled last year due to pressure from the U.N."

"I didn't know that, sir," Hanson said. "I suggest that we go ahead with preparations and see what happens in the next week or so. We can always cancel if it becomes necessary."

"Agreed. Let's meet Friday morning in my office at nine a.m."

"Yes, sir."

They said goodbye, then Hanson accompanied Muzzeti to his new office, which had been cleaned after the forensics crew finished with it. Sergeant Danowski greeted them.

"Good morning, sirs."

"Morning, Danowski. This is Captain Muzzetti. He'll be moving in here today. He has his own clerk, so I'm assigning you to me temporarily.

You can go over Captain Beasley's papers with me, then you'll be assigned to Lieutenant Kent."

"Yes, sir."

"Show Captain Muzzetti where everything is, then report to my office."

"Yes, sir."

"Captain Muzzetti."

"Yes, sir?"

"I'll see you, your officers, and senior N.C.O.'s at 1400 in the conference room."

"Yes, sir."

Carver called Hanson a few minutes later and mentioned a working luncheon for all medical department heads on Friday that he was scheduled to attend. He invited Hanson to address the meeting and gave him the topic, security issues and their ramifications.

"Glad to, sir."

Carver was surprised at Hanson's casual response.

"I thought you'd be excited at the opportunity to address so many important people."

"I've briefed generals, sir, so I'm used to high-level exposure, but I appreciate your thoughtfulness. Do you want me to focus on security concerns in the Enclave, or the broader issues that affect the nation?"

"How about a combination, but not too detailed. We're all very busy."

"I understand, sir. I'll keep it simple."

"That's not what I meant, Major," he said irritably. "These are highly educated people who are politically active. You won't have to talk down to them."

"That's not what I meant, sir. As you know, foreign and domestic affairs are interconnected and incredibly complicated, so I don't want to make a lengthy presentation. I'll focus on some specifics that we may have to deal with."

"Good. I'll see you Friday."

Hanson thought that Carver still sounded a bit annoyed when he hung up. He shrugged it off because it was time to let Carver know that he wasn't a dumb jarhead in awe of medical doctors, just because they had a few degrees. He had graduated from one of the great engineering schools in the country and had an M.A. in international relations. He had also seen too many bad doctors during his military career to retain any illusions.

He remembered reading Arrowsmith lifetimes ago at the Academy with its portrait of an idealistic doctor, but he had never encountered a dedicated physician. Of course, that didn't necessarily mean there wasn't one out there, somewhere, but he knew the difference between fiction and reality. He made a mental note to give the doctors a presentation that would spell out some of the many vulnerabilities that posed a threat, both in the Enclave and for the rest of the country. He doubted that it would shake them out of their comfort zones, because he was familiar with how civilians shied away from harsh facts. But he concluded with a smile that it might be fun to give them something to worry about beside budgets, and who had more influence in the get-ahead game.

He didn't have much time before the 1400 briefing, so he caught up on some overdue paperwork, then headed for the conference room. When he entered, Jed called, "Attention," and the officers and N.C.O.'s stood up snappily. He looked them over for a minute and recognized some of the newcomers from previous postings.

"At ease. I assume you've had a chance to get acquainted …?"

There were murmurs of agreement.

"Good. I see an officer I don't know …"

After a moment's hesitation, a grizzled Gunnery Sergeant shoved the nervous officer forward and hovered protectively behind him. Hanson hid his smile at the papa ursine, who he knew from Iraq, who was guarding his cub.

"2nd Lieutenant …" his voice broke into a squeak that made everyone laugh, except his gunny, who glared at them, then the officer continued in a firmer voice, "Robert Bernstein reporting, sir," and his gunny gave him an approving pat.

"Welcome aboard, Lieutenant," Hanson said.

"Thank you, sir."

As he looked the sergeants over more carefully, he nodded to several old-timers who he knew and made a mental note to check out a few who looked competent.

"Sometime tomorrow I'll meet with you newly arrived sergeants and we'll get better acquainted …"

There were several 'thank you, sirs', and other comments of appreciation for the recognition.

"This is our current situation. The Arabs may seek revenge for the suicide bombing and we've got to make sure they don't do anything in the Enclave. Lieutenant Kent will issue maps of the Enclave to all of you. I want you to study every inch of it and get to know it on the ground. You are not, repeat not, to talk to any reporters, under any circumstances. Be polite to everyone and if you can't handle something, call for help. You will not use force unless you are attacked … Don't get attacked."

This brought a round of laughter.

"We're in a very touchy situation and we have to be extremely careful not to make things worse. Lieutenant Kent will assign your duties. That's all for now. Welcome aboard. Dismissed."

16

T HURSDAY MORNING was the first time since U.N. Day that Hanson didn't feel that there was an imminent crisis. He reviewed the new officers and N.C.O.'s service records and noted which ones had Iraq or other combat experience. Danowski had been very helpful in bringing him up to date on company business and he decided to promote him and keep him as his clerk. He assigned his old clerk to Al, who he knew could use the competent clerk as she adjusted to her new rank. Carver called him after lunch and told him about the medical visit to the vets.

"They were so eager and cooperative that it's hard to imagine them as suicide bombers …" He paused, but Hanson didn't comment. "Anyhow, most of them need extensive treatment, or therapy and we started the process. I just hope we'll be able to follow through on what we began."

"So do I, sir. Thank you for your efforts. They really deserve your help."

"We're trying."

"I know, sir."

"I'll see you in the morning, Major."

•   •   •

The meeting with the sergeants turned out to be fun, an unexpected treat for Hanson. The newcomers, a typical Corps mix of men, women, black, white, Hispanic and Asian, were gung-ho for the new duty station. It was understandable after living in tents in upstate New York and freezing their butts off.

"The odds are probable that we won't see any action here," Hanson said, "but you never know. I will rely on you to keep your snuffies ready, but under control at all times …" There were nods and sounds of agreement. "Get to know the local cops. They've been very helpful and they're on the front lines. If any of your troops are disrespectful, discipline them …" More nods and sounds of agreement.

"We may have trouble when the results of the investigation of the suicide bombing are presented to the U.N …" There were sneers and sounds of contempt. "We must get along with the bluefish at all costs. I'll keep you posted about events. In the meantime, if you have any problems with your new quarters, speak to Lieutenant Davis."

"We'll suffer with them, sir," gunny ursine said with mock pathos.

Everyone laughed and Hanson grinned. "It's good to see you again, Le Beau. How are things at home? "

"Cajuns are still an oppressed minority, sir."

"Not in the Corps, gunny. I'll see you later."

He went back to his office and finished the security plan, emailed it to Carver, then summoned Danowski. "I've decided to keep you as my chief clerk and a promotion to Staff Sergeant goes with it, unless you'd rather work for Lieutenant Kent."

"No, sir. I'd like to work for you, sir, and thank you for the promotion."

"Good. Notify all officers to meet me here in fifteen minutes and send someone to the mess hall for a turkey sandwich on rye."

"Yes, sir. Will that be all, sir?" Hanson looked at him probingly for a moment.

"I get the feeling that I can rely on you."

"May I speak frankly, sir?"

"Shoot."

"I hope the Major won't hold my working for Captain Beasley against me. The clerks rolled dice for it and I lost."

Hanson couldn't suppress a grin. "What do they call you?"

"Ski."

"You have a choice this time, Ski."

"Thank you, sir. I'll do a good job for you."

"Alright. First arrange for someone competent to cover for you when you're out. Second. Draw up a plan for a battalion headquarters staffing. You'll be the ranking N.C.O."

"Yes, sir,"

"Dismissed."

His officers made some minor suggestions for improving the security plan for the Halloween Ball, but nothing significant. This made Hanson worry for a few moments that they might be missing something important, then he shook off the negative thoughts and called Lonigan, who never seemed to be off duty. "I just emailed you a security plan for the Halloween Ball. You'll be in charge and will replace Guardwell personnel with your officers. The Marines will be nearby in support. If you think of anything I missed, let me know."

"Thanks for another thankless job, pal," Lonigan joked.

"Just like a cop, grumbling about a chance to mingle with the elite." They laughed comfortably together.

"By the way, congratulations on your promotion, Major. Only a jarhead could go up the ladder that fast. One day you're a sergeant, the next a major. I wouldn't be surprised if you're a general by Monday."

"If I am I'll have you drafted into the Corps."

"No, thanks. I'll call you later, after I go over your plan."

The security plan seemed functional, so Hanson moved on to other business.

"Captain Muzzetti. Give us a rundown on the equipment and personnel of Weapons Company."

"Yes, sir." Without referring to notes, Muzzetti recited their status. "Our mortar platoon is about twenty percent understrength but is the largest platoon in the company. Our heavy weapons platoon is short some Humvees, but still mission capable and our anti-armor teams are led by the cockiest corporals in the Corps ..." They all laughed knowingly.

"Our javelin platoon is short missiles and is thirty percent understrength. I've transferred some people from our headquarters element, but they're not fully trained yet. Our N.C.O.'s are capable, but we're short six or seven slots. Some corporals are ready for promotion, but we've had a personnel freeze. All told, we're about twenty five percent understrength and most of the snuffies have little or no field experience, but we're mission-ready, sir."

"Good report, Captain."

"Thank you, sir."

"Draw up a list of what you need and give it to Lieutenant Kent. We'll see what we can get you. In the meantime, arrange a joint patrol schedule with Lieutenant Davis, foot and Hummers during the day, heavier vehicles at night. Make sure your noncoms understand that this isn't Baghdad. We don't want anyone getting trigger-happy."

"Yes, sir."

"Prepare a list of N.C.O.'s and snuffies who are ready for promotion and give it to Lieutenant Kent. Once you're settled in, we'll see what we can do."

"Thank you, sir."

"We're just about ready with our security preparations for the Halloween Ball and Election Day. We'll review Veterans Day later next week. Our biggest concern for these events is the perimeter security of the Enclave. Lieutenant Kent and Lieutenant Davis will take you and your N.C.O.'s in small groups on the one-dollar tour. Take notes and mark any likely infiltration spots on your maps and we'll review your observations together. I'll see you at dinner. Al. Stay here, please."

"Yes, sir."

The other officers saluted and left. "We need to make some changes in the mess hall, Al. Tell Danowski to arrange an officers table and a senior N.C.O.'s table. Now that we're becoming a battalion, it's time for some formalities."

"Yes, sir."

"What do you think of the new officers, Al?"

"They seem capable, sir, even the puppy."

He grinned at the nickname. "He should be. He went to a good school."

"What was it like at the Academy, Sam?"

He thought for a moment. "It was innocent."

"That's a strange thing to say about a military school."

He shrugged. "First they scared the shit out of us, then they worked our asses off, but it was organized, disciplined and structured. After graduation, many of my classmates had trouble adjusting to the chaos of the real world."

"Did you?"

"Not really. For me the Academy was a vacation from a confused society. Later some of us accepted the role of bringing stability out of the disorder. I'm not sure how effective we've been, but I know I've tried my best, just as you did."

"Thank you, Sam," she said gratefully.

•   •   •

Dinner that evening was intended to establish the separation between the ranks and it accomplished that goal without strain. Previous training asserted itself and the enlisted personnel accepted the change as condition normal, including table service for the officers. It helped that they were preoccupied with adjusting to a horde of newcomers who had to be scoped out. There was an amusing moment when Kyle and Tyrone arrived. Tyrone knew that his father had been promoted to lieutenant, but he was unaware of the separation of the ranks.

"Permission to dine with my father, sir?"

"Of course, Tyrone."

"Thank you, sir," and he went to the senior N.C.O.'s table.

"You're supposed to eat with the officers," gunny Le Beau growled.

"What are you talking about, gunny?" Tyrone asked.

"I guess you forgot. Your Dad's been promoted. He's an officer now, sprout."

Some of the sergeants laughed, but Tyrone ignored them. Hanson was proud of Kyle when he didn't react to the teasing of his friend. He also knew that he would have to discuss the new arrangements with him that night. Tyrone rejoined the officers' table and coolly said, "Good evening, sirs. ma'am," and they proceeded to have a pleasant meal.

When they finished dinner, Kyle asked, "Any chance of your coming home with me tonight, Dad?"

Hanson looked around, caught Al's eye and announced loudly, "I don't see why not. The battalion is in good hands." He stood up, said goodnight and walked out with Kyle.

"That was pretty clever of you, Dad."

"What do you mean?" he asked innocently.

"I know what you're up to. In one short statement you let everyone know they're part of a battalion, which will make them feel much more secure than being in an isolated company."

"I hope the officers catch on as fast as you did."

"You also established the confidence you have in your new battalion XO."

"Al will make a fine officer. I'll try to promote her as quickly as possible."

"Can I ask you a personal question, Dad?"

"Shoot."

"How come you never had a thing with Al?"

Hanson grinned at the term, 'a thing'. "It wouldn't have been fair to her or me. I'm her C.O. It would be an abuse of my rank and everyone would know it. I'd never do a thing like that."

Kyle thought about that for a moment as they walked home. It was a soft October night and the Sycamore trees, still with leaves, rustled gently in a mild breeze. For a brief interval the tumult and ferocity of the world was far removed and they were just a father and son, talking together as fathers and sons had since time immemorial.

"You know she worships you, Dad."

"I hold her in the highest esteem, Kyle. She's one of the bravest Marines I ever served with. I wouldn't dream of exploiting her or jeopardizing her career."

"Then what do you do about sex? Mom's been dead for a long time. Don't you get the urge?"

"Sure. When it's convenient, I'll visit a woman now and then. Otherwise, I exercise self-control. I manage."

"Would you ever get married again?"

Hanson stared at him. "How would you feel if I did?"

"Your choice, Dad. Just as long as she's not younger than me."

They laughed at that. "Not to worry. I have no plans."

They reached the apartment building and Hanson was satisfied to note that Marines were on guard. He paused and exchanged some pleasantries with the detail, who seemed glad to see him. They also greeted Kyle fondly.

"All quiet, Munez?" Hanson asked the corporal in charge.

"Yes, sir. I've just taken the night duty from Sergeant Berenger, but there was nothing to report on his tour."

"Are there only two shifts?"

"Yes, sir."

"Twelve hours each?"

"Yes, sir. But we're managing."

"I'll make some changes in the morning. We should run six-hour tours, with several breaks to preserve maximum alertness and efficiency.

We'll set up video cams in strategic locations and the guard detail can alternate monitoring the screens. We'll have two person patrols sweep the area at irregular intervals."

"Sounds good to me, sir."

"The more I think about it, the more I like that for the barracks. I'll set up the same schedule there. Goodnight, Munez."

"Night, sir. Night, Kyle."

Once the door of their apartment closed behind them, Hanson let out a sigh of relief. "If you don't mind, son, I'm too tired for any serious conversation that isn't an emergency. I'd like to watch an old movie, unwind a bit, and get to bed early."

"That's fine with me, Dad. What would you like to see?"

"How about 'Amadeus'? That's one of my favorite period films."

"Sure. You don't like war movies, do you?"

"Not really. They're mostly Hollywood glamour vehicles that make heroes conquer all. I do like intelligent anti-war movies like *Paths of Glory*, directed by Stanley Kubrik."

"I don't know it."

"It's about World War I. A French regiment in the trenches is given orders by its general to capture an impossible objective, while he's comfortable behind the lines in a luxurious chateau. When the attack fails, he orders soldiers shot for cowardice. You should see it. It's in black and white."

"I like color. What about Marine films?"

"I like *Full Metal Jacket*, also directed by Kubrik. It shows the insanity of war. Now how about the movie?"

"You got it, Dad."

17

CARVER CALLED HANSON early Friday morning and suggested that they cancel the 0900 briefing and instead conclude the luncheon meeting with a briefing for all the department heads. "I think it would be useful to let everyone know what we're dealing with. Do you have any problem with that?"

"No, sir. They should be as concerned as we are with our situation and be aware of the extent of your responsibilities."

Carver chuckled. "You're becoming quite a politician, Major. Too bad you didn't use some of that tact with the president."

"She betrayed her trust, then stirred up a hornet's nest of enemies and didn't defend us against them."

"Did you ever see a hornet's nest, Sam?"

"No. But I've seen the human equivalent."

"I did when I was a kid growing up in Georgia ..." Carver said dreamily. "Man, they were fierce. If they get after you, the only way to stop them is to kill all of them ... I'll see you at lunch."

"Yes, sir."

•   •   •

Al and Muzzetti brought him a priority list of equipment needs and a suggested promotion roster. They reviewed promotions first because it only required simple approval of the recommended personnel. Hanson outlined what determined their equipment priorities. "We have to be prepared to deal with multiple tasking, but the odds are probable that we won't fight pitched battles against organized military units. The biggest change for your company, Captain Muzzetti, will be in your mortar platoon. They'll have to do guard and patrol duty, and there's not much chance of training with their tubes in the near future."

"They won't be happy about that, sir."

"None of us are happy with the current situation, Captain."

"Yes, sir."

"We'll concentrate on requesting fuel, small arms ammo, communications gear, night vision gear and body armor. Al. Finalize the list with Captain Muzzetti, then give it to me this afternoon and I'll have Danowski process it for urgent priority."

"Yes, sir."

"I'll see you later. I've got to brief some doctors."

•　　　•　　　•

The luncheon was the standard, high-ranking civilian get-together and proceeded with predictable regularity, with one exception. The quality of the food was delicious. Diners had a choice of prime rib, swordfish, or roast turkey with all the trimmings. Hanson noted that most of the diners ordered the prime rib, indirectly sustaining the profits of Pfizer as they achieved high cholesterol status.

The speakers mostly congratulated themselves for the efficient functioning of their departments and deplored the recent suicide bombing. Several speakers attributed the attack to temporarily disturbed individuals and blamed Captain Beasley, United States Marine Corps, for not detecting and preventing the incident. Carver glanced at Hanson, possibly expecting a passionate outburst in defense of the dead Marine, but Hanson sat there stoically and didn't reveal the resentment he was feeling.

When it was Hanson's turn to speak, Carver introduced him to a smattering of applause. "Thank you, doctors, ladies and gentlemen. Our country is faced with the greatest crisis since the Civil War, but this time it's a foreign threat that requires a firm national resolve if we are to survive and bequeath a stable country to our children."

He paused for the obligatory applause, then continued, "I am heartened by the capabilities of numbers of Americans who are determined to preserve their country. One benefit of these trying times comes to mind. Lawyers have been replaced in the public esteem by doctors …" A burst of hearty laughter segued into enthusiastic applause.

"On a more serious note, we are in great danger from enemies emboldened by our growing display of weakness in confronting the threats that imperil us. Very much like the plight of the Roman Empire in the fourth century A.D., when the barbarians were no longer awed by their power."

The audience stirred restlessly at what could be interpreted as a militaristic declaration, but Hanson reassured them with his next statement. "Whether or not we once sought hegemony, as our enemies claim, is no longer pertinent. Now we seek to take our place in the family of nations and, as always, represent the benefits of democracy."

There was more applause for his soothing words. "However, many countries have conveniently forgotten how we always helped the world in times of disasters and emergencies, regardless of our national interests. In their fear of the threat of terrorism, former allies turned their backs on us, despite the shield we provided them with in their time of need." A ripple of unease went through the audience. "Today we are a wounded giant, unsure of ourselves and our place in the world. The suicide bombing on U.N. Day by our veterans is a reflection of the desperate weakness that affects us all."

In the silence that pervaded the dining room at this remark, Carver stood up and went to the podium. "Major Hanson will now brief us on the security situation in the Enclave. He will answer any questions at the conclusion. Major."

"Thank you, Doctor Carver."

He proceeded with a description of current conditions, possible threats and how they would deal with them, then described arrangements for the Halloween Ball and Election Day. He finished the brief summary, then asked, "Any questions?"

There was a lengthy silence and Carver was about to conclude the session when Dr. Van Meer spoke up. "Very competent presentation, Major."

"Thank you, sir."

"What are your politics?"

"Sir?"

"We're familiar with your unfortunate conflict with President Beaumont. Who will you be voting for?"

Hanson smiled politely. "The candidate of my choice, sir."

Dr. Van Meer started to get annoyed and Carver intervened before tensions could arise. "We know you have pressing duties, Major. Thank you for your presentation."

"You're welcome, sir."

Once he was back in his office, Hanson told Danowski to tell Al, Jed and Captain Muzzetti to come to his office in fifteen minutes. He also asked him to call the manager of the cineplex and let him know that they would be visiting and there was no need for alarm. A few minutes later Danowski reported the tasks done.

"By the way, sir. I have the battalion headquarters staffing roster whenever you're ready for it."

"Thanks, Ski. We'll get to it next week. For now, I want you to go over our equipment priority list with Lieutenant Kent and advise her what we can get immediately. Small arms ammo and gas are on top of the list. I have a feeling that you have friends in headquarters and supply."

"I can call some buddies."

"Good. Check our supply of uniforms and cold weather gear. It'll get cold in a few weeks. Check our food supply sources and make sure we also have three months of M.R.E.'s."

"Yes, sir."

"One more thing. I'll make a new guard duty and patrol schedule. Once you type it, distribute it to officers and senior noncoms."

"Yes, sir."

"How do you like the job, Ski?"

"So far, so good. Just don't go hanging yourself when I get to liking it."

Hanson grinned at his irreverence. "If you ever find me that way, it ain't suicide."

Al, Jed and Muzzetti showed up a few minutes later and he told them they were going to look at the cineplex on Second Avenue, and a polling station on East 29th street. He thought of something and buzzed Danowski.

"Yes, sir?"

"Call Captain Lonigan and get a list of all the polling stations in the Enclave."

"Yes, sir."

They left the office and walked up 30th street to Second Avenue. The street still had its greenery, due to the lengthy Indian summer. A large weeping willow tree on the manicured lawn of Kips Bay Houses looked sad and lonely, living up to its name. Kids were coming home from school. Shoppers were carrying their packages. Workers were heading for the late afternoon shift at the hospital complex.

There was an illusion of normalcy that could almost make one forget the crushing burden of a disintegrating economy that was wearing out its resources and its people.

There were no surprises at the cineplex. The large concrete planters used as barriers were already in place and the service road was closed. Heavy drapes covered the glass frontage, except for the main doors, which would be shielded by a temporary pavilion entrance. They inspected the main lobby, the basement lobby, and the mezzanine lobby, all of which seemed functional for the occasion.

Hanson didn't bother with the floor plan for the caterers or the musicians, leaving that to the party organizers. They did walk around the shopping strip that included the cineplex, and Hanson assigned a roving patrol to cover the area behind the building on the Kips Bay Houses grounds. No one had any questions or suggestions, since they had already covered almost all of the potential problems. They were amused when Jed paused to flirt with a couple of muscle chicks coming out of the gym near the cineplex.

The polling station was on the ground floor of a Phipps Houses building on East 29th street, between First and Second Avenues. Captain Lonigan met them there and they agreed that sawhorses were sufficient to protect the entrance. They walked into the garden area behind the building and found a delightful surprise. There was a small waterfall that ran into a mini stream with birds bathing, drinking and chatting away.

Al mentioned that she was a birder and pointed out cardinals, doves, blue jays, robins and a number of other species that the others had never seen. The hard-bitten Marines and the police officer watched and listened for several minutes to the lovely and melodic spectacle of nature, displayed in a gap in the concrete cliffs of mid-town Manhattan.

Captain Lonigan broke the reverie that had affected them. "I've got to get back to the stationhouse. I'll station an officer out here in the garden and I'll have men on the corners. I don't think the Marines should have a visible presence. If you could have them nearby, but out of sight, that should work."

"The polls are open from 0700 to 2100, right?" Hanson asked.

"Right," Lonigan answered.

"Al."

"Yes, sir?"

"Assign two squads for the polling station, one from Captain Muzzetti's company and one from Jed's. The first squad will take the duty from 0700 to 1400, the other from 1400 to 2100."

"Yes, sir."

"Find a good place where they can wait nearby. We'll use the same staffing at all the polling stations in the Enclave."

"Yes, sir."

"Anything else you can think of, Mike?" Hanson asked.

"No, Sam. Let's talk tomorrow about preparations for the Halloween Ball."

"Sure."

•　　　•　　　•

At dinner in the mess hall that evening, a passionate discussion went on at the senior N.C.O.'s table about the presidential primaries. Most of the sergeants argued bitterly that the governor of California, Frederick Dunkelwasser, who had been given a special dispensation to run, narrowly lost the republican nomination to Zachary Plant, former governor of Florida, and would have made a better president. The opposition contended that Plant was more qualified and would better support the military.

Opinions bounced back and forth, and the only point of agreement was that they'd both make a better president than Valerie Beaumont, who had presided over the mess that their country was in. Some of them were indignant that Valerie was daring to run again, and they explored the limits of imagination and language in referring to her. One remark that amused Hanson was a silly limerick, unexpected from a rough and tumble Marine, 'Valerie don't deserve her salary'.

The debate was relatively tranquil, because they all knew that come Election Day, Plant would beat Valerie. Then the Freddie-Zach debate would be over, until Zach messed up something that Freddy's supporters cared about. Quiet descended soon after and they finished the meal in peace.

18

S ATURDAY MORNING, Kyle and Tyrone went to a costume shop on Broadway, a few blocks south of 23rd street, just outside the Enclave. The store also specialized in magic supplies and practical joke implements, which the boys carefully inspected. "Look at this, K. It's a whoopee cushion."

"What's that?"

"When someone sits on it, it farts," and he squeezed it, producing the obvious sound.

"Oh."

"Here's some fake doo-doo."

"Some what?"

"You know … Fake shit."

"Doo-doo? Give me a break. Can we look at something else besides ass products?"

"Alright," Tyrone said sulkily. "How about this one. It's an electric buzzer that you put in your hand that gives someone a shock when you shake hands."

"I don't know anyone I'd use it on," Kyle commented. "Do you?"

"Not really."

"Then let's go look at the costumes."

There were over a dozen large racks tightly packed with costumes, as well as counters, shelves, boxes, closets, and wall hooks, all of them bulging with a colorful display of every type of costume imaginable. The boys browsed through rack after rack of period costumes, each more elegant than the last. Tyrone selected a nobleman's costume, a style from just before the French Revolution. Kyle was tempted by a Roman Legionary's outfit, but finally decided on a dashing pirate costume. Both boys felt cheated that the swords weren't real and got a resounding 'no' when they asked the salesman if he had any real swords.

With the help of the salesman, they selected masks that would cover most of their faces, and period hats that would add to their disguises. They tried on the complete costumes and Tyrone said, "See. I told you no one would recognize us." After a careful look in the mirror, Kyle was forced to agree.

•   •   •

Mavis and Jennifer had been carefully modifying their costumes for a week. At Jennifer's suggestion, they rented similar Dolly Madison type gowns, with big hoop skirts. Mavis' was pale yellow, Jennifer's was lilac and they would go as sisters. With the costume shop's permission, they altered the necklines to show more of their breasts. They both knew that the display would rile overly protective fathers, but they assumed that if necessary they could handle pliant Dads.

They had selected appropriate accessories, wigs, jewelry and cloaks, as well as elegant masks that added to their allure. "Don't we look sexy and full of mystery," Jennifer murmured, as they studied their reflections in the mirror. "I think I'm showing too much breast," Mavis whispered.

"No way. You have to show enough to arouse passion. We'll be in a protected environment and you're masked. Only your dad will know who you are."

"That's what I'm afraid of," Mavis said.

Jennifer studied her friend for a moment. "I have an idea. Let's get dressed at my house. This way your dad won't know what you're wearing."

"What about your dad?"

"He never notices anything but his medical computer programs. No one will know who we are. We'll be the mystery beauties."

"I can't wait. It's going to be so exciting," Mavis exclaimed.

"Especially when we select a ripe young intern to service you," Jennifer said suggestively.

"Are you serious?"

"Absolutely. I can't think of a safer way to introduce you to womanhood."

"What about love?" Mavis asked weakly.

"There's plenty of time for that once you know how to deal with a man."

"It sounds so cold and calculating," Mavis protested.

"Nonsense. It's healthy, enjoyable and necessary. You'll see. Now come here and let me undress you. Once you get accustomed to a young stud, I'll have to wait in line for you, if you even want me anymore."

"Oh, Jen. You are bad."

•   •   •

Dr. Carver tried on his costume, then posed dramatically in front of his bedroom mirror, the white Greek chiton flattering his still muscular, large body. "Eat your heart out, Hippocrates," he muttered, turning to see the side view. He debated whether or not to carry the caduceus, then decided against it so his hands would be free. He adjusted the gold ringlet on his head and pronounced himself satisfied with his appearance.

The image of Dr. Yi, the senior staffer in his department, clad in a diaphanous veil that revealed the sensual body that her hospital whites only hinted at, flitted through his mind. He shook his head to disperse the disturbing thoughts about someone who he saw every day, but he kept seeing her tantalizing mouth that he found himself staring at too often during rounds. He wished for an idle moment that there was someone with whom he could discuss his attraction to Mei, but there wasn't. And there was no harm in thinking about her, was there?

•   •   •

At Hanson's request, Danowski summoned all available officers and N.C.O.s to the conference room for a final review of security preparations for the Halloween Ball. Once they were assembled, Hanson stood up. "The smoking lamp is lit, ladies and gentlemen. This will be the last briefing before the Halloween Ball Monday night. All personnel, except those on duty, will have this afternoon and Sunday off ..."

Yays and whistles punctuated his remark. "Of course you can't leave the Enclave ..." There was a chorus of groans. "And you'll have to be models of behavior. No drinking, no fighting, no public displays of anything that will reflect badly on the Corps, especially no problems with civilians ..."

"Then what's left for us to do, Major?" gunny Le Beau asked plaintively.

"You can wear civvies and pretend to be human for a while …" They all roared with laughter. "Seriously. You can have a beer or two, talk to your preference in men or women, have a quiet, good time and stay out of trouble. Keep your cell phones on at all times, since you're subject to immediate recall. Dismissed."

•   •   •

At his request, Al, Jed and Muzzetti lingered after the others left. "What do you have for us, boss?" Al asked.

"I want you to go over every little detail of the plan for Monday night, Al. Make sure that we have everything in place. Let me know right away if there's a problem."

"Yes, sir."

"Jed. I want you to go over the distinguished visitor protocol with Captain Muzzetti, so he can brief his troops on appropriate behavior."

"Yes, sir."

"Captain Muzzetti. They call you Muzi, right?"

"Yes, sir."

"Muzi. You must impress on all your personnel that we are in a high visibility zone, with a frequent U.N. presence. We cannot afford any negative incidents or complaints that will disturb the Enclave or Washington. All personnel must consider themselves ambassadors at all times. Make sure your troops understand this."

"Yes, sir."

"We're on a tightrope here, boys and girls, and it's up to us maintain our balance. I'll see you at dinner."

•   •   •

Jed drew Al aside as they left. "Can I talk to you for a minute, Al?"

"Yeah. What's up?"

Jed shuffled his feet in an awkward, embarrassed manner. "I don't know quite how to say it …"

"Then spit it out."

"Okay. I'm not sure how I feel about being an officer."

"What do you mean?"

"It's like … I miss the camaraderie of the sergeants and I don't know if I'm really officer material."

"Don't be ridiculous, Jed."

"That's easy for you to say. You should have been an officer from the beginning. Me? Now I'm the oldest second lieutenant in the Corps."

Al understood what he was going through and tried to be reassuring. "As far as camaraderie goes, once you get to know the new officers, you'll find the same esprit that binds us all."

"I don't know …"

"I do. Remember when you first became a sergeant?" He nodded. "You joined a new rank and you quickly made a place for yourself," she pointed out.

Jed pondered that for a moment. "We'll come back to that. What about being officer material?"

"You've been working as an officer for years, Jed. You just didn't have the rank. It may take a couple of weeks for you to get used to it, but you will."

"How do you know that?"

"Because I know you. You're a natural born leader and you've always accepted responsibility."

"But I don't have enough education to be an officer."

"Bullshit. You'll do fine. Once you go to O.C.S., you'll learn what you need. In the meantime, start reading officer's training manuals."

"What makes you so sure?"

Al was getting a little exasperated. "Do you trust Sam?"

"Sure. With my life."

"Does he know what he's doing?"

"All the time."

"Well he made you an officer, didn't he?"

"Yeah. I guess you're right."

"Enough said?"

"Yeah."

"Then let me buy you a cup of coffee."

"You're on. Thanks, Al."

●　　　●　　　●

General Griffin called Hanson just as he was leaving his office. "How are things going, Sam?"

"Good, sir. Muzi's company has moved in without making waves, and the battalion is shaping up. We haven't heard anything about the Arabs and the streets are quiet. We're ready for the Halloween Ball and Election Day, and we'll finalize preparations for Veterans Day next week."

"I got your security plan for the events and I think you've covered everything."

"Thank you, sir. The only real threat would be Arab suicide bombers and I think they'll wait for the results of the U.N. hearing."

"I hope so, because Beverly and I are coming to the Ball."

"How is the commander, sir?" They both chuckled at her nickname.

"She's fine and looking forward to seeing you."

"Give her my love, sir. What costume will you be wearing?"

"An 1812 Marine. I've been wearing the same costume for almost thirty years and it still fits, although it's a bit snugger now."

"I'd still like you at my side in a hot LZ, sir."

"Thanks, Sam. I'll see you Monday."

A few minutes later, Carver called Hanson with startling news. The Secretary-General of the U.N., Mohamed ElBaradei, would be attending the Halloween Ball. This automatically meant that the U.S. Ambassador to the U.N., Will Blunt, would certainly attend, as well as many other notables, political and otherwise.

"Isn't it wonderful?" Carver gushed. "This will give us an opportunity to mend some of the relations that were damaged by the suicide bombing."

"Yes, indeed," Hanson said.

"You don't sound very enthusiastic, Major. Don't you see how this can benefit the Enclave?"

"Yes, sir. But it creates some security problems. I wish you told me earlier."

"He just accepted our invitation this morning," Carver said frostily.

"I was under the impression, sir, that this was a local affair. If I knew that important personages might attend, I would have prepared a different security plan."

There was a lengthy silence, then Carver said, "I see. I hadn't thought about the implications of the secretary-general attending. I'm sorry for being abrupt with you when you were just trying to do your job."

"That's alright, sir. I suggest we deal with the new situation immediately."

"Right. What do we have to do?"

Hanson thought for a minute. "First. If you will email me the list of everyone who was invited, I'll factor them into the revised security plan."

"I'll do it right now."

"Please have your secretary call every notable on the list on Monday morning and get a confirmation if they're coming. In the meantime, I'll prepare a plan as if everyone on the list is coming. I'll meet with my staff shortly and revise the plan. I'll email it to you and we can discuss it further, if you have any questions."

"Good. Anything else?"

"Yes. You might want to talk to your colleagues about how to handle any uninvited guests the secretary-general might bring, such as unfriendly Arabs."

"I see what you mean. I'll get back to you."

Hanson buzzed Danowski on the intercom and told him to have Captain Muzzetti and Lieutenants Kent and Davis report to his office immediately. He got the email list from Carver a few minutes later and scanned the names with growing apprehension.

Almost all the notables who were at the U.N. Day ceremony were on the list. He began outlining a revised security plan that required cutting off more of the area on Second Avenue, near the cineplex entrance. The metal detector would now be mandatory for all the entrants and he started considering how to deal with the armed guards of the notables, especially the Arabs, who would be very reluctant to either give up their weapons, or remain outside, while their principals cavorted inside, remote from their protective cordon.

His officers came in a few moments later and after greetings, he asked them to be seated. "I want you to listen to this conversation, then we'll deal with the problem." He called Captain Lonigan, who was still at the precinct house.

"What new crisis do you have for me now, Sam?"

"You'll love it, Mike. The secretary-general is coming to the Halloween Ball."

A string of profanity followed. "Why didn't you tell me earlier, Sam?"

"I just found out five minutes ago."

"Oh … How do we handle it?"

"I'm revising the security plan to include him and possibly some of the Arabs. I'll email the guest list to you that I just got, and send the security plan as soon as it's done. We'll have to coordinate with the various protective details and I think you better deal with them."

Lonigan cursed heartily, then said, "It's a fine state of affairs when the cops are more acceptable than the Marines."

"Yeah. Maybe they'll be some changes after Election Day. By the way, who are you voting for?"

"Anybody but Valerie, probably Plant. What about you?"
"The same. Let's keep in close touch, Mike."

19

T HE NEXT TWO DAYS saw a whirlwind of new security
procedures for the Halloween Ball. In an unexpected and
unpleasant surprise, Will Blunt's secret service detail gave Hanson and
Lonigan the most trouble. Every other security chief accepted the plan
of cutting off traffic on First and Second Avenues, and on 33rd and 30th
streets to establish a perimeter around the cineplex.

Blunt's chief of security, a disgruntled older operative, who grumbled
incessantly that he should be on the president's protective detail, insisted on
sniper teams on every building, from the U.N. to the cineplex. After several
irritating discussions, he reluctantly approved Hanson's suggestion for
posting Marine snipers at only a few strategic locations. He begrudgingly
accepted that the police would check each window that faced the cineplex,
rather than the FBI When he finally walked away, still mumbling that he
should be shielding the president, Lonigan said hopefully, "Maybe we'll get
lucky and he'll take a bullet for Blunt before he gets here."

Hanson grinned at his friend's sardonic humor. "Don't count on it."

"Well maybe the press will get it," he said, pointing at the clique
of reporters and camera crews, like vultures alerted to the arrival of
newsworthy prey.

•   •   •

Somehow, all the preparation problems for the event big and small were resolved by the time the first guests began arriving early, at 8:30. The last night of October was cool and clear, with a gentle breeze that rustled the remaining leaves on the sickly New York City Sycamore trees. A full harvest moon blazed down brightly, as if encouraging witches to arrive on their broomsticks.

Limousines pulled up to the cineplex entrance, disgorging an array of monsters, skeletons, aliens, cartoon characters, various animals, lavish gowns, and all types of period costumes. Dozens of pigeons that nested on the ledge above the cineplex were awakened by the exuberant arrivals.

From Hanson's vantage point in his Humvee, parked diagonally across the street, he idly wondered who would get the first liberal donation of pigeon droppings, hoping that it would be the secretary-general, or one of the despised Arabs. He smiled to himself at his silly thinking and settled down for a long watch. "We'll be here for a while, Tico, so catch a nap when you can. I'll wake you if I need you."

"Thank you, sir … Is it true that the President's coming tonight?"

"Where'd you get that idea?"

"Latrine gossip, sir."

"That's all it is, Tico. She won't be here." But he couldn't help thinking to himself, 'That's all I'd need, just as my career is being resurrected.'

All the medical department heads had arrived early and had waited patiently to greet their guests. Whether by arrangement or chance, most of them were wearing white, ancient Greek costumes. They reminded Hanson of a chorus of old men in a Greek tragedy, solemn and full of themselves.

He monitored the arrivals through his binoculars, curious to see who he'd recognize. He assumed that the secretary-general would come with a large convoy, but he wasn't certain if any of the Arabs would be with him. He watched a group of young men that included Zorro, a Viking, a pirate, Merlin the magician, a French nobleman and several others whose costumes looked vaguely familiar. They paused at the entrance to allow two elegantly attired young women in long gowns to precede them. Judging by the interest level of the men, the women were very attractive.

A few minutes later a convoy of black S.U.V.'s pulled up. A security detail fanned out to fend off the press and the secretary-general emerged, resplendent in Arab robes, followed by other Arabs. Hanson suppressed a curse when he saw their ethnic attire and hoped it wouldn't provoke someone with a resentment for all things Arab into doing something stupid.

He listened on the radio as Lonigan informed his officers inside the complex that the secretary-general would be entering momentarily and urged heightened alertness. As part of the modified security plan, Hanson had sent Al to the ball in a milkmaid costume, as well as several other women Marines also in costume. He called her and told her the secretary-general was on his way in. "How do things look so far, Al?"

"Calm, but not quiet. The notables are on the second floor mezzanine and the music there is big band, meant for dancing. There's a room nearby that's blaring classic 'gangsta' rap. It's awful."

"Is that your only complaint?"

"Well, No. There's this really obnoxious skeleton who keeps pinching me and asking me to demonstrate my milking technique. I'm ready to deck him."

Hanson chuckled. "The perils of farm life."

"Thanks for your sympathy."

"Stay alert."

"Yes, sir."

•　　　•　　　•

Kyle and Tyrone had entered with a group of noisy, already well lubricated interns. Although they had to pass through a metal detector, for some reason, in a strange lapse of security, they weren't asked to show their invitations. This obstacle had been the only thing that had worried them about getting inside.

Now that they were in, the boys went about the business of finding girls. Tyrone had prepared Kyle who would pretend to be an intern if asked, and to respond to any questions about medicine with, "I just toil at the hospital. I'd rather you told me about you."

At first Kyle said he was reluctant to lie, but Tyrone's logic had been unassailable, "We're not invited and we're underage. If we're unprepared to deal with those problems, we'll be rejected and thrown out, or worse. If you want any shot at a girl, you're going to have to lie."

After considering their circumstances he was forced to agree. "Okay. But I don't want to overdo it and get caught."

"Don't worry. Keep it simple. Do as I told you and all will be well. Now let's have some fun."

•   •   •

Men of all ages started flocking to Mavis and Jennifer from the moment they arrived. Jennifer kept sending her eager suitors for glass after glass of champagne, and Mavis began to feel like she was floating. She was accustomed to male interest, especially the lower varieties on the street, and the urgent, high school boy lust. This evening she felt like a woman, perhaps pursued by mature men for the same reasons as adolescent's yearning, but treated with respectful ardor, rather than raw lechery.

Disguised by the mask and costume that revealed desirable femininity, but concealed her age, she experienced the power women exercised over men that had kept the species reproducing since it first came down from the trees. She still was uncertain about Jennifer's insistence that she lose her virginity to a carefully selected intern, because it seemed so cold and calculating, but flirting in this protected environment was very exciting.

•   •   •

Dr. Carver and Dr. Van Meer made their way through the crowd to meet the secretary-general and escort him to the notable's table. Carver studied the costumed party goers as he went, trying to locate Mavis. He enjoyed seeing the colorful and vivacious costumes, especially after the drabness that prevailed in the crisis of recent days. The energy and exuberance beginning to permeate the gathering was already affecting him.

He moved to the entrance with a bounce to his step. The idea kept flitting through his mind that perhaps he'd meet a beautiful woman and have the well-deserved indulgence of a brief fling. He had never been able to reconcile his responsibilities for his daughter and the obligations of his profession to his desire for the opposite sex. He just never seemed to have enough time left over for the opportunity to have an affair. But as he stepped forward to welcome the secretary-general, the thought ran through his head that tonight could be different.

•   •   •

The secretary-general waved at the clamoring press and ignored their frantic questions. He paused at the entrance to give the crowd a chance to observe his splendor. It wasn't just his costume, the rich robes in the green and gold colors of Islam. There was a mystique about the head of the U.N. that awed and impressed even those who knew that he had limited power and was often manipulated by nationalistic governments for their own ends.

The peculiar confluence of the dependency on oil in industrial countries, with oil currently quoted at $237 a barrel; the enhanced political influence of OPEC; and the dwindling of American economic and military might, elevated the stature of the U.N. beyond its real strength. He had attended this American Halloween ritual that should be despised by all good Muslims, to flaunt his position before the weakened Americans, who once condescended to him and resented his lack of support for their anti-nuclear crusades against Islam. Now it was their turn to bow and scrape to him.

At the last moment, Dr. Van Meer put on a burst of speed to get to the secretary-general ahead of Carver. "Good evening, Mr. Secretary-General," Van Meer crooned. A step behind him, Carver repeated the greeting and bowed courteously.

The secretary-general fluttered a hand loftily and looked around the room. "I see people drinking what I assume to be alcohol. Since it is forbidden to me, I would prefer not to be near it."

"Of course, Mr. Secretary-General," Van Meer gushed. "You'll be at the distinguished visitor's table on the mezzanine, where alcohol isn't allowed."

"Please lead the way, Dr. Van Meer," the secretary-general said piously.

Carver couldn't help smiling to himself at their guest's hypocrisy about the Muslim prohibition of alcohol. It was rumored that the secretary-general was partial to hashish, and frequently indulged in an intoxicant not forbidden by the prophet. He wondered for the thousandth time as an African American if there could ever be reconciliation to the differences that separated people.

As they made their way through the crowded floor, the throbbing pulse of a bass beat permeated the air. Couples were pressed together, front to back, in the latest dance craze, the 'barge', where one partner towed the other, and others temporarily joined in. The practice of showing a lot of flesh, that by 2009 had reached the point of revealing almost the entire body, had gone through an extreme reaction and concealment was now the general rule.

They passed Frankenstein, a pyramid, a gaucho, his and her Draculas, Lincoln, Teddy Roosevelt, a caveman, and women in all types of gowns. All of them were modestly covered, except for a hint of breast in the younger women. The entourage paused in front of a belly dancer, possibly the only woman in the room whose charms were amply displayed. Carver noted the instant interest of the secretary-general, who remarked to Van Meer, "Perhaps you can get her to dance for us later."

Van Meer lamely tried to explain that she was a guest, not an entertainer, but wilted under the secretary-general's cold stare.

"I'll see what I can do, Mr. Secretary-General," he replied nervously.

•   •   •

Kyle and Tyrone had made their way through the three floors of the party, checking everything out. At Tyrone's suggestion, they stayed in the lower level.

"The ground floor's not cool," he had explained. "Everybody's coming and going too fast to make contact. The mezzanine is for those old folks, who want to think about the past. The lower level's for us, 'cause there's slow dancing and we'll have a chance to talk to girls."

Tyrone had been right so far, so Kyle agreed. When they got off the escalator, Tyrone said, "Let's split up. We'll do better alone," and he was gone in an instant.

Kyle hesitated for a moment, then realized that no one knew who he was, so he could be anyone he chose. Emboldened, he slowly moved through the crowd, surveying the women, bowing politely when noticed, and nodding to the men, who suddenly seemed much less threatening. He was too shy to speak to any of the women who were available to dance, so he hovered like a wallflower hoping for a chance meeting.

•   •   •

Mavis and Jennifer made their way through the crowd, basking in the attention showered on them by an admiring flock of suitors. Mavis saw their fathers escorting the secretary-general upstairs, and whispered to Jennifer, "I just saw our dads go upstairs. Let's go downstairs, so they don't notice us."

"Lead on, and don't trip on the tongues of our followers."

They giggled at her accurate assessment of the eager men doting on them, then assumed a more mature air as they made their way to the escalator. They paused to let a camel pass, with pungent smoke leaking out of its humps.

"That ain't hay they're burning," Jennifer quipped.

Before Mavis could respond, a skeleton popped up in front of her and poked his face near her breasts.

"I'm looking for some flesh to hold my bones together," he entreated.

Jennifer shoved him away. "Beat it, you crude bag of bones."

He slunk off and Mavis whispered, "Stay near me tonight, Jen."

"You got it, hon."

•　　　•　　　•

Dr. Van Meer successfully maneuvered the seating so he was next to the secretary-general, with a seat on the other side left vacant for Ambassador Blunt. Carver rightly assumed his immediate host duties were over, so he drifted through the crowd, idly looking for Mavis and greeting acquaintances. There was a brief stir at the door when the Mayor of New York, Roberto (Robbie) Ramirez, entered.

Carver had met him several times, so he said hello and directed him to the mezzanine to join the secretary-general. Robbie's usual laid-back image was belied by a flashy matador's costume that provoked snickers from some as he swashed along, waving cheerfully to anyone who met his eyes. Ambassador Blunt entered a minute later, in a sober business suit, and Carver steered him into Robbie's ample wake.

Carver felt a tug on his arm and looked down at a diminutive Rubik's cube. "Hello, little puzzle. What do I get if I solve you?"

"Aren't you forward," a familiar voice responded.

"Mei," he said, slightly abashed. "I didn't recognize you."

"What would you have done if you knew it was me?" she asked throatily.

He hesitated for a moment, then plunged in. "I would have asked you to dance."

"How gallant, Doctor. I accept. I understand we have a choice of music."

"Yes. There's big band music on the mezzanine and slow dancing downstairs. What's your preference?"

She tucked her arm on his. "Let's start with the big band and work our way down."

They eased their way to the escalator and a skeleton popped up in front of Mei.

"I'd like to play with your parts," he cackled.

Carver gently fended him off and as they rode up, Mei whispered, "That will earn you a reward, noble physician."

20

B Y ELEVEN O'CLOCK, almost all the guests had arrived and the reports from inside were reassuring to Hanson. Some of the notables grumbled about the demands from the press for interviews, but he knew they loved the attention. Lonigan had joined him in the Humvee and they had chatted casually about potential Veterans Day problems while monitoring the radio.

Hanson was getting restless and decided to go inside and see what was happening at the Ball and get something to eat from what he knew would be a lavish buffet. He made a last radio check with his personnel, both inside and on the street. They all reported that everything was calm, so he walked across the street, moving quickly to elude the press and the pulse of loud music that drew him in the door.

Even when he was a child he hadn't gone to parties, except very staid military gatherings for wives and children, so this colorful spectacle was a delightful novelty. He watched the costumed couples moving to the beat of rap music and actually felt a jolt of pleasure from their obvious enjoyment of each other on a light-hearted evening.

After eating a little too much of the unaccustomed delicacies of crab and lobster, Hanson wandered through the crowd, appreciating the diversity of the costumes and the good spirits of the revelers. It was a nice change from the usual atmosphere of strain and tension that he was used to seeing. He went up the escalator to the mezzanine and paused, watching the mostly sedate dancers shuffle back and forth to the moderately controlled beat of what looked like a cha-cha. He turned down invitations to dance from several older women with grey hair and faded expectations.

One of them said forlornly, "You look so nice in your soldier costume."

"I'm a Marine, ma'am, but thank you for the compliment." He turned and bumped into a tall, exotic Japanese geisha in an exquisite black and white kimono, who had moved close behind him.

"The lady is right. You do look nice in your soldier suit," she teased.

He started to get annoyed, then recognized who it was. "Tish. What are you doing here?"

"I'm a guest. Aren't you glad to see me?"

"Sure. But it's a surprise."

"A good one, I hope."

"Oh, yes."

She moved closer to him and whispered in a sexy voice, "Why don't you ask a geisha to dance."

"I'd like to, but I can't," he answered regretfully. "I'm on duty."

"You'll look like you're in costume to the people here. Who's to know?"

"Some of my troops are in disguise in costume, and many of the officials know me. Besides, I don't slack off when I'm on duty."

She smiled winningly. "You haven't said a word about how I look. Have you lost interest in me already?"

"Definitely not. I just can't do anything about it right now. If it's not too late for you, maybe we can get together when things wind down here."

She posed alluringly. "What do you have in mind, Major?"

He found himself ill at ease with the casual banter that was a part of the man-woman get-acquainted process that he had become unused to. "I haven't had a date with a woman for a long time. I'm feeling a little self-conscious."

She quickly switched gears. "You're doing fine, Marine. I'll call you when I'm ready to leave and we'll talk then."

He watched her move into the crowd and felt an urge to go after her and hold her close. He suppressed it with a sigh and headed for the notable's table. He passed Carver, who was dancing with a small Rubik's cube, and nodded politely. Carver stopped dancing and went to him, Rubik's following at his side.

"Good evening, Major. How are things going?"

"So far, so good. I'm just taking a brief look around, to make sure everything's secure."

"That's one of the things I like about you, Sam. You're very thorough."

Hanson decided he could be equally as informal. "Why thank you, Carv. I feel the same way about you."

The men smiled at each other, realizing that they had reached a more personal level in their relationship. "Let me introduce Dr. Yi," Carver said. "She's one of our finest physicians. Mei. This is Major Hanson."

"A pleasure to meet you, Major. I've heard of your dispute with the President."

"I hope you won't hold it against me, Doctor."

"Absolutely not. It was romantic, defying the most powerful person in the world."

"I'm no Don Quixote, if that's what you mean."

"Not at all. I meant that I thought you acted very honorably."

Before he could reply, they were interrupted by Dr. Van Meer, who greeted him brusquely. "Good evening, Major. I don't think it's a good idea for you to come to the notable's table. The secretary-general was told of your presence by one of his Arab companions and he would prefer not to meet you."

"Then I'll avoid him, Doctor," Hanson said coolly. "I'll just take a look downstairs, then leave you to your guests." He bowed courteously and went to the escalator.

"Was that necessary, Philip?" Carver asked. "The man is doing an exemplary job for us and he's a rising star in the military. You dismissed him like a common employee."

"First of all," Van Meer snapped, "he's still in disgrace in Washington …"

"Probably only until tomorrow's election," Carver interjected.

Van Meer ignored the interruption. "Second. He is in the Enclave and for practical purposes he is our employee. Third. We don't want to further aggravate the secretary-general after that deplorable suicide bombing. I should think you'd understand that."

Carver bit off a snide response and merely said, "I get your point," as Van Meer abruptly walked off.

Mei sensed Carver's agitation about the incident and guided him back to the dance floor, where she led him into a slow rhumba. "You were smart not to confront him," Mei whispered. "He sees you as a threat to his influence, because you're younger, smarter and more vigorous."

He began to relax. "How do you know I'm smarter?"

"Because you chose me," she replied.

"As a doctor?"

"That and other things," she answered enigmatically.

A rush of desire for her went through him and he drew her closer. He felt the heat of her body through her costume and began to get an erection. She reached down and patted him gently.

"It's nice to see I'm appreciated. What are we going to do about it?"

With an effort, he brought himself under control. "I can't do anything now. I still have to deal with our important guests."

"Then later. Your place or mine?"

He smiled. "Ladies choice. Now let me introduce you to the secretary-general, Ambassador Blunt and the mayor."

•   •   •

As he rode down the escalator, Hanson felt a twinge of regret for having to leave Tish. He paused for a moment on the main floor and watched the more energetic guests moving furiously to the rap beat. Despite the air conditioning going full blast, many of the dancers were sweating profusely. Alcohol and drugs were adding to the urgency of the frenzied pace. He saw the omni-present skeleton approach a cowgirl who was dancing with an Indian. The skeleton must have been his obnoxious self because the cowgirl shoved him so hard that he tripped and fell.

A colorful clown helped him up and after a brief conversation they wandered off together. Hanson idly wondered if the skeleton had finally lucked out and the thought flashed through his mind that maybe he'd luck out with Tish. He went down to the lower level, where couples were slow-dancing and he noticed some of the youngsters who he had seen come in earlier. It was obvious that the only tensions here were sexual and he headed back to his Humvee without talking to anyone else.

•   •   •

Tyrone had danced with four or five women but couldn't make any kind of connection with them. The last one, a beautiful woman in a light purple gown, had quickly pushed him back when he moved too close. When he tried again, she shoved him away, made a cutting remark, 'Find a teeny-bopper to neck with', and walked off. He was getting progressively more urgent to find a cooperative woman and he prowled the floor, not realizing that his too obvious hunger turned off the available women.

It didn't help that the women were vastly outnumbered by the men, so they could pick and choose. On one of his trips to the bathroom, some of the interns he had come in with were popping 'Delirium', the current designer drug of choice. It removed inhibitions, but severely drained one's energy, so users kept drinking restorative beverages. They offered him some, but he declined and decided to go upstairs and try for a hip-hop girl. He waved goodbye to Kyle, who was dancing with a woman in a light yellow gown, that except for the color looked just like the one that the woman who blew him off was wearing.

Kyle didn't even notice that Tyrone had left. He had hovered on the sidelines, too shy to approach a woman until he saw the one he had been dreaming of. She was surrounded by admirers, but he was drawn to her by an overwhelming force that freed him from restraints. He went to her and asked her to dance. She looked at him for a moment through large brown eyes that he instantly got lost in. He didn't hear the murmurs of resentment from his rivals. He boldly offered her his hand and a shock went through him when she took it. He sensed that she felt something similar and they moved onto the dance floor, oblivious to everything but the wonderful feeling of being together. When the music stopped, they stood there holding hands.

"I'm Kyle."

"I'm Mavis."

"You're the most beautiful girl I've ever seen," he blurted.

"How do you know I'm not ugly under this mask?" she teased.

"It wouldn't matter. I never felt this way about a girl before."

"How old are you?" she asked.

He didn't consider lying. "Sixteen. I'll be seventeen soon. How old are you?"

"Fifteen."

They didn't feel any pressure to leave the dance floor. When the music started again, they moved close and were completely carried away by the feeling of togetherness that washed over them.

Jennifer had been watching Mavis dancing with the pirate with growing impatience, as it became apparent that they were getting involved. She had intended to select a man for Mavis, so she decided to find out who this one was. She went to them and tapped Mavis on the shoulder, who turned to her with a bemused look on her face.

"I'm going to the ladies room, Mav. Come with me."

Mavis followed her in a daze, only pausing to say to Kyle, "I'll be back soon."

"I'll wait for you," he replied.

As soon as the bathroom door closed behind them Jennifer demanded, "Who is he?"

"His name is Kyle."

"What does he do?"

"I don't know."

"How old is he?"

"Sixteen."

Then Jennifer exploded. "Are you crazy? He's just a kid. We're supposed to get you a man tonight, not a boy."

"I can't help it, Jen. I'm really attracted to him."

"You haven't even seen what he looks like yet. What if he has a face full of pimples?"

"I don't care. Please don't be angry with me."

Jennifer slowly relented. "Alright. But I'll keep an eye on you. Don't do anything stupid."

Mavis hugged her. "Thanks, Jen."

21

I T WAS A LITTLE AFTER MIDNIGHT and the atmosphere at the ball was still calm. Hanson began to relax and his thoughts wandered to Tish. He was just picturing how she'd look without her kimono, when he got a radio call from Lonigan.

"Sam. This is Mike. One of my officers reported some people in costume on Lexington Avenue and 30th street, possibly heading for the cineplex. I thought I'd let you know."

"Thanks, Mike. Have your men monitor them and tell your men at the cineplex to check them out if they show up."

"Okay." Lonigan radioed an update a minute later. "Three men in black capes and masks just crossed Third Avenue and are continuing east. I'll let you know if they turn into bats and flap off," Lonigan joked.

"Only tell me if they fly this way." Hanson replied. "Then I'll issue wooden stakes to the troops."

"What about the rest of the Enclave?" Lonigan asked, mock indignantly. "Aren't you going to protect them?"

"It's your responsibility tonight, Mike … Just a minute. I see them. I'll call you back."

The three men, walking quickly, crossed Second Avenue and passed the Humvee without giving it a glance. They were wearing cheap masks and plastic capes, and they were all wearing sneakers. They just didn't look like normal party-goers to Hanson, so he went on high alert and radioed Lonigan.

"Mike. They look suspicious. Alert your men at the door." He turned to Tico, who was waiting expectantly. "Pull around and follow them." He checked his sidearm, then called Al. "Have your people move to the front entrance. There are three possible hostiles in black masks and capes heading that way. I'll meet you there."

"We're on our way," Al confirmed.

The men were halfway across the avenue, when one of them turned and saw the Humvee following them. He must have said something to his companions, because they walked faster.

"Tico. Speed up and cut them off. Have your weapon ready," Hanson ordered. "Aye, aye, boss," and he reached for his M16.

The media, suddenly aware of the growing security activity, looked around for the cause of the alert. When the Humvee got closer the men broke into a run and drew pistols from under their capes. Hanson yelled into the radio "Weapons showing," and drew his pistol.

The men put on a burst of speed and got to the cineplex at the same time as the Humvee. The police had deployed in front of the entrance and Al and her Marines just got there when the men opened fire. The police and Marines instantly returned fire and two of the attackers fell. The third, slightly wounded, pulled a grenade and Hanson shot him just as he threw it at the entrance.

"Grenade!" Hanson yelled.

Everyone hit the ground, except several reckless camera persons. The grenade rolled past the entrance and blew up in front of the large glass window with a tremendous explosion. The glass shattered, but most of it was blocked by the heavy drapes covering the windows. Hanson quickly checked his people and the police, who were uninjured, save for minor cuts and abrasions.

"Stay alert," he ordered. "There may be more of them." Then he went to see what happened inside.

The concussion had knocked down some of the crowd who had been standing near the window, but none of them appeared to be badly hurt and Hanson made his way past them, heading for the mezzanine. The explosion had rocked the building and alarmed the partygoers, abruptly shocked back to reality, who were now streaming to the emergency exits.

If it wasn't for the seriousness of the situation, Hanson might have laughed at the sudden migration of the colorful herd. But as he got to the top of the stairs, what had been a reasonably orderly evacuation turned ugly. The secretary-general's Arab security detail, guns drawn, brutally shoved people out of their way as they rushed their charge to an emergency exit that led to 30th street. The yells of outrage and screams of pain from the people knocked aside panicked the crowd, who stampeded wildly to the exit. The Arabs fired in the air to clear the way and clubbed anyone who impeded them. They even shot several people in their final effort to get to the door.

Hanson watched in helpless frustration as once again Arabs shot Americans. He couldn't reach them, so he resisted the urge to shoot some of them. He managed to reach the notable's table, where Ambassador Blunt's security chief had kept his boss waiting until he could clarify the situation. Hanson quickly explained what happened.

"Three attackers opened fire at the entrance and one of them threw a grenade. They were killed by the police and Marines, who have secured the area."

"Who are they?" Mayor Ramirez demanded.

"We haven't had time to investigate yet, sir," Hanson replied patiently. "Right now, I suggest you call your drivers and have them meet you in front, then follow me downstairs and out the front door, where your transportation will be waiting."

"Are you sure it's safe?" Dr. Van Meer asked in a frightened voice.

"Yes, sir. The police and Marines have everything under control and they're guarding the neighborhood," Hanson answered reassuringly.

Before anyone else could object, Carver said, "Take Major Hanson's advice and follow him out of here. I've got to find my daughter," and he rushed off.

"Are you the notorious Major Hanson?" Blunt asked.

"I would prefer not to be known as notorious, sir, but I might be the person you're referring to."

Blunt grinned. "I wouldn't want to aggravate my boss, but I'll try to get you a commendation for the way you handled this incident."

"It might be better for both of us if you don't draw any attention to me right now, sir, but thank you for your appreciation ..."

Mayor Ramirez interrupted indignantly. "How were those terrorists able to get so close to us, Major? Someone's going to pay for this negligence."

"The men approached the entrance in costume," Hanson explained. "There was no way to know their intentions, Mister Mayor. The police and Marines responded in their usual exemplary manner. There was no negligence. However, you might want to do something about the secretary-general's Arab bodyguards. They shot several of your guests in their rush to get out."

Dr. Van Meer had been pacing nervously. "I think Dr. Carver's right about our leaving immediately. We can all understand the Arab's reaction after the recent suicide bombing." Hanson felt a surge of rage at the cavalier dismissal of American lives, but fortunately, before he could react, Blunt took Van Meer's arm.

"We can discuss this further, once the events of tonight are clarified, Philip. Now it's time to go," and he led him away.

The mayor followed and Hanson escorted them out the door, along with General and Mrs. Griffin, who he hadn't had a chance to talk to and he whispered that he'd call him later. The notables, ignoring the press, got in their limousines, and sped away, lamenting another evening ruined by violence. Hanson watched them drive off, then turned to Lonigan, who was waiting impatiently.

"Sorry about that, Mike. I had to see the big birds off."

"Alright," he growled. "Can we go over the situation now?"

"Sure."

"Ladder 7 and Engine Company 16 responded quickly and are checking the premises. The battalion chief doesn't think there's any further hazard, but he'll get back to me. My officers are assisting the evacuation and are on heightened alert in the neighborhood. That's about it for the moment."

"Well done, Mike. Now all we have to do is survive the media."

•   •   •

Mavis and Jennifer were just coming out of the bathroom when the explosion shook the building. Jennifer reacted coolly, calmed the people around them and guided them to the exit. Mavis responded to her example and kept repeating, "It's alright. Don't rush," until others echoed her and they averted a panicky stampede. The lighting hadn't failed and they made their way in an orderly fashion through a corridor that led to an exit behind the cineplex. The girls were carried along by the flow of the crowd and a few minutes later found themselves on 33rd street. There didn't seem to be any point in going back to find out what happened, and the Ball was definitely over, so they decided to go back to Jennifer's house.

"I don't know anything about that boy, except his name," Mavis said. "How will I find him again?"

"Don't worry," Jennifer counseled. "If he cares enough, he'll find you."

"I hope so," Mavis said wistfully. "I really like him."

•   •   •

Kyle had been waiting in a rapturous trance for Mavis' return. By some inexplicable occurrence he had found the girl of his dreams and was swept away by love at first sight. Even more wondrous, she seemed to feel the same way. When the explosion went off he instantly guessed it was some kind of terrorist attack. It never crossed his mind that it could be an accidental detonation of some kind.

He had heard enough explosions, real and in training, to know what it was. He immediately looked for Mavis and caught sight of her yellow gown for an instant, but then she was swallowed up by the rapidly exiting crowd. He tried to make his way to her, but the frightened people were wedged tightly together, and he couldn't reach her. By the time he got outside she was gone and he walked home in a daze, wondering how he would find her again.

•   •   •

Carver went to each level of the cineplex in search of his daughter. She didn't answer her cell phone and his task was even more difficult since he didn't know what costume she was wearing. By the time he got to the lower level everyone was gone, except for police officers checking the premises to be sure that no one was left behind.

He was worried about her and decided to ask Hanson to confirm that she wasn't on the injured list. He called Hanson and was relieved when he told him her name wasn't on the list. Then he remembered that she was planning to spend the night at Jennifer's house and he called and left a message on the Van Meer house phone for her to call him.

He made a mental note to insist that she carry her cell phone at all times, then smiled at the absurdity of ordering a teenage girl to use her phone. As he made his way up the stairs he thought of Mei and decided that he would call her as soon as he knew Mavis was alright.

When Carver got outside, the media was behind the yellow crime scene tape and they yelled his name. "I'll have a media conference in my office at eleven o'clock in the morning. That's all for now." He saw Hanson conferring with Lonigan and joined them. He listened to the end of Hanson's report to General Griffin.

"The only real casualties were some of the guests who were shot by the secretary-general's Arab bodyguards in their rush to get out. There were no fatalities and Dr. Carver will request an FBI investigation of the incident, so you should call your sources. It's ironic that we're killing Armenians to protect Arabs … Yes, sir. I know they're terrorists. Thank you, sir."

He disconnected and turned to the others. "So much for our plans for a fun evening, gentlemen," he remarked.

"Have we learned anything about the attackers yet?" Carver asked.

"They appear to be Armenians," Lonigan replied. "At least the I.D. in their wallets has Armenian sounding names. It'll take a few hours to verify their identities if they're in the crime register. If not, it'll take a little longer to run DNA analysis."

"Is there any chance they're not Armenians?" Carver asked.

Lonigan shook his head. "I doubt it. Why would anyone want to impersonate Armenians?"

Carver shrugged, then looked questioningly at Hanson.

"I agree with Captain Lonigan," Hanson answered. "Their target must have been the secretary-general. The important question is how did they know he'd be here? I think the FBI should check that out."

Lonigan nodded agreement.

"Well you two seem to have everything under control, so I'll leave things in your capable hands. Good night, gentlemen."

"Good night, Doctor," they echoed.

Carver started for home, then gave in to an impulse and called Mei. "I just finished at the cineplex and for the moment everything's under control. We'll probably hear from the secretary-general tomorrow with wild accusations about the attempt on his life."

"Who were the attackers?" Mei asked.

"They seem to have been Armenians."

"Then who else would they be targeting?"

"Hanson thinks it was the secretary-general, but it could also have been Ambassador Blunt, or the mayor. They were both involved in the St. Vartans decision."

"What do you think?" she asked.

"The secretary-general," he answered. "I'm sorry that our evening was spoiled," he said regretfully.

"It's not too late," she offered.

"Thanks, but I still have to make sure my daughter's alright. I'll see you tomorrow."

"We'll try again. Goodnight, Carv."

He resumed the walk home, dejected about Mei and fretting about Mavis, when his phone rang.

"It's me, Dad. I'm alright. I'm spending the night at Jen's house. We helped people evacuate after the explosion. What happened?"

"I'll tell you tomorrow. Please oblige me in future and carry your cell phone at all times."

"Yes, Dad. Goodnight."

He immediately thought of Mei and called her. "Is it too late to change my mind?"

"Hurry, Carv."

•　　　•　　　•

By one a.m. the last ambulance had driven off with the only gunshot victim who required hospitalization, although the wound wasn't life threatening. The other victims had been treated on site and sent home. The media had finally dispersed, after recording every drop of blood, yet frustrated by the lack of interviews.

The bodies of the assailants had been taken to the Medical Examiner's office, conveniently located on 30th street. Hanson and Lonigan made a final sweep of the cineplex, before they left to survey the neighborhood. Then Hanson dismissed the Marines, commending them for a job well done and reminded Al to be sure they were ready for their early deployment at the polls. He also praised the police officers for their alertness and quick response.

Although he knew there would be repercussions from the attack, Hanson was satisfied with the performance of the security force. The neighborhood seemed to be sleeping peacefully and the enhanced police presence on the streets was reassuring. When they finished their tour, he dropped Lonigan at the precinct and realized that he was too tired to go see Tish. It was after 0200 and he had to be up by 0500 for the deployment to the polls. It was even too late to call her, so he told Tico to take them to the barracks in the hope of getting two hours sleep.

22

A T 0530, AN EXTRA CUP of mess hall coffee snapped Hanson wide awake, then he met with his officers and senior sergeants for a final review of the Election Day plan.

"As you all know, the only probable complication will be if the Arabs do something to disrupt the voting process. Keep in close touch with your police liaison and be ready to deploy instantly. Any questions?" There were none and he was about to dismiss the troops when he remembered an announcement that he had to make. "To those of you who haven't submitted your absentee ballots and still wish to do so, see Sergeant Danowski before 2100. He will be available until then."

"Who should we vote for, Major?" a sergeant asked.

"The candidate of your choice," Hanson answered.

"What if we want to vote for President Beaumont?" another sergeant asked.

"That's up to you," Hanson replied.

"Don't be a jerk," gunny Le Beau growled to the offending sergeant. "She's the one who got us in this mess."

Before this could become a debate, Hanson ordered, "Dismissed … Al. Meet me in my office in ten minutes."

"Yes, sir."

Hanson went to his office and reminded Danowski that personnel would be coming in until 2100 to submit absentee ballots. He called Lonigan, who confirmed that all their preparations were underway. Al came in a few minutes later.

"You wanted to see me, boss?"

"Yes, Al. I want you to coordinate all our field troops at the various polling stations."

"But, Sam. I want to be with my platoon," she protested.

"You're not a grunt anymore. You're the battalion exec. I need you to take on more of those responsibilities to prepare you for higher command."

"Higher command?" she squeaked.

"Should I translate that into English?"

"No, Sam. I just didn't think I was qualified."

"You're a great combat leader, Al, and for all practical purposes you commanded a line company. You just didn't consider the implications."

"You're right, Sam. It never crossed my mind that I could be an officer, let alone a commander. I was an N.C.O. and a woman."

"You're also a fine Marine who can go a lot further than you ever imagined."

"I don't have a field marshal's baton in my pack," she quipped.

He grinned. "I'll get you a bigger pack. Take charge of the command center."

"Yes, sir. What will you be doing?"

"I'll take a little vacation," he joked. At her shocked look, he said, "I'll check the various sites, then relieve you later, so you can do a field check. Now get going."

"Yes, sir."

•   •   •

Tyrone knocked on Kyle's door at 7:30 a.m. "Rise and shine, you pirate." When Kyle didn't answer immediately, he knocked louder. "Let's go. Let's go." Kyle opened the door and almost got a fist in the face.

"Take it easy, your highness. I don't need facial restructuring."

"Then hurry up. There's just enough time to have breakfast at the mess hall before school."

"How can you worry about such a trivial thing when I'm in love?"

"Even lovers have to eat," Tyrone grumbled.

"I think I'll live on love."

"Fine. I'll stick the I.V. tube in when you pass out. But right now, I'm hungry. Humor me. Grab your jacket and let's get going."

"If you insist."

"I do. Now move it."

The first day of November was a cool, clear fall day and the air for a change felt fresh and clean. On their way to the mess hall Kyle suddenly leaped forward and broke into a run.

"Everything feels great this morning," he yelled over his shoulder, as Tyrone raced to catch up to him. He abruptly stopped. "How am I going to find her?" he wailed.

"What's her name?" Tyrone asked.

"Mavis."

"Her last name?"

"I don't know," he moaned. "What if I never see her again? I couldn't stand it. What'll I do?" he asked in despair.

"You can start by controlling yourself … Do you know anything else about her?"

"Her age. She's fifteen."

"That's a start. That means she's in high school and we'll know someone who'll know her."

"Do you really think so?" Kyle asked hopefully.

"Definitely. Now can we eat?"

Thus reassured, Kyle raced off again. "Let's hurry. I'm starving."

•   •   •

Mavis woke up with Jennifer tucked tightly against her. Jennifer had made passionate love to her after they came home from the Ball. It was still exciting for Mavis, but she kept thinking about Kyle, the dashing pirate, and the electric thrill that had run through her when he touched her. She hadn't revealed her secret thoughts to Jennifer, who didn't seem to notice any difference in her response. After Jennifer had fallen asleep, she lay awake for nearly an hour, fantasizing about Kyle and imagining romantic encounters that she knew were silly, but nevertheless were delightful.

In one of them she was the daughter of a Spanish grandee, traveling on a galleon to meet her father, when the ship was captured by pirates.

Kyle, the ruthless captain of the cutthroat crew, took her to his cabin, where despite her fear, she was instantly attracted to him.

Jennifer's teasing voice snapped her out of her reverie. "What are you daydreaming about, girl, or shouldn't I ask?"

"I was thinking about Kyle," she gushed, "and how handsome and gentle he was. His touch sent chills through me. Oh, Jen. I've got to see him again. How'll I find him? I don't know anything about him, except his first name. I'll die if he just disappears into thin air."

Jennifer was torn between pity and scorn, but concern for her friend won out. "First of all, nobody dies of love. Hunger, disease, murder, but not love …"

"You don't understand how I feel," Mav protested.

"I know you're infatuated. I've been there. Maybe not as intensely as you, but I understand."

"Do you? Then help me find him."

"Alright," Jennifer said soothingly. "I'll ask around. Someone I know will know him."

"Do you really think so?"

"Yes, Mav. We'll find him for you."

"Thanks, Jen. You're the best friend I ever had," and she hugged her fiercely.

•   •   •

Carver woke up slowly, stretched, wondered for a moment where he was, then felt something warm against him. Mei was sound asleep, flat on her back, arms at her side, legs together, almost as if at attention, except for the slight smile of well-being on her face. He knew he had the same look on his face and smiled broadly at the feeling of well-being that possessed him.

After the death of his wife, it had been a while before he made love to another woman. Somehow, it hadn't been very satisfactory, so it seemed easier to control his needs, rather than go through the complications of dating. He had wanted Mei from the first day he met her but had refused to give in to his feelings. She had seemed to emanate subtle signals that indicated she felt the same way. Her intelligence, competence and beauty won him over, but he resisted her out of discipline and the reluctance to take advantage of his position. But reason had flown out the window and he had succumbed to desire.

A warm hand on his thigh, slowly sliding upward, brought him back to the moment. Mei was staring at him with big, jet-black eyes that gleamed with an enchanting mixture of mischief and lust that aroused him instantly. Her hand reached his penis and as she began to insistently squeeze, it stiffened.

"Something has come up, Doctor," she whispered throatily.

"What do you suggest we do about it?" he asked huskily.

"We'll have to examine it closely."

And she got on top of him and they made love until they both came in a rush. They lay there comfortably, until he remembered his responsibilities.

"I've got to get to the hospital. Can I take a quick shower?"

"Yes, Doctor. But what are you going to wear? You'll look funny in your toga."

"I'll take a cab home and change there."

He was luxuriating in the hot water when Mei slipped in. The sight of her aroused him and he lifted her onto him and plunged inside her. They came wildly at the same time, then soaped each other quickly and rinsed off. As they were dressing, he said awkwardly, "We'll have to be very careful to avoid improprieties."

"You mean you've never had an affair with any of the willing doctors or nurses?"

"Never."

"Don't worry, Carv. We'll be very discreet."

Once he got to the hospital, Carver found it difficult to concentrate. His mind kept wandering to Mei and how she looked and tasted. An angry phone call from the secretary-general brought him fully awake.

"We are very disturbed and outraged at the attempt on my life," the secretary-general yelled. "Is there no law and order in your land, Doctor? Perhaps the U.N. should get more involved in maintaining order."

"First of all, Mr. secretary-general," he replied soothingly, "it has not been determined that you were the intended target of the attack. This morning I will be requesting an FBI investigation of the incident and I suggest we wait for their findings before leaping to any conclusions. Second, I assure you we are quite capable of maintaining law and order. None of the attackers got close enough to threaten you. The only danger was from your bodyguards, whose irresponsible shooting wounded several innocent bystanders."

"They were trying to protect me," the secretary-general snapped. "We will discuss this further when we hear from the FBI," and he hung up without saying goodbye.

Carver immediately called Hanson. "The secretary-general just scorched me about the attack last night. I'm going to call the FBI as soon as we disconnect. Is there anything you want me to say or not say?"

"Just tell them what you know, Carv, and refer them to me. If you can, request Royce."

"I thought you didn't like him?" Carver asked in surprise.

"I don't, but he's media-hungry and knows how to cover his ass. Since it's the FBI's mission to prevent domestic terrorism, he'll have to find a way to make it seem like an isolated incident that security forces on site dealt with efficiently."

"What if he doesn't understand our need to defuse the situation?"

"Don't worry, Carv," Hanson chuckled. "I'll suggest the party line subtly."

"By the way, Sam. Your people handled the attack exceptionally well. I'll let everyone concerned know that."

"Thanks, Carv. Be sure to credit Lonigan and his cops. They did a fine job."

"I will."

Hanson had a ton of paperwork to get through, despite Danowski's best efforts to spare him as much as possible. He told Danowski to hold all calls except emergencies, otherwise he knew he would never start. There were endless supply requisition forms to be signed that he had quickly learned to trust Danowski to prepare.

There was a two-hundred-page draft of an FBI report about the suicide bombing on U.N. Day for his comments. He couldn't help wondering how they had the time to produce such a ponderous document. Promotion forms had to be endorsed and forwarded to headquarters for final approval and his troops were eager for the higher rank. This was the part of the job that Hanson found most boring, though he had to admit to himself that it wasn't as distasteful as ass-kissing in Washington, D.C., or even worse, bootlicking the Arabs in the U.N.

•　　　•　　　•

Kyle managed to irritate several of his teachers during the morning with his whispered inquiries to his classmates if they knew a girl named Mavis. His calculus teacher, Ms. Colon, finally reached the limit of her patience when he leaned across the aisle and asked a classmate something.

"Kyle. If you can't pay attention to the lesson, you can leave the class."

Kyle sat up abruptly. "I'm sorry, Ms. Colon. I meant no disrespect."

"You're my best student. What's wrong with you today?"

Without thinking, he blurted, "I fell in love last night at the Halloween Ball. There was an explosion and the girl left before I learned her last name, or where she lived." He ignored the class's laughter and the words tumbled out. "I've got to find her and I'm asking everyone if they know her. Do you know a girl named Mavis?"

She smiled indulgently. "No, Kyle. I wish you good luck. Now can I get on with my class?"

"Yes, Ms. Colon."

At lunchtime, in the cafeteria, he enlisted Tyrone to go table to table, except for their enemies, the doctor's sons, asking if anyone knew Mavis. No one knew her and for a brief moment he imagined some kind of conspiracy to keep them apart. He took a deep breath and had to smile at his crazy suspicion and decided not to confide it to Tyrone. One part of him tried to be rational, but another part was verging on losing control, and he was beginning to worry desperately that he wouldn't find her. Tyrone sensed his distress and tried to calm him.

"Take it easy, my man. We'll find her. We've just begun our search."

"I'm trying, but it's driving me wild. I've got to find her."

"We will. Just be cool … Hey. I've got an idea. Ask your dad if you can look at the invitation list."

"I can't ask him. I wasn't supposed to be there."

"What about asking Sergeant Danowski? He must have a copy."

"I'm glad I have a smart friend. Thanks, Ty. I'll see him right after school."

•   •   •

Mavis alternated all morning between elation and despair. One moment she was ecstatic about how she felt, the next she was depressed, fearing she wouldn't find Kyle. She was moping in her science class, while her teacher, Mr. Singh, was rhapsodizing about his favorite subject, string theory. No one in the class had the math to grasp what he was talking about, but it never stopped him from droning on. He was immersed in describing how supersymmetry posits the existence of a set of elementary particles, photinos, squarks and selectrons, which hadn't been discovered yet.

Somehow, he got on to the disaster of the Large Hadron Collider. When it was finally restarted in 2013 in Geneva, Switzerland, something went wrong and the colliding of protons by seven trillion volts of energy apiece caused its total destruction, including almost half of Geneva. "It was a great loss to science …"

Mavis interrupted him in a flash of outrage. "More than 100,000 people were killed, Mr. Singh," and she stormed out of the class. Jennifer followed her and heard Mr. Singh say in confusion to their retreating backs, "Some physicists believe that the people have been transferred to another dimension, caused by the protons colliding and creating a black hole …"

"Wait up there, girl," Jennifer called. "You're losing it."

Mavis burst into tears. "I feel terrible. Poor Mr. Singh. He really didn't do anything wrong. I better go apologize."

"You can do it tomorrow," Jennifer advised. "Right now, we better start our search for the mysterious Kyle, before you freak out completely."

"Thanks, Jen. I'm sorry to bother you so much. I am losing it."

"There, there. Don't worry. We'll find him."

"How?"

"My Dad has a copy of the invitation list. We'll start with that."

"And if he's not on it?"

"We'll ask around. Someone will know him. It's just a matter of time before we find him."

"Are you sure?" Mavis asked in a childlike voice.

"Yes, hon. He either came with someone on the list, or he knew about the Ball and snuck in. We'll find him."

"I hope so, 'cause it's tearing me apart."

"He better feel the same way," Jennifer muttered.

"I know he does," Mavis insisted.

"We'll see."

23

A L CALLED HANSON at 1100 and informed him that all the unit reports confirmed conditions were orderly at all polling stations. "The only thing that's unusual is the turnout," she said. "I talked to cops at several polling stations and they all said the same thing, the voter turnout is enormous. Jed told me that this nice old lady at the First Moravian Church on Lexington Avenue and 30th Street told him that she's been working there since 1860 …"

"Since when?"

"Well, 1960, if you want to quibble. She said she never saw a turnout like this. She actually heard lots of people complaining bitterly about Valerie while they were waiting in line, and no one defended her. If that's any indication of this election, we'll have a new president before the night's over."

"We don't know what's going on anywhere else and it's a big country," he said cautiously.

"I can hope, Sam."

The paperwork was becoming intolerable, so he decided to get out and see for himself what was going on at the polls. He told Danowski to hold the fort and have Tico meet him in front with his Humvee. He called

Lonigan and arranged to meet him for lunch at the Moonstruck Diner, on Third Avenue and 31st Street. He walked outside where he found a horde of reporters and camera crews who instantly recognized him.

"Major Hanson. Major Hanson," they clamored. "Tell us about last night."

Then they yelled over each other so it was impossible to understand their questions. After a minute, he held his hands up for silence.

"Special Agent Royce of the FBI is in charge of the investigation. I'm certain he will inform you of his findings. Thank you." Then he turned to go.

A strident blonde grabbed his arm. "Tell us how you feel about Valerie."

He removed her hand. "I have nothing to say," and he got into his Humvee, ignoring their demands for him to make a statement that they could blow up into controversy.

"You handled them gabbers pretty good, boss."

"Thanks, Tico. I don't think they were happy with me."

"The only time they're happy is when there's some kind of disaster and they can tell us how much they care."

Hanson looked at his young driver in surprise. "That's a pretty cynical attitude about the media."

"Most of them are traitors and bloodsuckers. They always treat our enemies fairly, but they treat us like criminals. If they had to defend this country with their lives, they'd sing another song."

Although Tico's explanation was simplistic, Hanson understood his feeling of betrayal and was forced to admit that he often wondered why the media was so harsh on America, one of the few places in the world where they could attack their own country with impunity. He couldn't think of anything that would change Tico's mind, so he said, "Let's go to some polling stations. Start with the senior center on 29th Street, between First and Second."

"Yes, boss. I gave my absentee ballot to Ski. Did you?"

"No. Thanks for reminding me. I'll do it when we get back."

"I voted for Zack," Tico said proudly. "Who're you voting for?"

Hanson grinned. "I think you know."

The line of voters stretched from the middle of 29th Street to the corner of Second Avenue. Tico pulled up in front of the building and Hanson debated whether to go in. A police officer standing at the entrance walked to the Humvee and saluted.

"How're ya doin, sir?"

Hanson returned the salute. "Good. What about you?"

"Good."

"Everything quiet?"

"Yes, sir. The only disturbance was when some people in line chased away a Beaumont campaigner for being too close to the polls."

"Did anyone object?"

"Not that I heard."

Hanson looked at the orderly line. "Is it always this crowded?"

"No, sir. I've been in the precinct for six years and it's the first time I've seen anyone waiting outside."

"Thanks, officer. Have a good one."

The cop saluted. "Semper fi, sir."

"Were you in the Corps?"

"Iraq in '03."

Hanson stuck out his hand and they shook hands, then he told Tico, "Next is the church on Lexington and 30th Street." As they drove off, he thought about how many good people still worked for America and hoped they partially made up for those who only worked for themselves.

The line at the church was much longer than at the senior center. It went around the corner and up 30th Street all the way to Park Avenue South, yet it was orderly and relaxed. He watched for a few minutes and noted how patiently everyone was waiting. He felt a warm glow at the reassuring sight of citizens exercising their franchise, without fear of intimidation or reprisal.

Although he had become disillusioned about the equality of democracy because he knew that the few still exploited the many, he still recognized that it was a system that protected the many from the few better than any other form of government. His doubts about the system never caused him to question his commitment to service. He had taken an oath to support the constitution when he still had faith in the rightness of America. Some of his ideals may have tarnished as he learned how his country could be as abusive as others, but it was still better than any other that he had seen and he was bound to defend it.

He visited most of the polling stations in the Enclave and conditions were similar; long lines, orderly behavior, patient waiting. When they headed for the Moonstruck Diner, he invited Tico to join him for lunch.

"I better stay in the Humvee and monitor the radio, boss, but you can bring me a ham and cheese sandwich and a Coke, if it's not too much trouble."

"You got it." He made a mental note to promote Tico to staff sergeant, and to find out a little more about his ambitions, if any. Lonigan was already at the restaurant and, after exchanging greetings, Hanson called Al and asked what was going on.

"Agent Royce and those Navy investigators were here. I made an appointment for you with them for 1500. Agent Madison looked disappointed that you weren't here. Is it considered fraternization if you work for the same government?"

"I can remember when junior officers were more respectful," he said mock fiercely.

"Then you better promote me, boss."

He laughed. "Anything else?"

"Nothing that can't wait."

"I'll see you at 1400, Al."

Lonigan suggested they compare impressions of the day's events and they both agreed, 'so far, so good'.

"At one polling station on 33rd street, there was a line halfway around the block, before it even opened," Lonigan said. "The officers assigned there were a little embarrassed that some of our citizens got there before them. It's the same all over the Enclave."

"Can you call other precincts in Manhattan and find out what kind of turnout they're getting? It's the most liberal borough in the city, so it'll confirm what we're seeing here."

"Sure, Sam. I have family on Long Island. I'll call them too."

"I've got to get back for a meeting with the FBI and navy investigators. I'll try to monitor CNN and I'll let you know anything interesting."

"Do you want me to go with you?"

"No, Mike. If they know how well we're getting along they'd use it against us. See you later."

When he returned to headquarters he released Al so she could go into the field.

"Thanks, boss. Muzi asked if he can come along, if you don't need him for anything else."

"Sure. Who's the duty officer when he leaves?"

"Jed."

Hanson laughed. "I can guess how he feels about that."

"You'd be surprised, boss," Al said. "He takes his duties as an officer very seriously and is up late each night studying the manuals."

"How do you know what he does late at night?" he asked mock suspiciously.

"You've got a dirty mind, boss. I know what he's doing because we talk a lot more than we used to and I'm reading the same manuals."

"I'm glad to hear that, Al. It further confirms why you two are officer material."

"Thanks, Sam. Can I ask you a personal question?"

"Shoot."

"What kind of future do we have in the Corps?"

"The Corps takes care of its own. As General Griffin is my guardian angel, I'm yours, and I foresee rapid promotion. Now get out of here, before I put you on desk duty."

"I'm gone, boss."

Danowski brought him up to date on all important battalion business, including the absentee ballots.

"Most of the troops have given me their ballots and I'll have one of my clerks remind everyone else."

"Good. Make sure they don't pressure anyone who to vote for. It's their choice."

"Sir. We won't tell anyone who to vote for, but we sure as shit want them all to vote."

Hanson grinned. "You wouldn't happen to know who they're voting for?"

Danowski grinned back. "I could make a good guess and it wouldn't be a certain president who isn't high in our esteem."

Hanson recalled how articulate Danowski was in all their conversations and made a mental note to look at his personnel jacket. "What was your background before the Corps, Ski?"

"I wanted to be a computer systems engineer, but in my third year in college my job was outsourced and I couldn't afford to stay in school."

"Why the Corps?"

"The challenge. I figured if I could hack it here, I could do it anywhere."

Before he could ask more, the sergeant of the guard buzzed and told him the FBI was outside.

The investigators greeted Hanson warmly, especially Royce, appreciative that he had been allowed to shine in the media spotlight. Tish had a professional demeanor, but when the others were looking at Hanson's post-action report of the attack at the Halloween Ball, she mouthed 'Call me'. He felt an immediate surge of pleasure but suppressed it when he noticed the keen eyes of Captain Evans regarding him.

"I think I speak for all of us," Royce said pontifically, looking at his colleagues for approval, "when I say you and your security forces prevented what could have been another embarrassing incident."

"It's interesting," Hanson remarked, "that no one seems concerned about the Americans who were wounded, or the people whose church was stolen by the Arabs."

Royce was startled by Hanson's comment, but responded reasonably, an indication that he no longer considered Hanson an enemy.

"You know as well as I do, Major, that they were terrorists, and in this case they were treated accordingly. If they had a legitimate grievance, they should have taken it to the courts."

"What kind of justice could they expect there?" Hanson asked bitterly.

Before Royce could answer, Evans interjected, "These are difficult times for our country, and you know the constraints imposed on us as well as anyone. There's always injustice and possibly more so in a democracy, where citizens expect more from their government. But the reality right now is that we've lost a lot of our power and can no longer act unilaterally. The U.N. and certain individual nations are infringing our sovereignty. We should never forget that nothing is more important than preserving the independence of our country. Perhaps a new president will reestablish our position in the world."

There was a momentary silence while they considered his statement.

"It's easy to blame Valerie for the mess we're in," Hanson remarked, "but I don't know if a new president can do any better."

"I thought you hated her for what she did to you," Agent Madison said in surprise.

"Sure. But that was personal. There are much bigger issues than my feelings of betrayal, or anger at a president's mistakes. Our nation is in such a state of decline that I don't know if it can be saved, and it started way before Valerie."

"That could be interpreted as disloyalty by some people," Commander Hooper said snidely.

Hanson glared at him. "I've put my life on the line for my country many times, and will again, while you'll be snug in your office shuffling paper."

Hooper turned red, but before he could retort, Evans interceded. "I'm sure Commander Hooper meant no disrespect for your service. Why don't you tell us what you meant?"

The question seemed sincere to him, so Hanson decided to explain. "After World War II, Eisenhower warned us about the threat of the Military-Industrial Complex. No one warned us of the dangers of corporate consumerism. Everyone was conditioned by TV to want more and to buy more. For a while we were so prosperous that it seemed like the American dream was possible. But when our steel and automobile industries became obsolete, it was more profitable for the industrialists to invest in other country's industries, rather than expend capital to upgrade ours.

"While the activists were protesting the war in Vietnam, the country was being sold abroad. The oil industry trained us to use more and more cars and to consume more and more energy, until our economy was inextricably linked to a controlled fossil fuel. By the time people started noticing outsourcing, it was too late. Our industries had mostly gone abroad and left us with low paying service jobs and collapsed pension funds. We couldn't pay our service people, police, fire, or military, decent wages, but we built billion-dollar airplanes and multi-billion-dollar ships. We consumed, or let others consume our essential resources."

He realized that he had said much more than he intended and fell silent. Evans was staring at him curiously, and said, "That was an interesting theory," then trailed off vaguely, possibly implying 'for a jarhead'.

"Even Marines are allowed to think, Captain, despite the disapproval of some of their superiors."

Evans grinned disarmingly. "I didn't imply criticism. I happen to agree with much of what you said ... Have you attended the War College?"

"No, sir. I've been too busy fighting wars."

Evans chuckled. "So I gather. I'll forward a recommendation that you be assigned there when you're between wars."

"Thank you, sir. Don't you think you should wait for the results of the election?"

"Have you been following it in the Enclave?" Madison asked.

"Yes. As of 1300, there was a huge turnout, mostly for Plant. I'm expecting an update for the rest of Manhattan and Long Island soon. I haven't had a chance to check the rest of the country on CNN."

"I think we've gotten away from our business here today," Royce reminded them. "We need to include all the pertinent facts that will go into our final report of the Halloween incident."

"You have my report," Hanson said. "I suggest you interview Captain Lonigan and any individual police officers or Marines who were involved. They were the only participants or witnesses to the incident. Any comments by the secretary-general, the mayor, or any other guests will be second-hand and prejudiced, since they didn't witness the incident."

"We already interviewed Captain Lonigan and read his report," Royce said. "It substantially agrees with yours and we don't think further investigation is called for. After we make final revisions, we'll present the report to the secretary-general. I think that concludes our business," and Royce abruptly walked out.

Hanson rose and saluted Evans and Hooper and they walked out. Tish quickly whispered, "Call me," then followed them.

24

T HE AFTERNOON ROUTINE was so normal that it didn't seem like Election Day, with so many future consequences at stake. Reports flowed in from the polling stations and were uniformly the same, long lines, orderly crowds, and anti-Valerie sentiments. The only significant change happened a little after 5 p.m. when people started to leave work and head for the voting booths. By 6 p.m. the lines were so long that the Board of Elections wisely decided to keep the polls open until 10 p.m., to allow for people waiting in line who hadn't gotten in to vote yet.

The only unpleasant incident in the Enclave occurred at a polling station when an Arab woman, who turned out to be an American citizen, was confronted, then threatened and might have been assaulted, but for the speedy intervention of alert police officers.

By 7 p.m. CNN was already predicting a landslide win for Zach Plant, despite the fact that most of the polls across the nation were still open. Hanson followed the news on the monitor in the mess hall while eating dinner. He began to believe that his nemesis, Valerie Beaumont, would soon be losing the reins of power that had allowed her to give him so much grief. It took an act of rigid self-discipline to keep from thinking about what her departure would mean for him. However, the broader implications for foreign policy were legitimate arenas for speculation.

His biggest fear was that the boys and girls in the Pentagon hadn't yet learned that their multi-billion-dollar ships and planes weren't as important as the men and women who had to do the nation's dirty work. Not enough of the big brass accepted that the days of massive armies storming across battlefields were over and large navies no longer met in battle on the high seas. Would it take a national disaster for the brass to see that the world had changed? That, he knew, was the question.

At 9 p.m. eastern standard time, Valerie conceded the election. The nation rejoiced because the Bible-thumping Plant had prevailed and would soon enter Washington in triumph. For better or worse was anyone's guess and Hanson knew that it could be worse but couldn't help heaving a sigh of relief that She would soon be gone. Al called him at 2200 to report that the last voters were in the booths and the polls would be officially closed within minutes. Lonigan called him a few minutes later and confirmed that all the polling stations had closed and he was dismissing his officers.

"We seem to have pulled it off without a hitch, Sam."

"That's always nice. Tomorrow's shaping up as an administrative day, so how about we get together for lunch on Thursday and discuss Veterans Day?"

"You got it, Sam. I'm glad we didn't need your Marines today."

"Me too, Mike."

Al knocked on his door a few minutes later and summarized the day. "The troops weren't called out, although they were ready for anything. I dismissed them without any announcements and told them they'd be on the regular duty roster tomorrow."

"Good. Any problems?"

"Just some loud catcalls when they heard that Valerie conceded," she answered with a grin. "I'm glad she's gone, boss."

"Apparently so are a lot of other people. Keep in mind that she's still with us until January, and a lot could happen between now and then."

She looked confused. "Like what?"

"What if Plant, our new V.P., Condi, and the Speaker of the House had a fatal accident? Valerie might try to retain power until another general election could be scheduled."

"Is that legal?"

"No, Al, but she's a ruthless person … Ah. None of that tonight. You did a good job today. Dismissed."

She saluted sharply. "Thank you, sir."

He called General Griffin and made his report. "Everything went off smoothly here, sir. No problems at the polls. The investigators left happily and I'm shutting down here, except for the night detail. The Enclave is secure, sir."

"Well done, Sam."

"Thank you, sir."

"Did you happen to notice that we got a new president tonight?"

"Yes, sir."

"As a way of celebrating I'm promoting you to lieutenant colonel." Hanson was silent for a long moment. "Did you hear me, Sam?"

"Yes, sir. Can you do that?"

"That's what generals do. You'll find out someday."

"Do you really think so, sir?"

"Yes. The Corps will always need warriors. Goodnight, Sam."

"Goodnight, sir." Hanson looked at his watch, saw it wasn't too late and called Kyle. "How're you doing, son?"

"Alright, Dad," he answered listlessly.

"What's wrong, Kyle?"

"Girl trouble. I'll tell you about it when you get home."

"Maybe I should save my news for another time."

"What news?"

"I'm being promoted to lieutenant colonel."

"That's great, Dad. Congratulations. You deserve it. Maybe you'll buy me a celebration drink at the officers club tomorrow night."

Hanson laughed. "If we only had one, son. I'll see you in a bit."

Hanson checked the duty roster for the morning, called the sergeant of the guard, who reported 'all quiet', then turned off his office light. On an impulse, he called Tish. When she answered, he quickly said, "If I'm calling too late, tell me."

"It's not too late and I have some spaghetti and a nice bottle of wine, if you feel like a midnight snack."

"That sounds great. Where do you live?"

"The Hotel Tudor, on east 42nd Street."

"I know where it is. I'll be there in fifteen minutes."

He said goodnight to the guards, went out and walked north on First Avenue. He called Kyle, who still sounded depressed.

"Listen, son. If it's alright with you, I won't be home for a while."

"Another crisis, Dad?"

"Believe it or not, I have a date."

"You're kidding?"

"No."

"Who is she?"

"An FBI agent I met recently."

"At least she isn't a Marine. It is a she?"

Hanson laughed. "Yes, Kyle. I'm not gay yet."

"Just checking, Dad. How do you feel about gays?"

"Regardless of preferences they're part of our society, so I accept them in the Corps."

"You do?"

"As long as they do their duty, like everyone else. We can talk about it later."

Kyle felt good for his father and hoped that he met someone special. He knew there had been women in his father's life since the death of his mom, but they never seemed more than a brief distraction. He had to laugh at the thought of his dad getting it on with an FBI agent. Silly but amusing images floated through his mind and he cracked up picturing her slapping the cuffs on him.

The diversion only lasted a few moments, then the terrible ache that possessed him since he lost sight of Mavis the other night gripped him with unreasoning anguish. 'What if I never see her again' kept flashing through his mind, with an agony that felt physical. He hadn't eaten all day and was surprised that he managed to sound under control when he talked to his dad. He knew he was close to losing it.

•   •   •

Mavis lay awake, while Jennifer slumbered contentedly beside her. Jennifer had made love to her earlier and she had submitted, all the while thinking of Kyle and the rapturous feeling of being close to him, the heat of his body, the succession of thrills when they touched each other, the certainty that he was that special one. All of a sudden, a terrible feeling that she wouldn't see him again wracked her body in a paroxysm that made her gasp. She started to cry, trying not to make noise, but Jennifer woke up.

"What's wrong, hon? Do you have cramps?"

Mavis threw her arms around her and sobbed brokenly. "I'm so miserable. I want Kyle and I'm afraid I'll never see him again," and she bawled like a baby.

Jennifer looked at her in exasperation, then softened as she felt the extent of her friend's despair. "There, there, hon. We'll find him. You'll see."

"You promise?" Mavis asked in a child's voice.

"Yes, Mav. Now relax and go to sleep."

• • •

Carver was delighted with the peaceful outcome of Election Day, since he was the department head who was responsible for the complement of Marines, and they had performed to everyone's satisfaction. His working relationship with Hanson was a major improvement over Captain Beasley. He was even beginning to like the man and he had discovered unexpected depths in the hard-bitten warrior. He had no doubt that the new administration would reward Hanson and reflect well on himself, and it reassured him that he was getting more comfortable dealing with the politics of the Enclave. He recognized that he owed some of the recent stability to Hanson and made a mental note to help his career, whenever possible. He started to call Hanson, then noticed how late it was and made a written note to call him in the morning and discuss Veterans Day.

He sat back in his recliner and took a sip of the chilled natural Rhine wine, and actually relaxed for the first time since leaving Mei the other morning. Images of her exciting naked body flitted through his mind and he became aroused. The familiar sensation of frustration that was not to be satisfied moved through him, but this time he had an opportunity to deal with it; Mavis was spending the night at Jennifer's house again.

He wondered for an idle moment what the girls did together, considering how often they were in each other's company, then assumed they talked endlessly of girl things. Despite his new-found confidence, it took him a minute to pick up his phone and call Mei. When her answering machine clicked on he felt a spasm of jealous rage and started to disconnect, but he forced himself to leave a message.

"Hi, Mei. It's Carv. I just called …"

She picked up her phone. "I was just thinking about you, Doctor. I need another consultation."

"When?"

"Right now, Carv."

"I'll be right there."

•　　　•　　　•

After being indoors all afternoon and evening, Hanson found the walk up First Avenue refreshing. It was a clear, cool, early fall night and the air was breathable for a change. He paused at 40th Street, the northern boundary of the Enclave, and stared at the U.N. building for a minute. He couldn't help reflecting on the ideals they professed and the bitter realities of what they accomplished.

He begrudgingly admitted that sometimes the U.N. actually did some good and they had successfully intervened in several cases of ethnic cleansing, at least in white countries. The third world was an altogether different story. They were definitely an improvement on the long extinct League of Nations but were hardly a world body that would alleviate universal suffering and injustice.

The U.N. building was far enough away from other nearby buildings so it looked isolated and aloof, detached from human suffering. He shook his head in momentary despair for the millions whose only hope for the future was that fragile institution, then shrugged off his dark brooding and headed for the Tudor Hotel.

The hotel lobby was understated and he paused to appreciate the aged wood paneling. The desk clerk stared at him haughtily when he asked for Tish's room number.

"Is this an official visit, sir? I don't think the military has any jurisdiction here."

The clerk was short, plump, soft and pale, with a sycophant's face that was ready to snarl or cringe in the service of his masters. Hanson had met the type in a dozen countries and had long since lost any pity for the type of lackey who surrendered his soul to his economic superiors.

Hanson automatically used the authority tone. "Notify Ms. Madison that Major Hanson is here."

"There's a soldier here asking for you, Ms. Madison and I don't know what he wants." She obviously told him to mind his own business in no uncertain terms, judging by his reddened face. "Yes, ma'am. I'll send him right up. Thank you, ma'am." He turned to Hanson. "Suite 804, sir."

Hanson leaned across the counter. "If I come back in an official capacity, know the difference between a soldier and a Marine."

"Yes, sir," he said tamely.

Tish was waiting at her door when he got out of the elevator. "You managed to scare froggy," she said archly.

"Who's that?"

"Our officious desk clerk, who tries to intimidate all but the rich."

Hanson laughed. "I never let toadies bother me."

"Froggy, not toadie," she corrected.

She was wearing a white satin lounging suit and he admired her for a moment before going inside. She didn't move out of the way and he found himself pressed against her. The heat of her body aroused him and she pulled him closer.

"It's about time we got together," she said throatily, then kissed him passionately.

They seemed to float into the bedroom, shed their clothes and fall on the bed, locked in a tight embrace that quickly led to an urgent joining. They made love several times and Tish finally held up her hands.

"No more. I surrender."

He grinned. "It's the training, ma'am."

She laughed. "We'll have to discuss the rules of engagement."

"Later," he mumbled, as he reached for her again.

25

C ARVER, IN A DARING MOMENT, decided not to go to the hospital Wednesday morning. Of course it had nothing to do with being comfortably sprawled in Mei's bed, with her snuggled closely against him. He reviewed his obligations for the day and concluded that nothing was so urgent that it couldn't be postponed. He slipped out of bed without waking Mei and made the necessary phone calls.

He called his administrative assistant first and instructed him how to handle various appointments and problems. Then he called the veteran's ward and told the nurse that he and his staff would be there at 9:00 a.m. tomorrow morning. Lastly, he called Hanson and canceled their morning meeting. Hanson sounded as lazy as he did and invited him to join him and Lonigan for lunch on Thursday, at 1 p.m. at the Moonstruck Diner, to finalize plans for Veterans Day. He accepted, disconnected, then crawled back into Mei's warm, cozy bed.

•　　　•　　　•

Hanson would have smiled broadly if he knew that he and Carver were lolling in bed, instead of diligently pursuing their duties. He stretched luxuriously, careful not to wake Tish and silently sighed with satisfaction. This was the first time since the death of his wife that he felt really fulfilled by another woman. He worked his way out of bed without waking Tish, who was entangled in the sheets. He went into the living room where he had shed his uniform the night before and clucked reprovingly at himself for having left his pistol on the floor. He called Danowski, who reported all quiet, then told him he wouldn't be in until the afternoon. He called Al and told her he wouldn't be in until later and not to bother him, except in the event of terrorist attack, or a declaration of war. He fended off her efforts to find out where he was and endured her nosey questions patiently.

"You sound mighty relaxed, boss. Should I guess what you're doing?"

"None of your business. By the way, you're promoted to first lieutenant."

"Gee, boss," she said teasingly, "at this rate I'll outrank you in a few months."

He laughed. "Not quite. I've been promoted to lieutenant colonel."

He heard her draw in her breath. "Congratulations, Sam. You deserve it. You're the finest officer in the Corps."

"Thanks, Al. I'll call you later."

      •   •   •

Kyle was not having a good day. The tensions at school between the doctor's sons and the Marine's sons had been simmering for months. Only because cooler heads, especially Kyle's, had prevailed over the rush to battle because of the doctor's kids' snotty remarks and 'accidental' jostling in the hallways, had conflict been avoided.

The two groups were in distinct contrast. The privileged sons of doctors sported the assurance of money and social status, favoring designer clothes and accessories, but were untested in the arena of life. The Marine offspring had lived on bases in foreign countries, wore PX attire, moved every few years, had faced crises, even danger, and had developed self-reliance. They bitterly resented being condescended to by kids they viewed as soft and spoiled by the crutch of the economic security of their parents.

From their first day at school, the Marine boys were taunted and sneered at, nicknamed the 'warmongers', instead of being welcomed. Only Kyle's repeated injunctions to, 'ignore the insults, pretend you're in a hostile country and you have to get along with the natives, which we've done before', prevented the outbreak of violence. There had been dozens of minor incidents, but fortunately none had erupted into warfare. But anger was always close to the surface and tempers were always ready to explode.

The doctor's boys had dominated the school population for years by virtue of their father's positions. The Marine boys, the newcomers, who were superior athletes and most shockingly, scholars, threatened the status quo. Their more worldly experience appealed to the sheltered schoolgirls and irked the doctor's boys, who for the first time faced competition. As a further insult, the Marine boys called them 'peace pussies'.

It was just a matter of time before the complications of teen romance or sex led to hostilities. The gay boys had made overtures to the Marine boys and were publicly rebuffed, but accepted rejection gracefully. The straight doctor's boys started losing their girlfriends to the newcomers and resented it.

When Kyle and Tyrone began asking about a girl who was obviously from the hospital class, irritation flared into anger. A group of doctor's boys decided to teach Kyle and Tyrone a lesson. They were aware of the two boys' ability to defend themselves, so they made a plan to grab them one at a time and administer a beating.

One of their hangers-on told them that Tyrone had just gone into the boys bathroom, and they quickly prepared an ambush. Five of them, led by Derek, who was the most arrogant and obnoxious of the group, went to the bathroom, grabbed Tyrone, threw him down and kicked him savagely, over and over. They left him lying on the floor, battered and bleeding.

One of the Marine boys found Tyrone, called for help, then told Kyle what happened. Kyle saw Derek posing and preening for his friends and heard him bragging loudly about what he did to Tyrone. In a spate of fury he raced to him and knocked him down. Derek's friends tried to restrain Kyle, but he shook them off, then gave Derek, who was just getting up, a tremendous kick that sent him crashing into the wall. The loud crack of a bone breaking froze them all. The principal and a security guard arrived a moment later.

"What's going on here?" the principal demanded. "Who started this?"

Both factions blamed the other and the principal ordered them to his office, after instructing the guard to call for an ambulance. He listened to both sides, then dismissed the doctor's boys without rebuke and put Kyle on suspension. Kyle protested the unfairness of his treatment, but the principal ignored his objections.

"You are suspended from school until further notice. Have your father call me to make an appointment to discuss your case."

"What about Derek?"

"You'll be lucky if he doesn't file assault charges against you, considering what you did to him."

"But he and his friends attacked Tyrone," Kyle protested.

"I'll look into it," the principal said vaguely.

"That's bogus."

"I suggest you go home, before I call the police."

Kyle left, barely able to refrain from punching the principal.

•   •   •

Later that day, a girl friend called Mavis and told her about the fight at school between Kyle and Derek. She was thrilled that at last she knew where he went to school. However, she was disturbed by the fight, worried that Kyle was hurt and upset by his suspension. She was also concerned about the injury to Derek.

When she first moved to the Enclave he had tried to date her, but she was repelled by his haughty attitude of superiority. His ego was so big that he accepted her rejection without any disruption of his equilibrium, but he couldn't tolerate derision. A joke about him had made the rounds, that since his father was the head of the proctology section, he was the son of an asshole inspector. A girl who was jealous of Mavis told her friends that Mavis had laughed at him and made sure to spread the word. Ever since then, their relationship was distant.

Mavis immediately called Jennifer and asked her to get all the details of the clash, and if there was any way to get Kyle's cell phone number. After some cajoling, Jennifer promised to find out what she could and call back as soon as she knew something. Now that Mavis knew where Kyle went to school and that she should be able to contact him, instead of feeling relieved, she really became agitated.

"What if he's so upset about being suspended that he runs away and I never see him again?" she asked, then burst out crying.

It took a while for Jennifer to calm her down. "There, there. He's too young to run away."

"No he's not," Mavis protested. "He's almost seventeen. Boys run away younger than that all the time."

"He's not going to run away."

"How do you know?"

"Because school is too important. Now stop fretting," Jennifer insisted. "We know where he goes to school and we'll find him."

"Are you sure?" Mavis quavered.

"Yes."

"I'll die if I don't see him again."

"Don't worry. You will."

Jennifer wasn't happy about Mavis' infatuation with that silly boy, but she had already selected her for a future college roommate, on the basis of her tractability, social status and appearance. She would also make a convenient lover, once this immature boy episode was out of her system. So she called her network of friends until she learned all the dirt. She was shocked that the mystery boy was a Marine brat and felt confident that when she told Mavis it would end a brief chapter in teen romance. It took a while to learn all the details of the events of the day, but she was delighted that Derek finally got his comeuppance. She got an additional laugh when she realized that the Marine boy who got beaten up was the same boy who had tried to pick her up at the Halloween Ball. She made a quick decision not to tell Mavis the news right away, then called her and said she should have some news that evening.

•   •   •

When Kyle left school he went straight to the barracks and told his father about the attack on Tyrone, his retaliation against Derek and his suspension. Hanson's first thought was for Tyrone.

"How is he?"

"He's got cuts and bad bruises, but he'll be alright."

"And Derek?"

"His arm is broken."

As expected, Hanson wasn't happy. "We occupy a peculiar place in the Enclave and everything we do is carefully scrutinized."

"I know, Dad."

"The boy you injured is the son of a section head."

"I know, Dad."

"Do you realize the problems this could cause us? And don't say 'I know, Dad'."

Kyle resisted temptation. "I'm sorry, Dad. They really beat Tyrone badly and I would've been next. I went after Derek without thinking about other implications. I was furious that they hurt my best friend and I reacted."

"More like over-reacted. You broke his arm."

"I didn't mean to. There were five of them and there wasn't time for me to throw a glove in his face and challenge him to single combat."

"Don't be a smart-ass."

"Sorry, Dad."

Hanson stared at his son in exasperation. "Tell me what started this."

"Derek and his friends have been hassling all the Marine kids since we got here. I've been a peacemaker from the beginning, but what they did to Tyrone was too much."

"Did you ever consider telling me about the problem?"

"You had bigger things to contend with. I didn't want to bother you."

"I'm your father. What makes you think you'd bother me?"

"Come on, Dad. You've got serious battles to fight. This was just stupid kid stuff, until today. We've been through this before, especially in foreign countries. We always take shit from the locals. It's a fact of life. You know that."

Hanson nodded reluctantly. "I guess I do. I just didn't expect you to flip out."

"I defended my friend," Kyle snapped angrily. "Wouldn't you defend your troops?"

Hanson sighed. "Yes, son. I would … Well. I'll tell Jed, then talk to your principal and straighten things out. Once it's settled, I rely on you to avoid trouble."

"Yes, Dad."

It took a while to calm Jed, who wanted to confront the principal and teachers for allowing the atmosphere that led to the attack on his son. Then Hanson called the principal and arranged to meet him that afternoon, at 3:30.

The meeting turned out to be less than satisfactory. The principal was an affected product of private and Ivy League schools that had brainwashed him in the delusion that their graduates were superior creatures. He showed a disdain for the armed forces that revealed he placed them in the lower echelon of uniformed services, on a par with sanitation workers. He immediately got Hanson's hackles up when he prefaced the conversation with, "I've always been anti-military, but that won't interfere with my treating your son fairly, Mr. Hanson."

"First of all, it's colonel, not mister. Second, I won't let your anti-military sentiments prejudice me against you if I have to defend you from Arab terrorists. Finally, I require that you treat my son as fairly as you do anyone else. No more. No less. Do we understand each other, sir?"

"I think so," the principal answered reluctantly.

The principal stared at him warily, suddenly realizing that this wasn't the average father, apologizing for his son's peccadilloes and he spoke more cautiously.

"We had an unfortunate incident today that resulted in a student's arm being broken by your son, for which offense I suspended him."

"I see," Hanson replied neutrally. "Did you investigate the incident?"

"That was unnecessary. A dozen witnesses saw your son assault the boy."

"Did you inquire why my son attacked the boy?"

"I imagine over some disagreement that your son couldn't deal with, except by resorting to violence."

"I see. Do you have a list of these witnesses?"

"Of course not. This is a school, not a courthouse."

"Yet you judged and condemned my son without due process. Did you know that his best friend was brutally assaulted in the bathroom by the boy he fought with and four others, just moments before the so-called 'incident'?"

"Why, no."

Hanson was briefly tempted to ream the vapid jerk. They stared at each other for a moment, then Hanson resumed his questioning.

"Did you know that my son was a child of the military?"

"Why, yes."

"Did you know that the children of the military have been insulted and persecuted ever since they entered this school?"

The principal was getting distinctly uncomfortable. "Well, there have been rumors about some friction between the newcomers and the regulars, but it never amounted to anything."

"Today was more than a rumor."

"That's why I suspended your son, to show them that violence isn't the answer."

"Then why didn't you suspend the gang that attacked my son's friend?"

"I'm not one of your soldiers who you can order around," he blurted. "I don't answer to you."

"If I'm forced to go to the appropriate authorities and reveal your discrimination towards certain students," Hanson said softly, "it would hurt the school and the students. I'm certain you wouldn't want that."

The principal realized the possible ramifications. "Well. We wouldn't want to hurt the students."

"That's right," Hanson said encouragingly.

"And the school does treat everyone fairly," the principal said.

"I'm glad to hear that."

"Then I think it will be in the interests of all concerned to cancel your son's suspension."

"It's always reassuring to hear good sense prevail. Thank you," and he managed to walk out of the office without laughing at the twerp's bullshit.

26

THE VETERANS REALLY APPRECIATED getting medical services after years of neglect. They welcomed Carver and his staff raucously, cracking off-color jokes and bawdy comments that were meant to embarrass the female doctors and nurses. They were pleasantly surprised when the women gave back as good as they got.

They were particularly taken with Dr. Yi, who treated the vets as if they were naughty children, ordering them firmly to behave. Carver couldn't help smiling at the tiny doctor commanding the unruly vets who already adored her. This was still early in the examination process of the vets and the staff was engaged in a preliminary evaluation of each vet's condition, which would precede individual treatment.

After several hours, the examinations were progressing efficiently and the doctor jokes were becoming tedious, so Carver placed Mei in charge and left for his lunch appointment with Hanson and Lonigan.

Carver got to the restaurant first, ordered coffee and reviewed his clinical notes while waiting for the others. Hanson and Lonigan arrived a few minutes later and greeted him warmly.

"And how are my two security pillars today?" Carver asked.

"Relieved that there were no problems on Election Day," Lonigan said.

"Me too," Hanson added. "However, there is something I have to tell you before we discuss Veterans Day."

"Go ahead," Carver said.

"There was an unfortunate incident at the N.Y.U. Academy yesterday."

"What happened?"

"Some of the doctor's kids attacked a Marine kid and the Marine kid was badly beaten, and a doctor's kid got a broken arm."

"That sounds serious. How did it start?"

"There've been tensions between the two groups since the Marine kids started school. This experience taught them all a lesson in getting along and Mike made sure there were no legal problems, so I think we can consider the case closed. I just didn't want you to hear about it from someone else."

"You're sure there'll be no complications?"

"Pretty sure."

"Then let's move on to our next problem, Sam."

It was reassuring to Hanson that there was a functional level of trust between him and the doctor, so he confidently expressed his opinion that, at the moment, there didn't appear to be a specific reason to cancel the Veterans Day parade.

"There's always the possibility of a disruption, but unless intelligence warns us of a direct threat, we should consider that the security plan for the event should be sufficient. The two groups we have to be concerned with are the Armenians and the Arabs. I'll let Mike brief you about them. Mike?"

"The Armenians are now under surveillance by the FBI, so that means they could be anywhere," he said with a chuckle.

Hanson laughed, but Carver looked shocked.

"Are you questioning their competence?" Carver asked.

"They're good at some things," Lonigan explained, "but street smarts isn't one of them."

"Are you saying we have to worry about the Armenians?"

"Yes. They look like many other occidentals, so we can't profile."

There was a lengthy silence while Carver digested the implications.

"Let's come back to the Armenians after the Arabs," Hanson suggested.

"The Arabs are easier to profile," Lonigan continued, "despite the restrictions demanded by the U.N., the A.C.L.U. and other groups that advocate terrorist rights."

"That's a bit harsh, Captain," Carver said.

"You've seen what they do, Doctor. I'd like to see more concern with the victims of terrorists and have some leeway to fight fire with more than diplomatic protests."

"Do you want to suspend the constitution?" demanded Carver.

"The constitution wasn't written for terrorists. Once a terrorist decides to give his life for his cause, we're no longer dealing with ordinary crime or war. The only way to prevent deadly attacks is through better intelligence and pre-emptive action. It really comes down to us or them. The media and the liberal left just can't grasp that there's no negotiating with terrorists."

It was clear to Hanson that Carver wasn't opposing Lonigan, just trying to learn more about him, so he felt it was unnecessary to intercede. Carver cleared his throat.

"I want to hear more about your views, Mike. Is it alright to call you Mike?"

"Sure."

"Call me Carv. Now tell me yes or no to the parade." Lonigan looked at Hanson, who took over.

"The reality is very simple, Carv. The parade could always be a target for terrorists. The terror threat won't end because we cancel a parade. Besides, the reviewing stand uptown would be the most likely target.

"We'll set up multiple check points in the Enclave and shut most of the access streets to 23rd Street and Fifth Avenue to traffic and funnel the crowds to several screened entrance areas. We'll station police and Marines at all the access streets and deploy the National Guard and the police on the parade route. We'll also flood the entire area near the parade route with plainclothes and undercover personnel. We'll request the same security north of 40th Street."

The plan sounded effective to Carver, but something kept nagging at him.

"How do we know that it won't be another U.N. Day incident?"

"Nothing's ever a hundred per cent sure in life," Hanson stated, "but this time security won't be withdrawn at the last minute. I think we can contain the situation, but there are no guarantees. It's your call."

"Do you agree with him, Mike?" Carver asked.

"Yes, Carv. I have confidence in our people and we'll coordinate with the appropriate people north of the Enclave."

"I have to get final approval from the mayor and other officials. Is there anything we might be forgetting before I give them my recommendation to hold the parade?"

"We'll let you know if anything changes," Hanson answered. "Right now, we have the situation well in hand."

"I wish I was feeling as confident as you two," Carver muttered.

"We'd be pretty nervous if we had to run an operating room," Lonigan joked.

On that note, they arranged to meet Saturday morning, then went their separate ways.

•　　　•　　　•

When he got back to the barracks, Hanson sent for Al and Jed and confirmed that it was a go for the Veterans Day parade. They reviewed the security plan and agreed that the arrangements were basically the same as for U.N. Day, with the need to factor in possible threats from the Armenians and Arabs. When they finished discussing the plan, Jed brought up the school incident.

"I'm still pissed at how that principal handled the attack on Tyrone," Jed asserted. "I'm glad that he revoked Kyle's suspension, but that doesn't resolve the gang attack on my son."

Al, who had heard about the incident, calmed Jed, as usual. "Wouldn't you say that Kyle's breaking that boy's arm made up for Tyrone's injuries?" she asked.

"I guess so," Jed admitted," but it still leaves the question why the principal didn't do anything about the gang attack."

"I think we know the reason," Hanson said. "Prejudice against the military. I believe I reasoned with the principal ..." They grinned at the euphemism. "I'd like to schedule a visit to the school for the three of us," Hanson said. "We'll talk to the students and teachers and hopefully establish a better understanding of our mission."

Danowski buzzed him and said General Griffin was calling. Hanson told Al and Jed that he'd see them later and waited until they closed the door behind them. "Hello, General. How are you?"

"Good, Colonel. And you?"

"Appreciating being a colonel."

"It was a long time coming. Barring unforeseen circumstances, you'll be a full bird colonel in a few months."

"I guess that's called the fast promotion track, sir. What unforeseen circumstances do you foresee?"

The general laughed. "That's what I like about you, Sam. Your flexibility. If nothing drastic happens between now and the inauguration to disrupt the transfer of power, we should see major policy changes in the new administration."

"Why, General, if I didn't know better, I'd suspect you were implying that Valerie might not be ready to move on."

"Even though we're encrypted this line might be monitored, Sam, so let's not discuss improbables, but advisors to the new administration have recommended increased security."

"Does that include you, sir?"

"Yes, it does. But I'll tell you more when I see you in person on Saturday for dinner. Unless you have other plans?"

"I'd be honored, sir."

"Pick a nice restaurant and Beverly said you should bring a date. I'll call you tomorrow with specifics."

"Yes, sir."

• • •

Jed was still brooding about the assault on Tyrone, who had stayed home from school. On an impulse, he decided to check on him. "I'm going to drop in on Tyrone and see how he's doing," he told Al.

"How about I go with you?" she suggested.

"Cool. He'd love to see you."

"Nobody says cool anymore, Jed."

"What do they say?"

"I don't know. Let's ask Tyrone."

Tyrone was delighted to see Al and barely noticed his father, until his insistent questions got his attention. The most challenging one was what started the fight. "The peace pussies resented us from the beginning ..."

Al laughed. "Is that what you call them? No wonder they resent you."

"They called us warmongers from the first day," Tyrone protested.

"But was this the first time things got violent?" Jed asked.

"It was the first time there was more than bumping or shoving."

"Why?"

"Kyle and I were asking about a girl he met recently. She may be a doctor's daughter and that may have made them jealous."

"Just for asking about her?"

"Yes, sir."

"That seems pretty trivial. Was there anything else?"

Tyrone knew he couldn't reveal that he and Kyle went to the Halloween Ball, so he said innocently, "As far as I know, sir."

"Well Colonel Hanson, Al and I …"

"Colonel Hanson?"

"He was just promoted," Jed explained.

"That's great, sir."

"Now if I can finish?"

"Yes, sir."

"We'll be going to your school to talk to students and teachers to try to improve relations between the kids."

"That might help, sir."

Then Al came to the rescue.

"You can lecture him later, Jed. I'd like to visit for a few minutes before getting back to the barracks."

"Thanks, Al," Tyrone said gratefully.

•　　　•　　　•

Kyle went to Tyrone's house as soon as school let out. "How you doing, Tiger?" Kyle asked.

"Look who's calling who a tiger. I heard you broke Derek's arm."

"Well, I did get a bit carried away when I heard him bragging about what he did to you."

"Remind me not to get on your bad side," Tyrone joked.

"Seriously. How are you feeling?"

"Except for a sore chest and a strained hamstring, I'm okay. It's a good thing those pussies don't know how to fight. If they hadn't grabbed me from behind, I probably could have taken all of them."

"Maybe the whole school," Kyle said with a straight face, which made Tyrone laugh.

"Don't do that," he pleaded.

"What?"

"Make me laugh. It hurts."

"I didn't force you."

"Some friend you are. Wait 'til I'm better."

"Instead of threatening me, start thinking about how I can find

Mavis. Nothing's worked so far."

"You really got it bad for her, don't you?"

"Yeah."

"I'll be back in school Monday and we'll make friends with the pussies and ask them."

"What if they won't tell us?"

"Then we'll beat it out of them."

"That's what I like, Ty. A diplomatic solution."

"We aim to please."

•   •   •

Mavis was finding it more and more difficult to stay focused in Mr. Singh's science class. Despite his having accepted her apology for her recent outburst in class, and her promising to pay attention, she was increasingly irritated by his rapturous digressions.

He was babbling about a fusion device that accelerated hydrogen atoms and slammed them together to make helium. His description of the device's crystal, which was made of lithium tantalite and belonged to a class of materials known as pyroelectrics, was meaningless to her. She couldn't understand why he was babbling away about nuclear reactions when her heart was breaking. She wanted Kyle, not neutrons. She lost control as he explained how fusion could power spacecraft and yelled, "They'll just make bigger bombs," then burst into tears and ran out of the classroom.

Jennifer shrugged apologetically to Mr. Singh and went after her, leaving him bewildered and muttering, "Ms. Carver really shouldn't be afraid of scientific innovation."

Jennifer was getting slightly exasperated with her friend's mood swings and erratic behavior, but she rationalized that her peculiar actions were a byproduct of a very romantic, if silly, young girl. Having never experienced burning passion, Jennifer couldn't understand what Mavis was feeling and ascribed her extremes to misplaced role playing. She caught up to Mavis, who was aimlessly wandering the corridor.

"You did it again, hon. Mr. Singh's class will never be the same."

"Oh, Jen. I didn't mean to … I'm so unhappy."

Jennifer patted her consolingly. "There, there. You should be happy, not miserable. We know where your Kyle goes to school. You'll see him soon. You've got to be patient and try to control yourself."

"I'm really trying, Jen, but I can't help it sometimes … I wish I went to the N.Y.U. Academy. Then I'd be near him all day."

Jennifer smiled at the silly fantasy. "First of all, if you went there, you might never have liked him at all."

"Oh, no. I would."

"Second. You wouldn't have met me."

"Oh, no. That would be awful. You're my dearest friend."

"Then listen to me. You'll see him soon."

"Are you sure?"

"Yes."

"You promise?"

"Yes. Now let's go back to class."

"Yes, Jen."

•   •   •

The atmosphere at the mess hall that evening was more cheerful than at any time since they arrived at the Enclave. Hanson thought back to his earlier misgivings when the remnants of his decimated battalion were assigned to New York City. When General Griffin had described the mission, he had been shocked.

"But, General," he had protested. "Isn't that a violation of the Posse Comitatus Act of 1876, to use the military for domestic law enforcement? We could be prosecuted as criminals."

"First of all," the General had explained, "you're not being sent there to enforce the law. Your presence is a reminder to certain members of the U.N. that we are still a sovereign power and will not accept abuse of our citizens by extremist elements. Besides, most of what you'll do will be ceremonious and it'll give your troops a chance to recuperate from their recent setbacks."

"Are these legal and official orders, sir?"

"Yes, Sam. Don't you trust me?"

"I trust you all the way, sir. I don't trust some people in Washington."

He was just remembering his gratitude at the time to General Griffin for keeping him from a court martial and dismissal from the Corps, when Al interrupted his reverie.

"Excuse me, sir. Jed and I would like to speak to you."

"Sure, Al. What's up?"

"In your office, if you don't mind, sir?" Jed asked.

Every eyeball in the mess hall fastened on them as they left and the usual rumors that diverted the lower ranks of the military began to spread like wildfire. By the time they reached Hanson's office, Danowski was waiting attentively by the door, a concerned expression on his face.

"Anything wrong, Colonel? Are we going on alert?"

"What gives you that idea, Ski?"

"Latrine gossip, sir."

"I haven't been to the latrine yet, Ski."

"Yes, sir. Is there anything I can do sir?"

"Yes. Make some coffee, please."

Danowski walked away with a disgruntled look, thinking he had been left out of the loop.

After they settled down with coffee, Hanson remarked with a grin. "You've got the entire battalion worried. What's the problem, Al?"

"Sorry about stirring up the troops. It's Jed."

"What did he do?"

"I'd rather he told you."

"Good. Does he remember how to speak?"

"Don't rag on me, Sam," Jed pleaded. "This is difficult enough for me as it is."

"Alright. Tell me."

"I still can't get used to being an officer," he blurted.

"Why not?"

"Everything's different now."

"Has Al changed?"

"No."

"Have I changed?"

"No."

"Have the Sergeants changed?"

"No."

"Then what is it?"

"It's all this saluting and formality. I don't know if I like it."

"You didn't have any problems saluting before becoming an officer."

"I know, Sam. It just feels strange."

"Listen, Jed. You're a natural born combat leader. The next time we go into battle you'll feel fine. I know you've been studying the manuals. Is there anything you don't understand?"

"No, Sam."

"Then try it for three months. If you still don't like it, I'll demote you. O.K.?"

"Yes, Sam."

"Now get out of here, you two. I don't want to hear about this for three months."

"Yes, Sam," they echoed.

27

COLONEL WARRINGTON CALLED HANSON Friday morning in response to the email of the security plan for the Veterans Day parade.

"Your sergeant answered, 'Colonel Hanson's office'."

"That's right."

"When I first met you several weeks ago you were a sergeant. If I knew that promotion came that fast, I might have joined the Marines. I would have made field marshal years ago."

"We already have too many field marshals in the Corps," Hanson joked.

"Well I'm glad to hear about your promotion."

"Thank you, Colonel. I'd buy you a drink at the Officers Club, if we had one."

Warrington laughed. "The closest thing we have to an O Club at the armory is an illicit bottle in a locker. Between the homeless shelter at night and the children's school in the daytime we barely have room for roll call anymore."

"I thought the National Guard only served on weekends?" Hanson asked.

"That was in the good old days, before the Iraq war. We've been nationalized since then and the battalion is always on duty. There's a rumor going around that we're getting another battalion and I'll be promoted to brigadier general and command the regiment. But you know the Army and rumors."

"I hope it happens, then you'll buy me a drink."

"Thanks, Sam."

They chatted casually for a few minutes, two new friends comfortable together, then got down to business.

"I see that the security plan is basically the same as for U.N. Day, with the addition of checkpoints on the cross streets leading to Fifth Avenue," Warrington remarked.

"The checkpoints alerted us to the approach of the Armenian terrorists the night of the Halloween Ball," Hanson explained.

"I heard about that. Do we have to worry about the Armenians?"

"Yes. And the Arabs. Hopefully, we'll be able to intercept any threat before it reaches the parade, but the police are prepared to stop anyone who looks suspicious."

"Too bad we can't afford metal and chemical detectors on every corner," Warrington said wistfully.

"That would be nice, but fortunately we've got some well-trained cops who did a great job the other night. If you and I deploy our most experienced troops, we might get lucky."

"I hate to rely on luck," Warrington muttered.

"There've been times when that was all I had …" Hanson mused. "We're meeting with Dr. Carver tomorrow. Why don't you join us?"

"I just met him recently. What do you think of him?" Warrington asked.

"I like him," Hanson answered. "He's more of a doctor than a bureaucrat."

"Sounds good. I'll check my schedule and get back to you later."

The more Hanson thought about the checkpoints, the more he realized how vulnerable they were, He sketched out a revised plan, where police barricades with planters and sawhorses actually cut off each street entrance, forcing people to pass through a small opening, one at a time. He placed back-up units halfway down the block that would support the checkpoint in the event of any disruption. The police would man the checkpoints, the Marines would be the back-up units and the Guard and police would line the parade route.

He selected positions on 23rd Street, 34th Street and 40th Street for his Stryker vehicles and response force, and made a note to ask Warrington to request two helicopter gunships from the Army. He made another note for the police and Marines to make an advance sweep of the area the night before and set up the checkpoints at midnight.

He couldn't think of anything else at the moment and gave the revised plan to Danowski to email to his officers, Captain Lonigan and Colonel Warrington. He also told Danowski to request all officers to report to his office at 1500 to review the plan. That done, he went to the mess hall for lunch.

•   •   •

Everyone looked at Kyle strangely in school, at least it felt that way to him. The peace pussies regarded him warily after what he did to Derek. The girls were fascinated by the violent outbreak from someone who was usually reserved and attracted little notice.

The Marine kids were proud of the peacemaker who instantly sprang to the defense of one of their own. He didn't like the attention for the wrong reason and the more he thought about it, the more he regretted his impetuous attack on Derek. His image of himself as being cool and controlled was going through a drastic change.

He certainly wasn't cool about Mavis, who he couldn't get out of his mind and who he ached for constantly, only forgetting her for the few moments that he lost control and went after Derek. He made a mental note to work harder at self-control and to remain calm in tense situations.

Kyle's classes went by in a blur and he was barely aware of going from room to room for the next class. His teachers surreptitiously avoided meeting his eyes, as if he was a dangerous beast who might turn on them momentarily. He was oblivious to his classmates, who for differing reasons respected his isolation.

All he could think about was Mavis, with a brief distraction from her when feeling guilty about Derek. He decided to apologize to Derek as soon as he returned to school and felt slightly better.

The school day dragged on interminably, the clock maliciously moving slower and slower as he got more urgent to depart. Finally, the dismissal bell rang and he dashed out of class, sprinting for the street door, yelling "Gangway," to anyone in his way. He was too restless to do anything that required concentration, so he decided to go to the barracks and see if he could find someone for a karate workout, then pick up some Chinese food and bring it to Tyrone.

•　　　　•　　　　•

The officers arrived a little before 1500 and Hanson told them to be seated. Before he began the security review, he looked them over and was pleased with their attitudes. They were eager, attentive and not the least bit uncomfortable in the presence of their commanding officer. He thought back to several of his commanders when he was a junior officer who made a point of scaring their subalterns. He never felt intimidated, but he remembered several promising young officers whose careers were derailed because of their inability to deal with officers who wanted to be feared by their troops. He could never understand why a commander would think that way about an all-volunteer force. He believed that respect for the troops, an unswerving devotion to duty and always setting an example were the pillars of leadership. Early in his career he came to detest the chateau generals of World War I, who sent hundreds of thousands of men to their deaths to gain a few worthless yards of muddy ground, while they wallowed in luxury, twenty miles behind the lines.

Danowski brought him back to the present, whispering in his ear, "Sir. Your officers are assembled."

"Thank you, Ski."

He watched Danowski unobtrusively take a seat in the back of the room, automatically including himself in the officer's briefing. He made a mental note to remind Danowski that the privilege of being an insider also required keeping all information confidential. Then he turned his attention to his officers.

"I want to inform you that I'm very satisfied with your performance of your duties. I'm particularly pleased by your grasp of the sensitivities of our situation and how well you've made the troops understand our delicate position. We've had no problems with our civilian population and I want it to continue that way. Please remind your enlisted personnel that they'll get a warm welcome at the Soldiers, Sailors, Marines and Airmens Club, right here in the Enclave, on Lexington Avenue and 37th Street. There are also plenty of Irish bars on Third Avenue, where they'll feel at home ..." He paused for their laughter. "Lieutenant Kent will now brief you on the Veterans Day Parade."

Although he hadn't told her that she would do the briefing, Al didn't seem at all surprised.

"Thank you, sir. If you've all studied the revised plan that Sergeant Danowski emailed to you, I'll now go through it in detail."

Hanson listened carefully, as did all his officers. There were enough intelligent questions and comments to confirm the high opinion he was forming of them. When she finished, Hanson concluded the meeting.

"Sergeant Danowski will email the final plan to all of you. Please go over it thoroughly with your N.C.O.'s and sit in with them when they brief the troops. Captain Muzzetti. Please stay here. The rest of you are dismissed."

Danowski called, "Attention," and everyone stood, saluted and left. Only Al and Danowski remained behind.

Muzzetti had no idea why he was told to stay, but he looked completely relaxed, which Hanson appreciated. Al and Danowski also had no idea what Hanson wanted, but they had already mastered the inscrutable air of "staff" and waited as if they knew everything.

"I'm considering having a Marine detachment march in the parade," Hanson said. "If it happens, it'll be from your company. Do you have two platoons that are in top shape?"

"Yes, sir. My entire company is in shape."

"It's a two-mile march and we have to look as snappy at the end as we do at the beginning. Our Marines must look reassuring to our friends and dangerous to our enemies."

"I understand, sir. I'm confident we can do it."

"Good. Think about it, then talk to your N.C.O.'s about switching personnel from other platoons if necessary and get back to me later."

"Yes, sir."

When Muzzetti left, he turned to Al and Danowski. "What do you think? Are his troops up to it?"

"I think so, sir," Al said.

"I'll talk to the squad leaders and get their take," Danowski offered.

"Thanks, Ski. Now I want to discuss a few things with both of you."

Al and Danowski waited while Hanson gathered his thoughts. Danowski poured coffee for the three of them and accepted their nods of thanks. He was feeling better and better about his choice to stick with Colonel Hanson. When he was Captain Beasley's clerk, he was just a low-grade gofer and a punching bag outlet for the C.O.'s frustration.

Now he was a significant member of the battalion and was happy for the first time since joining the Corps. He was even toying with the idea of applying for Officers Candidate School and he intended to discuss it with the Colonel at the next convenient opportunity. He studied Hanson out of the corner of his eye and couldn't help appreciating the differences between him and Beasley. Out of all the qualities he had come to admire about Hanson, the one that impressed him most was that he was still the same man he had been when he was a Sergeant.

Al nudged Danowski, a reminder to stay alert.

"I'm meeting Dr. Carver tomorrow," Hanson explained, "and I want to resolve several problems. I'd like to get the Guardwell private security service out of the Enclave. They're not very efficient and their boss, Grant Browning, is an obstructionist pain in the ass. I'd like both of you to review their duties and advise me whether or not we can replace them with our troops. If you can do that by the end of the day, I'll go over it with Dr. Carver tomorrow.

"Next. The Enclave manager has been virtually invisible since the U.N. Day incident. I'd like to break the ice by giving him a simple request or report, before I invite him to the Veterans Day parade. See what you can come up with.

"Last. If Muzi's troops march, do they wear dress blues or camis? Check the condition of their blues and let me know if they're new enough."

"Will they carry ammo?" Al asked.

"Yes."

"Loaded weapons?"

"Yes, Al."

"Isn't that pushing the envelope, sir?"

"Yes, Al. But if anything happens, I want our boys and girls to be able to do more than spit at their enemies. Let's meet here at 1800 and we'll go over your findings, then have dinner at the mess hall. Dismissed."

•   •   •

Jennifer had been trying unsuccessfully to divert Mavis' attention from Kyle. She was honest enough to admit that much of her motivation was selfish. She wanted Mavis as a willing lover, who would also be dependant on her. She was enough of a realist to recognize that if the infatuated young lovers got together, there might be complicated, even serious consequences, considering their different backgrounds and upbringing. She briefly considered introducing Mavis to an attractive intern, but quickly rejected it, certain that he would be a poor substitute for her silly Kyle and it might further alienate her. Then she came up with a brilliant idea. She could open her father's ski chalet in Vermont and take Mavis there for a weekend. She would also arrange for two desirable interns to join them for a day. Perhaps the exhilaration of the outdoors, the slopes, cognac, cocoa, perhaps some pot, a complete change from the gloom of the city would work wonders on her friend.

•   •   •

Tyrone was glad to see Kyle and attacked the Chinese food voraciously. After they finished eating, they relaxed and played a video game for a while, 'Smash Al Qaeda', a covert operation to eradicate the terrorists. They casually chatted as they played, a pleasant change from the recent tensions.

"I've decided that I want to go to the academy," Tyrone said. "Now that my father's an officer, I'd stand a good chance of getting in if your dad recommends me."

"I'm sure he would," Kyle replied. "There's only one problem."

"What?"

"The academy's still closed. Maybe when the Plant administration takes over they'll reopen it," Kyle said wistfully. "Until then, all we can do is prepare and hope for the best."

"You said it," Tyrone said fervently.

"You've also got to work harder on your math," Kyle added. "Don't forget that the academy is an engineering school."

"I shouldn't have to do all that math," Tyrone griped. "I just want to be a mud Marine."

"The Corps wants officers with brains. You got 'em. You just gotta use them more," Kyle urged.

Tyrone's phone rang and he held up his hand to pause their conversation while he answered. He listened intently for a minute, then kept repeating, "Uh huh," over and over, which piqued Kyle's curiosity. Tyrone finally said goodbye, turned to Kyle and said, "I've got good news and bad news. Which do you want first?"

"There's been enough bad news lately. Tell me the good stuff."

"That call was from a girl I know who goes to Finch."

"What's that?"

"It's an exclusive girls school on the posh east side for the daughters of the upper crust."

"What does that have to do with me?"

"Mavis goes there."

"What?"

"You heard me."

Kyle started hopping around like a mad dervish, firing questions. "Does she know her? What's her last name? Where's the school? Does she have her phone number?"

"Take it easy, bro. That's all I know."

"This means I'll find her … What's the bad news?"

"You won't be able to see her until Monday."

"I can't wait 'til then. I'll go nuts."

"Cool it. We'll leave school early Monday and go meet her."

"It's like forever."

"I know, K. Just stay calm and you'll see her Monday."

"That's if I survive the weekend."

28

M AVIS ANSWERED THE DOOR to the Carver home and let Hanson and Lonigan in.

"Colonel Warrington will be along shortly, Ms. Carver," Hanson said.

"Then we'll wait for him. And please. Call me Mavis."

Warrington arrived a few minutes later and the Carver's Mexican servant, a sullen man who obviously resented Yankee imperialists, led him into the dining room. Carver greeted the latecomer, then told them that Dr. Van Meer would be joining them and asked if they would mind waiting for him.

They were all agreeable and chatted casually for a while. Mavis, acting as hostess for her father, served coffee and directed the servant to set out orange juice and croissants for their guests, which he did, casting simmering glares at the uniformed men. Lonigan was beginning to get annoyed at the insolent servant, but the arrival of Dr. Van Meer diverted him.

Mavis supervised the serving of bacon, eggs and waffles, then she and the servant withdrew, leaving the men to their conference. Hanson and Lonigan brought the others up to date on any recent events of significance in the Enclave. When they finished, Carver took over.

"Thank you, gentlemen. Now let's discuss the main topic of this meeting; the Veterans Day parade. Do we go ahead with it, or cancel? Why don't you start, Colonel Warrington."

"Certainly, sir. Unless there are some recent threats that I am unaware of, the security plan is thorough and I feel confident that we should go ahead with the parade as planned."

"Thank you, Colonel. Captain Lonigan?"

"I agree with Colonel Warrington. We demonstrated during the Halloween Ball that careful containment in depth worked. We can do it again."

"Thank you, Captain Lonigan. Any other thoughts before we hear from Colonel Hanson?"

"Now that you mention it," Lonigan quipped, "we have a lot of colonels around here. Maybe someone should make me one."

The burst of laughter eased some of the tension in the room.

Dr. Carver turned to Hanson. "Colonel?"

"I think we should appoint Mike a grand exalted poobah. That might take care of his colonel envy." This really cracked them up and they actually began to relax. "The security plan is excellent," Hanson said. "However, like all plans, it contains some wishful thinking."

"What does that mean?" Dr. Van Meer asked in alarm.

"We try our utmost to consider everything, but there's always the possibility of the unexpected. Our enemies spend full time thinking about how to hurt us. We have many diverse responsibilities that preoccupy us. If we plan well and everyone is prepared to deal with surprises, the advantage is with us and we should be able to successfully carry out the plan."

"I hear a lot of ifs and maybes," Van Meer said nervously. "Maybe we should be on the safe side and cancel the parade."

"We shouldn't give in to fear," Hanson urged. "That's the real enemy that saps our will to resist."

"What if people are killed?" Van Meer asked.

"43,000 Americans died in automobile accidents last year, Dr. Van Meer. We didn't stop driving. It's our duty to our country to rebuild the frayed fabric of the public will to support actions to preserve our future."

There was a lengthy silence as they considered Hanson's statement and it was clear that only Van Meer was apprehensive.

"Colonel Hanson is right, Phil," Carver said. "We have to stand up to the threat of terror, or the country will fall apart."

"That's easy to say," Van Meer retorted. "Will you take responsibility if anything goes wrong, Dr. Carver?"

"I thought we're all supposed to take responsibility," he replied. "We're here to decide on the best way to do it. The choice seems simple to me. We either trust our experts to handle whatever situation comes up, or we cave in to fear of terrorism. Have I oversimplified things, Colonel Hanson?"

"It is basically one or the other, sir."

"Then I vote for the parade," Carver stated. "What about the rest of you?"

Hanson, Lonigan and Warrington voted for the parade. Van Meer was silent.

"What about you, Phil?" Carver asked.

"I have misgivings."

"So do we," Carver said softly, "but we can't let that stop us."

"Then I reluctantly vote yes."

Carver let out a sigh of relief, then turned to Hanson.

"What do we do next, Sam?"

"You'll have to notify the mayor, the governor, and the White House of our decision. Then the mayor's office should confirm to participating organizations and the media that the parade will take place, rain or shine."

"Isn't that giving advance notice to possible disrupters?" Van Meer quavered.

"It is a public event, sir," Hanson responded. "Once the mayor knows, the whole world will know. There's no way we can keep this secret. Besides, we shouldn't want to. The more people that know, the bigger the turnout. This could be a great opportunity to demonstrate our solidarity as a nation and show our respect for the men and women of the armed forces who served our country."

"That's well and good," Van Meer snapped, "but what if there's a disaster? Then how will we look?"

"We'll deal with it to the best of our ability and show the world what we're made of," Hanson answered.

"I hope you're right, Colonel."

"Me too, sir."

Carver, buoyed by the unanimous decision, queried the rest of them, "Is there anything else that requires our attention?"

When the others shook their heads no, Hanson spoke.

"There is one thing, sir. We're considering having a company of Marines march in the parade with weapons and live ammo just in case they're needed for a reaction force. The question came up whether they should wear full dress blues or camis."

"What do you suggest?" Carver asked.

"Well, the Marine Band will be in dress blues and they always look smart. If the rest of the Marines are in camis, they might be an additional deterrent."

"I have no objections," Carver said. "Does anyone?"

"Do you think it's wise for them to have ammunition?" Van Meer asked.

"They'd be helpless without it," Hanson answered. "They're well led and well trained. They'll be an asset. I'll let General Griffin make the call."

"If there is no further business, I suggest we adjourn," Carver said. "We should meet Wednesday for a final review and we can talk before that if there are any problems. Thank you for coming, gentlemen."

•   •   •

Kyle hadn't slept much Friday night and by Saturday afternoon he was almost a nervous wreck. One moment he was burning with anticipation to see the girl who had so enchanted him. The next he was fretting that she might not feel the same way. The possibility of her not caring put him in a near panic. Wild thoughts flew through his head.

The most disturbing one was that he'd kill himself if she didn't return his feelings. He started considering various ways to commit suicide, with particular interest in the most attention-getting and the most painful. He began to believe that someone could actually die of love. Then a more rational part of his distressed mind tried to convince him that he was confusing love with rejection. He only got more confused. In desperation, he called Tyrone and babbled madly, with no idea what he was saying. Tyrone listened patiently, then urged, "Stay calm, bro. You'll see her Monday. Hold it together 'til then."

"What if she doesn't want me?" Kyle wailed.

"You'll have to accept it."

"What if I can't?"

"You will. But I think she wants you as much as you want her."

"You do?"

"Yes. Now be patient until Monday."

By the time Hanson came home, Kyle had exercised a modicum of control and managed, "Hi, Dad," without revealing how on edge he felt.

Hanson was too preoccupied with thinking about the security meeting with Dr. Carver to notice Kyle's tension. He was also preparing a mind set for dining with General and Mrs. Griffin, which would include a thorough inspection and interrogation of Tish.

This would be the first time since the death of his wife that he was bringing a woman to meet them and he was a little nervous about it. Beverly Griffin had been like a mother to him from his first year at the Academy, when then Major Griffin had been his tactics instructor and welcomed the intense young loner to his home. Despite the difference in their ages they became good friends instantly, recognizing the willingness in each other to go all the way for what they believed in. He loved the Griffins and he really wanted them to like Tish.

Kyle had been staring at him for a minute and he finally became aware of it.

"What's up, son?"

"What's up with you? You were a thousand miles away."

He didn't know how much to tell Kyle about his growing feeling for Tish, so he said vaguely, "Just woolgathering, I guess. I've been very involved in the security plan for the Veterans Day Parade."

"Is it on, Dad?"

"Yes."

"Do you think the Arabs will try anything?"

"I hope not, but we're preparing for any eventuality … I'm having dinner tonight with General Griffin and Beverly. Would you like to join us? You haven't seen them for a while. They'd love to see you."

"I don't think so, Dad. I've got something on with Tyrone. You give them my love though."

"Sure. How are you doing?"

"Okay."

"Are you settling down after that school fight?"

"Yes, Dad."

"Anything you want to talk about?"

"No, Dad."

"I've got to get dressed, son. I'm taking Tish to meet the Griffins and I don't want to be late."

"Have a good time, Dad."

Kyle heaved a sigh of relief that his father didn't notice how tense he was. If he had to talk about Mavis, he ached so much for her that he might have rambled on like an idiot or broken down and sobbed like a looney. In either case, he would have thoroughly alarmed his father, who couldn't help him anyway.

At least he could talk to Tyrone, who may not have understood how he felt, but was sympathetic out of loyalty. He thought about Tyrone's newfound desire to attend the academy and become a Marine officer, and a glow of pride went through him.

They had been best friends since third grade, in Bahrain. Afterwards, they were constantly moving to different schools on different military bases, sustaining each other in foreign lands. After the disaster in Saudi Arabia and the fears they shared for the fate of their fathers, they had become closer than brothers. If Tyrone became an officer there wouldn't be a social gulf between them that could threaten their relationship. On an impulse, he called Tyrone and told him he'd bring Thai food for dinner.

•   •   •

Hanson put on civvies, then called Tish.

"I'll pick you up in an hour. If you want to ride, I'll bring my driver and Humvee."

"I'd like to walk, if that's alright with you?"

"Sure."

"Where are we going?"

"A restaurant on Third Avenue and 36th Street, Hudson Place."

"Is it nice?"

"Yes. The General and Beverly will like it."

"You call her Beverly?"

"I call her Bev. She's been my self-appointed mom since the Academy."

"I guess it was different from the FBI Academy. You'll have to tell me about it sometime."

"Sure. I've got to call the general now and tell him where we're eating. I'll see you soon."

"Sam?"

"Yes?"

"Do you think he'll like me?"

"Absolutely."

"How do you know?"

"He loves a woman with a gun."

She giggled. "You're a dreadful man. Will Mrs. Griffin like me?"

"As long as she doesn't think you're after me for my money."

"You'll pay for that later. Will it bother them that I'm black?"

"Honey, General and Mrs. Griffin are African American."

He heard her intake of breath, but disconnected before she could respond.

He called General Griffin and confirmed their reservation for 1900 and gave him the name and address of the restaurant.

"Do you want me to send a car and driver for you, sir?"

"No thanks, Sam. Bev and I will catch a cab. By the way, I'm wearing civvies."

"Good idea, sir. So will I."

Griffin laughed. "You're already wearing them."

"How did you know that, sir?"

"Just common sense, which we both have. This is a convenient opportunity to be anonymous for a little while. We can use a short break from the pressure of the uniform."

"You're right, sir. As usual."

"Do I detect the buttering up of a senior officer?"

Hanson laughed. "No, sir. It's just that you know me so well."

"We've been through a lot together, Sam. You know me pretty well."

"It's been a great privilege for me to have you as a friend, Charlie. I don't know where I'd be without you and Bev."

Griffin chuckled. "Probably butting your head against some unmovable object."

"Following right behind you, sir."

They both laughed.

"We'll see you soon, Sam."

"I look forward to it, sir."

•   •   •

Tico was delighted when Hanson dismissed him and also gave him Sunday off.

"Just keep your pager on, in case of an emergency."

"Try not to have one, sir."

"I don't plan them, Tico."

"Some of the troops think you do to test our readiness."

"I'll see what I can do about a quiet night."

"Thanks, sir. I met this nurse at the V.A. Hospital and I'm crazy about her. I told her I'd see her tonight, if I didn't have the duty."

"Have a good time, then."

"Thanks, sir. You too," and he winked knowingly.

Hanson watched him run off and smiled to himself about how nothing could be kept secret from the Sergeants. He walked up First Avenue, which near the Midtown Tunnel had more small parks than other parts of the city.

It was a pleasant, warm evening, more like early October than November, probably courtesy of greenhouse effect, as well as the toxic emissions donated by cities in the Industrial Age. For the first time in a long time he felt like he left his worries behind when he walked out of the barracks.

29

TISH WAS A BIT NERVOUS about meeting General and Mrs. Griffin and kept asking over and over, "They're accomplished black people. What if they don't like me?"

Hanson offered various reassurances each time, but they didn't help. Finally, in exasperation at her refusal to stop fretting, he said, "Don't worry. If they don't like you, we'll invoke the traditional Marine solution."

"What's that?"

"A firing squad at dawn."

"You rat," she said and smacked him playfully on the arm. Some people nearby stopped and looked at them, uncertain if they were joking.

"It's alright," he said to them mock pitifully. "She abuses me all the time."

She smiled sweetly at their now bewildered audience. "And I'll keep it up, until he behaves." She turned to Hanson. "Get moving, before I hit you again."

"Yes, dear," he said meekly.

They walked off, giggling at their performance.

"You're a funny lady."

"You like what I did?"

"Yes. But I was thinking of something else."

"What?"

"First you were worried because they were white. Now it's because they're black. Make up your mind."

"I know how much they mean to you. I just want to make a good impression."

"Don't worry. You will."

Tish and Hanson got to the restaurant first and General and Mrs. Griffin arrived a few minutes later. They exchanged hugs and greetings, then Beverly inspected Tish carefully.

"Where are you concealing your firearm, my dear?" Beverly asked.

Tish was immediately flustered. "In my purse. I hope you don't mind. I'm an FBI agent and I'm required to be armed at all times."

"Not at all, my dear. I just wanted to be sure you were dressed properly. I suggest that you carry it on your person, rather than your purse. I always carry my pistol on my person. That way it's always there when I need it."

"You carry a gun?" Tish asked in surprise.

"Of course," Beverly answered seriously. "All intelligent people go armed these days. The general always does and so does Sam."

Tish turned to Sam. "Are you armed?"

"Of course," he replied in the same tone as Beverly. "You heard Beverly. She's always right."

General Griffin had been observing Tish and smiled at her.

"I'm glad that Sam picked someone familiar with weapons. This can be an unforgiving world for the unprepared."

Beverly nodded agreement. "We can no longer afford liberal squeamishness about guns. Our country is in a struggle for survival."

"Did you ever fire your weapon in anger, Mrs. Griffin?" Tish asked in fascination.

"Call me Beverly, dear. I don't discuss that in mixed company."

Hanson grinned. "Ask her to tell you about the time she shot the terrorist in Baghdad."

"Now don't bring that up again, Sam," Beverly said.

"Why not? It's my favorite story." He turned to Tish. "That's how she got her nickname in the Corps, 'quick draw Griffin'."

"I'd love to hear it. Please tell me, Beverly."

"I'll let Sam reveal my secrets and later I'll tell you some stories about him."

"That's not necessary, Bev," he said quickly.

"We'll see, young man. We'll see."

"I detect a not too subtle threat," Hanson said. "I better not speak."

"You better," Tish warned, "Remember what happened on the street?"

Beverly smiled. "I think you'll have a story to tell, my dear."

"Now see what you started," Hanson complained.

"You brought it on yourself," Tish said smugly. "Now let's hear the story."

Hanson looked at them ruefully. "We joke about it now, but it wasn't funny when it happened. I was a company commander and Colonel Griffin was our brigade commander. This was in 2007, during the Sunni-Shia civil war in Iraq. A truce had just been negotiated and for the first time in months Baghdad was quiet. Beverly had been staying in a secure hotel in the Green Zone and she suggested to the Colonel that they take a tour of the city, while the truce held. I told her it might not be safe, but she insisted. We drove around in an armored Humvee, with a Stryker escort and I was glad to see the city was calm. We passed a well-known Arab restaurant and Beverly requested we eat there. When I objected, she said no one knew we were coming, so it should be safe enough to just grab a quick bite. The restaurant was crowded and we created a stir, but it seemed alright when we sat down and ordered. The place seemed calm and we started to relax. The waiter brought a tray with our order, then suddenly dumped it on the Colonel and me, yelled, 'You die, Maline', just like the japs did in those old World War II movies, and drew a pistol."

"That's not what he said," the General and Beverly objected simultaneously.

"He said, 'Marine, not Maline," Beverly corrected.

"Do you want to tell the story?" Hanson asked.

"No," Beverly answered, "but don't make ethnic slurs about our former enemies, who are still our enemies."

"Okay. Anyhow. The Colonel and I were trying to throw off the plates and reach for our pistols, but this enterprising oriental gentleman had us dead to rights ..."

He paused dramatically and Tish demanded, "What happened next? Tell me. Tell me."

"If you insist. Bev drew a pistol from somewhere on her person, I never figured out exactly where ..."

"The belt behind my back …"

"Thank you, Bev. And drilled him right between the eyes. The best snapshot I've ever seen."

Tish looked at Beverly in awe. "Wow."

"It was a pretty good shot," Beverly admitted. "He was about to shoot the two men I love most in the world. I had to protect the boys." They all roared with laughter.

When they stopped laughing, Hanson said to Tish, "You haven't heard the end yet. Bev, pistol smoking in her hand, turned to the men in the room who were frozen in place and said in perfect Arabic, 'We'll be leaving now. Sorry we can't stay for dessert'."

Tish's jaw dropped. "Did you really say that?"

"It seemed like the right thing to say at the time," Beverly said modestly.

"That's the coolest thing I've ever heard," Tish blurted.

Beverly slipped an arm around her. "We're going to be good friends, my dear. Now let's go powder our artillery, so the boys can discuss business for a few minutes."

"Yes, ma'am."

"Call me Beverly, my dear,"

General Griffin watched the ladies walk away. "I'll be damned if I can figure out how she always knows we need to talk."

"I was under the impression that Marines were always damned, sir."

"It's good to see you happy, Sam. It's been a long time."

"Yes, sir. It has."

"You like this girl, don't you?"

"Do I!"

But before he could pour out his feelings, Griffin held up his hand. "I want to hear all about her, but right now update me before the girls get back."

"Yes, sir. Sir?"

"Yes?"

"They're women, not girls."

"How come we're boys?"

"Just lucky, I guess."

Hanson outlined the final security plan and recounted the substance of the meeting that morning with Dr. Carver and the others.

"So Van Meer gave you a hard time?"

"Not really, sir. He's a worrywart, and it's not the worst thing in the world to have someone like that requiring answers."

"Then everyone approved the parade?"

"Yes, sir."

"Do you have any misgivings?"

"Not more than a million or two, sir. The mayor's against ethnic profiling and we can't search everyone, which makes it more difficult, but we'll hope for the best."

"What can I give you?"

"Fifty more metal detectors and a hundred bomb sniffing dogs."

"I'll see what I can do, but don't count on it. I can give you two Wolverine vehicles for the parade."

"They might help. There is something for you to decide. Do the troops wear blues or camis, and do they carry live ammo?"

"What did you tell the doctors?"

"Camis and live ammo."

"Then that's what we'll do."

"Thank you, sir. Will you attend the parade?"

"I'll be at the one in Washington. Here come the girls. Is there anything else?"

"Yes, sir. They're women, not girls."

The rest of the evening was extremely pleasant and they lingered over coffee, until the maitre' d's desperate ESP messages for them to leave were finally accepted. They stood on the curb and chatted for a while and the general invited them back to the hotel for a nightcap.

"I have certain intentions towards you tonight, Charlie," Beverly purred suggestively, "so let's get rid of the kids."

The general almost blushed. "You are a very forward woman, Bev," he muttered.

"That I am. Now kiss that pretty girl goodnight and I'll kiss that handsome stud, and then we'll be on our way."

After affectionate farewells, Beverly put her fingers to her lips, let out a piercing whistle that instantly produced a taxi, then waved goodbye and she and the General drove off.

It started to rain lightly and Tish asked, "Your place or mine?"

Hanson leered.

"Yours is closer."

"Do you think I'm that kind of girl?"

"I hope so."

"Is it alright if we walk?"

"As long as it's quickly," he answered.

She slipped her arm through his and they walked up Third Avenue, ignoring a driver dispute that threatened to become violent over a fender bender incurred in the mindless race to the Midtown Tunnel. The warmth of her body aroused him sexually, and at the same time elicited an unexpected tenderness. He unconsciously walked a little faster and she put her arm around him, moving closer. They got to her building and the doorman rushed to open the door for them. When froggy the desk clerk saw her, he warbled, "Good evening, Ms. Madison," but his voice changed when he said, "Good evening, sir."

Hanson nodded politely and sensed the glare of resentment that followed him to the elevator. He ignored it in the anticipation of making love to Tish.

•   •   •

Kyle paced up and down Tyrone's bedroom, mumbling to himself that he didn't know what he'd do if he didn't see Mavis on Monday. Tyrone finally had enough of the disjointed rambling and said, "I thought I'd go crazy confined in here, but if I have to listen to you rave about Mavis much longer, I'll go nuts. Let's go for a walk."

Kyle was immediately apologetic. "I'm sorry, Ty. I didn't mean to bug you. Are you up to walking?"

"I'll crawl if I have to, as long as I get out of here."

"If it's because of me, I'll go home. I don't want you to hurt yourself."

"Don't worry, bro. I'll be alright. You can always carry me back if I collapse."

"Talk about the white man's burden. I wouldn't have let you eat so much if I knew I might have to lug you around."

"Is that anyway to talk to a future brother officer?"

"What if you flunk out of the Academy? Then I'd have carried you for nothing."

"What are friends for, K? Let's go."

Sergeant Wilkins, still a bit self-conscious about his new stripes, but proud of them, was in charge of the guard detail at their building.

Both boys had known and liked him for years and they were happy about his promotion. They greeted him cheerfully.

"Hey, Sarge."

"What's happening?"

"Just checking the detail, boys. You never know what those ragheads are up to."

"They're called gentlemen of mid-eastern persuasion these days, Sarge," Tyrone said.

"Is that what you have to call them now that your Daddy's an officer?"

Kyle burst out laughing and the others joined in.

"That was pretty good, Wilkie," Kyle said. "Next thing you know you'll be going to O.C.S."

"Not me. Your Dad'll probably bust me by next week."

"I don't think so. You'll make a great Gunnery Sergeant."

"Are you kidding?"

"No. Ask Ty."

Wilkins turned to Tyrone expectantly.

"Kyle's right," Tyrone confirmed.

"Well that's nice of you boys to say so. We heard about your fight at school. We're proud of you."

"I should have found a better way to settle it," Kyle replied.

"Sometimes you gotta fight. See you boys later."

Wilkins walked off to continue his rounds and Kyle turned to Tyrone.

"What do you feel like doing, Ty?"

"Let's go to that bar on Third Avenue and 37th street that's always jumping and see if we can get in. I've seen some great looking girls in there."

"I'm only interested in one girl."

"I know. I know. But you can back me up. You know girls don't go there alone."

"Sure. But I'm not getting involved with anyone, no matter what."

Whether it was their air of assurance, or a permissive bartender, no one asked for I.D. The place was jammed and it took a few minutes to reach the bar and order beers. The human tide quickly separated them and Kyle was content to drift with the herd and just observe the scene. He occasionally spied Tyrone talking up a storm to a girl and made sure not to catch his eye to be summoned for support duty. He knew the cover story, that they were interns at N.Y.U. He had insisted that they looked too young to be interns, but Tyrone was determined to meet an older girl.

There was a steady flow of pot and tobacco smokers, pill poppers and the usual Saturday night traffic. The coke sniffers generally used the bathrooms, so the dynamics in the room were constantly changing. No one paid any attention to Kyle and he preferred it that way. Once or twice he noticed a girl looking him over, but he didn't send out recognition signals. He was still nursing his first beer when somebody yanked his arm and he almost jumped out of his skin.

"Take it easy, bro. It's me."

He glared at Tyrone. "Don't sneak up on me like that."

"I wasn't sneaking. I've been trying to catch your eye for a while and you've been ignoring me."

"I didn't see you. What's happening?"

"I'm coming on to this girl who loves doctors. She has a great looking friend."

"No way. Can you get her home alone? Do you have cab fare?"

"Yes, Dad."

"Then I'm going to take off. I'll see you in the morning, Ty."

"Why don't you stay. It'll take your mind off you-know-who."

"No. You have a good time, but don't get into trouble."

"Yes, Dad."

The rain was coming down heavier, but Kyle didn't mind. While people were leaping into doorways, or scurrying under their umbrellas, he plodded along, oblivious to the downpour. He relished the dank chill as a physical torment that complemented the emotional anguish he was going through.

All he could think about was Mavis. Some partyers poured out of a bar on 35th Street and jostled him, but he barely noticed. One of them said something, but he ignored him and trudged on, heading for home. He walked east on 34th Street and turned south on Second Avenue. He passed a pizza place and the aroma tempted him. He stood at the counter in the dismal fast food joint and ate, all the time asking himself, 'Where are you, Mavis?' and wondering how he would endure until he saw her on Monday.

30

T HIS WAS THE MOST LUXURIOUS Sunday morning that Hanson had experienced in years. He woke up as usual at 0600 and called the duty officer, who reported all quiet. Tish hadn't stirred when he got up to make his call and she snuggled against him when, in a radical change of pattern, he got back into bed and went to sleep.

At 0800 the heat of her body aroused him and he rolled over and started to stroke her. She woke up just as he moved on top of her and slid inside her. She moaned softly and moved against him faster and faster, until they both came in a rush. Then they both fell asleep, locked in each other's arms. A little later, the smell of coffee snapped him out of a horrible dream about being trapped in a building in Riyadh, watching his troops get shot, one by one.

"Don't expect breakfast in bed every morning," Tish said, "but you've been so sweet that you deserve it."

"So service is dependant on performance? That sounds fair."

"That's not exactly what I meant," she protested, as she buttered a piece of toast, then fed it to him.

"Keep this up and you'll spoil me rotten. How can I resist a woman who serves breakfast in bed and carries a Beretta?"

"Do you want to resist me?" she asked, posing provocatively.

"At least long enough to eat."

"Well then, stuff yourself. Make me wait."

"This way I'll have enough energy to satisfy you."

She grinned. "I wouldn't worry about that. If I had to go to work today I'd look bowlegged … What would you like to do this morning?"

"If it's alright with you, I'd like to laze around and read the *Sunday Times*. I rarely get the opportunity to do more than scan it."

"Sounds good to me. News first, or magazine section?"

"News," he requested.

France seemed to dominate the headlines. Radical Islamist terrorists had suicide-bombed the Millau Viaduct bridge for the second time in a year, killing 42 motorists. Former president Jacques Chirac, who had dedicated the world's tallest bridge in December 2004, deplored the brutal attack.

After three years of making its way in the French legal system, the ban on the Hezbollah-run television channel, Al Manar, was lifted. The station immediately aired a Syrian produced anti-Jewish show, with a scene of a Jewish man demanding the blood of a Christian child to bake Passover matzo bread. French voters once again refused to ratify the Euro Union Constitution, ensuring that the establishment of a stronger Federal Union would be deferred for another year.

Hanson read with intense interest the French declaration of intent to withdraw from NATO, which they described as a moribund alliance. The lawsuit by French wine growers at the World Trade Organization against American vineyards, whom they accused of flooding Europe with inferior wine, elicited no sympathy from Hanson, who could only shake his head at the fickleness of the French.

The most outrageous news article reported that Germany's Chancellor, Angela Merkel, was preparing to sign a protocol with the Arab league of oil-producing states, pledging not to support any armed intervention in Arab nations, except if approved by majority vote in the United Nations General Assembly. 'Fat chance of that,' Hanson snorted to himself.

The UNICEF report on the condition of children in the world was depressing. According to the report, more than a billion children suffered deprivation worldwide, because of war, H.I.V./AIDS, or poverty. The report cited global military spending at a trillion dollars, while the cost of combating child deprivation would be a mere 60 – 80 billion dollars. The only item of amusement was the Honda Corporation's new version of its humanoid robot, Asimo II, which they called a personal care attendant for the aging Japanese population. The new model included all the traditional Japanese courtesies, as well as sensitivity to the particular problems of the aging. He had to smile at the image of the robot bowing politely, as it cleaned Japanese posteriors.

The domestic news was mostly about economic and trade issues, focusing on inflation, or the colossal national debt. There were stories about particularly gruesome murders that were gang and drug related. More disturbing were nightmarish murders of children that could only have been perpetrated by lunatics, nurtured by an overly permissive society.

He wondered how a nation could accept some of the horrors inflicted on its children without stirring biblical wrath against the evil monsters, who then took shelter in the protection of the law, as if they were human beings entitled to the same constitutional rights as other citizens. He knew how he would feel if his child was tortured, murdered and dismembered. He wouldn't be able to sit by for years as the sub-human's case wound its way through the legal system, all the while allowing him basic comforts. He would find a way to bring justice to the killer.

Tish interrupted his reverie.

"You're muttering, Sam. What's wrong?"

"Just some bad thoughts. Nothing to talk about."

"You must have a great store of anger built up after what you've been through. You can talk to me."

"Thanks, honey. That's nice to know. But I really don't need to unburden myself. I was just reacting to some of the stories about murdered children in the paper."

"You are a strange one, but the offer stands … I didn't tell you this before, but I admired the way you dealt with Agent Royce and the Navy investigators. You never lost your cool."

"I've learned a little about self-control over the years … Now, if you don't mind, I'm going to read the paper for a while longer. I'm through with the news section, if you want it."

She held out the magazine and book review. "Your choice." When he reached for the book review, she moved it so he touched her breast. One thing led to another and he never got to literary reading.

•   •   •

Carver had arranged to spend the day with Mei and was looking forward to her company. She had suggested they go see the Frank Stella retrospective at the Whitney Museum, and after the required but perfunctory anti-culture protest he agreed. They took a taxi up Madison Avenue and what had once been the most expensive street in the world looked shabby.

The office buildings had the dreary appearance of under-tenanted structures that were going to seed. When they passed 57th Street, half the shops were vacant and the restaurants were obviously struggling for survival. A few of the passersby still looked prosperous, but most of the people on the streets seemed to be wandering aimlessly in what may have been a confused search for now departed prosperity.

The museum wasn't crowded, which Carver appreciated. They were able to look at paintings without being jostled by the usual culprits, who once jammed museums to prove how cultured they were. Carver mentioned that he didn't know anything about art.

"It's like any of the arts," Mei explained. "Once you know something about it, you can decide if you like it or not out of choice, rather than ignorance."

"Are you calling your boss ignorant?" he teased.

"That's what you said," she replied. "Let's look at the Stella exhibition first and I'll tell you about the paintings, then you can make up your mind how you feel about them."

"Sounds good. How do you know so much about art?"

"I wanted to be an artist when I was a young girl. My father convinced me to go to medical school and try art later, once I was established."

"Any regrets?"

"None. Contrary to common belief about parental advice, my father was definitely right."

They started looking at the Stella's, which left Carver completely unmoved. Mei told him a bit about the artist and the paintings, but it didn't change his response.

"What are those black paintings supposed to be?"

"The artist was very young then and he was trying to redefine the nature of abstract painting."

"What's that mean?" he asked, pointing to a title on one of the black paintings, 'Die Fahne Hoch', from 1959.

"It means 'with banners high'. It's a line from a Nazi marching song, the 'Horst Wessel'."

"They were before my time, but I never cared for the Nazis," he growled.

"I don't think he was a Nazi, Carv. He was expressing himself artistically."

The paintings grew more colorful as the years progressed and they stopped in front of 'Jasper's Dilemma', a big 6' by 12' painting, from 1962, of colored squares on one side, and black and white squares on the other.

"Who's Jasper, and what's his problem?"

"It's probably another artist whose work we'll see later, Jasper Johns. I don't know what the dilemma is."

He walked on, muttering under his breath.

They stopped at a 1966 painting, BAFQ, a big, odd-shaped striped painting and he remarked, "It wouldn't even make a nice rug."

She ignored his comment and they looked at a group of paintings that she said were from Stella's Protractor series, mostly named for Asian cities. He inspected 'Sinjerli Variation IV', from 1968, which he found colorful, but bland, then went on to 'Agbatana', 'Quathlamba', then 'Saskatchawan', all big, colorful and bland. He paused at 'Double Scramble Orange' from 1977, another 6' by 12' painting.

"That looks like the same squares he painted years ago. This guy isn't very creative."

Mei was getting the message that Stella wasn't making it for him and didn't respond. She noticed that he was moving past the paintings faster now and she decided that they saw enough Stella. He stopped in front of 'Puerto Rican Blue Pigeon', from 1980, and after a moment, mumbled, "That just looks like a bowl of mush."

"I think it's time to look at the permanent collection," she said brightly, and they left Stella for what she hoped would be more appealing art.

Mei realized that Carver wasn't the least bit responsive to abstract art, so she concentrated on realism, starting with the Ash Can School. He nodded politely at her explanation of the first American movement that showed the grittier side of urban life. He liked the clean lines of the Precisionists but found the paintings cold and impersonal.

When she said, "They reflected the industrial harshness of the age," he wasn't impressed.

She bypassed Arthur G. Dove, her favorite abstract painter, and let Carver look at the Hopper's. They were the only paintings he showed any real interest in and he listened intently to her description of light, shadow and color. He was completely turned off by the Abstract Expressionists and she tried the Pop artists in her last effort at art appreciation. He thought most of their work was ridiculous looking, especially the Warhol Brillo Box and the soft Oldenburg sculpture.

"I guess I'm just a philistine," he whispered.

"We'll try the Metropolitan Museum of Art next time," she replied. "Perhaps more traditional painting will appeal to you."

"How about we try music, or dance? I always liked ballet."

"Maybe there's hope for you yet," she said with a smile.

•   •   •

Jennifer was annoyed when Mavis woke up crying on Sunday morning. She had been planning a sexual interlude, rather than a consolation session. It took a while to calm Mavis down and the effort consumed much of Jennifer's patience.

"You're so good to me, Jen. I don't deserve a true friend like you. I don't know what I'd do without you. I can't stand behaving like this. You must hate me."

"I don't hate you, Mav. But it is getting difficult to deal with you. Come here and I'll make you feel better."

Jennifer drew Mavis closer and started to pet her. She opened the buttons on her pajama top and caressed her breasts, then gently squeezed her nipples. She heard Mavis' intake of breath as she slipped her hand down her pajama bottom, found her clitoris and stroked it harder and harder, until Mavis came with a gasp. Then she guided Mavis' hand to her clitoris, which she let her stroke until she came, but she could tell that Mavis' heart wasn't in it.

Jennifer felt mildly satisfied and exasperated at the same time.

"I will find that boy for you, if only to get my tough-minded friend back."

"I have been acting like a wuss, haven't I?"

Jennifer laughed. "Either that, or it's first love."

"You do understand, don't you, Jen?"

"I guess so," she reluctantly admitted, "but I never felt that way. The idea of letting someone turn my life upside down is abhorrent to me. I wouldn't let that happen. There's too much I have to do to let myself be dependant on some silly boy."

"He's not silly," Mavis snapped. "He's wonderful. He's sensitive, kind, thoughtful, intelligent and handsome."

Jennifer hooted in derision. "You never even saw his face. Besides, you were only with him for a few minutes. How do you know what he's like?"

"I know. I could never feel that way if he wasn't special."

"Well, we'll find out soon enough, won't we? In the meantime, what shall we do today? Unless you'd prefer to mope around in bed all day?"

"No. Let's go out."

"You got it. We can go shopping."

"That sounds like fun," Mavis said, trying to be enthusiastic.

•　　•　　•

Kyle took the elevator to Tyrone's floor and knocked on his door. He hadn't been sure if he wanted to listen to his friend's admonitions to 'be cool' and 'wait for Monday', but he was the only person he could talk to about Mavis. Tyrone had been up for a while and was restless from too much home confinement.

"Let's get out of here, bro," Tyrone urged. "I'm going stir crazy."

"Where do you want to go?"

"How about Madison Square Park?"

"Did you forget what happened last time we were there?" Kyle protested.

"The Arabs aren't going to suicide bomb the dog run."

"It's chilly out. What'll we do there?"

"I've been thinking about trying to pick up a single mom in the playground."

Kyle shook his head. "You are one strange dude. Why a single mom?"

"Isn't it obvious? They're not virgins and they don't have husbands. They must be in need of a vigorous young stud like me."

Kyle laughed. "I guess if you can tolerate my raving about Mavis, I can watch you snuffle around old ladies in the playground. Let's move out."

•　　•　　•

Tish and Hanson spent the rest of the day in bed. They alternated reading the newspaper, eating, making love and dozing. When he got ready to leave in the late afternoon, she kept kissing and caressing him each time he headed for the door.

"Do you ever intend to let me out of here?" he demanded, mock sternly.

"Of course. I just changed my mind at the last minute. I'm always decisive when I'm on a case."

"Are you on my case?"

"Didn't you hear me say 'Welcome aboard, Marine', last night?"

He grinned. "I don't remember if you said it, but I certainly felt it."

"Don't make me pull out the old rubber hose and polygraph," she threatened.

He raised his arms. "I surrender. I'll confess. Don't torture me."

"Seeing you go feels like torture," she said seriously.

He put his arms around her and held her tight. "It feels that way to me, but I've got to go."

"I understand. When will I see you? And don't give me any of that 'long time no come see', Marine jive."

He laughed. "I wouldn't dare. Bev likes you too much. I'll call you tomorrow. Once the Veterans Day parade is over, I should have more time."

"You better, or I'll come gunning for you."

"On that gentle note, I'm leaving."

31

THE BRIEF REPOSE OF SUNDAY completely dissipated for Hanson by 0900 Monday. Every official who had anything to do with the parade—federal, state, city, or county—called him to contribute their ideas for security. He managed to placate them by expressing respect for their suggestions and proposing an urgent meeting of all those concerned on Tuesday morning, at 0700. The range of excuses would have been amusing, if the subject wasn't so serious, and only 'the dog ate my homework' was omitted.

He did listen carefully to every suggestion from the office of Homeland Security, an agency much criticized by ambitious politicians in their ruthless quest for office, blaming them as a scapegoat for America's ills. When Homeland Security signed off on their preparations, Hanson heaved a sigh of relief, then had Al call every involved agency and official to inform them of Homeland's approval of the plan.

He smiled when Al came in and told him how outraged some of the elected officials were, particularly Governor Krasner's aide, to be notified by a mere secretary. He laughed when she described their reactions after she informed them that she was a lieutenant in the

Marine Corps. "Krasner's aide threw a shit-fit and demanded to know why a higher ranking officer didn't call."

"What did you say?"

"I told him they were all in the field, attending to security duties. Then he asked me pathetically, 'Couldn't at least a Captain have called?' I answered that I was the only officer here, but I'd be glad to give him my name and serial number if he wished to file a complaint."

Hanson really cracked up at this.

"What did he say?"

"He mumbled that he'd tell the governor, but I didn't ask what."

"Al. You are definitely destined for higher rank."

"Why thank you, Sam. I learn from the best."

"Flattering your C.O. is not mandated in the manual. Now get back to your calls."

"Jawohl, Herr Oberst," she said sassily, clicked her heels, about-faced smartly, and exited.

The rest of the day would have been a nightmare of conflicting demands, except for Danowski's good sense and efficiency. He had separated the requests for action into different levels of priority, leaving any items he wasn't sure of for Hanson's decision. There weren't many. Hanson had come to depend on Danowski in a remarkably short period of time and was more than satisfied with his performance. When Danowski brought in the vehicle status report, Hanson told him to sit down while he looked it over.

"I see that all vehicles are operational, except for one Stryker. Any chance of it being ready for the parade Friday?"

"I'm on maintenance's back. I promised them a 48-hour pass if they came through. That is with your permission, sir."

"Sure. Add a bottle of whiskey from me, if they're ready."

"That should encourage them."

"You've done an outstanding job, Ski."

"Thank you, sir."

"If you decide to stay in the Corps, I'll recommend you for O.C.S. You'll make a good officer."

"Why, thank you, sir. That's good to hear. I've been thinking about it."

"Well let me know. You've been a big help around here and I think you're capable of doing more."

"I really appreciate that, sir."

•　　　•　　　•

Carver enjoyed rounds on the veterans' ward Monday morning. He was feeling incredibly relaxed after the weekend with Mei and took pleasure in watching her lead the medical team. The vets were eager for her approval and wagged enthusiastically when she personally examined them. He found it hard to believe that these were the same men who a short while ago were forced to become suicide bombers to get medical attention.

He understood that their circumstances weren't that different from residents of poverty communities who turned to violence and crime because they lacked essential services, and felt abandoned by their societies. He made a written note to discuss an outreach plan with the other department heads that would target the underserved in the Enclave.

He saw that rounds were progressing well and signaled Mei that he was leaving. She excused herself to the vet she was examining, who forlornly watched her walk away and escort Carver to the door.

"You seem to have everything under control, so I'm going to take the other team to the Arab exiles ward."

"Thanks for putting the women on my team, Carv. They really appreciate not being abused by the Arabs."

"It's the least I can do. Besides, it's a great object lesson for our people."

"Why?"

"Our men are a diverse interracial group, black, white, Asian, Hispanic. They see firsthand how the Arabs despise everyone, except other Arabs. It reminds our people why the melting pot is so precious. It's the best way yet devised for different people to get along."

"I want to hear more about this, Carv, but I've got to get back to my patients."

"I saw that last guy rubbing against you."

"Jealous?"

"Envious. See you later."

As usual, the Arabs were rude, surly and insulting. Carver forced himself to ignore crude provocations and continue with the duty of healing. He couldn't help thinking about how doctors were once regarded with the utmost respect, until the HMO's took control of the practice of medicine, and determined the kind of service doctors provided.

When money became the measuring stick of treatment, patients perceived doctors as any other service provider for hire, with barely a touch more appreciation for the persons who maintained their health care. His reverie was interrupted when his patient, a fat, overindulged Omani, grabbed his arm and yelled furiously at him. Carver pulled his arm away and turned to the interpreter.

"What's his problem?"

After an incomprehensible exchange of Arabic, the interpreter said, "His Excellency doesn't think you look attentive enough."

Carver suppressed the urge to strangle the fat pig. "Tell His Excellency that I was considering his medication."

This seemed acceptable and Carver finished quickly, then led his team to the next patient, who he knew would be equally offensive.

Despite more insults and abuse, they finally finished with the last patient. Carver dismissed the team so they could prepare their notes for the staff review. He was still smoldering from the assault of the fat Omani, but he was happy about maintaining self-control.

He started thinking about one of his intern's suggestions that they get an Arabic speaker on the team, even if he wasn't a trained medical person, so they'd know what the Arabs were saying. He had rejected the idea, calling it spying, but now he began to reconsider his snap decision. He made a note to discuss it with Hanson after the Veterans Day parade and explore the ethics of the idea. For example, if he overheard a plot to kill Americans, should he report it to the appropriate authorities? He quickly answered 'Hell, yes', then headed for the staff meeting with a jaunty walk.

•　　　•　　　•

It was a major effort for Jennifer to keep Mavis calm in school. She kept a careful eye on her in Mr. Singh's science class, where the poor man had been the recipient of several unwarranted outbursts. As a special treat if she promised to behave, Jennifer said she'd take her to lunch at a very trendy Italian restaurant, Destino, instead of eating in the school cafeteria. Whether from self-control, restaurant incentive, or other reasons, Mavis was functional all morning and was excited when they left school at lunchtime.

It was an unusually warm November day, with the temperature reaching 75 degrees and the scraggly east side trees still had most of their jaundiced leaves. They had left their coats at school and their youthful, shapely bodies attracted stares, particularly from a group of construction workers in front of an unfinished Third Avenue condo, who offered comments in an eastern European language that the girls ignored.

The maitre'd greeted Jennifer effusively and fawned over her as he escorted them to a table. He regally summoned the captain, the waiter, the bus boy and the sommelier, deftly palmed the twenty-dollar bill from Jennifer's hand as he kissed it, then bowed himself away with the suppleness of a servitor. Jennifer ordered for them without consulting Mavis and discussed French white wines versus Italian white wines with the sommelier, who was a rabid Italian partisan. After a lengthy comparison of various wines, Jennifer conceded the virtue of a Po valley offering and approved the sommelier's choice. He left wagging happily at another conquest of the crude Americans. The food was delicious and Mavis loved it all.

"You're so good to me, Jen. I'm sorry to be so much trouble."

"Don't worry, hon. As soon as you meet your dream boy, you'll return to earth." Before Mavis could protest, she continued, "I paged a boy I know who goes to the N.Y.U. Academy. He'll find out what time Kyle gets out of school and we can go there tomorrow and surprise him."

Mavis hugged Jennifer. "You're the best friend ever ... I don't know if I can wait until tomorrow."

"You better, or I won't take the call."

•   •   •

The only thing that kept Kyle from going off the deep end at school was looking out for Tyrone. This was Tyrone's first day back after the injuries from the "pussies'" attack. Tyrone refused to walk with a cane, so Kyle insisted on staying near him so he could help in the event of a problem. Although Kyle didn't think that the "pussies" would try anything hostile, he decided it was best to be alert. Besides, this way he had a captive audience to talk to about Mavis. Tyrone tolerated his friend's jabbering about her all morning, but by lunchtime his nerves were fraying from the constant 'Mavis this', 'Mavis that', declarations.

"Listen, K. If you don't stop running on about Mavis, I won't go with you to meet her."

Kyle gave him a hurt look. "Is that how you to talk to your best friend, who always looks out for you?"

"You know you can always depend on me, K., but you're driving me nuts. Now we'll leave school at 1400 and go to Finch, where you'll see your girl. Until then, stop babbling about her."

"I don't know if I can."

"Try."

They left school at 2:00 p.m. as planned. Kyle talked them past the door guard by telling him he was taking Tyrone to a doctor's appointment, and they rushed past him before he could ask for any documentation. They got to the bus stop on First Avenue just as the bus arrived and paid the five dollar fare with their personal account cards.

They sat down on the too narrow seats, designed and made in China for smaller bodies, courtesy of a Metropolitan Transit Authority contract. The days were long gone when an American company could have made the same seats, better and roomier, while providing Americans with jobs.

The bus detoured west on 42nd Street to bypass the U.N., which maintained tight security and limited American access to the alien island in mid-town Manhattan, even closing the bypass tunnel to traffic. The ride for the few blocks up Third Avenue, until the bus turned east on 50th Street to get back to First Avenue, was interminable. They got off at 66th Street and walked towards Park Avenue. They stopped across the street from the elegant townhouse that housed the Finch school and waited at a good vantage point for Mavis to appear.

Jennifer still hadn't been paged by her friend by the time classes ended, and Mavis was feeling depressed again as they walked out the door. Kyle spotted her instantly and yelled, "Mavis," and he rushed across the street to her.

An S.U.V. narrowly missed him by jamming on the brakes and managing to stop less than a foot away. Mavis screeched in horror, thinking the car hit him. She raced to him and they embraced in the middle of the street, babbling each other's names back and forth. Traffic piled up behind the S.U.V. and impatient motorists blew their horns with the usual urban talent. One particularly irate driver, with a flair for New York City humor, hollered, "Why don't you kids find a youth hostel and make out there, instead of blocking the street?"

Tyrone and Jennifer hurried to their friends and led them back to the sidewalk in front of the school, where an appreciative audience of the girl's classmates applauded the romantic moment.

Jennifer introduced the boys to her classmates and Tyrone looked each girl over carefully. Kyle, completely enrapt with Mavis, didn't notice them. The words poured out of him in a torrent.

"You don't know what I've been going through day and night, worrying that I'd never see you again. It's been driving me nuts."

"I've been feeling the same way," she gushed. "I didn't know if I'd see you again and I've been going crazy … But you're here now, and we're together."

They kissed passionately and their highly entertained classmates oohed and made encouraging or teasing remarks. Jennifer took them both by the arm and drew them apart.

"I'm enjoying the show also, but if it goes on much longer, someone from school will object and cause problems. Let's go to Central Park and you can get reacquainted there, with a little more privacy."

She started them on the way with a gentle push and followed them with Tyrone at her side.

Tyrone had been studying Jennifer intently.

"You're that beautiful girl from the Halloween Ball, who was dressed like Mavis. You're even more beautiful without the mask and costume."

Although she knew she'd never consider dating such a young boy, Jennifer was pleased by his flattery and decided to at least talk to him.

"I'm Jennifer," she said, and held out her hand.

"Tyrone." He held her hand until she disengaged it.

"Are you also from an army family?"

"Marine," he gently corrected.

"What's the difference?"

Before he could explain, Kyle and Mavis reached the corner and were about to walk into Madison Avenue traffic. Tyrone and Jennifer quickly grabbed them and made them wait until the light turned green.

"You can walk now," Tyrone said loudly, then turned to Jennifer. "We may as well go to the zoo, since we're already keepers."

"That's witty," she said. "You boys may not be complete barbarians."

"Kyle and I came down from trees long ago," he grunted. "Gave up animal skins for chinos."

She laughed. "You're much too young for me, but perhaps we can be friends."

"Wait'll you see my winning ways."

"They won't win you anything, but you're amusing."

They reached Fifth Avenue without problems, crossed the street and entered the zoo at 64th Street. Kyle and Mavis were so absorbed in each other that they didn't see Tyrone buying ten-dollar tickets for each of them. Tyrone selected a bench in the sun, guided them to it and said, "Both of you sit here. Don't wander away. We'll pick you up later."

Jennifer nodded her approval and Kyle absently replied, "Yes, Dad."
Mavis echoed, "Yes, Dad."

Tyrone and Jennifer laughed, then walked away without the pre-occupied lovers even noticing their departure.

"What do you want to look at?" Tyrone asked.

"Let's go to the reptile house first. It'll remind me to keep a careful eye on you," she teased.

He put on a wounded expression. "Is that what you think of me, a snake in the grass?"

She giggled. "Don't forget that you tried your line on me at the Halloween Ball. Do you expect me to trust you?"

"At least give me a chance," he urged in his most sincere voice.

She looked him up and down appraisingly. "We'll see. Just don't be too pushy."

"Yes, ma'am."

"And don't call me ma'am."

"Yes, beautiful one."

Now that Kyle and Mavis were finally together, they sat with their arms tightly holding each other, too overcome with joy to speak. They gazed into each other's eyes, oblivious to anything around them. They both started speaking at the same time, then fell silent.

"You first," Mavis said.

The words tumbled out of him.

"All I think about, day and night, is you. I've been going crazy, afraid that I'd never see you again. I haven't been able to concentrate on anything and I've been driving Tyrone nuts. When he found out this week where you went to school, I almost went out of my mind with impatience. I don't know how I got through classes today. On the way here my heart was in my mouth. The same questions kept running through my head; 'What if she's not there?' 'What if she doesn't want me?' When I saw you come out the door I had to go to you, even if you didn't want me."

She kissed him lovingly, then said, "I thought I'd die when you ran into the street and that car almost hit you. I've been going crazy also, babbling about you day and night. It's a wonder Jennifer doesn't hate me because all she hears is Kyle this, or Kyle that. I don't even know your last name."

"Hanson. What's yours?"

"Carver."

"Your father's a doctor?"

"Yes."

"I think my dad works with him."

"Major Hanson's your father?"

"Yes. But he's Colonel Hanson now."

"My Dad likes him. That should make it easier for us to see each other," she said gleefully.

"My Dad likes him, but he might feel differently about the military if it involves his daughter."

"My Dad's not prejudiced," she snapped.

"I didn't say he was. I just hope he likes me."

"He will," she reassured him. "Before we do anything else," she suggested, "let's exchange cell and email info."

"Sure." They took out their pda. phones, and recorded each other's contact data. That done, they sat quietly, content to be together.

Tyrone and Jennifer rejoined them an hour or so later and informed them that the zoo was closing. Kyle and Mavis got up in a daze and followed their friends to the exit, not really listening as Tyrone and Jennifer discussed the animals they had seen. Tyrone was particularly upset.

"Yeah, some of them are cute. But they're in prison for life, just for our amusement. It's not fair."

"There's no habitat left for them anywhere," she reminded him. "This way we're saving their lives."

"That's no life, to be gawked at and teased. I'd rather be dead."

"Maybe they feel differently."

"They didn't have a choice," he growled.

"Would you rather they were in somebody's trophy room or starving to death?" she asked reasonably.

"I don't know. I'll have to think about it."

They reached the street and Jennifer announced, "I have an errand to run. Will you come with me, Mavis?"

Before she could respond, Jennifer started dragging her away. Mavis called back to Kyle, "Call me tonight."

"Yes," he answered and watched her disappear in the distance, certain that he would see her again, missing her already.

"Was she everything you expected?" Tyrone asked.

"More."

"Good. Maybe you'll be cool for a while."

32

T HE ENCLAVE MANAGER, who hadn't been heard from in days, called all Enclave people involved with the parade for an emergency meeting at his office in a non-descript building on Park Avenue South and 26th Street. Hanson was immersed in troop dispositions for the parade and tried to beg off, but the manager insisted. When Hanson got there, he saw many of the familiar faces he had been working with, most smoldering with annoyance at being summoned so abruptly.

He joined Lonigan and Warrington, and waved to Carver and Van Meer, who were huddling with the other medical department heads, obviously as unaware as the uniformed personnel why they were there. Dr. Van Meer was beginning to turn from a slightly indignant shade of light pink to a moderately irate rosé at the outrage of being kept waiting, when the manager made a self-important entrance, followed by Grant Brown, of Guardwell Security, who was smiling smugly.

The manager slowly looked at his assembled guests, whose irritation grew in the drawn-out silence.

Van Meer demanded curtly, "We changed our schedules to come here. Now stop playing games and tell us why we're here."

"Thank you, Dr. Van Meer," the manager replied loftily, ignoring Van Meer's impatience. "I summoned you here to propose a change in plans for the Veterans Day parade." A murmur of surprise ran around the room, but before anyone could respond, the Manager continued. "I thoroughly reviewed the plan with our security consultant, Mr. Brown." Brown bowed and actually seemed to expect a round of applause, which was not forthcoming. The manager ignored the rising tension in his listeners. "I know how concerned we all are with the recent security failures, so Mr. Brown and I have devised a way to avoid any further embarrassment. I'll let him present our recommendations."

Brown stepped forward, full of himself, and struck a manly pose. "We're all too aware of the security lapses since the police and military took charge." He pretended not to hear the growls of anger from the men in uniform. "In order to prevent any further incidents, we propose that the parade begin on 50th Street, so there will be no involvement in the Enclave."

He threw a triumphant look at Hanson, then stood there proudly, waiting for the ovation of approval. The manager moved next to him, eager to share in the anticipated appreciation.

Carver shook his head in disgust. "Mr. Brown. You are an idiot. The Enclave is an integral part of the parade, and you suggest we cancel our part and put the responsibility elsewhere. With the approval of my colleagues," he looked at his fellow department heads, who nodded agreement, "please remove all Guardwell personnel and equipment from the Enclave immediately."

"You can't do that. We have a contract," Brown protested.

"It's canceled for cause."

"I'll sue you."

"See you in court. Captain Lonigan. Escort Mr. Brown out."

"With pleasure, sir."

They all watched as Brown stormed out.

"Captain Lonigan," Carver said.

"Yes, sir?"

"Please assign a detail to make sure the Guardwell people leave without a fuss."

"I'll go myself, unless I'm needed here?"

"I think the meeting's about over," Carver replied.

Lonigan left, but before the others could leave, Van Meer said coldly, "There's one more item." He turned to the manager, who was trembling visibly. "Brown's not the only idiot. We overlooked your egregious mistakes on U.N. day, but this is the limit. With the approval of my colleagues," who again nodded agreement, "you're fired."

The manager slunk out the door a dejected man, only pausing to ask plaintively, "Will I get severance pay?"

Van Meer shooed him away without another word, then said, "This impromptu meeting allowed us to settle two problems that will now let us function more professionally. The police and military will immediately assume all former Guardwell responsibilities for Enclave security and report to Dr. Carver. Next week I will appoint a search committee for a new manager. Thank you all for coming."

Hanson walked out with Carver, who asked, "Any comments, Sam?"

"I admired your subtlety." Carver laughed and Hanson joined in, then added, "I was impressed by Van Meer's decisiveness."

"Don't ever underestimate him. He may be a worrier, but he's a great doctor and a top-notch administrator."

"Thanks, Carv. What a relief to be rid of those two. Things'll run a lot better without them … I hope you'll be on the search committee."

"I will … I must tell you I'm still worried about the parade. Do you really think we'll be safe?"

"We'll do our best. The system worked on Halloween. We'll have more resources on Friday and we'll be prepared to the best of our abilities. There's always a risk in any public activity these days, but we don't have positive choices. Either we stand up to terrorism and suffer the damages they may inflict on us, or we give in and become helpless victims. I will always fight rather than quit."

"Me too."

"You'd have made a good Marine."

"Thanks, Sam. I appreciate that. How about we meet Wednesday morning, instead of tomorrow?"

"Sure. 0900. I mean …"

"I know what time 0900 is. See you then."

•   •   •

Kyle had slipped into a world of his own when Mavis left with Jennifer. Tyrone led him to the bus like a watchful parent with a not overbright child. Tyrone's consolation was that for the first time in days he didn't have to listen to him drivel about Mavis. The dumb, rapturous expression on his friend's face told it all. He was swept away by love and lost to reason. During the short ride down Fifth Avenue, Kyle didn't notice the evident decay on the once resplendent avenue. Even Saint Patrick's Cathedral desperately needed a cleaning. Once they passed the Empire State Building, which somehow never regained its stature after 9/11, the stores and commercial loft buildings were shabby, mostly fast food and cheap clothing outlets.

The boys walked east on 33rd Street and the quality of the buildings didn't improve until they reached Lexington Avenue. When they got to their building, Tyrone greeted the Marine guards, but Kyle passed them in a daze. Tyrone sighed in relief when his friend's apartment door closed behind them.

Kyle sank into the couch and stared blankly at the wall.

"What do you feel like doing, K?"

"Huh?"

"Come in, earth," Tyrone teased. "Do you want to have dinner at the mess hall?"

"I don't think I can deal with people today. What if we just order Chinese food?"

"Okay. But you have to pull yourself together and function. You should feel a lot better now that you've seen your girl."

"Now I can't wait until I see her again. I'll go to her school tomorrow and we'll go someplace where we can be alone."

"If today's any example, you and Mavis need keepers. I better come along with Jennifer, just to make sure you don't get into trouble."

"No, thanks, Ty. It'll be my first chance to be alone with her and I don't want to waste it. I'll be aware of what's going on around me."

"Are you sure? You almost got run down today and you and Mavis would have walked into traffic if we didn't stop you."

"Don't worry. I'll be alright. Now let's order some food."

•　　　•　　　•

Hanson invited Warrington to join him for dinner in the Marine mess hall, but he got an urgent call from Danowski. "You better come back to your office immediately, sir. Some of the Guardwell people confronted the Marine guards at our apartment building and words were exchanged. It might have gone further, but the Marine's M16's outgunned the Guardwell pistols. It's probably over, but I think you should speak to Sergeant Wilkins, who was in charge of the guard detail."

"A good idea, Ski. I'll be there in ten minutes. Well done."

"Thank you, sir."

Hanson turned to Warrington. "I'll have to cancel my invitation. There's been some trouble with Guardwell. Let's try for tomorrow evening."

"I'll look forward to it, Sam."

Warrington waved goodbye, as Hanson rushed off and hit Lonigan's button on his cell phone as he went.

"Mike? It's Sam. There's been an incident with Guardwell and some of my Marines. Can you get your cops to monitor all Guardwell personnel until they leave the Enclave?"

"Sure, Sam."

"Thanks."

When he got to his office there was a call waiting, a furious Grant Brown.

"It wasn't enough that you got our contract canceled, but your men are bullying my people. This will all come out in court."

"First of all, Mr. Brown, women make up a good part of our ranks, so we call our people troops. Second. My staff reported that your people confronted my Marines."

"They only reacted when they were provoked," Brown yelled.

"What were they doing at our building? They had no business there." Hanson waited for a response, then continued when he got none.

"Anything that happened to you was brought on by your negative attitude and your unwillingness to cooperate. The police will supervise the withdrawal of your personnel and if there are any further incidents, they will be arrested. I will be holding you personally responsible for any disturbances and will make sure the police arrest you in the event of any occurrence. Do we understand each other?" But Brown had already disconnected.

Hanson called Kyle and invited him to dinner at the mess hall, but Kyle said he'd see him later. The mess hall was crowded and the enlisted men's tables were buzzing indignantly at the affront by Guardwell to the Corps. The N.C.O.'s tables were quieter, as the more experienced heads assessed the performance of their colleagues and wistfully expressed regret that they didn't bring home some scalps. The officer's table was quiet and Jed discussed the incident and used it as an example of how they had to be ready for anything.

Al nodded approval and added, "Remind your troops that we're in a civilian area and they should only discharge weapons when absolutely necessary. They've got to be smart and careful." She saw Hanson approach. "Anything to add, boss?"

"No," he replied. "Please continue to share your experience with the rest of your fellow officers, who I am pleased to say, are performing well. Now. What's for dinner?"

Hanson hadn't spent as much time in the last few days with his officers as he would prefer, so he took advantage of having most of them at the same table. Once everyone was well into their meal, he casually asked the table at large,

"What have the sergeants been saying about the parade?"

He noted with amusement that Jed and Al looked to Captain Muzzetti for the first response, thereby putting him on the spot.

"They're looking forward to it, sir," he replied. "The general feeling is that they want to strut their stuff and nobody better mess with them."

"Are they aware of the security problems?"

"As far as I can tell, sir. I have a meeting scheduled tomorrow after morning formation for officers and N.C.O.'s. We'll review the plan thoroughly again."

"Do you think we're overdoing it, Muzi?"

"No, sir. We can never prepare enough these days."

"That's true. Do either you or Al have anything to add, Jed?"

"No, sir," they echoed.

"Then what's for dessert?"

Danowski was waiting for him when he got back to his office with a mound of papers for his signature. He kept a straight face when he came to the last one, Danowski's application for O.C.S., which he signed and returned without comment. Danowski was disappointed that his commander apparently hadn't noticed the document that was so important to him and started walking out dejectedly.

"Ski."

"Yes, sir?"

"Start studying the officer's handbook."

"Yes, sir. I already have. Thank you, sir," and he whooped as he left.

Hanson made a written note to promote Danowski to second lieutenant after the parade. The man had quickly become invaluable and was ready for some real authority. Lonigan called and reported that all the Guardwell personnel had left the Enclave without incident, beyond Brown's repeated threats to sue everyone.

"One of my officers almost clubbed Brown when he jostled him."

"I hope you commended him, Mike."

"That I did."

"Will you join me for breakfast in the mess hall at 0700?"

"Yes. I'll see you then."

There were still a hundred things to be done, but Hanson realized that they could wait, so he called Tish.

"I may be able to get out of here soon. Do you want company?"

"Long time or short time, G.I.?"

He burst out laughing. "Do I have to decide now?"

"No. Come over as soon as you can and don't abuse froggy."

"Yes, ma'am."

He found himself humming as he called Kyle, who sounded a lot more upbeat when he answered.

"You sound like you rejoined the human race, son. How are you?"

"Great, Dad. Simply great. I can't tell you how good I feel."

"I can hear it in your voice. What're you up to?"

"Ty and I ordered Chinese food and we're just going to hang out for a while."

"I may not be home until late. Is that alright?"

"Sure, Dad. Going to see your girl?"

"Yes."

"Cool. When do I get to meet her?"

"Soon."

"I hope I approve of her."

Hanson chuckled. "I love you, son."

"I love you, Dad."

•   •   •

Kyle and Tyrone talked for a while about what it would be like at Annapolis, then Kyle started getting that lost in cloud Mavis look.

"I'm going home, K. I've got calculus homework due tomorrow. I'll see you in the morning."

Kyle was already reaching for his phone as Tyrone left. When Mavis answered, Kyle was silent for a moment, loving the sound of her voice.

"Who is this?" she demanded.

"It's Kyle. I never heard you on the phone before. You sound wonderful."

"Oh, Kyle. I've missed you terribly. It seems like years since we parted."

"I miss you too. I'll pick you up after school tomorrow and we can go somewhere, then have dinner together."

"Oh, yes. I can't wait."

"Neither can I. I didn't know it was possible to feel this way."

"Neither did I, Kyle. All I can think about is you."

"Me too."

"You better be there, or I'll go mad."

"I will … I'll dream about you tonight."

"And I of you. Goodnight, my love," she whispered.

"Until tomorrow."

He disconnected in a trance hearing her last words over and over, 'until tomorrow'.

33

MORNING FORMATION had been very smart, and no one had missed it for sick call. Captain Muzzetti dismissed the troops, then met with his officers and Sergeants. Jed scheduled his meeting for 1400. When Hanson entered the mess hall at 0700 the snuffies were lively and cheerful.

He could remember other times, when everyone was as grim as death can make troops who have seen too much of war's destruction. Smiles and friendly waves greeted him as he made his way to the officer's table, pausing for a few words with some of his veterans, who were proud to be singled out by their C.O. The ranking mess sergeant, Carstairs, a grizzled lifer who once had to drop his pots and pans and grab a rifle in Saudi Arabia, took his breakfast order personally and paused to chat.

"Is it true that Danowski's bucking for officer, sir?"

Hanson kept a straight face but was inwardly amazed at the efficiency of the sergeant's intelligence system. He wistfully thought how nice it would be if military intelligence was half as effective.

"You'll have to ask him, Carstairs."

Lonigan joined him just as Carstairs walked off, looking hurt.

"What's with him, Sam?'

Hanson grinned. "I wouldn't add to latrine gossip."

"That might be a misdemeanor. Your people look happy this morning. Not like my weary cops."

"We have a different mission, Mike. We probably won't get shot at today."

A private brought Hanson's orange juice and took Hanson's order.

"Don't I rate a sergeant?" Lonigan joked.

Hanson started to explain that Carstairs was sulking when his cell buzzed.

"Hanson."

"This is Sergeant Jefferson at the front gate. Two Wolverine combat vehicles just arrived on a flatbed truck."

"Sign for them and direct them to the motor pool behind the building. Alert maintenance to meet them."

"Yes, sir."

"Good news, Mike. Two heavy combat vehicles just arrived. We'll station one near the reviewing stand. The other will follow the Marine Band."

"That'll help, but I'm still worried."

"Me too, but we're committed."

Danowski was sporting a big grin when he got to his office. "The FBI is lending us ten metal detectors for Friday."

"How did you wangle that?"

"You don't want to know, boss."

"What about personnel to operate them?"

Danowski shook his head. "One instructor. But he swears it only takes a few minutes to master it."

"Well done, Ski. Do you have a contact there?"

"Up to a point. What do you need?"

"A suicide bomber profiler to spend the day with us Thursday and brief everyone who's deploying."

"I'll get right on it, sir. Don't forget to call General Griffin and remind him about the dogs."

"Thanks, Ski." He called the general and thanked him for the Wolverines. "They'll make a great deterrent, sir. Any luck with the dogs?"

"The Navy's promised six teams. They'll arrive Thursday morning. You'll take care of them?"

"Yes, sir."

"I'm still working on D.E.A. for some of their dogs. I'll let you know if they agree."

"Thank you, sir."

"Bev and I enjoyed meeting Tish, Sam. Let's do it again soon."

"Our pleasure, sir."

•   •   •

The veterans were excited when Carver's medical team entered the ward. They were looking forward to the parade on Friday and the chance to remind the spectators of their service to their country. They had an entirely different attitude from the belligerence and distrust at the first meeting. Carver looked at each patient's chart, which had been another neglected task, but let the medical team function under Mei's supervision. Her competence and confidence reassured him that her advancement would not be because of their personal relationship. He watched the hard-bitten veterans, ignored for so long, eagerly greet her and babble away like infatuated children. He realized that he was no longer needed there, so he took half the team, those who required more supervision, and led them reluctantly, though he didn't show it, to the privileged Arab's ward.

They went through the metal detector and the usual body search, an indignity that they all objected to, especially the women. The translator, Mussa, a servile Jordanian, always urgent to please his masters, counted the doctors, then demanded to know where the rest of them were.

"We brought the specialists today," Carver answered glibly.

He watched in amusement, without showing it, as Mussa explained the situation to Prince Ahmed, the ranking Saudi, who all the other Arabs deferred to. The explanation proved acceptable and the prince gestured for them to proceed with a regal wave of his hand.

Again, Carter studied each patient's chart, lingering longer on those of the more important personages, but left the examinations to his residents, who had been prepared to deal with their inflated egos. There didn't seem to be any unusual problems, so Carver let his mind drift to a paper he was writing for the New England Medical Journal, but he continued to monitor the resident's progress.

They finished the last examination and the senior resident, who only lost her cool when she was being pawed by the security guard, signaled they were through. Carver told Mussa to inform the patients that he would see them Thursday morning and started to lead the team out. Prince Ahmed barked an imperious command to Mussa, who beckoned to Carver.

"His Highness would like a word with you."

Carver told the team he'd meet them in the conference room and turned to the prince.

"What can I do for you, Your Highness?"

The prince said something and Mussa translated, "Are you going to the military parade on Friday?"

"Yes, Your Highness."

This time he made a longer statement. "There is a rumor that a dissatisfied Arab with a grudge against doctors may attempt to shoot someone at the parade. Perhaps you shouldn't attend."

"Do you have more specific information, Your Highness?"

The prince shook his head and Mussa translated. "Regrettably, that is all."

The prince turned his back and Mussa led Carver out the door.

As soon as he was on the elevator Carver called Hanson.

"Sam. This is Carv. Listen. I just heard something a minute ago that you need to know. My most important Arab patient, Prince Ahmed, a Saudi, told me that an Arab with a grudge against doctors might try to shoot one at the parade. He cautioned me to stay away."

"Anything else?"

"No. What do you think?"

"He was obviously giving you a warning. Do you think I should talk to him?"

"It wouldn't do any good and it would dry up an information source. What should we do about it?"

Hanson thought for a moment. "We'll see if we can ratchet up security a bit more. We just got metal detectors from the FBI and we're getting bomb-sniffing dogs from the Navy. I hope to have an FBI profiler on Thursday who will review what to look for. We should be alright. It might be a good idea for Captain Lonigan and Colonel Warrington to join us in the morning."

"Sure. Let's have breakfast at my house at 8:00 a.m. I'll see you then."

"Thanks, Carv."

•   •   •

Kyle didn't pay attention in class and Tyrone had to remind him several times to at least look like he was interested in calculus. He moved from class to class in a daze and only Tyrone's careful guidance kept him from wandering the halls aimlessly. He ate something at lunchtime at Tyrone's prompting but didn't notice what it was. The rest of the day passed in a haze and the closer it got to 2:00 p.m., the more restless he became. The recalcitrant bell finally sounded and he dashed for the door, startling his history teacher, Mr. Spangler, with whom he had a running feud, with his abrupt departure.

Tyrone raced after him and caught up to him at the street door and grabbed him by the arm.

"Hold up, bro."

"What is it, Ty? I'm in a hurry."

"You're in no condition to go off by yourself. I'll go with you."

"No need, Ty. I'm cool."

"That's whack. You're out of it."

"I'll be fine. Besides, no one says whack anymore."

"I'm worried about you, K."

"Don't worry. It's alright."

"Call me later?"

"Yes, Dad."

•　　　•　　　•

Mavis, much to Jennifer's delight, almost seemed her normal, outgoing self again. She actually was engrossed in her class work and most surprising, actively involved in the discussions in science class. Mr. Singh was mourning the loss of the large Hadron Collider in the disaster of 2013. "The accelerator might have found evidence of particles disappearing into the extra dimensions demanded by string theory," he said wistfully. Mavis raised her hand.

"Yes, Ms. Carver?"

"Does that relate to supersymmetry?"

He looked at her in astonishment, then positively glowed.

"Supersymmetry is predicted by string theory, but there are thousands of models of supersymmetry, so it will be hard to figure out which is right. Do you follow that?"

"Not really, Mr. Singh, but I'm working on it."

"It's a pleasure to have you back in mind, as well as body, Ms. Carver."

"Thank you."

Jennifer led Mavis to the cafeteria for lunch and once they were seated with their salads, asked, "What got into you in Singh's class?"

"I felt so badly about how I treated him last week that I decided to make his day."

"You made his month. How did you come up with that supersymmetry question?"

"The topic is in the book. It seems that physicists are always arguing about one theory or another and this one seemed interesting. It was either that, or landscape."

"I didn't think you wanted to be a gardener, Mav."

"You're such a tease, Jen. Landscape is about a meta-universe …"

"Stop right there. Save it for Mr. Singh. I want to talk to you about Kyle."

"Only if you don't say anything bad about him."

"Alright."

"Promise?"

"Yes. I don't know if you should see him alone."

"I'm a big girl, Jen," she protested.

"I know, but you're infatuated. You might get into trouble."

"Don't worry. I'll call you before we elope."

"Mavis Carver …!"

"Just kidding. He's picking me up after school and we'll get acquainted."

"That's what I'm afraid of."

"I'll be alright."

•   •   •

Kyle saw her come out the door and his heart beat faster. He stood there and watched her look around, until she saw him across the street. Instead of running to each other, as in so many movies, they were fixed in place, gazing raptly, eclipsing the passing cars and people. After an eternity of two minutes, they turned and walked up the street towards Fifth Avenue. Looking across at each other, until they reached the corner. Kyle beckoned to her and the closer she got, the more beautiful she looked.

He reached out his hand and she came into his arms, a snug fit. They kissed and it was sweet and sexy, welding them together to the amusement of passersby, to whom the lovers were oblivious. When they drew apart it was a painful separation and only the looks of adoration they exchanged convinced them that they would not lose each other.

It was a raw, cold day, with a threat of rain or snow that could not cleanse the particles of pollution that infested air breathers, human and other, striving for survival in the harsh city. They walked uptown, absorbed in the explorations of each other that usually preceded the commitment of love. After walking a while, Kyle noticed that Mavis was beginning to get cold. They were at 78th Street, so without asking, Kyle led her to the Metropolitan Museum of Art. By the time they got to the 81st Street entrance she was shivering and he rushed her inside. At the ticket counter, he ignored the thirty-five-dollar admission charge and gave the clerk, a prissy looking old woman whose frosty blue hair radiated disapproval, an offering of one dollar each.

"Admission is thirty-five dollars, young man," the clerk said snippily.

"It's a suggested amount, ma'am," he responded, taking the admission buttons that she reluctantly dispensed.

Mavis didn't react to the clerk's attitude, already assuming that Kyle could do no wrong. She went to the elevator, willing to go anywhere with him and she didn't notice the art they passed. She only became aware of her surroundings when they were seated in the café.

"I'll get coffee," Kyle murmured, and she followed him with her eyes as he left their table.

Her stress and tension since their first separation had evaporated and she was filled with the certainty that she belonged with Kyle. She had to smile when she remembered Jennifer's comment that she was infatuated. Enchanted was more like it. Kyle returned with coffee and saw her smile.

"What?" he asked.

"Something Jennifer said. She doesn't understand how I feel about you."

He laughed. "Tyrone doesn't understand how I feel about you. I don't know if anyone would understand."

Her look would have melted the remaining ice in Antarctica.

They didn't talk for a long while, holding hands, growing closer, watching the snow that began to fall slowly etch the Central Park trees with white smears that looked like a skin disease. They lost track of time and it started to grow dark as the snow subtly beautified the park. A recording announced the museum would be closing in fifteen minutes, snapping them out of their reverie.

"We have to go," he whispered. "It's too cold to be outdoors, so if you're hungry, we can take a taxi to a restaurant near where you live, then it won't be a problem later if it snows heavily."

"That sounds good."

"What kind of food do you like, Mavis?"

"That's the first time you said my name."

"It's a beautiful name."

"My friends call me Mav."

"Hi, Mav. My friends call me K."

"Hi, K," and she leaned over and kissed him.

"Do you like French food?" he asked.

"Yes."

"There's a nice little restaurant off Third Avenue, on 33rd Street."

"Let's go."

Despite the snow and it being rush hour, they managed to get a taxi immediately. The bearded, angry looking Arab driver glared when Kyle told him their destination and mumbled something they couldn't hear that they ignored. Traffic grew heavier as they went downtown and by 63rd Street it slowed to a crawl. The driver muttered louder and louder, cursing the American pigs and infidel dogs who were preventing his passage, but Kyle didn't reveal that he understood Arabic.

Traffic came to a complete halt at 58th Street and the driver's cursing grew so loud that Kyle reached out and shut the safety partition, provoking a snarl of indignation. Mavis snuggled into Kyle's arms, and they were content to be together. They didn't speak, enrapt in their feelings.

When the taxi stopped in front of the restaurant, Kyle sent Mavis inside while he paid the driver, concerned that the mad Arab might be confrontational. But he accepted the exorbitant fare and the tip with a sullen glare, then roared off in the night, another hate America immigrant who took our bounty and cursed us for it.

Mavis was already seated when he entered the tiny restaurant. Although it was in a decaying traditional New York City tenement, the place was spotless, with a certain rough charm, and the staff was neat and clean. There were only a dozen or so tables, but the service was on a par with good, upscale restaurants. The bus boy quickly brought water and said he'd bring hot bread.

The waiter took their drink order, after handing them menus. Kyle suavely ordered two glasses of the house chardonnay and his age wasn't questioned. They didn't notice what they ate, totally absorbed in each other, and they sat long after they were done eating, gazing in each other's eyes. Their waiter told the rest of the staff about the young lovers and won everybody over. The room was narrow and the staff found various pretexts to observe the youngsters. Their waiter even brought them a complimentary glass of wine. But time flew by on spiteful wings and soon it was time to go.

They walked to Mavis' house in a near trance. Kyle barely noticed their surroundings, an unusual lapse from his normal vigilance. They stood on the steps of her townhouse, locked in an embrace that they hoped would never end, but it was late and they had to part.

"Will you meet me after school tomorrow, Kyle?"

"Oh, yes. I wish it was tomorrow already."

"I'll dream of you tonight and see your face when I'm awake, until we're together again," she whispered.

"It hurts to leave you," he responded.

"I know," she said, "but you're part of me now."

"And you of me."

They kissed tenderly and she turned to go.

"One minute more," he urged.

She came back and kissed him sweetly, then went in. He walked home in a daze, repeating her name silently, over and over, Mavis, Mavis, Mavis. He passed the Marine guard at his building without hearing his greeting. He didn't even think of stopping at Tyrone's apartment. He unlocked his front door, went straight to his room, managed to undress, got into bed and fell into an instant, blissful sleep.

34

M AVIS ANSWERED THE DOORBELL and admitted Hanson and Lonigan. "Good morning, gentlemen. My father is waiting for you in the dining room. Please follow me."

A few moments later Warrington arrived and after Mavis led him to join the others he was still grumbling.

"What's wrong, Colonel Warrington?" Carver asked solicitously.

"That blankety-blank Marine sentry had the gall to demand my I.D."

Hanson tried to suppress a grin, but Warrington noticed and glared at him.

"Colonel Hanson was kind enough to assign Marine guards to all medical department heads, since we got rid of Guardwell," Carver explained. "I'm sure the girl meant no disrespect."

"She's a combat trooper, not a girl, Doctor Carver," Colonel Warrington retorted, "and I'm sure she was pulling my chain."

"She was just doing her job, Colonel," Hanson said. "I would have reamed her if she didn't check everyone. I don't think she meant to tweak the Army."

Warrington finally smiled and said begrudgingly, "Nervy kid. I don't know if I would have stopped a full bird colonel at her age."

"It's time for breakfast, gentlemen," Mavis suggested and they followed her to the table.

The maid, Antonia, a dark-haired, lively looking beauty from Nicaragua, a refugee from the civil war, took their breakfast orders. Warrington followed her fluid hips with his eyes, and Hanson thought; *The old dog. I better check if he came on to the sentry.* They didn't talk much until the meal was finished and Antonia served coffee.

"Why don't you bring us up to date, Sam," Carver requested.

"Sure. We borrowed extra metal detectors from the FBI and we're expecting a profiler to be with us tomorrow. We should be getting six bomb sniffing dogs from the Navy. We have two heavy duty combat vehicles that should work as a deterrent. Everybody, police, Army and Marines know what to do. The parade organizers have been slow to take our suggestions. If you could have Dr. Van Meer call them …"

"I'll do it right after we're finished," Carver said. "Anything else?"

"You should tell Mike and Oliver about the Arab warning," Hanson said.

"What warning?" Mike asked.

"When I was finishing my rounds, Prince Ahmed, a Saudi royal, warned me that an Arab who was angry with doctors might be a threat."

"Did he give you any details?" Lonigan asked.

"I'm afraid not. Do we have to worry about this?"

"Of course," Hanson stated. "We'll keep an eye on anyone who looks the least bit Mid-Eastern. If we're lucky it'll be a warm day and people will leave their winter coats at home."

"Why?" Carver asked.

"That way we can see what they're wearing or carrying," Lonigan replied.

"If there's nothing else now I suggest we meet the same time tomorrow morning for a last-minute review," Carver said.

Mavis escorted the guests to the door and when Hanson was leaving, she said quietly, "Colonel Hanson. I know your son, Kyle."

"Are you in his class?"

"No. We just met recently, but I'm in love with him, and he with me."

He looked at her in surprise. "Aren't you both a little young for that?"

"We grow up quickly these days."

"When did you two meet?"

"At the Halloween Ball and we've been thinking about each other ever since."

"I didn't know Kyle was there. How did he get an invitation?"

"He came with his friend. When the explosion went off and we were separated, I was afraid that I'd never see him again. I thought I'd die until I saw him Monday."

"You've only seen him twice?"

"Three times and it feels like we've been together always."

"I think you kids are being a bit hasty. Does your father know?"

"No. He's been so busy. But I'll tell him after the parade."

"I'll talk to Kyle then."

"Please don't be angry with him, Colonel."

"I won't. But I think we should all have a serious talk. Good morning, Ms. Carver."

"Call me Mavis," she said to his departing back.

As soon as he was outside, Hanson called Danowski and ordered him to have all officers and N.C.O.'s meet him in the conference room in twenty minutes. He stopped at his office to take care of several clerical chores, then, followed by Danowski, went to the conference room.

"Attention," Danowski called, and all personnel snapped to. "At ease, ladies and gentlemen. Be seated."

A few late comers straggled in, murmuring the reason as they went by, but Hanson understood that they had to leave various duties to attend the sudden meeting. When Danowski signaled that everyone was present, Hanson began.

"I sent for you because we've been advised that an Arab may have a grievance against doctors and might pose a threat at the parade."

He paused a moment to assess the response and was gratified to see everyone sit up a little straighter.

"Now that I have your attention I want to talk to you about profiling. It's considered politically incorrect to profile according to race or ethnicity. On Friday, I don't care what you do to spot threats. Be alert at all times. You don't have to look at little old blue-haired ladies too carefully, but study all males over fourteen, and pay particular attention to anyone of possible Mid-Eastern origin. Look for signs of nervousness; furtive glances, tension, sweating, twitching, restless movements, anything revealing undue stress. Detain anyone who looks suspicious for closer inspection. It's up to you to prevent anyone who is a possible threat from getting close to the parade."

His people were concentrating intently, so he gave them some time for the importance of what he was saying to really sink in.

"Sir?"

"Yes, Al?"

"Do we have the legal authority to detain anyone?"

"Every Marine detachment will have police officers accompanying them and your instructions will be written up in the orders of the day."

"Thank you, sir."

"Any other questions?"

Captain Muzzetti raised his hand.

"Yes, Muzi?"

"How good is this information, sir?"

"It really doesn't matter. We have to assume that the threat is real and act accordingly. We don't want any kind of incident to disrupt the event and further display our vulnerabilities to the world." He saw heads nod knowingly and realized that he was getting through to them. "Friday will be a test of how we can protect our own. I want all of you to be sharp. Better to be overly cautious and check out the slightest suspicion thoroughly. If you offend anyone, apologize. If that's not enough, refer them to me. Any further questions?"

There weren't any and Hanson nodded to Danowski, who called, "Dismissed."

Jed and Al lingered to talk to Hanson and he gestured for them to follow him. They went to his office and he told Danowski to lock the door and see they were undisturbed. He didn't say anything when Danowski joined them and he turned to Jed and Al.

"What's on your minds?"

"Go ahead, Al," Jed urged.

"We're worried about parade conditions outside the Enclave, boss. The official parade liaisons aren't communicating with us, and they're not as concerned as we are about security. We can't find out how well they're prepared."

Hanson took out his cell and hit Lonigan's number.

"Mike? This is Sam. My people aren't getting the cooperation they need to properly coordinate security outside the Enclave on Friday. Can you call your counterparts and ask them to talk to my people? Thanks, Mike."

Next he called Dr. Carver. "Carv? This is Sam. We're having some communication problems with the parade organizers. Can you talk to them? Thanks, Carv." He turned to Jed and Al. "Let me know if you haven't heard from them by 1000 tomorrow. I'll see you in the mess hall for dinner."

•　　　•　　　•

School was fun for Kyle for the first time since the conflict with the "pussies". He enjoyed a spirited discussion with his history teacher, Mr. Spangler, a rabid anti-war activist, who singled out the Marine boys for sarcastic comments. Kyle and Tyrone had nicknamed him "Spangles", for his chi-chi style of dress and affected mannerisms.

The topic had been what "Spangles" called the American imperialistic wars for oil in the Mid-East. Kyle took exception to many of "Spangles" opinions, which were often highly emotional and rarely based on fact. One of "Spangles" most annoying qualities was never letting a student respond without interrupting and making derisive remarks. He frequently referred to the military as mercenaries of the fascist warmongers. This time Kyle responded that he was a bigot. This offended "Spangles", who called him a neanderthal pup.

"You'll change your tune when you need a policeman, firefighter or soldier to save your ungrateful ass," Kyle retorted.

The bell rang and everyone dashed for the door, before 'Spangles' could reply.

"You really laced into him there," Tyrone said, as they headed for their next class.

"I'm tired of listening to his stupid prejudices. He has this warped view of the world and he blames America for everything that's wrong with it. If he lived in some of the places we did and saw the terrible things that go on there, that only our military protects us from, he'd get down on his knees and give thanks that we still had a reasonable shot at survival."

"You were a bit confrontational, bro. What if he gets back at you with a low grade?"

"I've aced my tests and term paper, Ty. So he knocks a few points off. I'll still get an A."

"I hope you won't be as testy in calculus class."

"How could I? It's not based on opinion. It's fact, logically organized. Unlike the 'Intelligent Design' theory, which requires blind faith and arbitrary opinions, calculus is provable and demonstrable. That's why I love it. An asshole like 'Spangles' can't just decide that something isn't so and get away with it."

"You're hanging tough again, dude. Mavis must be good for you. Now let's get to class."

•   •   •

Jennifer couldn't decide whether to be happy or annoyed at Mavis' return to good spirits. She resented the effect that Kyle was having on her friend, who she wanted to be dependent on her. Yet she loved the inner glow that made her friend so beautiful. They hadn't spent time together for days and Jennifer was just beginning to realize how much she wanted to be with her. Her consolation was in the expectation that puppy love would soon be over, consumed by its very intensity, and her friend would return to her.

In the meantime, she would try to keep things in perspective and not let any of her agitation show. This was made easy by Mavis' not noticing much in her state of infatuation, while bubbling over with happiness. Jennifer admonished herself to wait patiently until the fires of love burned out, without alienating Mavis by impatience.

The most amusing change that Jennifer noticed was Mavis' renewed interest in science class. Mr. Singh, formerly listened to more as a drone of a distant insect, was suddenly fascinating. Mavis got more and more involved in his once boring, obtuse physics lectures. She listened raptly as he discussed an aspect of string theory.

"We should consider the perplexingly small value of the cosmological constant, a force that seems to be accelerating the expansion of the universe. Perhaps there is a random distribution of values of the constant, often known as the authropic principle, but many scientists reject this, preferring fundamental physics, giving rise to the East Coast-West Coast split."

Mavis raised her hand.

"Yes, Ms. Carver?"

"Why is it called that?"

Mr. Singh beamed. "Because a lot of the scientists come from Stanford or Princeton."

"Which do you favor?"

"East Coast. I went to Princeton. If there are no more questions, the next assignment will be to read the chapter on the loop quantum gravity theory."

On their way out of class, Jennifer asked Mavis, "Do you really understand what Singh is talking about?"

"I don't get all of it, but I'm working on it."

"You don't need physics in medical school … You are still planning to be a doctor?"

"Of course I am, Jen. I just love the challenge of physics. It forces me out of my comfort zone and makes me exert my mental muscles."

"Just as long as you don't neglect your physical muscles. We haven't worked out together since the day before the Halloween Ball."

"I know, Jen. I feel terrible about it, but so much has been happening. I'll stabilize things by the weekend, and we'll get back to our normal schedule."

"I hope so, Mav. I've given up many of my friends to spend time with you."

"I know, Jen. You've been so good to me. I really love you."

Mavis' obvious sincerity appeased Jennifer and the girls made their way to the next class, arm in arm, happy with each other.

When the girls left school, Kyle was waiting across the street. Jennifer saw Kyle first and nudged Mavis.

"There's your new flame," and she started to walk away.

"Why don't you come with us, Jen?"

"I'd just be in the way. Call me later if you feel like talking," and she waved to Kyle and left.

Kyle rushed to Mavis and hugged her, spilling both their books.

"I missed you," he said.

"I missed you too," she responded.

They clung to each other, oblivious to the stares of Mavis' classmates or passersby.

They had no awareness of time passing, until Mr. Singh went by and said teasingly, "Ah, Ms. Carver. I see you are practicing cling theory. Hee, hee." He smiled at her fondly and walked off, delighted with his wit.

"Who's that?" Kyle asked.

"My physics and calculus teacher."

"I like physics and calculus. You must be pretty smart. Are you planning a career in science?"

"Medicine. I'm going to be a doctor. What about you?"

"I'm going to the Naval Academy, if it reopens, and become a Marine officer."

Mavis looked at him curiously. "What do you mean 'if it reopens'?"

"One of the conditions of the Treaty of Tehran in 2015 was the closing of the American military academies."

"What will you do if the academy doesn't reopen?"

"I'll become a Marine officer another way."

"Like your father?"

"I only hope I can be half as good as he is."

"You admire him?"

"He's a hero and a great leader … What about your father?"

"He's the head of cardiology at N.Y.U. in the Enclave."

"My father talks about him all the time. He really admires him. Is it because of him you want to be a doctor?"

"Partially. I also promised my mother I would study medicine."

"She must be very proud of you."

"She died in the flu epidemic of 2013, along with my two sisters."

"I'm sorry."

"No need. I'm used to her being gone and she's always in my heart. What about your family?"

"My Mom and older brother also died in the flu epidemic."

"I'm sorry, Kyle."

"We have things in common, good and bad."

"We have a lot to learn about each other," she said.

It was getting chilly as the day wore on and Kyle realized that they had been standing in front of Mavis' school for so long that it would soon begin to get dark.

"It's too cold to stay outside. What would you like to do?" he asked.

"I don't care, as long as I'm with you."

"I want to be alone with you, but we can't go to my apartment, because the Marine guard might recognize you."

"What about your friend Tyrone's place?"

"He lives in the same building. What about your house?"

"We can't go there because of guards and security," she replied.

"I don't have enough money for a hotel," he said reluctantly.

"Even if you did, they wouldn't take us without luggage."

He shook his head in frustration. "We'll have to find someplace, but for now, let's go to a movie. We can sit in the back and pretend to be alone. I don't know this neighborhood too well. Where's the nearest cineplex?"

"On Third Avenue. It's a short walk."

They walked slowly, arms wrapped tight around each other, ignoring the cold, pausing briefly at each corner to kiss. By the time they reached the cineplex, the kisses had changed from sweet to urgent. He bought tickets to the movie that he hoped would have the lowest attendance possible, 'The Son of the Taiwanese Avenger', a sequel in the dreadful series about the Chinese conquest of Taiwan.

The earlier films in the series were all poorly shot, badly acted, limply directed and beneath the scorn of the lowest level of reviewers. There were only two patrons in the house and the film was already in progress, but one man was sitting only three rows from the rear and he turned at the latecomer's arrival. Kyle assumed he would return his attention to the film once they were seated, but he kept slyly checking them out. Kyle tried to ignore him and started kissing Mavis, but he was aware that their neighbor was more interested in them than the movie.

Mavis sensed Kyle's growing annoyance and whispered, "Don't worry. The movie's almost over. After he leaves we'll have some privacy."

She kissed him tenderly and held his hand. The touch of her warm hand made him forget his irritation. They waited until the end of the film, but the now intrusive stranger didn't leave.

"Maybe he just wants to see the credits," she said hopefully, even though they were in Chinese.

But after fifteen minutes of commercials, none of which were the least bit appealing, the feature started and the man remained welded to his seat.

"Let's change seats," Kyle urged and they moved to the farthest corner in the row, but the man kept watching them. Kyle glared lasers at him, without effect, and said, "I'm going to ask him either to move or stop watching us."

"Don't," she asked. "It might lead to an argument and that would spoil things for us. Let's go now and we'll have to find a place to be alone another time."

•　　•　　•

When Kyle got home he was surprised to find his father there.
"Hi, Dad. What are you doing here?"
"I live here, remember?"
"I hadn't noticed lately."
"Very funny. You know what I'm dealing with."
"Just teasing, Dad."
"What have you been up to?"
"The usual."

"Is the usual named Mavis?"

"How do you know about her?" Kyle asked in surprise.

"Secret intelligence. She told me this morning at her father's house. You understand that this could be a very delicate situation ..."

"I love her, Dad, and she loves me."

Hanson was silent as he considered his reply ... "You're too young to get married and too smart to do anything stupid, so just make sure you don't make waves."

"Then you're not angry at me?"

"Of course not. You're a fine boy and she seems to be a fine girl. You're lucky to have each other."

"Thanks, Dad. I love you."

"I love you, son. I've got to get some sleep. Tomorrow will be a busy day. Goodnight, Kyle."

"Goodnight, Dad."

35

HANSON TURNED COMMAND OVER to Al, then went to Dr. Carver's house. They were just sitting down to breakfast when they heard loud explosions. Hanson, Lonigan and Warrington rushed for the door and a moment later Hanson's cellphone rang. He paused and listened while Al told him that a bomb went off at the barracks entrance, that she was going there to assess the damage and that's all she knew. Then he issued orders.

"First clear your immediate area. Have Jed lead a platoon to our apartment building, then detach squads to patrol the thirties from First Avenue to Fifth Avenue. Have Muzzetti lead a platoon to the Vet hospital, secure the building, then patrol 23rd Street. Hold the rest of the battalion on standby 'til I get there."

He could hear gunfire and explosions over the phone and Al's voice was more urgent.

"We're taking fire, boss. Gotta go."

"I'm on my way," he said.

"We heard more than one explosion," Lonigan said.

"One was at the barracks, which is under attack," Hanson answered. "Put all your men on alert, Mike, but don't send them out until we know who we're fighting. They're not heavily armed enough to take on automatic weapons and RPG's. We'll stay in touch."

"I'll go to the armory," Warrington said, "and organize all available troops. Let me know what we can do."

"Will do. Carv. I'll let you know what's happening as soon as I can," Hanson said, as he headed for the door.

"Good luck, Sam," Carver called after him.

The three men rushed out and Mavis followed.

"Colonel Hanson," she yelled. "I heard you say your building is under attack. Is Kyle alright?"

He didn't pause and called over his shoulder, "I'll have him call you," and he jumped into the Humvee that Tico had waiting at the curb. "Grab your weapon, Tico. The barracks is under attack, but we'll go by our building on the way."

•　　　　•　　　　•

Kyle was just getting ready to leave for school when he heard an explosion and a moment later the building shook. He instantly knew what happened and grabbed his father's spare pistol, some extra clips and dashed into the hall where he met Tyrone, equally armed.

"Let's go downstairs, Ty, and see what's going on."

"Right behind you, bro."

They raced down the stairs to the lobby and saw that it was in shambles. They could see three or four attackers in ski masks firing at someone behind the lobby desk, near the entrance. They opened fire instantly and hit two of them. The other two ducked behind a sofa and one of them fired at the boys, who threw themselves to the floor. The other one tossed a grenade at the counter, but it flew back a moment later and exploded, killing the last two attackers. Wilkins' head cautiously peeked out from behind the desk.

"Mornin', boys," he drawled. "Thanks for the help."

"What about our other guys?" Kyle asked.

"They bought it, but they took a bunch of those rags with them. I gotta call headquarters and report."

The boys slumped down on the steps, after-action shock setting in. They ignored the frantic questions from the residents who were straggling into the lobby, pointing out Wilkins and sending them to him.

•　　　　•　　　　•

The gunfire and explosions at the barracks entrance was getting louder. As soon as Al issued Hanson's orders to Jed and Muzzetti, she grabbed her M16 and headed for the fighting. Danowski followed her and they met Carstairs in the hall.

"We can't keep meeting like this, Al. I mean Lieutenant," he muttered.

She didn't slow down but flashed him a grin.

"We'll understand if lunch is late."

She saw Nakamura, who was looking bewildered.

"Naka. Take your platoon out the back and as soon as you're sure the area is secure send one squad around 30th Street to the front entrance, and another around 29th. Move."

"Yes, sir. I mean ma'am." He took off at a run, calling for his gunnery sergeant. The gunfire was getting louder and she saw Lieutenant Bernstein heading for the entrance, carrying his M16.

"Bob. Get your men and form a perimeter in the main corridor. Use desks and whatever else you can find,"

"Will do," he yelled and dashed off.

Just then, a group of attackers in ski masks and camis, firing AK47's, burst into the corridor. Al fired back and some of them went down, but the others kept firing. Carstairs yelled, "I'm hit," and slumped down.

More attackers charged in and Al and Danowski retreated, still firing, until they reached the improvised perimeter, where they took cover. The two groups exchanged fire and Al was about to organize a counter-attack, when gunny Le Beau charged out, cradling an M60, and laid down a devastating burst of fire that cleared the corridor. A minute later, Nakamura led one of his squads through the front entrance and they finished off the remaining attackers. He gave her a snappy salute.

"Lieutenant Nakamura reporting, ma'am. All resistance is over."

"Good job, Naka. Make sure all of the rags are dead or handcuffed and check our casualties. Where's Sergeant Jefferson?"

"He and the rest of the guard detail outside are dead. It looks like the explosion got them."

"Have their remains brought inside," Al ordered. "Then patrol First Avenue from 28th Street to 32nd Street."

"Yes, ma'am.

•   •   •

It was only a few blocks from Carver's house to the Marine's apartment building, but it seemed to take forever. Hanson urged Tico to go faster. He had a horrible image of finding his son dead in a slaughterhouse that was typical of terrorist attacks. They sped around the corner at Second Avenue and Hanson's pulse raced faster when he saw the signs of an explosion at the entrance.

He couldn't hear any gunfire, but fearing the worst, drew his sidearm, jumped out of the Humvee followed by Tico and ran into the building. He saw Kyle and Tyrone sprawled on the steps and for a moment his worst fears possessed him. His heart pounded and he rushed to them, then realized that they were alive. A tremendous feeling of relief surged through him.

"Are you boys alright?"

He started to check them for wounds.

Kyle said, "We're okay, Dad. You better check Wilkins. I think he's hit."

Wilkins had been checking the attackers for survivors and turned to Hanson.

"I've just got a flesh wound, sir, but the rest of my detail didn't make it," he said mournfully.

They looked at each other, sharing the loss of comrades that they both knew so well.

Just then Jed and his platoon arrived and Hanson told him to take over.

"See that Wilkins gets medical help and make sure that everyone's accounted for."

Jed saw the boys and asked urgently, "Are they alright, Sam?"

"They're fine. They did well. I've got to call Al."

She reported that everything was under control at the barracks, all the outside guards were dead and she'd give him details when he got there.

"Did you hear from Muzzetti?" he asked.

"Not yet, Sam."

"I'll see you in five. Call me if Muzzetti checks in."

He headed for the entrance, but paused when Kyle called him.

"Dad. Wilkie saved everybody here after his detail was killed. He deserves a medal."

"We'll have time for that later, son."

"The boys were the real heroes, sir," Wilkins said. "Those rags just about had me, when these two came out of nowhere, blazing away like wild. They got two of the rags."

"Well done, Wilkie. We'll have a lot to talk about later. Now I've got to go."

After Hanson left, Wilkins turned to Kyle with a smile. "That's the first time your dad didn't call me 'snail'."

Tico had the Humvee waiting when he came out.

"Barracks, sir?"

"Yeah."

"How'd we do there?"

"Jefferson and the outside guard detail are dead. I don't know about the rest."

They pulled up in front of the building a minute later and Hanson saw that the explosion had blown in the metal gates and destroyed the guard post, but hadn't caused major destruction to the solid brick structure. He told Tico to keep the motor running and went inside, where he found Al and Danowski inspecting the damage.

"Casualties?" he asked.

"Four dead and six wounded, Sam. The four were Jefferson's outside detail. They didn't have a chance. We're taking care of the wounded and the rest of the troops did well, except gunny Le Beau."

The big bear of a man was standing nearby, still cradling the heavy machine gun in his large paws, looking embarrassed.

"His gung-ho charge prevented the rags from overrunning us. I'm putting him in for a silver star."

"Later. Well done, Al. Now I'm going to the vet hospital to see what happened to Muzzetti."

"Any orders, sir?" Al asked.

"Any live prisoners?"

"Two, sir."

"Put them on ice, out of sight and tell our people not to mention them to anyone. We'll interrogate them later."

"Yes, sir."

Ladder 7 was arriving as Hanson walked out of the barracks and he waved to the firefighters. He called Lonigan and asked him to send police to the apartment building and barracks and arrange for ambulances. It only took a minute to drive down First Avenue to the Veterans hospital.

When they got there, Hanson saw a squad of Marines deployed at the undamaged entrance and two Marine bodies laid out on the ground.

"Who's in charge?" he demanded.

"I am, sir. Staff Sergeant Delotte," she replied.

"What happened here?" he asked, pointing to the bodies.

"I don't know, sir. They were both dead from gunshots when we got here. We straightened their bodies. Captain Muzzetti left us here and led the rest of the platoon inside. There was a lot of firing going on, but it's just about died down now. That's all I know, sir."

"Carry on," he said, and hurried inside, alert because he didn't know what to expect.

Tico was right behind him, head swiveling back and forth, ready for action. They took the stairs to the second floor, the vet's ward, where they found another squad guarding the door. Several bodies with ski masks were crumpled on the floor outside the door to the vet's ward.

"Any casualties?" he asked.

"None of our people here," the Sergeant in command answered, "but you gotta see what happened inside, in the vet's ward."

"Is it bad?"

"You better see for yourself, sir."

Hanson walked into the ward, expecting to find a bloody massacre of the vets. Instead he saw six or seven dead bodies sprawled on the floor, but they all wore ski masks. The vets were gathered in a corner brandishing weapons, yelling in triumph and bragging about their kills, or singing exuberantly and passing bottles of liquor around. The strangest sight was one legless vet in a wheelchair pouring liquor into the mouth of a quadriplegic.

"Attention on deck," one drunken vet called.

An equally drunken quadriplegic yelled, "Sorry I can't snap to, sir."

Hanson didn't know whether to smile, curse, or cry.

"It looks like you boys had quite a party here."

"We had a battle. A real, live fuckin' battle. Now we're havin' a party," the same vet who called "attention" replied. "You're welcome to join us, sir. Have a snort." He offered a bottle.

"I have to see what's going on upstairs, but I'll join you later."

"We'll still be here," the vet said.

Hanson gestured for Tico to follow him, and they headed for the stairs.

"Those guys are too much," Tico commented.

"You're absolutely right, but quiet now, until we know what's going on upstairs."

They found Marines on each of the floors, who told Hanson that everything was secured. On the top floor, the door to the Arab's ward had been blown in. The Marines outside told Hanson that the fighting was over and he went inside. He found Muzzetti standing next to a pile of bodies, surveying the devastated ward.

Blood was everywhere; walls, floor, beds and ceiling. The hazy air stank of cordite, and bullet holes had ventilated the walls. Shredded bedding floated everywhere and was beginning to settle on the bodies like tarnished snow.

"Did you take any casualties?" Hanson asked.

"Two of my people have flesh wounds," Muzzetti replied. "Eight attackers are dead. Two are wounded and in restraints. We don't have a count of the patients yet. My medics are seeing to the wounded. We took them by surprise. I guess they didn't expect us to get here this quickly."

Hanson looked around the ward, visualizing the fight.

"How did it happen, Muzi?"

"As far as I can tell, about twenty attackers killed the sentries outside, then split into two groups. One went to the vet's ward, and the other came up here. The vets had an arsenal and they must have heard the gunfire, because they were ready for them. They shot the shit out of them …"

Hanson nodded. "I saw the results. They were celebrating their victory when I got there and invited me to join them."

"Think they'll invite me, boss?" Muzzetti joked.

They exchanged tight grins. "I'll put in a good word for you. Go on with your report."

"I left troops on each floor and got here with two squads. The attackers had blown the door with an RPG and were shooting it out with the remaining bodyguards who weren't killed in the blast. The defenders had dragged beds and night tables into a corner and were making a last stand when we hit the door. The rags forgot to leave a rear guard and didn't even see us until we opened fire. We took them out quickly and it was over in a minute or so. Our troops did great under fire for the first time."

"I expected no less of Marines. Well done, Muzi."

"Thank you, sir."

One of the prisoners was glaring at Hanson as he walked by and muttered something about "an infidel dog and his whore of a mother". Hanson smiled pleasantly, then said in fluent Arabic, "We shall talk later, oh defiler of the law. You will not be happy." Hanson pointed him out to Muzzetti and said loudly, "Take good care of that one, he has informed for us before." He walked away, as the Arab vehemently protested his innocence to his companion, who averted his gaze.

There was only one bodyguard left alive and he was seriously wounded. Hanson patted him on the arm and said in Arabic, "I hope those who you protected were worthy of your faithful service."

The man just shrugged weakly. Hanson turned to the patients. Some were dead and most were wounded except for a few, including Prince Ahmed.

"Thank you for saving us, Colonel Hanson," the prince said in Arabic.

Hanson stared at him blankly, until the prince repeated his thanks in English.

"I thought I heard you speaking Arabic to my guard?"

"You're mistaken, sir."

The prince stared at Hanson strangely, who was already looking at the survivors. There were more than he expected.

He said to the prince, "Your guards fought bravely and saved those of you who are lucky to be alive."

"They did what they were paid for," the prince responded indifferently.

"They gave their lives for you. They deserve some appreciation."

"We look at things differently in the East. We do not place the same value on life as you do in the West, because you are corrupted by worldly pleasures."

He knew that the prince was trying to provoke him and smiled pleasantly.

"I think what you really mean is that we in the West respect the rights of others and admire someone who sacrifices himself for another."

The prince sputtered with rage. "How dare you. Do you know who I am? I'll call your ambassador to the U.N. and inform him of your affront to the Arab people."

Hanson laughed and pointed to the dead attackers. "I think you affronted the Arab people. Why don't you complain to the Caliph in Iraq?" And he turned and walked away, gesturing to Muzzetti to follow him.

Once they were in the hall, he told Muzzetti, "Make sure the hospital is secure. The doctors are on their way and should be here momentarily. Send a detail to 23rd Street and have them patrol the immediate area. I'll have the police relieve them later.

"Have two of your men put the prisoners in my Humvee and instruct everyone not to mention them to anyone. I'll send Lieutenant Bernstein here. As soon as you're satisfied that everything's secure leave him in charge and meet me at headquarters. Tell Prince Ahmed that we'll provide a police guard, until he can make other arrangements."

"He won't like that, sir."

Hanson grinned. "Let him complain to Valerie."

Muzzetti laughed heartily and Hanson felt his liking for the man grow a little more.

"These are the same people who betrayed us in Riyadh, Muzi. The only loyalties they have are to their own well-being. As soon as the Saudis are sick of islamic extremists, they'll buy their way back, then turn on us again."

Muzzetti looked around to be sure that no one could hear him.

"I could have the men finish them off, sir."

"No, Muzi."

"Why not? You said they'll be our enemies again."

"Because right now we may be able to use them to find out who sent the attackers. We'll determine their fate later."

36

W HEN HE GOT OUTSIDE, Hanson looked at his watch and was surprised that it was only 0837. It had just been thirty minutes since the explosions signaled the three attacks. He called Carver and briefly described the situation.

"Everything's quiet now, Carv. I'll call you later with a complete report."

"One question, Sam."

"Shoot."

"How will this affect the parade tomorrow?"

"I don't know yet. If these events were self-contained and nothing else happens, there's no specific reason to change plans. Let's discuss our options later, when we've had time to assess the event."

Next he called General Griffin and briefed him on the situation.

"It's obvious, sir, that we've got to barricade the entrances to all our facilities. All our dead were from the guard details."

"We'll have to consult the mayor's office, but draft a plan, Sam."

"Yes, sir."

"What about tomorrow? Do we cancel?"

"It's not my call, sir."

"I know. Opinion?"

"Unless something changes, we should go ahead."

"Anything else?"

"Yes, sir. We have some prisoners. I'd like to interrogate them."

"No torture, Sam."

"No, sir."

"Let's talk this afternoon."

Tico was waiting with the Humvee and it only took them a minute to get back to the barracks. Fire, police and ambulance vehicles jammed First Avenue and Hanson picked his way through fire hoses, emergency equipment and rubble to get to the entrance. Special Agent in Charge Royce and a worried-looking Tish waited there. Royce tried to attract the attention of several reporters and ignored Hanson. Tish rushed to his side.

"Are you alright?"

"Yes. But we lost some of our people."

"What happened, Sam?"

"Three groups of Arabs attacked three different sites that Marines were guarding. Their main effort was at the V.A. hospital, targeting the vets and the Saudi exile's ward. The vets had weapons and managed to kill all their attackers. They were having a drunken celebration when I left them. On the Arab's ward, the Saudi guards put up a good fight and all but one of them was killed. My people got there just in time to save most of the exiles, who didn't even put up a fight. Their leader, Prince Ahmed, didn't appreciate his guard's sacrifice, just like so many privileged Arabs who don't recognize the worth of their followers … Ah. I'm just rambling on. We lost good people, but it could have been worse."

Before Tish could say anything, Royce called him and gestured for him to join the impromptu media interview. Hanson shook his head, declining to participate in what he knew would be a who's to blame session. Royce glared, but Hanson ignored him, turned, and walked into the building, picking his way carefully through the debris at the entrance, pausing to look at the body bags being brought inside. He couldn't stop thinking about Jefferson, another veteran of the escape from Riyadh; another Marine who would be missed. Al walked up to him and stood quietly, until the body bags were taken out to the morgue.

"We've seen too much of that, Sam," she said quietly, "and there's something real wrong when Arabs are attacking us in our own country with impunity."

"At least we got all of them, Al."

"You know what I mean."

He sighed. "Yes. Maybe the new administration will make some changes. Until then, we do what we've always done."

"What's that?"

"Die for our country."

Royce's blaring voice shattered their moment of mourning.

"This is quite a mess. A real black eye for our relationship with the Arabs."

"How do you figure that, Agent Royce?" Hanson asked ominously.

"They'll be upset that so many of their nationals were killed."

Hanson stared at him in amazement. "They attacked an American hospital, our homes and our military installation. They murdered American citizens. I don't think we should be concerned that they'll be upset."

"You don't understand the big picture," Royce said patronizingly. "We're trying to rebuild our image and make friends in a world that is no longer intimidated by our power."

"I understand that when someone is shooting at me, he's not my friend," Hanson responded. "The Marines who died today, on their own soil, were defending their country. They weren't concerned with our image. They died doing their duty. You do remember what duty is."

Royce shook his head, pityingly. "You're like so many military men, who don't realize how complicated the world is."

"You're like so many civilian bureaucrats," Hanson retorted, "who never heard a shot fired in anger and sneer at the people who protect them."

He walked away, leaving Royce fuming at being lectured.

Tish followed him, apologizing for Royce.

"Don't mind him, Sam. He means well. He just doesn't understand what's really happening in the world. He's a paper pusher, not an investigator. When the new president appoints a new director of the FBI, he'll be reassigned back to the office."

"We have his type in the military, Tish. They're not all bad. They're just not very sensitive to front line problems."

"Try to deal with me then."

"Sure. Why are you here?"

"The Bureau has the lead in the investigation of domestic terror incidents, especially in federal installations. We'll take charge of the prisoners."

He stiffened noticeably. "I don't think there are any."

She sensed his change of attitude and was alarmed.

"You mean they're all dead? Isn't that unusual?"

"Not in terrorist attacks. They don't surrender easily."

She stared at him suspiciously.

He stared back at her, tension mounting between them, until Al came up to him, saluting formally.

"The bomb dog teams just arrived, sir, with a Lieutenant Commander Lansing in charge. Is there any reason not to quarter them?"

"No, Al. I'll go talk to them, then I'll let General Griffin know they're here. Now, please escort Agent Madison to my office. I'll join her there in a few minutes."

"Yes, sir."

"By the way, Agent Madison, this is Lieutenant Kent," and he strode off, leaving the two women regarding each other with an instant surge of antagonism.

•   •   •

"This way, Agent Madison. And don't touch anything. N.I.S., that's the Naval Investigative Service, will be here soon and they won't want the crime scene disturbed."

Tish bit back an angry comment. "I understand, Lieutenant. I am an FBI investigator."

"That's very nice," Al said disdainfully, "but you don't have to show me your badge. Follow me, please," and she led the way, before Tish could reply.

When they got to Hanson's office Al introduced Danowski to Tish.

"This is Sergeant Danowski. Ski. This is Agent Madison of the FBI If she needs anything before Colonel Hanson returns, see to it."

"You're not waiting?" Tish asked.

"I have duties to attend to, Agent Madison."

Al walked out, back straight, annoyed at herself for reacting that way to Madison, thinking, *She probably thinks I'm jealous, or something. What does Sam see in that tabby?*

Tish controlled her anger when she realized that Danowski was staring at her.

"Is something the matter, Sergeant?"

"No, ma'am."

"Then why were you staring?"

"No offense meant, ma'am. Rumor has it that you're Colonel Hanson's girlfriend and I guess I was curious."

She was speechless for a moment … "Where did you get that idea? Did Colonel Hanson tell you anything?"

"Oh, no, ma'am. He wouldn't do that. There aren't many secrets on a military base."

"Does Lieutenant Kent think that?"

"I wouldn't know, ma'am. Can I get you a cup of coffee?"

"Yes. Thank you."

Tish brooded while she waited. She suspected that some prisoners were still alive and that Hanson was intending to interrogate them away from anyone who might object to his methods. She was seeing him in a different light then that of the tender, thoughtful lover who had swept her away. Images of Lieutenant Kent kept recurring in her mind, and she was surprised at the hostility she was feeling towards that competent, obviously trusted, and attractive officer … *Why I'm jealous. That's ridiculous. He wants me, not her.* She shook her head to clear it of the petty thoughts, when much bigger issues were arising.

"Anything wrong, ma'am?" Danowski asked.

"No, Sergeant. Everything's fine."

But it isn't, she said to herself. A gap was opening between her and Sam, one of two very different perceptions of the law. She felt a sense of dread that she was going to lose the man she had come to love so much, in such a short time.

Danowski was cleaning his M16 and cheerfully whistling a country western tune as he worked.

"Do you always clean your weapon in the office?" she asked.

"No, ma'am. Only when I use it."

"You were in the firefight?"

"Yes, ma'am."

"Did you shoot anyone?"

"I hope so, ma'am."

"Were there any prisoners?"

"I don't know, ma'am. You'll have to ask Colonel Hanson."

She looked at him appraisingly. "You think a lot of Colonel Hanson, don't you?"

"Yes, ma'am. He's the best."

"You wouldn't want to see him get into trouble, would you?"

"No, ma'am."

"If he did something bad would you report him?"

"Like what, ma'am?"

"Say prisoner abuse."

"I don't think he'd do that without a good reason."

"What if what he did was illegal?"

"Then it would depend, ma'am."

"On what?"

"The circumstances, ma'am."

"You don't volunteer much, do you?"

"No, ma'am. Not when you're fishing for info to use against the Colonel."

"If he tortures those prisoners, you could be accountable, Sergeant."

"I don't know anything about prisoners, ma'am. You should take that up with the colonel," and he ostentatiously turned his back and continued cleaning his rifle.

When Hanson walked in a few minutes later and sensed the tension in the air, he knew that something happened between Tish and Danowski. He made a mental note to question Danowski later.

"Lieutenant Kent will be escorting Agent Royce here in a few minutes. Why don't we wait for him before talking further," and he reached for some paperwork.

Tish didn't reply, torn between wanting nothing to interfere with her feelings for Hanson, yet fearing that a conflict of interest was forming. She resolved to do her duty and follow the letter of the law, so she would maintain a clear conscience. Hanson ignored her and called General Griffin, speaking quietly so Tish couldn't hear him.

"The FBI suspects we may have prisoners. I denied it. Does this create a problem, sir?"

"Not yet, Sam. Stay in close touch."

Then he called Kyle and passed on the message from Mavis, again speaking quietly so Tish couldn't hear him. He was amazed at how quickly he placed her in the category of naïve civilians who hadn't the faintest understanding of how ruthless the war on terror had to be. He thought with regret that she probably couldn't grasp the concept that terrorists weren't protected by the Geneva Convention.

Agent Royce stormed in, complaining at the top of his voice about being restricted from access to the entire facility.

"We have just concluded a battle, Agent Royce," Hanson explained patiently. "Once we've assessed the situation, we'll make certain that you can inspect anything you like. In the meantime, you might want to prepare a press release for a major media interview that we should arrange shortly."

Royce immediately forgot his anger and swelled noticeably with importance. "Perhaps you should join me," he offered condescendingly.

"I don't think so, Agent Royce. You're a much better spokesperson than I am."

"Then I'd better prepare. Do you have an office I can use?"

"Certainly. Sergeant Danowski will see to your needs and he'll stay with you as long as you're here."

"Thank you, Colonel. Come along, Agent Madison. We've got work to do."

Danowski led them to a nearby office, with Tish marveling at how deftly Hanson had calmed Royce and at the same time avoided a showdown with her.

Jed burst into Hanson's office a moment later.

"Did Wilkins tell you what our boys did?"

"Briefly."

"When those crazy kids heard the bomb go off, they grabbed the house guns and rushed downstairs. Wilkins was the only survivor of the explosion and he was wounded. Four attackers were firing at him and they were just about to finish him off when our boys opened fire, killing two of them. The remaining two ducked and tossed a grenade at Wilkins. He tossed it back and got them, but our boys saved the day. If they hadn't responded, those rags might have massacred everyone in the building. They'll make great Marines someday."

Hanson got a haunted look. "I once hoped our children would have a safer world than ours. Maybe they'll do a better job than we did."

"We've done a pretty good job so far, Sam, considering the world we inherited."

This was a new, philosophic side of Jed that confirmed Hanson's belief that he was officer material, and he certainly had a better view of the big picture than Royce. He smiled to himself at the thought of Royce, who. like so many ego-driven small minds, conceived of the military as automatons, who blindly obeyed their leader's orders, without thought. *It's a pity,* he mused, *that there was such a misperception of the warrior, who was a dwindling minority in the military. If only America understood that democracy was preserved by the willingness of citizens to risk their lives for their nation.* He sighed and Jed assumed he was still thinking about the boys.

"Don't worry, Sam. They're alright. It's too bad we can't give them medals."

"Let's just make sure they know how much we admire and respect them."

"You got it, boss."

They looked at each other, sharing a special moment of pride in their sons that didn't require any further comment. Then it was time to get back to business.

"What's the situation at the apartment building?"

"We removed our dead and the rags and sent them to the morgue. I left a squad there and the rest of the platoon is patrolling the area. There's no major damage to the building and we sent for a replacement door. Police officers are on the scene and they're keeping the street clear. That's about it. What happened here?"

"Al organized the defense and they killed all but two of the attackers. Do not mention to anyone that we have prisoners."

Jed nodded knowingly. "Yes, Sam."

Hanson, confident of Jed's support, continued. "Jefferson and the rest of his guard detail were killed in the bomb blast, but after the initial attack, the only one seriously wounded was Carstairs and he should make it."

Jed smiled tightly. "Let me guess. He grabbed his rifle and headed for the action, right?"

"You know Carstairs."

"There aren't too many of us old timers left, Sam," Jed mused.

"That's what they pay us for, Lieutenant."

There was a knock on the door. Al entered, followed by Muzzetti.

"Hi, boys," she said cheerfully. "We survived another rag attack." Muzzetti looked horrfied at her casualness with her commander.

"It's alright, Muzi," Hanson said lightly. "She'll be exactly the same when she's the first woman Commandant of the Corps."

"She? She? I'll remember that sexist remark when I'm commandant and post you to Iceland."

"We don't have a base in Iceland," Hanson joked. "Now let's have your report."

She was immediately serious. "All the wounded have been treated and they elected to return to duty," she said with pride. "Carstairs and Wilkins were taken to the N.Y.U. Emergency Room and the resident assured me that their wounds weren't life threatening. The explosion destroyed the main gate and we're rigging a temporary barrier. You'll have to consider later what to replace it with. Our two prisoners are shackled to the beds in separate sergeant's rooms and we put Muzi's two prisoners there also. We're going to run out of room soon."

Al was silent for a moment, then looked directly at Hanson.

"The FBI is going to be a problem. That Agent Madison is determined to find out if there are any prisoners."

"I know, Al. She wants to take them into federal custody."

"We can't let her do that, sir. Even if the feds don't release them immediately, we'll never find out who sent them."

"Suggestions, Al?" he asked.

"Let me and Jed interrogate them."

Hanson turned to Muzzetti. "You didn't hear that, Muzi."

"No, sir."

"This is your chance to withdraw, Muzi, before you become an international criminal. No one will hold it against you if you leave."

"If you don't mind, sir, I want to stay. I like the company."

"Welcome aboard, Muzi," Jed said warmly. "I thought you looked like a criminal. I hope you know that this can get ugly."

"I didn't join the Corps for a beauty contest, Jed." Muzzetti replied.

Hanson gave them a minute to appreciate the feeling of camaraderie, then turned to Muzzetti.

"Report, Muzi."

"The V.A. hospital is secured. I had a squad search every nook and cranny for possible attackers. I don't know how, but the vets killed nine attackers, yet only two of the vets received flesh wounds …"

"God is an ex-Marine," Jed interjected, and they all grinned at the irreverent comment.

"All of the royal's bodyguards were killed, except one. Three royals were killed, five were wounded and fifteen attackers were killed. I brought the two prisoners here."

"Did anyone see them?" Hanson asked.

"No, sir. And I instructed my troops not to mention them to anyone. I left a squad in the building with Lieutenant Bernstein in charge and the rest of the platoon is patrolling the area."

"Bob did good here, boss, before I sent him to the hospital," Al added.

"Thanks, Al. Well done. All of you," Hanson commended. "Now we've got to find a place to stash the prisoners, before the FBI finds them. Any ideas?"

They discussed the problem for a few minutes but couldn't come up with an immediate solution. Hanson ruled out suggestions of the barracks, the police station, or the Armory and explained why they weren't practical. Danowski had drifted in and was listening intently.

"I have a suggestion, sir."

"Shoot, Ski."

"Put the rags in one of our Strykers, secure them and have them driven around the Enclave, until the FBI leaves. Then move them into the basement here. There are rooms down there that haven't been used for years. The walls and doors are thick. Security won't be a problem and nobody ever goes down there, except for scheduled maintenance. We could keep them there as long as necessary."

Al, Jed and Muzzetti were nodding enthusiastically.

"See to it, Al," Hanson ordered.

"Yes, sir."

"Have Lieutenant Danowski assist you."

"Yes, sir," Al said, while Jed and Muzzetti nodded approvingly at the battlefield promotion.

"Thank you, sir," Danowski said fervently when he got over the sudden surprise. "You won't regret it."

"Let's hope you don't," Hanson replied.

37

K YLE WASN'T QUITE CALM ENOUGH to call Mavis. He and Tyrone had been sitting in the lobby on a bullet ridden sofa, waiting for the medics to evacuate Wilkins. They had been holding their pistols, not sure what to do with them, until Kyle slipped his into his waistband and Tyrone followed suit.

"We should have armed ourselves a long time ago, K. This is cool."

He stared at Tyrone, trying to assess his aplomb.

"We just killed two men, Ty. How do you feel about it?"

"Like I did what had to be done. What about you?"

Kyle thought for a moment. "I did what had to be done. I'm not happy that I killed someone, but I know what I did was right, and I'll do it again if I have to. I just don't want to feel casual about killing."

"Neither do I, bro. I guess we're part of the team that does the dirty work now."

"Our Dads might have something to say about that, Ty."

The medics were finally evacuating Wilkins, who had refused to go until he told everyone how the boys came charging into battle, guns blazing, and saved his ass. He had praised the boys extravagantly, first to Hanson, then to Jed, who were both horrified that their sons were in a gun battle and could have been killed, yet proud that they saved the lives of Wilkins and the residents.

Hanson had left Jed to take the after-action report from Wilkins, who, after describing the explosion and his retreat into the lobby, repeated over and over, "I was hit in a couple of places and the rags just about had me, when the boys arrived like the cavalry to the rescue."

Jed told him to take it easy, instructed the boys to come to headquarters later to make their report, and left. As the medics carried Wilkins out, he yelled loudly, "They did the Corps proud today."

Tyrone smiled at Kyle.

"I guess we're not going to school today, bro. What do you feel like doing?"

Kyle looked at his watch and it was only 9:30 in the morning, yet it seemed like the explosion was hours ago.

"Let me call Mavis. She was worried about me."

Mavis was in science class and she had been fretting, not sure if Kyle was alright. She excused herself to the obviously annoyed Mr. Singh.

"I'm sorry, Mr. Singh. This is very important. My boyfriend was in an explosion this morning and I've got to know that he's alright."

"You're excused, Ms. Carver, but please don't make a habit of taking calls in class."

"I won't. Thank you, Mr. Singh."

As she rushed into the corridor, Jennifer smiled at her encouragingly, yet thought to herself, *I just hope that boy is dead, rather than wounded. If he's dead, we can have a nice funeral and after an appropriate period of mourning, while I console the bereaved, we can get on with our lives.*

Mavis sighed with relief when she heard Kyle's voice.

"You're alive. I've been so worried. I didn't know what to do. Are you hurt? You're not saying anything. Are you alright?"

"You haven't given me a chance," he replied.

Then they both laughed.

"Tell me what happened," she said.

He carefully considered his response. "There were some terrorist attacks in the Enclave this morning …"

"I know that," she interrupted impatiently. "I want to know what happened to you."

"If you'll let me finish, I'll explain."

"Go ahead."

"A group of Arabs attacked my building. Two of our Marine guards were killed when a car bomb went off at the entrance. Sergeant Wilkins was wounded and retreated into the lobby, fighting off the attackers. Tyrone and I helped him and …"

"You were in the fighting?"

"Yes."

"Are you alright?"

"Yes."

"I was so worried about you. I knew you were in danger."

"It's over now," he said reassuringly, "and I'm alright."

"Will I see you after school?" she asked.

"No. I have to help clean up here, then go to Marine headquarters and make a report. I'll call you later and we can talk, and I'll see you tomorrow."

"Do you have to go?"

"Yes. I love you, Mav."

"I love you, Kyle."

Tyrone had been politely pretending not to listen during the phone conversation.

"You're really stuck on that girl, aren't you, bro?"

"I never felt this way before, Ty. One minute loving her is the most wonderful feeling ever, the next it's an anguish, worrying if she feels the same way. Did you ever feel like that?"

"It sounds like the crush I had on Al for years," Tyrone said lightly.

Kyle laughed and Tyrone joined in.

"You know I had a crush on her also," Kyle admitted, "but this is different."

"I know bro, I was kidding. I can tell how serious it is. I'll help you any way I can."

"Thanks, Ty."

"I've had enough of hanging around the O.K. Corral. Let's get out of here. We can keep in touch with headquarters by cell."

"Sure, Ty."

Kyle looked outside and said, "It just started raining and it's cold out. Let's get changed. Whoever's ready first knocks on the other's door."

"You got it. Are you bringing your pistol?"

Kyle thought quickly. "I guess we better, just in case they want to see them at headquarters."

"Yeah, bro. And it wouldn't hurt to be armed if the rags aren't through for the day."

•   •   •

Carver had been on the phone since shortly after the explosions. First, he spoke with the mayor's office, then to Dr. Van Meer, followed by brief conversations with the parade coordinators. Everyone had been hypertense. It took a good deal of effort to keep them calm, from making snap decisions to cancel the parade. He repeated the same reason to each of them, "This may not have anything to do with the parade. Colonel Hanson and the FBI are investigating the incident. We should wait until we hear from them later this afternoon before reaching a conclusion."

The most difficult person had been Mayor Ramirez's executive assistant, a tightly wound woman who reflected the uncertainty of the administration when faced with complex problems. He had been particularly soothing, reassuring her that they had time to wait for the results of the investigation and they didn't have to make a decision until late in the day.

The most disturbing call was from the secretary-general's office. An under-secretary from Libya demanded to know what happened, then didn't listen to his explanation. Carver was forced to endure an arrogant lecture that concluded with Khalid el-something threatening to send in peacekeepers if America couldn't maintain order in the Enclave. Then he disconnected.

It had taken an effort not to reply harshly, but his position as a department head required, among other chores such as the practice of medicine, that he play punching bag to the U.N. He wondered, not for the first time, if he had made a wise choice in becoming a department head with all its political responsibilities. He shook his head throwing off the distracting thought but filed it away for consideration at a more quiet time. He made some notes about who to talk to later, then called Mei. She confirmed that she and her team were at the V.A. hospital tending the wounded and he told her that he'd be there soon.

•   •   •

Hanson was about to leave for the N.Y.U. emergency room to see Carstairs and Wilkins, when Danowski buzzed and told him that Royce and Madison were waiting to see him. He suppressed his irritation and put on a professional look.

"Send them in, Ski."

Royce was bubbling over with enthusiasm for the anticipated press conference.

"I have a draft ready, Colonel Hanson, with a short statement from you. I think you'll approve of it."

"I'm sure I will, Agent Royce, but I don't think it's a good idea for me to appear in uniform. If you do it alone, it will assure our U.N. friends that the military isn't manipulating anyone."

Royce visibly inflated.

"Well we wouldn't want to give any negative impressions. I think I can manage without you."

"I'm confident you can. Now if you'll excuse me, I have to visit my wounded in the hospital."

"Of course, Colonel," Royce crooned. "I arranged the press conference for noon, in case you change your mind."

Hanson headed for the door, but before he could get there he saw Tish nudge Royce.

"One moment, Colonel," Royce said. "Agent Madison informed me that you may have some prisoners. If so, they would be under our jurisdiction."

"My people are still sorting out the bodies. If we have any prisoners, we'll turn them over to you. You might want to have a team on call in that eventuality."

"I'm convinced you have some prisoners," Tish blurted.

"What makes you think that, Agent Madison?" he asked coolly.

"Just a very strong feeling."

"Are you accusing Colonel Hanson of concealing prisoners?" Royce asked.

Tish looked flustered. "No. I just want to be certain that everything's done properly."

"That's very commendable in a young agent," Royce said, "but until you have evidence to the contrary keep your suspicions to yourself."

Hanson nodded curtly and walked out the door. Al was waiting for him, flanked by Gunny Le Beau and two snuffies.

"What did Le Beau do now, Al?"

"Nothing sir. I want him and his detail to accompany you and Tico, until we're certain that there won't be any more attacks."

Hanson snorted. "Then he'll be with me for the rest of my life." He turned to Le Beau. "You're the ugliest babysitter I've ever been stuck with."

"That's alright, sir," Le Beau retorted. "You're not the prettiest baby I ever minded."

The two snuffies waited for the colonel to ream the brash gunny and tried not to look surprised when Hanson just grinned and said, "Let's go."

Tico was waiting at the curb with the Humvee and Hanson signaled him to follow them for the one block walk to the E.R. The two snuffies went first, walking alertly, as if they were in Indian country.

"The kids did pretty well today, didn't they, Cajun?" he said to Le Beau.

"Yeah. Some of them ain't kids anymore, sir."

Hanson left the snuffies in the Humvee with Tico, and he and Le Beau went inside. They could hear the commotion from the waiting room. Carstairs and Wilkins had the E.R. in an uproar. The resident rushed to him and complained bitterly that Carstairs was disrupting everyone with loud demands for beer, and Wilkins was molesting the nurses.

"Those soldiers seem to think this is a playground. Could you please tell those wild men this is a hospital and we require order and quiet. If they don't behave I'll have them removed and they can seek treatment elsewhere."

Hanson gestured to the agitated resident to follow him to an empty cubicle, and he reluctantly complied.

"I'm sorry that my men's behavior has disrupted the E.R. I'll have a word with them. They were just in a gun battle and are experiencing the after-effects."

"That's no excuse for their hooligan behavior."

Hanson looked at the young man in exasperation. "They defended our fellow citizens against Arab terrorists," he said softly, "who may come here next, when you'll need those men to defend you."

"That's not the point," the resident insisted.

"Then let me be blunt. If you attempt to remove them, I'll have you out of here so fast your head will spin and your next job will be treating penguins in Antarctica." The resident was open-mouthed, and Hanson added, "By the way. Those men are Marines, not soldiers. You better learn the difference if you want to get along with them."

Carstairs and Wilkins were in adjacent cubicles, jawing away, having a great time. When they saw Hanson, they both saluted, looking absurd, lying on their backs in hospital gowns.

Carstairs was high on painkillers and bellowed, "Hi, ya, Colonel. I cheated General Death again. I bet I've got more purple hearts than any cook in the history of the Corps."

Hanson found it difficult to keep a straight face and turned to Le Beau. "What do you think, Gunny? Is he right?"

"I don't know, sir. I think he'll have to get shot a few more times before making that claim."

"Whadda ya mean, Le Beau?" Carstairs protested. "This'll be my third gong. No other cook got three hearts."

"I know he is the big liar, sir," Le Beau said, "but he may be right this time."

"Who are you calling a liar, you frog eater. Wait'll I get out of here."

"Take it easy, Carstairs," Hanson counseled. "I wouldn't want you to hurt Le Beau." They all laughed at the absurdity of that. "Now I want you to quiet down and stop calling for beer. They need quiet here, so they can take care of their patients."

"Yes, sir," Carstairs muttered. "You're no fun, sir."

Hanson turned to Wilkins. "And you, Wilkie. Stop assaulting the nurses. They're professional personnel with important jobs to do and you're interfering with their duties."

"Yes, sir. Carstairs is right, sir."

"About what?"

"You're no fun, sir."

"Once you two are on your feet and out of here, I'll see that you get leave and can have some fun. Until then, conduct yourselves properly and obey the doctors and nurses."

"Aye, aye, sir," they said in unison.

Hanson walked away, followed by Le Beau. The resident ran after them.

"Colonel. Colonel."

"Yes?"

"I'm sorry about our misunderstanding. I didn't realize that they're like children. You won't have any more complaints about them."

He knew that the doctor was trying to make amends. He said pleasantly, "They're not children, Doctor. They're adults who just escaped death and they'll face it again. That's what they're paid for. Don't you hospital folk do silly things to deal with stress?"

"Why, yes."

"Then just talk to them if there's a problem. They'll cooperate. Now have a good day."

When they got outside, Hanson signaled Tico to follow them, then called Al, as the two snuffies jumped out of the Humvee and led the way.

"Have the prisoners been moved yet, Al?"

"They're just getting ready to leave the motor pool now, sir."

"Good. Have Jed take a Humvee with them, as if they're going on patrol. As soon as I get there I'll have Gunny Le Beau give the FBI a complete tour of the installation."

"Why Le Beau?"

He answered loudly enough for Le Beau to hear him. "Because he can be charming and pretend to be dumb."

Le Beau obligingly put on a dumb expression. Just as they got to the barracks entrance, a Humvee crossed First Avenue at 29th Street, followed by a Stryker, with Jed in the turret. He saw Hanson and nodded as they drove away. Hanson was relieved that the prisoners wouldn't be discovered by the FBI but felt the too familiar ache of losing someone he could love. He knew the gulf between him and Tish couldn't be bridged.

•　　　•　　　•

Royce was so engrossed in preparing for the press conference that Tish took it upon herself to investigate if there were prisoners. She started questioning the privates and corporals. They all said they knew nothing about prisoners and referred her to their sergeants. She made a particular effort to put one corporal, a young black girl, at her ease in the hope of creating a bond between them. The girl refused to respond and declared, "I don't know about no prisoners."

"They're human beings," Tish exclaimed in exasperation. "They have rights. Don't you care about that?"

"I care about my family, my squadmates, the Corps, my country and God. I don't care about anyone who attacks them."

Tish's efforts to question the sergeants were equally unproductive. They all knew nothing. Tish attempted to question the officers she encountered, but they also knew nothing. She complained bitterly to Al.

"Lieutenant Kent. I'm not getting the cooperation I require."

"Take it up with Colonel Hanson," Al replied coldly. "He'll be here in a few minutes."

Tish managed to control her annoyance until she saw Hanson, then blurted impatiently, "Your people aren't cooperating with my investigation."

"What seems to be the problem?"

"Everyone I question doesn't seem to know anything."

"Maybe they don't. Maybe there's nothing for them to know."

"I demand access to any part of this facility that I want to inspect."

He nodded curtly. "Gunny Le Beau. Escort Agent Madison through the installation. Let her see whatever she wants."

"Yes, sir. Are you ready, ma'am?" Le Beau asked.

"I also want to question anyone who may have some knowledge of prisoners," Tish added.

"Let Agent Madison question anyone she cares to."

"Yes, sir."

Tish turned to Le Beau. "Do you know anything about any prisoners, Sergeant?"

"No, ma'am. And it's Gunnery Sergeant, ma'am."

"See what I mean?" she said. "That's the kind of response I'm getting."

Hanson shrugged. "Gunny Le Beau. After Agent Madison concludes her inspection, escort her out of the installation."

"Yes, sir."

Tish glared at him and stalked off, back stiff, radiating anger. She knew that even though she might see him again officially, their personal relationship was over.

38

CARVER DECIDED TO WALK to the V.A. hospital so he could see the effects of the attacks for himself. At the Marine's apartment building, the clean-up crew was hard at work; and, except for the doorway, the damage appeared minimal. The Marine headquarters and barracks building was intact, but parts of the front gates were gone and there was a lot of rubble near the entrance. Emergency crews were still at work, so he didn't go in.

He was pleasantly surprised that there was no exterior damage at the V.A. hospital. After he showed his credentials to the guards he went inside to the vet's ward, where the signs of the gun battle were evident. Bullet holes pockmarked the walls and ceiling in the corridor and perforated the door. The sounds of raucous revelry blared loudly. He opened the door to a wild scene of doctors trying to coax the drunken vets back to bed so they could be examined.

The vets with functional hands and arms were attempting to fondle the women doctors, while fending off the men doctors. The armless and quadriplegic vets were propped up in bed, sucking through straws on liquor bottles, and their bodies were draped with rifles and grenades. It was the most surreal sight he had ever seen.

Mei had been losing control of the situation and was running out of options to calm the vets when she saw Carver.

"Thank god you're here. These characters are going berserk. I don't know what to do with them."

"Alright. I'll see what I can do." He picked up a bedpan and banged on it with a metal water pitcher, until he got everyone's attention. "Good morning, gentlemen. Congratulations on your victory."

This elicited a loud cheer and shouts of, "Thanks, doc,"

"You shoulda been here,"

"We kicked Arab ass, Doc,"

"The Corps rules."

Carver responded calmly, "I wouldn't have been much use to you. I'm a doctor, not a soldier."

"We're Marines, doc. Not soldiers," one vet yelled.

Another chimed in, "Hey. Let's make Doc an honorary Marine."

This met with general approval and a chorus of, "Yeah"s, and "Right on"s.

"Thank you, gentlemen. I'm honored to accept." But before they could respond he quickly continued, "But let's do it another day, after we've had a chance to examine all of you. Your health is very important to us. Now if you'll all go back to your beds, Doctor Yi and her team will help you."

Mei watched in amazement as the unruly vets quietly returned to their beds.

"I don't know how you did it, Carv, but thank you. I was at my wits end."

"Glad to help. Check the wounded first and get the liquor away from those quadriplegics before they go into cardiac arrest. And ask the vets to put their weapons away, before there's an accident."

"Yes, Carv." She looked around to be sure no one could hear her. "My team was scheduled for a visit at nine a.m. If we got here early we might have been caught in the battle."

"I'm glad you weren't," he said with relief.

"These guys may be crazy," Mei whispered, "but what they did was incredible. All of them are handicapped in some way, but they fought off a surprise attack and none of them were killed or seriously wounded."

He nodded agreement. "Take good care of them, Mei. They deserve it."

"Yes, Carv. Will I see you tonight?"

"I'll try. You know I want to. A lot happened today and I may not be able to get away. I'll call you later." He waved to the vets and left.

•   •   •

Tish finished her inspection of the Marine barracks and headquarters, burning with frustration. She had no hard evidence that she was being deceived about prisoners, except a gut feeling. She had inspected the sergeant's rooms and found bloodstains, which aroused her suspicions. But Le Beau explained that they had brought wounded Marines there during the firefight. Some of the basement doors were locked and she demanded access.

Le Beau sent for keys without making a fuss and she found the rooms unoccupied. She finished looking everywhere else, then checked each of the headquarters' offices, including closets. But when she got to Hanson's office, Danowski would only let her look from the doorway. This led to an unpleasant confrontation. She insisted on looking in the closet, which he reluctantly agreed to. The closet was empty and she started towards the desk to inspect Hanson's papers, but Danowski stopped her.

"This room is off limits, Agent Madison," he said, and refused to let her continue her search.

She suppressed her annoyance.

"I could return with a warrant," she warned.

"Then do so, Agent Madison," he replied calmly, then requested Gunny Le Beau to escort her to the street. So she left, angry at her failure and convinced that Hanson had thwarted her.

The sky had turned very dark when Tish got outside. She was surprised to see Royce holding his press conference on the sidewalk, rather than in the building's conference room. She moved close enough to hear him, but not so he would notice her until he was finished.

He concluded his prepared statement by saying, "The terrorist attack this morning was a cowardly assault on innocent women, children, and hospital patients. All the resources of the FBI will go into the efforts to bring the planners and organizers of this dastardly deed to justice. Questions?"

Tish saw several reporters snicker at his use of "dastardly". They were interrupted by the departure of most of the fire trucks and Royce waited patiently for the last one to leave. The crew of Ladder 7 finished their final inspection, said goodbye to the Marine guards, then drove off.

"Sorry for the delay, folks," Royce said. "I'll take your questions now." There was a lengthy silence that was becoming embarrassing, until he finally got a question.

"*New York Post.* Do you know who the attackers were and where they came from?"

"Not yet. We're still in the first stages of our investigation. I will notify you when I have further information. Next."

"*The Times.* Do you think this is a matter for the International Criminal Court?"

"It might be, once we establish the identity of the terrorists and their country of origin."

"That's not what I meant," *The Times* said pompously. "I was referring to the Marines who killed so many people today."

Royce shook his head. "There seems to be some kind of misunderstanding," Royce replied righteously. "The Marines were attacked. They defended themselves and innocent civilians. Besides, as you well know, the United States of America is not a signatory of the International Criminal Court treaty."

The tone of the interview suddenly changed and Royce was put on the defensive.

"*Newsweek.* Don't you think that it's a disgrace that the United States is the only country not to sign the I.C.C. treaty?"

"That's not my call. I'm a Special Agent of the FBI, not a politician."

"*Village Voice.* You're a law enforcement official. You should have an opinion. Every American who believes in law and order should want that treaty. Why should America be the only exception?"

"You may recollect, ladies and gentlemen of the media," Royce said placatingly, "that President Beaumont approved the treaty, but congress overrode her decision. I'm sure that if she had been re-elected, she would have advocated for the treaty. Now we'll have to wait and see how the new administration deals with the problem."

"We can guess how war-mongering Plant will act," the *New York Times* said cynically.

"That's not fair," Royce asserted. "Give the president-elect a fair chance before condemning him. Now thank you all for coming. I've got to get back to the investigation."

●　　　●　　　●

Shortly after Tish left, Hanson called Al and told her to report to him immediately. She arrived a few minutes later than he expected.

"Sorry for the delay, boss. I was just making a final sweep of the installation, to be sure we didn't have any uninvited guests."

"Good. Ski. Wait outside and be sure we're not disturbed."

"Yes, sir. Can I help in any way? I'll do whatever has to be done."

Hanson realized that Danowski knew what he was planning and wanted to be involved.

"Thanks, Ski. I appreciate that. Dismissed."

"Yes, sir."

Al waited until the door closed behind Danowski.

"He's a good kid, Sam."

"I beg your pardon, Captain. He's not a kid. He's an officer and gentleman, even though not yet by an act of congress."

"Did you say captain?"

"Yes. You need the rank to be battalion exec. I'm promoting Jed to first lieutenant and he'll command Alpha company. We need a platoon commander for heavy weapons. Any suggestions?"

"Let me think about it. I'll get back to you later today."

Hanson studied her intently until she finally asked, "Are you already regretting promoting me to captain?"

He grinned. "No, Al. You earned it. I want to make you aware of the possible consequences of interrogating the prisoners illegally ..."

"I know what we're doing, Sam."

"Please don't interrupt me, Captain."

"Yes, sir."

"Agent Madison is convinced we have prisoners ..."

"What's with her, Sam? I thought you two ..."

"That doesn't matter now. If we're discovered, we could be charged, arrested and tried for war crimes."

"But we're not signatories to the International Court," she protested.

"Valerie wouldn't protect us. Anyone involved will be at great risk, so if you want to change your mind ..."

"I know what has to be done, Sam. So does Jed."

"Glad to have you aboard, Al."

"Thank you, sir."

"Select a guard detail to assist us. Make sure they're volunteers who understand what they're getting into."

"Yes, sir."

"Anything else you can think of?"

"No, sir."

"Then have Jed bring the prisoners in and make sure nobody sees them, then lock them up in separate, secure rooms in the basement."

Half an hour later, Al reported to Hanson, "The prisoners are secured, sir, and await your disposition."

"Good. Do you and Jed have a plan?"

"Yes, sir. Good Marine, bad Marine. Jed will start all of the interrogations and grow increasingly angry and threatening. If he gets the information, fine, otherwise I'll intervene and try the soft, save yourself pain approach."

"What questions?"

She looked at him wryly. "You know as well as I do. Name of country or organization that sent you. Names of individuals who sent you. Is there anything else we need to know?"

"It would be nice if they implicate the U.N., but the powers that be would never allow that hot potato to become public. I'll visit each prisoner with Jed and encourage them to talk. This way, if there are any repercussions, the chain of command will be clear."

"You don't have to do that, Sam."

"Of course, I do. I'm not going to let the lower ranks be punished for war crimes, the way it happened in Vietnam and Iraq, while the commanders who were responsible got away with torture and murder. Clear?"

"Yes, sir."

"Then let's go."

•   •   •

The basement was dank and filthy from years of neglect. The obsolete heating system was fueled with coal, so black dust pervaded the air. Jed had posted guards at the basement entrances, all lifers, who had lost comrades in Arab attacks. He met them at the door of the first temporary cell and signaled Al to move out of sight before he opened it.

"Ready, Sam?" she asked.

"Yes. I'll talk to them first, then leave them to you."

The first prisoner was a sullen Saudi, who refused to even look at Hanson, let alone acknowledge his questions and it was obvious that he was hard core Al Qaeda. The second one was almost a clone of the first, except he stared at them with fanatic's eyes, full of hate. The third prisoner was noticeably afraid and Hanson assured him that if he talked, no one would know and he'd be treated well.

The fourth prisoner was the one from the hospital who had cursed Hanson. He glared rabidly at Hanson and unleashed a string of profanities.

Hanson smiled wolfishly and said in Arabic, "No one knows you are here and no one will help you. Your insults will be on your own head," and he turned to Jed and said in English, "This one will require special treatment," then he walked out, leaving Jed with the prisoner.

Al was waiting at the end of the hall.

"How did it go, sir?"

"We've got three hardcases and one weak one. The one in the fourth cell cursed me at the hospital, but he may be vulnerable."

"Don't worry, Sam. We'll get at least one of them to talk. What'll happen to them afterwards?"

Hanson looked around to be sure no one but Al could hear him.

"That's up to General Griffin and his bosses. If the prisoners talk and we can bring them to public trial, we'll see what happens."

"If they don't talk?"

"Then they're of no use to us and an embarrassment to our country. We'll try them and sentence them here and they'll probably get a bullet in the back of the head, KGB style. Can you live with that, Al?"

"Yes, sir. But I don't think it's a good idea for us to try them. That would make it official and it could be used against us."

"What do you suggest?"

"If they're of no further use, we should just execute them."

"Could you do it?"

"Yes, sir."

He knew that she and Jed were hard core enough to do whatever had to be done, so he just nodded and said, "We'll decide later."

Jed stood over the cursing Arab who finally looked at him. "Why do you, a black man, a third world brother, serve these white devils?" the Arab asked.

"You shoot, bomb and kill my comrades, regardless of their color," Jed replied. "You are not my brother."

"I am a true believer. I do Allah's will against the crusader infidels, who are the enemies of Islam."

"The Koran forbids the slaying of innocents, so you are the infidel."

"You have read the Koran?"

"Many times. But enough idle talk. You will answer my questions when I come back."

"And if I don't?"

"Then you will suffer before you die, and you will not see paradise."

"Who are you to tell me that, a nigger who blindly slaves for his masters?"

Jed shook his head in disgust. "Just a moment ago I was your brother, but now you insult me. You who have strayed from the true path of Islam would not understand. I will leave you for now. Think, so that you may repent of your sins against Allah."

"I curse you and the mother who bore you."

"When I return, you will speak differently," Jed promised.

Jed joined Al and Hanson in the corridor.

"What do you think, Jed?" Hanson asked. "Which one is the best bet?"

"The first two are a waste of time, except if we had several weeks."

"We only have a few hours," Hanson said.

"That's what I thought. The third one is scared, so I'll concentrate on him ..."

"That's the one that Sam mentioned," Al said.

"The fourth one is also a possibility," Jed continued. "He talks tough, but it's all surface. He'll crack under pressure."

Hanson nodded. "When I talked to him at the hospital he was defiant, but he got very nervous when I said in front of the fanatic one that he had informed for us in the past. I think you have the two to work on."

"What about the other two, Sam?" Al asked.

"They're of no further use. Let me talk to General Griffin about them."

Hanson moved away from them, then called Griffin.

"We have four prisoners, sir. Two may talk, the other two are useless. Can we dispose of them?"

"Can you do it so it appears they died in the firefight?"

"Yes, sir."

"Do it then. Let me know as soon as you learn something."

"Yes, sir."

Jed and Al had been waiting for him attentively.

"We'll shoot the two with M16's," Hanson instructed, "then the guards can take them to the morgue. List them as died of their wounds. I'll do the shooting."

"No, Sam. Al and I will do it," Jed insisted.

"Then you'll be as guilty as I am of crimes against humanity, at least in the judgment of the U.N."

"They're terrorist scum who wanted to kill our families. I can live with that," Jed said.

"If there was any justice in the world," Al added, "we wouldn't have to do this."

"Alright," Hanson agreed. "Don't talk to them, just shoot them. Three or four shots each, in the belly and chest, so it doesn't look like an execution. Are you both sure you're up for this?"

"Yes, Sam," Jed replied.

"What happened to KGB style, Boss?" Al quipped.

"Never mind that. We're at great risk here and we'll get no support from Valerie if this were to become public."

"She's such a wimp," Al snapped. "Why can't she see that we're in a life and death struggle for our country's survival?"

"There's a short and a long answer to that, Al, but it doesn't matter now. We're on our own. Let's go," Hanson ordered.

"Aye, aye, sir," Al and Jed said.

It only took a few moments to shoot the two prisoners. Al opened the first door and Jed did the shooting. Jed opened the second door and Al did the shooting. Then Jed called the guards and announced loudly, "These two died of their wounds. Bag them and take them to the morgue."

Less than five minutes later the bodies were gone and Jed went to the third cell.

"Stay somewhere to the side, where he can't see you until he's scared enough," Jed told Al, "then intervene."

The prisoner was cowering in a corner when Jed approached. He stood over him menacingly and he could see the man shivering.

"What were those gunshots?" the man quavered.

"We found some of your fellow terrorists and they chose not to surrender."

Jed was tempted for a moment to say they were executed and put a further scare into the already frightened man. He thought better of it when he considered that they might keep this one alive for testimony.

"What about the other prisoners?"

"They died of their wounds. Now no one knows you're here. No one will save you. If you do not answer my questions I will torture you."

"What will you do to me?" the man asked tremulously.

"I will start with my knife and cut off your toes, then I will cut off your feet …"

"I will tell you whatever you want to know."

Jed looked triumphantly at Al. "I think he's ready for you."

Al took out her notebook, then said softly to the prisoner, "You are wise to talk to us. This way he will not hurt you."

"Do all Americans speak Arabic, even the women?"

"Many of us do. Now what is your name?"

"Adel Rashid."

"What country are you from?"

"Saudi Arabia."

"Are you a member of Al Qaeda?"

"Yes. But they made me join."

"What do you mean?"

"They came to my village and told our sheik that two of our young men must go with them. I and my good friend Safwat were picked. He was killed in a training accident. I did not want to be a jihadist. I was a religious student. But I had no choice. Either I obeyed or they would kill me."

Al realized that she had a willing informant. "If we protect you and give you a new safe life in America, will you answer whatever we want to know?"

"Yes. Oh, yes."

"I will leave you for a few minutes and return with a video camera for your statement."

"Please take the savage one with you."

Al made a quick decision. "I am his superior officer. I will order him not to harm you."

"Thank you, kind lady soldier."

Al related the substance of the interrogation to Hanson.

"So you think he'll spill his guts?"

"Yes, sir. He's terrified of Jed."

Hanson called Griffin. "We have one prisoner who's willing to talk, if we protect him."

"Will he name names?"

"Yes, sir."

"Does he know what happened to the other prisoners?"

"No, sir."

"What do you think, Sam? Will he be believable to the FBI?"

"I think so, sir. Captain Kent will take his statement on video. Then, with your approval, I'll notify the FBI to collect him."

"What about your remaining prisoner?"

"He'll die of his wounds, sir."

"That seems to cover everything … This may give you another chance with Tish."

"I don't think so, Charlie. Our moral and philosophical differences are too great. She thinks even terrorists are entitled to a fair trial. She just doesn't understand we're fighting for survival."

"Too bad, Sam. I liked her."

"So did I, Charlie. I'll call you when the video session is over, sir."

39

THE NO LONGER NEEDED PRISONER was disposed of like the others, after Al finished videotaping the remaining prisoner's statement. Hanson called General Griffin and informed him of the results.

"This was a well-designed operation they were preparing for months, sir. The prisoner named names that go all the way up to the Saudi intelligence directorate. Their main objective was the V.A. hospital and the Saudi royals. The attack on the barracks was to keep us occupied and they thought there wouldn't be any resistance at the apartment building once they killed the guards. We were lucky there, and they were unlucky when they hit the vets at the hospital first. What do you want us to do with the prisoner and videotape, sir?"

"Make a duplicate copy of the tape and put it in a safe place, call Agent Royce and tell him you found one survivor, who you interrogated and videotaped."

"They'll be pissed, sir."

"Well, we can't always make everybody happy, Sam."

"What about the parade, sir?"

"Did we learn of any threats?"

"No, sir."

"Proceed as planned."

Doctor Carver was understandably nervous about approving the parade right after the terrorist attack.

"I'm just not sure, Sam. What if something terrible happens tomorrow? I'd never forgive myself."

"I understand, Carv. May I speak bluntly?"

"Of course."

"What happened today was planned months ago. It's doubtful that it's connected in any way to the parade."

"Can we be sure of that?"

"No. But nothing will happen tomorrow spontaneously. We're too well prepared for that. If there's a long-term operation targeting the parade, we are as ready as possible for it."

"What are the chances that there'll be an attack tomorrow?"

"The same as they were yesterday. It's up to us to decide whether or not to go ahead with it."

Carver took a deep breath. "What do you recommend?"

"General Griffin thinks we should go ahead. So do I."

"And if something terrible happens?"

"Then it'll be one more affliction on our poor country, Carv."

"Alright. I'll notify everyone involved that the parade should go on. Do me a favor, Sam."

"Sure. What?"

"Triple check our security."

•   •   •

Danowski informed Hanson that Agent Royce, Agent Madison and two guard types were outside and that Royce wanted to see him before taking custody of the prisoner. Hanson wasn't in the mood for what he knew was coming, but he had to resolve any questions about the prisoner. Royce was his usual grating self.

"I see that your secretary is a lieutenant now. Promotion comes fast around here," he commented sourly.

"Lieutenant Danowski isn't a secretary. He's our supply and logistics officer."

"Whatever. You notified us that you had a prisoner."

"That's correct."

"Yet you told us earlier there were no prisoners."

"At that time there weren't."

"Then where did this one come from? Did you conjure him up from thin air?"

"No, Agent Royce. There was another group of four terrorists who opened fire when we discovered them during a sweep of the V.A. hospital. There was one survivor, who we'll now turn over to you."

"You mentioned that you questioned him?"

"That's correct."

Tish had been listening impatiently and blurted, "Who gave you the right to question him?"

Hanson looked at her calmly. "We had to find out if there were any more terrorists hiding nearby who might be planning attacks."

"Did you torture him?" she demanded.

"Of course not. We're Marines, not savages."

"Why don't I believe you?"

"We've had him in custody for less than an hour. That's hardly enough time for torture."

"I wouldn't put it past you," she said bitterly.

Hanson turned to Royce. "Your young assistant is worked up over nothing. When you collect him you'll see that there isn't a mark on him."

"Then why did you make the videotape?" she exclaimed triumphantly.

"It was to insure there would be a record of the attack, if the FBI gave in to pressure to do a cover-up."

"Are you implying that we won't do our jobs?" Tish asked shrilly. Hanson shook his head.

"Agent Royce. I don't have time to listen to her hysterical accusations …"

"Why you …"

"That's enough Agent Madison," Royce ordered. "Colonel Hanson. We would like to take our prisoner."

Hanson keyed the intercom.

"Lieutenant Danowski. Escort the FBI to our prisoner. Have them sign for him, then escort them out of the building."

As they left, Tish turned back and whispered, "You haven't heard the last of this."

He just shrugged.

•   •   •

Carver was getting tired of reassuring members of the parade committee and government officials that the terrorist attack had nothing to do with the parade. He managed to remain patient, despite responding to the same question over and over, "No. I can't guarantee that there won't be an incident tomorrow." The most difficult conversation was with Mayor Ramirez's frenetic assistant. She kept demanding to know if he would assume responsibility if anything went wrong.

"Don't try to avoid your responsibility. It's not my decision. I gave you my recommendation and I'll repeat it one more time. I think we should go ahead with the parade, but it's the mayor's call. Have I made myself clear?"

"Well, you don't have to take an attitude," she said tartly. "I'm just trying to look out for the mayor."

"Then tell him not to be so wishy-washy and make a decision. I'll wait to hear from you."

He was still sitting at his desk brooding when Mei came in.

"Why so glum, oh exalted man of medicine?" she asked playfully.

He managed a weak grin. "I'm just a little worn down from the complications of the job. I actually used to treat patients. Now I negotiate with politicians. That wasn't what I had in mind when I became a department head. I thought I'd be able to innovate new treatments. Instead, I spend time kissing ass."

"Once you get used to the system you'll find a way to do the important things," she consoled.

"I wish I could be sure of that."

"Take my word for it."

"What makes you so certain?"

"I've seen you with patients and staff. You're a great doctor and a great teacher, and you'll do a superb job as a department head."

"Why thank you, Doctor. It's nice to be appreciated."

"You're welcome, Doctor. Perhaps you could show your appreciation tonight at my place."

This time he really grinned. "I'd like that."

"Good. Now for a lighter moment. Today was the first time that the Arab royals didn't grab my ass."

They both laughed.

"I'll try to arrange regular terrorist attacks on their ward."

Carver and Mei chatted companionably until it was time for the staff meeting to review the events of the morning. Mei summarized the activities of her team at the V.A. hospital.

"We treated two vets for minor gunshot wounds. One of them was a paraplegic and he didn't even know that he was shot. We certified that all the attackers on the vet ward were dead. We treated five Saudi royals and one bodyguard for gunshot wounds. The bodyguard was severely wounded, but no vital organs were hit and we evacuated him to the E.R. Between the Marines and the bodyguards all the attackers were either killed or died of their wounds shortly after. The Marines took two of their wounded to the E.R., one from the apartment building and the other from the barracks. I'm pleased to report that our staff performed their duties optimally."

"Thank you, Doctor Yi," Carver said. "Well done to all of you. Barring emergencies, all of you take the rest of the day off," which brought a cheer. "But keep your pagers on," he added, which brought a groan.

Carver was feeling much better when he got the call from the mayor's assistant and she confirmed the parade was on. He was relieved that the problem was resolved and was pleasant to the woman for the first time, which probably caused the note of suspicion in her voice.

She had even called all the involved officials, except for those in the Enclave, leaving notifications up to him. He reminded her that he'd see her on the reviewing stand in the morning and said goodbye amiably. He called Hanson and officially confirmed that the parade was on and expressed his final anxiety, "I only hope nothing goes wrong, Sam."

"We'll do our best."

"We better. Do you want me to call Captain Lonigan and Colonel Warrington?"

"I'll do it, Carv. I have to review last minute procedures with them anyway."

"Will I see you on the reviewing stand, Sam?"

"Probably not. I'm going to march with the troops for a ways, then I'll be in my communications vehicle. But I'll stay in touch."

Carver called Doctor Van Meer, soothed his apprehensions, then decided to take the night off and spend it with Mei.

•   •   •

Warrington was an old trooper and responded tersely, "We'll be ready."

"Good. Why don't you have dinner with me at our mess hall tonight at 1800? We'll talk more."

"See you there, Sam."

Hanson couldn't help thinking back to how the National Guard used to be looked down on by the full-time soldiers, until the Iraq war, when they did their share and paid with their blood. Lonigan was a bit more worried.

"What do you think, Sam? Was today step one, with something bigger planned for tomorrow?"

"I have no information either way to reach a conclusion. Does the police anti-terror unit have any intel?"

"Nothing solid. They promised to stay in close communication and call me instantly if anything shows up on the screen ... What's your gut feeling, Sam?"

"I just don't know. Today they attacked soft targets, with virtually no security systems. Tomorrow we'll have metal detectors, bomb dogs, access will be restricted through well-staffed checkpoints, and our people will have a heightened sense of alertness. The only thing that worries me is the individual suicider. It's almost impossible to defend against the loner who's willing to give his life ... Have dinner with me and Colonel Warrington at our mess hall, at 1800 and we'll review the final arrangements."

"Sure."

Hanson buzzed Danowski. "Ski. Have Al, Jed and Muzi come to my office and you join us. By the way, we need a sergeant to replace you as chief clerk. Let me know your recommendation." While he waited, Hanson went over the security plan for the parade for the hundredth time.

The only area that he wasn't completely confident about was Central Park, adjacent to Fifth Avenue. As he traced the topography of the park on the map, he saw too many places that afforded cover to a potential sniper or RPG attack. He made a written note to ask Lonigan to review protective arrangements with the park precinct. He knew that the FBI and police SWAT teams were securing all buildings that faced the parade route, but he couldn't help brooding about how many there were and how many vantage points they offered. Even with the heightened security alert, it was impossible to check every last office and apartment.

A horrible thought occurred to him and he mentally kicked himself for not spending enough time considering the department stores and shops on Fifth Avenue. He made another note to review the procedures in place.

Al, Jed, Muzzetti and Danowski came in to find him pacing up and down in agitation.

"What's wrong, boss?" Al asked.

"We may not have thoroughly covered the department stores."

"Everybody has to go through checkpoints to get there," Jed responded.

"What about the night before?" Hanson asked.

Al pulled out her security plan, turned to the appropriate page and read aloud, "FBI agents will sweep all commercial buildings that front Fifth Avenue, before the parade commences. But it doesn't say what time."

Hanson immediately called Agent Royce.

"This is Colonel Hanson. Some of the parade officials are concerned that the department stores and other commercial establishments could be infiltrated by terrorists the night before the parade. They would like your agents to sweep the buildings this evening, then monitor traffic through tomorrow." He listened to the reply, nodding.

"I know it's a huge job, but think about how we'd look if someone snuck into Saks with a bomb … You're right. We've got to do it."

Al looked at him admiringly when he disconnected.

"You'll become a diplomat yet, boss."

"That'll be the day. I want all of you to review the plan again. We'll meet here at 2000 for a final review. Dismissed."

•   •   •

Kyle and Tyrone wandered aimlessly around the Enclave for a while, trying to digest the events of the morning. It had been a roller coaster ride of exhilaration, fear, savagery, commitment to action and satisfaction at having met the test. They didn't talk much, sharing the unique aftermath of combat and the glorious feeling of being alive.

They knew that they had passed the plateau of teenager and had suddenly become young men. It was even reflected in their walks, which were no longer childish displays of their manhood. Instead, they showed a new confidence, with an attitude of self-possession that indicated they were secure in their abilities and didn't have to prove anything.

They reached Madison Square Park and Tyrone said, "Remember the last time we were here, on U.N. Day?"

Kyle nodded.

"Wouldn't it be great if we could lead a platoon in the parade tomorrow?" Tyrone murmured.

"Someday, bro."

"Do you really think so, K?"

"Yes. I do."

It started to rain and the mild November day became chilly.

"Let's go to the E.R. and see Wilkins," Kyle suggested.

"Do you think they'll let us in?"

"Sure. We can always claim we're family."

"I'm a little dark for that," Tyrone quipped.

"You know what they say, Ty."

"What?"

"There's one dark secret in every family."

They burst out laughing and a floodgate of emotion built up since the attack in the morning burst open.

"I wasn't thinking about anything in particular when we went downstairs this morning," Tyrone confided. "I knew we'd have to fight and I was ready."

Kyle nodded agreement. "There didn't seem much to plan. I just reacted."

"Me too, K. Now that you've had time to think about it, how do you feel about killing your first man?"

"The same. I did what had to be done. I'm just glad they tossed the grenade at Wilkins, not us."

"Me too," Tyrone said. "We didn't have any cover and it might have wasted us."

"Let's hope we're always that lucky," Kyle said fervently.

By the time they reached the E.R. it was pouring. They ducked inside the First Avenue entrance, shaking off water like bedraggled pups. The triage nurse, barricaded behind the plastic shield, asked in a bored voice, "Yes?"

"We're here to see Sergeant Wilkins," Kyle answered.

"I hope you brought some tranquilizers, or some rope to tie him down. He's pinched every nurse in the hospital, including me," and she rubbed her backside for emphasis.

"Why don't you give him some tranquilizers?" Tyrone asked.

"I don't dare. I'd give him enough to kill him. Go right in," and she buzzed the door open.

Wilkins was delighted to see them and yelled at Carstairs, who was asleep on painkillers, until he woke up.

"Here they are, Carstairs. The boys who saved my life, then everyone else's in the building."

"Couldn't you have been a few minutes later," Carstairs growled, "then I wouldn't have to listen to him."

Wilkins and Carstairs exchanged insults for a while, only pausing for Wilkins to brag about the boys to the doctors and nurses. When the boys had enough of the two Marine's grumbling, they said goodbye and headed for the mess hall.

It got very quiet when the boys walked in. Every Marine they passed stood up and saluted them. By the time they reached the officer's table almost everyone in the room was standing at attention.

Al stood up, saluted the boys, then said, "My fellow Marines, I give you the true heroes of today; Kyle Hanson and Tyrone Davis." The shout of "Hoorah" was almost deafening, then Al continued, "There's no award or decoration that we can give you, except our thanks and well done."

The "Hoorah" that followed was even louder than the first one. Hanson and Davis bursting with pride, stood and saluted their sons, then hugged them fiercely. Neither fathers nor sons noticed what they ate that evening. Although Hanson was reluctant to end the special moment, he knew he had a final security review meeting.

"I hate to break this up, boys, but we have work to do. I'd like you to spend the night at the barracks."

Jed nodded agreement. The fathers hugged their sons again, then fondly watched them leave the mess hall, congratulated by all the Marines, especially the N.C.O.'s with families in the apartment building.

Danowski led the boys to Carstair's room, which they were surprised to find was clean and neat.

"Feel free to use Carstair's refrigerator and tv," Danowski offered, "but don't touch his liquor."

"We won't, Ski," Tyrone promised.

"That's Lieutenant Danowski to you, boot," Danowski said.

The boys snapped to attention and said in unison, "Yes, sir."

"At ease, men," Danowski said, eyes twinkling. "Just thought I'd try my rank out. Goodnight."

When he left, Tyrone remarked, "Everyone becomes a hard ass in the Corps," then added, "Quite a day, huh, bro? Feel like talking about it?"

"Yes. Just let me call Mavis first."

"That'll be an all nighter," Tyrone teased.

"No. I just want to let her know I'm alright and tell her that I'll see her tomorrow."

When he reached her, Mavis was delighted to hear his voice and would have happily chatted all night, but Kyle said they'd talk tomorrow. Mavis said she'd be sitting with her father on the reviewing stand in front of Saint Patrick's Cathedral and they arranged to meet there.

40

A T 0545, DANOWSKI WOKE HANSON, who was sleeping in an empty sergeant's room.

"Morning, sir. It's time. Here's some coffee." It was still dark outside and the security lights were barely visible in the heavy rain. "A helluva day for a parade, sir."

"At least it's not freezing, Ski. Anything new to report?"

"Not really, sir. Just before he left last night, the FBI profiler complained bitterly that he waited around all day and only a few officers and sergeants attended his briefing."

"Did you explain that we had a few emergencies earlier?"

"Yes, sir. He seemed to think his lecture on identifying terrorists took priority over fighting them."

Hanson chuckled. "I guess we lost another friend at the FBI What else?"

"The sergeants and officers will be getting up at 0600. The rest of the troops at 0615. Breakfast is scheduled at 0630. I suggest we have inspection in the squad bays and assemble in the mess hall, rather than the courtyard."

"Good idea, Ski. Most of us will spend a good part of the day getting soaked."

The mess hall was bubbling with energy when Hanson got there. The atmosphere was a curious mix of sorrow for the Marines killed yesterday, satisfaction that not one terrorist escaped, and grim determination to show the flag today. The knowledge that they'd be marching in the rain didn't dampen their enthusiasm.

The troops sat in squad units this morning and Hanson looked them over as he made his way to the officer's table. They looked smart, fit, ready to go and a feeling of pride washed over him. His officers stood when he got to the table.

"As you were." He looked at Al. "Anything new to report?"

"No, sir. No new developments since last night. You asked me to remind you to get the up to the minute police intel from Captain Lonigan."

"Thanks, Al. I'll call him after breakfast. Jed."

"Yes, sir?"

"Put two more squads around the lighting ceremony at Madison and 23rd Street."

"Yes, sir."

"Al. Convey my respects to all officers, N.C.O.'s and troops and tell them well done yesterday."

"Yes, sir."

After breakfast, the kitchen staff removed the tables and the battalion assembled. Since they were less than a half-strength battalion and it was a large room, they managed to muster, despite being crowded.

Hanson walked through the ranks, followed by Al and Danowski, and nodded approval at what he saw. He was pleased that Muzzetti's company was looking good, although they weren't as experienced as Jed's. Gunnery Sergeant Le Beau, standing at attention in front of his platoon next to Lieutenant Bernstein, saluted smartly.

"Question, sir?" Hanson nodded. "Do we have to march in our ponchos, sir? We'd rather have our arms free, just in case anything happens."

"Does the rest of your platoon feel that way, Le Beau?"

He saw Le Beau nudge Bernstein, who replied, "Yes, sir."

"Good idea, Cajun." He turned to Muzzetti. "What about the rest of the company, Captain?"

"They feel the same way, sir."

"Then let's march without ponchos, Captain."

"You're marching with us, sir?"

"At least part of the way, Captain, but I'll stay out of your way, behind the colors."

"It's an honor to have you march with us, sir."

"Thank you, Captain Muzzetti. Captain Kent."

"Yes, sir?"

"Dismiss the battalion."

"Yes, sir."

Hanson made all the last-minute calls, including the Department of Defense parade hot line, which had received what sounded like crank threat calls. He spoke at length to Lonigan, who had nothing new to report. Every security unit that wasn't already in place would take up positions by 0700.

There was nothing new on the threat board and, except for the weather, conditions seemed favorable. Lonigan grumbled a bit about the rain making it easier to conceal things under raincoats, but they both agreed that as long as the checkpoints screened everyone thoroughly, there shouldn't be a problem.

"Let's stay in close touch all day, Mike," Hanson suggested. "I'll be marching with the troops for a while, but my Humvee will be alongside and I'll respond quickly to any problem."

"Only a jarhead would want to walk around in this downpour," Lonigan quipped.

"It's better than pounding a beat and shagging apples from some helpless storekeeper," Hanson retorted.

They both laughed companionably.

"Let's hope there's no trouble today, Sam."

"Amen."

"I'll be moving around the parade area, Sam, and I'll always be nearby."

"Come march with us, if you feel like it."

"No, thanks. The only marching I do is when my wife orders me to bed."

"Later, Mike."

Tico was waiting for him with the Humvee, along with the two Marines Al had assigned as bodyguards.

"Where to, Boss?"

"The Armory on 25th Street."

The soldiers at the entrance saluted Hanson and as he went inside he heard them questioning Tico about the terrorist attack. Warrington was concluding his final security review, and he introduced Hanson to his officers.

"Anything new we should be aware of, Colonel Hanson?"

"Just some crank threats, but after yesterday's attacks we should all be extra alert."

"I'm sorry for your losses, Sam. Please convey our regrets to your troops."

Hanson listened carefully to the last few minutes of the briefing and couldn't think of anything that was overlooked. He saw that the commander of the company that would march, Captain Rollins, was bursting with pride at being selected. His respect for the officer grew when he said, "Colonel Warrington. I didn't issue live ammo to two of my squads because they're mostly green kids."

"I'm sure they weren't happy about that."

"No, sir."

"Well, we all know what we have to do. Dismissed."

The officers saluted and left, some casting awed glances at the legendary Marine.

"Coffee, Sam?"

"Yes."

"I appreciated your calling me 'sir' in front of my officers."

"The man and the rank merit it."

"Thanks. Anything more you can think of that we can do?"

"Not really. Where will you be today?"

Warrington's eyes twinkled. "Marching with my troops, of course."

Hanson grinned. "Why doesn't that surprise me? I'll be marching also. Let's keep in close touch. The Marines are marching in the middle of the parade, so we can respond in any direction. Your company is near the front. Can you deploy them in squads on Fifth Avenue when they reach the end?"

"Yes. Any reason?"

"After yesterday, the more security coverage we have the better. If you can send another platoon to the park for the lighting ceremony, that would be helpful."

"Can do. Did you know that this is the shortest parade in the history of Veterans Day?"

"Tell you the truth, Oliver, this is my first time. I've been so involved in crises that I'm looking forward to just marching for a while. What's the significance of the lighting ceremony?"

Warrington got a faraway look.

"Actually it's called the Eternal Light Monument Ceremony, commemorating the end of World War I ... When I got back from 'Nam' in '72, everybody despised the military."

"You must have just been a kid."

"I was eighteen and I had already seen death and an incredible waste of resources. I couldn't afford college, so I joined the Guard and they paid my tuition. I discovered that I really liked the Army, so later I went to O.C.S. and became an officer ...

"Since the 69th is the closest military unit to the parade, we're always involved. My platoon was at the lighting ceremony in '73 and people actually spat on us. I never forgot that. It made me realize that too many people don't understand how violent the world is. They're so sheltered, even spoiled by the protection our country gives them, that they can't accept our failings."

Hanson nodded. "That may change now that we're the victims of foreign aggression."

"I hope so, Sam, before it's too late for our poor beleaguered country."

A staff officer interrupted Warrington for a minute with a problem, then he continued.

"The lighting ceremony includes speeches, the laying of memorial wreaths and a ceremonial firing of a rifle salute. Disabled vets get priority seating, but they didn't let Vietnam vets sit until Reagan was president.

"Then Valerie, after her draft-dodger husband's heart attack in 2012, banned them again in the Washington parade. That woman has absolutely no sense of shame."

"At least she'll be gone in two months and hopefully Zach will rebuild the military."

"If the U.N. lets him, Sam. They're lording it over us now ... November 11th through November 17th, is supposed to be 'National Veterans Awareness Week'. There should be educational efforts in elementary and secondary schools to teach students about the contributions and sacrifices of veterans, but it's not happening. We should also be teaching our kids that in a world filled with nationalistic and ethnic hatreds, we have to be strong to survive."

"You're preaching to the choir, Oliver."

Warrington shrugged. "Sorry, Sam. It still bugs me. We better get going."

Tico drove Hanson to Madison Square Park, where he did a walk-through, then they slowly drove up the complete parade route, ending at 59th Street and Central Park.

Hanson was reasonably satisfied with the security arrangements he observed and hoped that good efforts and communication would provide a thorough shield. It was still raining hard when he got back to the barracks at 0830. Al reported that Jed's company would take their positions by 0900, and Captain Muzzetti's company would form up at 0930 and reach 23rd Street by 1000.

"Good. What about the metal detectors and bomb dogs?"

"Metal detectors are in place and dog units will be on station by 0900."

"Good. Anything new?"

"No, Boss. Why don't you relax for a few minutes. Everything's under control."

"I forgot how, Al. If all goes well today, I'll relax tonight."

Al looked around to make sure no one could hear her.

"Ready for a laugh, Sam?"

"I could use one about now."

"Carstairs called me and asked if he and Wilkins could join the parade on their stretchers."

They both laughed.

"I hope you told him no."

"You should have heard him gripe."

"I can imagine. I'll be in my office."

Danowski kept him informed of the departures of various units to their duty stations, and he talked at length to General Griffin who was going to march in the Washington D.C. parade.

"I didn't want to tell you this earlier, Sam, because I knew it would aggravate you."

"Go ahead, sir."

"I'll just read it to you. 'By executive order from the White House, November 10th, 2015. To all units marching in the Veterans Day parade in Washington, D.C. There will be no carrying of weapons or participation by armed vehicles. This day is meant to commemorate the service of veterans. Any display of weaponry could be considered offensive to the peaceful community of nations'."

"I know you're not kidding, sir."

"I wish I were. Valerie persuaded most of the foreign embassies to attend the parade and she doesn't want to appear warlike, especially since the ambassador from the peace-loving People's Republic of China is attending."

"I thought I heard it all from this administration," Hanson growled. "If she had won another term, she'd have us equipped with sling shots and pea shooters."

Griffin laughed heartily. "Thanks, Sam. I needed that. I've got to go. Let's hope for an uneventful day."

•   •   •

At 0945 everything seemed under control and Hanson decided to go to the lighting ceremony. He had Tico drive down First Avenue, then across 23rd Street to the park. Muzzetti's company was forming on 23rd Street and all the security posts were alert, so the morning was shaping up efficiently. The ceremony was already underway and the Ambassador to the U.N., Will Blunt, was speaking about the need for peace and cooperation in the global village.

Hanson tuned out the fine sentiments that he felt would have been more appropriate on U.N. Day, and thought about the executive order banning weapons in the Washington parade. He shook his head in disgust at what he considered to be another act of political cowardice by Valerie.

He noted that Blunt had finished and Mayor Ramirez was speaking and listened for a few moments, but it was the usual collection of platitudes. He surveyed the crowd and spotted Agent Royce and Agent Madison escorting Ambassador Blunt to a limousine. Tish saw him and elaborately looked the other way.

The rain gradually diminished, and fog rolled in, cutting visibility to fifteen or twenty feet. Hanson could still hear the speakers, but they were just vague shapes in the distance. He called Al and told her about the latest problem, then instructed her to contact all units and urge them to be extra alert. He called Lonigan, who was on the other side of the memorial.

"This is all we needed, Mike. I put my people on heightened alert. Can you think of anything else we can do?"

"I'm placing more officers on Fifth Avenue, but that's about it. Did you ever read that poem by Carl Sandburg about fog?"

"No. I read his Lincoln book at the Academy. I didn't know he wrote poetry. You're full of surprises, Mike."

"Yeah. I read a book or two. He wrote, 'The fog creeps in on little cat feet'. I don't know what made me think of that, but I hope it creeps out soon."

"Me, too. We don't want the fog of war today."

There didn't seem to be anything that Hanson could do in the park, so he decided to join Muzzetti's company. He called Al and told her that's where he'd be if something else developed. It took him a few moments to find his Humvee in the thickening fog.

Then they circled the park, creeping along at five miles per hour, with virtually no visibility, despite their powerful headlights. He had a sudden idea and called Lonigan.

"Can you get someone to turn on the streetlights?"

"That's a good idea. It's either Public Works or the Department of Traffic. I'll get someone on it. I see that a lot goes on under your helmet, Sam."

"It does more than keep the rain out. How soon do you think we can get the lights on?"

"That depends on who's in charge. If it's someone functional, it might be as simple as pushing a button. Otherwise …"

"I get it. I'll have all military vehicles turn on their headlights. Have your officers use their flashlights."

"Jawohl, Herr Oberst."

"Sorry, Mike. I was thinking quickly."

"That's alright. I'm glad someone is."

When they got to First Avenue and 23rd Street, he told Tico that once they started marching to drive ahead of the company but stay close. Muzzetti's troops were standing at ease as he pulled up and he heard Le Beau growl, "Once we start, the only sound I want to hear is your boots hitting the ground in perfect cadence. Clear?"

"Oorah, Gunny," the troops responded.

One voice called out, "But we can't see nothin', Gunny."

"Marines ain't got to see when they're marching," Le Beau answered. "If there's any of that sloppy Army shit I'll personally discuss it with you later."

"Oorah, Gunny," they repeated.

He found Muzzetti conferring with his officers.

"Everything all right, Muzi?"

"Yes, sir. We're raring to go."

"Good. If anything happens, have your platoons form a perimeter, until you know what to react to."

"Yes, sir."

"Unless I give you a direct order, you're in command, no matter what happens."

"Yes, sir. You can rely on us, sir."

"I'm beginning to learn that, Muzi. Carry on."

For the moment, Hanson had absolutely nothing to do for the first time in weeks. He stood there in the fog feeling completely cut off from the rest of the world, even though he knew it was an illusion. The normal sounds of city life were absent. He could hear the faint voices of the sergeants getting their troops into line, but there was no yelling or cursing, just quiet efficiency.

His mind wandered to thoughts of battles fought in the fog and the chaos and confusion that ensued, especially in the pre-mechanical age, when armies groped towards each other and clashed blindly. He recalled that Gustavus Adolphus was killed in the fog by friendly fire, following his great victory in the battle of Leützen, in 1632. The death of that great commander changed the outcome of the Thirty Years War, as well as the political map of Europe. He wryly asked himself, not for the first time, 'how could fire be friendly'?

He felt the same familiar sense of detachment that preceded a battle, when all preparations were done and all that was left was waiting. He knew from bitter experience that not everyone responded well to the tension of waiting, with death ahead, eager to collect the legions of the slain. He felt fortunate that so many of his people had been tested in the furnace of conflict and had emerged confident in their abilities to deal with the mission.

He had to smile at the thought of the mission today. What was the mission? To march from here to there, then return to the barracks after an uneventful day? Or would there be something more consequential? Another terrorist attack that would surprise a military still yearning for a decisive, massive assault on an enemy army, so they could proclaim victory, a la World War II? He shook his head to dismiss these unwanted thoughts and just waited patiently, thoroughly enjoying the brief isolation of the concealing fog.

41

A LIMOUSINE WAS WAITING for Carver and Mavis in front of their house, instead of the usual Lincoln Town Car. When they got in, Dr. Van Meer's cordial welcome indicated their growing friendship. Once they were seated, Jennifer opened a bottle of champagne and poured for everyone, ignoring her father's disapproving look.

"Oh, poo, Daddy. If we're going out in this miserable weather to a parade that we won't be able to see in this fog, at least we have to celebrate."

"What do we have to celebrate?" Van Meer grumbled.

"Lots of things," she replied sweetly. "First of all, I'm with two of the greatest doctors in the world who are helping to hold our country together …" Carver watched in amusement as Van Meer melted with the flattery. "Second. I'm with my best friend. I could go on with lots of reasons, but I think you get the idea."

Van Meer shook his head. "You're a manipulative devil, just like your mother, but she is special and so are you. Well, let me offer a toast. To good friends and stability, so we can practice medicine."

They murmured, "Hear, hear," clinked glasses and drank, enjoying the unexpected treat as they drove uptown.

The limo stopped at the security post on Madison Avenue and 51st Street. Van Meer grew uneasy while the bomb-dog team inspected the vehicle. He became even more nervous when the dog sniffed him suspiciously.

"Is that absolutely necessary?" he asked the security officer. "I'm afraid of dogs."

"Don't worry, sir," the young naval Lieutenant said reassuringly, while he checked out the two girls. "Lizzie's a sweetheart. She wouldn't hurt a ladybug."

"Would she bite me if she smelled explosives?"

The officer smiled and shook his head. "Oh, no, sir. She doesn't bite. If she smells explosives she'll freeze and point. Then we bite," and he growled mock ferociously.

"Now, if you'll be kind enough to step this way and pass through the metal detector, I'll have someone guide you to the reviewing stand. Even though it's in front of Saint Patrick's Cathedral, it could be hard to find in this fog. Your limousine will be waiting for you here, whenever you're ready to leave."

"Thank you, young man. Are you a Marine?" Van Meer asked.

"No, sir. Did I sound that dumb?" Jennifer giggled and didn't see Mavis glare at her. "I'm a naval officer, sir. Have a nice day."

"What a nice young man," Van Meer remarked, as they walked towards Fifth Avenue. "Do you think all the military officers are that bright?" he asked Carver.

"I don't know about all of them, but I've been working closely with the Marines lately and I've been very impressed with their abilities."

This earned him an approving smile from Mavis, who slipped her arm through his.

"Now that you mention it, Carv," Van Meer remarked, "that Colonel Hanson seems quite capable. He handled that Halloween incident very efficiently. I hope you expressed our appreciation. He might have made a good doctor."

Carver grinned. "It might amuse you to know that he said I might have made a good Marine. I'll be sure to tell him what you said."

Their guide said loudly, "Watch your step ahead, ladies and gents. There's a slab of concrete sticking up and you don't want to trip."

"Thank you," Carver said.

"Are you a naval officer?" Van Meer asked.

"No, sir. I'm a Marine corporal."

"Did you resent what that officer said about the Marines?"

"No, sir. Those Navy types spend all their time sailing around, doing nothing, so they envy us, because we do things."

Van Meer didn't know who to believe, so he just murmured, "I see."

Their guide left them at the reviewing stand, where an usher led them to their seats in the dignitary section and gave them cushions.

"The parade should be here in a few minutes. If you can't see anything at first, you'll hear the band that leads the way. I'm Reggie and I'll stop by periodically to see if you need anything."

Carver and Van Meer greeted some nearby notables, including Mayor Ramirez and Ambassador Blunt. Jennifer was busy flirting with one of Blunt's aides, so Mavis took the opportunity to call Kyle. When she heard his voice, a warm glow rushed through her.

"I can't hear you. Mavis? Is anything wrong? Speak to me, or I'll disconnect and try you."

"Don't hang up, Kyle. It's me."

"Why didn't you say something?"

"I was so happy to hear your voice that I couldn't speak. I want to see you so badly. Are you coming to the reviewing stand?"

"Yes. I just have to pick up Tyrone and we'll be there soon."

"Hurry. I miss you."

"I'll rush."

•　　　•　　　•

Tyrone wasn't quite ready and Kyle urged him to hurry.

"Move it, bro. Mavis is waiting for me."

"Be cool, K. The more you make a woman wait, the more she'll appreciate you."

Kyle laughed derisively. "Where did you get that from, a fortune cookie?"

Tyrone put on a look of mock indignation. "Is that any way to talk to your elders?"

"If you don't get your ass in gear, Ty, I'm going alone."

"Patience, little mantis. I'm ready. I just wanted to be sure I looked my slickest for any honeys I might meet."

"Alright. Alright. Let's go."

They raced down the stairs and got outside just as a Humvee pulled up. It was one of the Marine security patrols and the boys knew the sergeant leading the detail.

"Hi, Sergeant Vasquez. Are you heading uptown?" Kyle asked.

"Yeah. Where are you boys going?"

"The reviewing stand at Saint Patrick's. Can we catch a ride with you?"

"Get in. We just stopped by to check on things after yesterday's attack. You guys did fine. We're all proud of you."

The boys got in and as they started to drive, Tyrone whispered, "You know, Nita, I had a crush on you ever since Bahrain."

She looked at him sternly, then bopped him on the head.

"Button it, sprout, or I'll tell your dad."

He held up his hands in surrender. "You got it, Sarge."

•   •   •

The Marine Band had been tuning up for a while and some of the Marines in Muzzetti's company, in the concealment of the fog, kept making derisive remarks about their musicianship. Hanson casually listened without paying much attention, just occasionally noting a particularly witty comment. The only one he actually smiled at was one young Marine's quip, "You old bugle heads should get with it. If you had any real rhythm you could play hip-hop music, then I could rap while we march."

This caused a burst of laughter that drowned out the musicians indignant, unamusing replies. Le Beau's voice penetrated the laughter.

"Steady, boys and girls. We don't want to get into disagreements with the musicians."

This brought an even bigger outbreak of laughter and a young female Marine yelled out, "You call them musicians, gunny? My high school band played better than that."

This evoked a howl of outrage from the band members, but before it could go further the band got their marching orders and stepped out smartly, playing their first marching tune.

Less than a minute later, a parade marshal told Captain Muzzetti that it was time to go. He passed the word to Le Beau, who called, "Company, ten-hut … Forward, march."

The company moved out at a lively pace and Hanson got into step behind the colors, moving at an angle so he could keep the Humvee ahead of him in view. It didn't take long to fall into the peculiar rhythm a cohesive unit can produce that leads to a rapture of the march. He was possessed by that unique feeling of belonging to an extended body of troops that provided an almost spiritual nourishment to its obedient parts.

The fog had thickened even more, so visibility was limited to a few feet in any direction, but he could sense the presence of the troops behind him. The sound of their purposeful marching had a calming effect, and he gave himself up to the flow of the march, which began to ease his built-up tensions.

Even though he couldn't see very far, Hanson could hear the thud of the boots hitting the ground in unison and the sound of the stirring march music with unusual clarity. The Marine Band started a march that he hadn't heard since his Annapolis days, and his thoughts drifted back to that earlier period of innocence and expectations. The image of one of his classmates flashed into mind, a passionate young man who urged his fellow midshipmen to aspire to be poet-warriors. After graduation, the youngster had, at his own request, been posted to the Bureau of Ships.

In an indulgence that he hadn't allowed for years, he thought back to his Academy roommates. Tommy and Rick were the live wires in the room. They did everything full speed ahead and damn the obstacles. They invented more pranks, broke more rules, got more demerits to work off then any midshipmen in the class. They were hotshots and naturally wanted to be jet fighter pilots. Tommy crashed and burned in flight school training at Pensacola. Rick went to American Airlines after the carrier force was downsized. Vinnie was the most laid back of the four roommates. He was sober, calm and deliberate, which made him eminently suitable for nuclear missile subs, because 'Boomer' duty required a cool head and clear judgment. He was beached in 2008, when most of the 'Boomers' were decommissioned. The last Hanson heard of him, he was working for an insurance company in Kansas, as far from the sea as he could get.

Hanson hadn't noticed when the column turned right onto Fifth Avenue and picked up the pace. They were approaching 27th Street and he made a mental note not to lose track of what was going on. He called Lonigan, who reported no incidents and no new intel of possible threats. Hanson told him they should talk every ten to fifteen minutes, then disconnected.

His brief serenity was shattered a minute later when he got a call from Sergeant Vasquez informing him that Kyle and Tyrone had been detained at the security checkpoint on 51st street, for carrying concealed weapons. For the hundredth time he wondered if it had been a mistake not to have ever spanked his headstrong offspring.

"I told the FBI puke," she explained, "that the boys were temporarily authorized to carry weapons by our commanding officer, because of a terrorist threat to their lives."

He shook his head, not sure whether to praise or rebuke her, then the father in him took over.

"Let me talk to the FBI puke, Sergeant."

"Yes, sir," she said happily.

"This is Colonel Hanson. Who am I talking to?"

"Agent Vitelli, sir."

"What seems to be the problem, Agent Vitelli?"

"We detained the subjects when they passed through the metal detector carrying concealed weapons."

"First of all, Agent Vitelli, they are not subjects, but members of the Marine Corps family. They were in the company of a Marine detachment, weren't they?"

"Yes, sir. But they don't have the legal right to bear arms."

"Do you know who I am, Agent?"

"Yes, sir. You're one of the security coordinators of the parade."

"You would make my job easier if you give the weapons to the Marine Sergeant and we will assume responsibility for them."

"I don't know if I can do that, sir."

"Why not?"

"Because there's been a violation of the law."

"Agent Vitelli. You can either cooperate with us and you'll receive a commendation for your alert attention at a checkpoint, or I'll have you taken into custody by my Marines for interfering with our security procedures."

"Can you do that, sir?"

"You don't want to find out, son."

"In that case, sir, I'll release the detainees and their weapons to your sergeant."

"Thank you, Agent Vitelli. Please put the sergeant on."

Hanson considered whether to rip the boys a new one on the phone or wait until later. He decided there were too many people around, so when Sergeant Vasquez put Kyle on the line he told him to obey her orders and have her call him as soon as they were past the checkpoint.

The column had just passed 34th Street and the fog was still too thick to see very far. For a moment Hanson wished he could just march undisturbed in it for a while, but duty took over. He called Lonigan, who had nothing new to report. Warrington called him a minute later and reported that his troops had reached the end of the parade route and his squads were deploying to Fifth Avenue.

"It felt great, marching with the troops," Warrington exclaimed.

"I know. I'll see you tonight at the party at the Waldorf."

As the column was approaching 42nd Street, his cell rang and it was Sergeant Vasquez, now in charge of Kyle and Tyrone.

"Sorry for the delay, sir. The FBI puke kept having me sign release forms. I hope you don't mind, sir. I signed them Chesty Puller."

He couldn't suppress a laugh. "Doesn't that sound a bit sexist, Sergeant?"

"I'm secure in my womanhood, sir. I'll escort the boys to the reviewing stand and make sure they don't get into trouble. Should I give them their guns?"

"No, Nita. Well done."

"Thank you, sir."

•　　　•　　　•

All the distinguished guests had arrived, and some were sipping hot coffee, while others were nipping at flasks of stronger beverages. The high-ranking military officers were huddling as far as they could from Ambassador Blunt, as if to escape the taint of the soon-to-depart Beaumont administration that they felt had so weakened the American military. No foreign ambassadors or dignitaries were present, which was an indicator of the country's fallen prestige.

Blunt's protective detail was so casual that it suggested the liberal democrats had become so ineffectual that even the usual crazies didn't want to assassinate them. Agent Madison had nothing to do until the ambassador left, so she struck up a conversation with Mavis. Some of

Madison's bitterness seeped out when she mentioned her frustration in dealing with the Marines and it alerted Mavis.

"The most difficult of them all is that Colonel Hanson," Madison muttered. "And his son is a cowboy, just like his father. Did you hear about their wild west shootout yesterday?"

"I don't know Colonel Hanson well," Mavis replied coldly, "but I like him and I'm in love with his son. So please go complain about the Marines to someone else," and she turned her back on the astonished Tish.

Mavis, still fuming, put her arm around Jennifer.

"Did you really mean it when you said I was your best friend?"

Jennifer kissed her on the cheek affectionately. "Of course. You'd be a perfect friend, if you'd only get over your infatuation with that boy."

Mavis shook her head emphatically. "You don't understand. I can't help myself. I think about him night and day. If I can't have him I'll die. It was love at first sight, just the way it happens in books."

"Maybe it isn't infatuation," Jennifer admitted grudgingly. "It could be first love, which can be exciting, but you're still a girl. What are you going to do, elope with him?" she teased.

This lightened the mood and they both laughed.

"I know we're too young for marriage or living together, but if I was older that's what I'd do."

"At least you haven't lost your mind completely," Jennifer said. "I suggest you see him for a while, to see where it goes. But you should also date other young men, just for a contrast. After all, he's not much older than you. His feelings could change after a while and he could break your heart."

"He'd never do that." she protested.

"How can you be sure?" Jennifer retorted.

"I just know it."

Mavis sensed Jennifer's growing impatience and changed the subject.

"Did you hear about what Kyle and Tyrone did yesterday morning?"

"No. But knowing that brash Tyrone I could guess."

"Not this time. You heard about the terrorist attack yesterday, didn't you?"

"That's all everyone was talking about last night."

"Well the terrorists attacked Kyle's building and they killed all the Marine guards with a bomb, except one. Kyle and Tyrone heard the explosion, grabbed their father's guns, ran downstairs and fought the terrorists. They killed two of them and saved everyone in the building from being massacred. They were heroes. Does that sound like something a boy would do?"

"No," Jennifer reluctantly admitted, "but that's not what I'm talking about. I'm glad he's brave and I know he's smart, otherwise you wouldn't care for him. All I'm trying to make you understand is that you and he are too young for a serious relationship."

Mavis was starting to get annoyed with her friend, but she was diverted by a summons from their fathers. Dr. Van Meer had the girls greet Mayor Ramirez, Ambassador Blunt, the governor's representative, the head of the Veterans Association and several other notables. Van Meer had an usher summon the generals and admirals, who fussed over the girls, but were courteously distant to Ramirez and Blunt.

Then the generals and admirals quickly retreated back to the other side of the reviewing stand, where they continued their whispered criticisms of the Beaumont administration. The officials and the girls chatted pleasantly for a few minutes, then Mayor Ramirez went to the microphone and the parade was temporarily halted for his speech.

He mouthed the usual phrases about the service of the armed forces in the past, and the need for the incoming administration to respect our fellow dwellers in the global village, in order to build a prosperous future for all humanity. The reference to the global village drew an approving smile from Blunt. Ramirez apologized for the absence of a jet fighter flyover, a tradition of the parade, due to the fog. "That's one occurrence that can't be blamed on the Democrats," he quipped. There was no response, so he said loudly, "Let the parade continue."

•   •   •

The fog lifted slightly, so it was possible to see which units were passing the reviewing stand. An Army contingent marched by earlier, with their band playing "As the Caissons Go Rolling Along". The Navy was right behind them and their band had played "Anchors Away". The parade resumed with the Air Force unit and they were almost strolling, rather than marching, to the tune of "Off We Go Into the Wild, Blue Yonder". The generals and admirals got into a verbal dispute as to which service looked sharpest. For once the Army and Navy were on the same side, and one admiral described the Air Force contingent as being less disciplined than cub scouts.

This provoked defensive replies from the Air Force. The seemingly good-natured dispute went on for a bit, to the amusement of the other guests, who were unaware of the underlying seriousness of the interservice rivalries. Civilians couldn't be expected to understand that the real enemy was always the other service branches, competing for funds and prestige.

42

THE FEW WORLD WAR II VETERANS, mostly in their late eighties and in wheelchairs, sat up straight as they reached the reviewing stand. Some of them had tears in their eyes, brought on by the respectful salutes of the generals and admirals. By some coincidence, the veterans from the V.A. hospital were just ahead of the Marine Band and they kept up a constant banter with the non-combatant musicians.

The oldest and most bitter vets were from Vietnam. The rest were mostly vets from both of the Iraq wars. Their cynical comments got louder as they lingered in front of the reviewing stand, then they broke into a chant, "We are the forgotten men," which they repeated over and over.

A parade marshal, dispatched by a distraught parade official, tried to quiet them, but this only provoked them further and the chant grew louder and louder. The marshal threatened to have them removed from the parade.

One grizzled vet slipped an M16 from under the blanket on his stretcher and growled, "Don't make me remove you, sonny," which prompted the marshal's instant retreat.

•   •   •

Kyle, Tyrone, and Sergeant Vasquez finally got to Fifth Avenue just as the Marine Band, a block away, started the Marine Hymn. The three of them began to hum the familiar tune, 'From the Halls of Montezuma'.

"In a few years, I'll march ahead of my Marine platoon to that tune," Kyle enthused.

Tyrone simply said, "Amen, bro. I'll be there with you."

Sergeant Vasquez smiled fondly at the two boys. "I'll be a gunny by then," she said, "and after what you did yesterday, I'll be honored to serve with you."

The boys felt ten feet tall after that and Kyle impulsively took her arm.

"Thanks, Nita. Let's go salute some Marines."

They walked the short distance to the reviewing stand and Kyle saw Mavis. He hurried towards her and she started towards him. Out of the corner of his eye he saw two people appear out of the fog, their faces frozen in a horrible scream, as they ran towards the reviewing stand.

It happened so quickly that it barely registered that they were Arabs. An alert police officer tried to stop them and they struggled for a moment, but despite the officer's efforts, just before they reached the reviewing stand, they detonated themselves in a tremendous explosion. As the fireball rushed at him, Kyle didn't have time to finish the warning he started to shout, "Mavis ..."

●　　　●　　　●

Hanson heard the explosion from two blocks away and instantly turned to Muzzetti.

"That could be at the reviewing stand. Send two platoons ahead, double-time, to set up a perimeter north of the explosion. Have the rest of the company set up from here on. Don't let anyone leave the area until they've been security checked. Move." Then it registered that Kyle was there. "Oh my god. Kyle." He raced ahead to the Humvee and jumped in. "Get going, Tico."

He tried to call Kyle, then Vasquez, but there was no answer. He called Lonigan and told him to send for emergency services and have his cops check everyone leaving the area.

"It sounds like a bad one, Sam."

He was trying to compartmentalize his worry about Kyle and didn't bother answering and disconnected.

They only got a block or so, when the chaos on the avenue and people running in every direction forced them to slow down. Hanson was too agitated to wait and hopped out of the vehicle and ordered his two bodyguards to come with him.

"We don't know what's going on, so stay alert," he ordered, "but don't get trigger happy. There are a lot of panicky people around here right now."

The competent looks on the young Marines' faces told him that they understood. Images of Kyle kept flashing through his mind and he forced himself to concentrate on what had to be done.

•   •   •

He moved quickly and when he got to 50th Street he could see smoke and flames. He kept whispering a mantra to himself, "Be safe, Kyle." Then he smelled the familiar, sickening odor of explosives and burned flesh, and hoped that Kyle wasn't dead.

People were screaming and the wounded were staggering around aimlessly, already succumbing to shock. Sirens from the first responders added to the din. The scene was a glimpse into hell that he had seen too often in his military career. And he knew that once again it was innocent Americans who were the victims of heartless terrorists.

He didn't stop to help anyone, because his job was to prevent further attack and hopefully to stop any attackers from doing more harm. A lot of the V.A. hospital vets had been caught in the blast and his two troopers started to go to their aid.

"Leave them for the medics," he ordered. "We've got to secure the area and make sure there are no follow-up attacks."

The troopers nodded grimly, their faces already black from the smoke, then followed him to the blast area near the reviewing stand.

He looked around carefully and couldn't see an immediate threat, but he also couldn't see Kyle. He slowly scanned the stands that were on fire in several places, but didn't seem badly damaged by the explosion. Then he saw Carver, tears flowing, desperately clutching a body to his chest and he knew it was Mavis.

He suppressed an impulse to go to his friend and stayed alert, waiting until he received word from Muzzetti that the area was secure. He again called Kyle and Vasquez, and again there was no answer. Medics, police officers, firefighters and volunteers were helping the wounded to an improvised aid station for triage assessment. The heartbreaking task of pulling out the dead hadn't begun yet.

Muzzetti joined him a few minutes later and reported that the perimeter had been secured from 47th Street to 53rd Street. Just then, the EMTs carried a body past them, charred beyond recognition. He fervently offered a silent prayer that it wasn't Kyle. Muzzetti gaped at it, then turned aside and retched. He wiped his mouth, then turned back to Hanson.

"Sorry, boss. I never saw one like that."

"I've seen a lot of them and I always feel that way. Try not to show it to the troops. They don't expect us to show human weakness."

"Yes, sir. I've heard that when a body was burned by napalm in Vietnam, our troops called it a crispy critter. I never understood such callousness."

It took a great effort for Hanson to reply, "People can get used to anything."

A camera crew from Al Jazeera jostled him as they maneuvered for a better shot of the gory scene. Hanson wondered for a moment how they got there before the other media, then he shook off the idle thought, shoved them aside and growled, "Watch where you're going, you vultures."

The camera crew slunk off, then one of them turned and gave Hanson the finger. He shook his head in disgust.

"It's bad enough that the American media attack our way of life all the time," he said to Muzzetti, "but we shouldn't have to tolerate a network that supports any enemy of America, as well as terrorists. They make me sick."

Jed rushed up just then and reported that he had circled the entire perimeter.

"No one's getting past the security checkpoints, unless they have wings."

He looked at the destruction around him for a moment and his glance lingered on the bodies of the vets who had been killed by the explosion and flames.

"Those poor guys," Jed murmured. "After all they've been through, to get it like this."

"At least they got some of the rags yesterday," Muzzetti said.

Hanson ignored their comments and asked, "Do we need reinforcements?"

Muzzetti waited for Jed. "I don't think so, Sam. The attack seems to be over."

"Alright. Muzi, you're in command here. Have Nakamura monitor south of 50th Street and have Bernstein take the north. Stay in close touch."

"Yes, sir."

"What do you want me to do, Sam?" Jed asked.

"Give me a minute." He called Lonigan, who reported all quiet in other sections of the city.

"I'll be there in a few minutes, Sam, so you don't have to face officialdom alone."

"Thanks, Mike. Bring Colonel Warrington, if he's able to join us."

He saw that the fire department had the flames under control and the media circus was getting underway. The camera crews were battling with their rivals to get closer for the bloodiest, most disturbing footage, with, as usual, no concern for the loss of life, as long as it was hot news.

He saw the Al Jazeera crew poking its camera into the shredded bodies of some of the vets and he resisted the impulse to shoot them. The thought sprang into mind again, *How did they get here so quickly?* and he made a mental note to look into it. He saw CNN arrive and realized that the event would be flashing all over the world in minutes. He called Al, gave her a quick update, and told her to get all the troops at headquarters ready to move, in case they were needed. Then he called General Griffin and that update took a bit longer.

Jed had been waiting impatiently for orders and when Hanson, with a growing feeling of dread, finally turned to him, he shocked him with the look on his face.

"What's wrong, Sam?"

Hanson stared at his good friend and comrade in arms and took a deep breath. "I may have bad news, Jed. I think our boys may have been killed in the explosion."

Jed became rigid. "What? How do you know? Have you seen their bodies?"

"No. But they were with Sergeant Vasquez and I haven't been able to reach them."

"Let's go find them, Sam."

The two men went to the reviewing stand, carefully inspecting every wounded or dead body they passed. They found three bodies near the stand that were badly burned, but still identifiable. They looked at each other in horror.

"Tell me it's not them," Jed pleaded.

Hanson knelt and looked at them carefully, trying to maintain control, while in his head he kept screaming, *No. No. No.* He wasn't aware that tears were pouring down his face as he turned to his friend.

"I'm afraid it's them, Jed," he said, his voice cracking. "Our boys. And Nita Vasquez."

"Why our boys, Sam? They're just kids … Are you sure it's them?" he asked brokenly.

"Yes."

He put his arms around Jed and they stood there crying, oblivious to whatever was going on around them.

Carver lurched to them, the broken body of his daughter pressed tightly to his chest, his robust frame already shriveled.

"My beautiful Mavis is dead," he gasped through his tears.

Hanson put his arms around Carver. "My son is dead. So is Jed's son. Those monsters robbed us of our precious children."

Carver stared at him blankly, then slowly knelt and put Mavis' body next to the boys. "I know you have things to do," he whispered. "I'll stay here and guard them, until they can be moved."

With a tremendous effort, Hanson struggled to bring his raging emotions under control. "I'll arrange to have them taken to the barracks, until we make arrangements …"

He started to walk away and Jed stopped him, his face a tortured mask of suffering.

"Why did it happen to them?"

Hanson was feeling the same anguish. "I don't know, Jed."

"They were all we had, Sam. We're all alone now."

They looked at each other, good friends tested by so many battles, now bound by even more painful ties. "We'll send them in my Humvee," Hanson said.

Hanson sent one of his bodyguards to tell Tico to bring the Humvee. The remaining bodyguard said softly, "I'm very sorry, sir. They were great kids. Real Marines."

Hanson stared at him, while he tried for enough calm to cover the gaping wound.

"Thanks, Carlos."

When Tico got there, they carefully loaded the bodies of Kyle, Tyrone, Mavis and Nita Vasquez into the back of the Humvee.

"Take them to the barracks, Tico. I'll have a detail waiting for them."

"I should stay with you, sir," Tico said.

"It's alright, Tico," he said gently. "Come back as soon as they're unloaded."

He called Al and told her the terrible news.

"Oh, no, Sam. Not the boys," and she burst into tears, crying for the first time since he had known her. "How did it happen, Sam?"

"I'll tell you later. Tico is bringing them to the barracks. Have a detail meet them and put them in an empty sergeant's room."

"Yes, Sam. I'll come back with Tico."

"Stay there, Al. We don't know what else may happen. I may need you to coordinate things."

"Yes, sir."

Hanson, Jed, and Carver stood there in a daze and watched the Humvee drive off with their children. The reality of their deaths was almost overwhelming. Hanson was the first to speak.

"I've got to check on Captain Muzzetti. Jed. Get a count of the wounded and dead and make sure they're being tended to. I'll set up my command post next to the reviewing stand in the Wolverine. Come there when you finish."

"Yes, sir."

Jed drew himself up slowly, saluted and walked off.

"Carv."

"Yes, Sam?"

"I'm so sorry for your loss."

"And I for yours ... Mavis was all I had. How do you get over the loss of your only child?"

"I don't know yet ... Kyle was all I had ... We'll have to learn ... Right now, we have work to do. Will you check on the condition of the distinguished guests?"

"Yes, Sam."

"Meet me at the Wolverine when you're ready."

"Yes, Sam. Why do you call it a Wolverine?" he asked in a childish voice.

"Because it's fast and deadly."

"Thank you, Sam."

He watched Carver walk away and felt the same burden of loss weighing him down. He knew that the only way he could endure the anguish he was feeling would be by painstaking attention to duty.

He looked around and saw that the initial chaos was being brought under control and he called Muzzetti.

"Report, Muzi."

"No new incidents, sir. The perimeter is secured and everyone in the area is being checked by the police and FBI, before they're allowed to leave. There's one small piece of good news, sir. Gunny Le Beau apprehended an Arab woman who was wandering around in a daze. He thinks she may be a suicide bomber who couldn't handle it."

A momentary jolt of elation surged through Hanson.

"She could help us find out who sent them. First. Order him to immobilize her so she can't detonate her explosive belt. Then get the nearest Navy bomb team to disarm her device. Make sure they understand that they're not to tell anyone about her. Secrecy is vital."

"Yes, sir."

"Once she's disarmed, put her in the Wolverine near you and take her to the barracks. Instruct Le Beau that they're not to let her be seen. A detail will be waiting for her. Carry on."

"Yes, sir. Sir?"

"Yes?"

"I'm very sorry about your son."

A stab of agony ran through him. "Thanks, Muzi."

He called Al and told her that Le Beau was bringing a prisoner.

"Have a detail waiting for her, then put her in total isolation. Make sure that everyone knows they're not to discuss her with anyone. We'll interrogate her later."

"Yes, Sam. How are you holding up?"

He took a deep breath. "I don't know yet, but I'm doing what has to be done," and he disconnected.

He went to the Wolverine and established his command post. Muzzetti came in a few minutes later.

"The detail is on its way to the barracks, sir. Orders?"

"Have Nakamura and Bernstein make sure that each security checkpoint is functioning properly and have them stay in close communication with you. Let me know if there's any kind of problem."

"Yes, sir. How do you think those bombers got past our security?"

Hanson's face formed an implacable mask. "I don't know, but we'll find out. Right now, we've got to take care of the situation here."

"Yes, sir. Just so you know, sir. Even though you haven't known me for very long, I'll do anything you ask."

Hanson looked at him and liked what he saw. "Thank you, Muzi. We'll make a criminal of you yet."

He had dreaded calling General Griffin because there would be a certain finality once he told him the tragic news, but he ordered himself to punch the button.

"Charlie. I have something terrible to tell you … Kyle's been killed. Your godson is dead."

There was a long silence, then Griffin asked in what was suddenly an old man's voice, "How did it happen?" Hanson managed to tell him the little he knew, then they didn't speak for a while.

"Beverly and I will catch a flight and be there in a few hours," Griffin said slowly.

"Don't come here, sir."

"Why not, Sam? He's family."

"I know, sir, but we have a prisoner to interrogate and it may get messy. I want to know who sent them and how they got through security, then I'm going to teach them that they can't attack us with impunity. We're going to be way out on a limb with this one and I don't want you getting chopped off with us."

"I appreciate your concern, Sam, but I have as much of an obligation as you do. Any action, however subject to later interpretation, will include me. Do we understand each other?"

"Welcome aboard, Charlie."

43

J ED CAME BACK to the Wolverine with a preliminary list of the dead and wounded.

"Except for us and the vets, casualties are minimal. The count is nine dead, twenty-two wounded and three of the wounded are critical. Apparently, a cop stopped the bombers before they could reach the reviewing stand, but that's not confirmed yet. For some reason the explosion wasn't very big … I guess it could have been worse."

Then he realized what he said and his voice cracked. "My god, Sam. How could I say something like that?" and tears started to flow down his cheeks.

Hanson made an effort to console him. "Try to take it easy, Jed. It's going to take a lot of time for us to get used to losing our children. Meanwhile, we have things to do, no matter how we feel."

"Yes, Sam," Jed replied in a childlike voice. "Just kick me if I forget myself."

"There's no need to beat up on yourself. We have to do our duty. That's all we have to hold on to right now. It's the only thing that'll get us through this."

"Yes, Sam … What do you want me to do next?"

"Help Muzzetti monitor our security patrols."

"Yes, sir … Thank you, Sam."

Carver walked over a few minutes later, a shadow of his former larger than life self.

"I checked on the notables," he said hesitatingly, then trailed off and just stood there.

"Yes, Carv?" Hanson encouraged.

"Oh … Yes. Some people in the first row were wounded, but none of them are life-threatening. A lot of the others were knocked over by the explosion and some got superficial burns and temporary deafness, but there were no serious injuries. The only exception was Ambassador Blunt, who got a very large splinter in his gluteus maximus."

"What's that?" Muzzetti asked.

"His ass," Carver replied, then he got a strange expression on his face. "Maybe the splinter came from an ecologically certified tree." He looked at the others as if they thought he was crazy. "I don't know what I'm babbling about. Am I making any sense?"

"Don't worry, Carv," Hanson soothed. "We're all in a state of shock. We'll have to find a way to live with our loss."

"Can I stay here with you for a while?" Carver asked pathetically.

"Yes, Carv," Hanson replied gently.

Lonigan and Colonel Warrington arrived and the first thing they did was to express their condolences.

"I'm terribly sorry for your loss, Sam, Jed, Doctor Carver," Lonigan said. "They were wonderful kids."

The three fathers murmured their thanks. Then Colonel Warrington offered his regrets for their loss.

"It's always a tragedy when kids are killed. It's even worse when they're special and belong to friends."

They were silent for a while, each of them lost in his own thoughts. Hanson forced himself to pay attention to what was going on around him and noticed that the Wolverine was becoming too crowded for efficient functioning. He decided to expand the command post and remain in the area until the situation was clarified. He looked around and concluded that the nearby stores would be too isolated from the site of the attack.

"Muzi. Have some of your troops attach a tarp to the Wolverine, get some tables and chairs and set up some heaters, so we can work here."

"Yes, sir," Muzzetti replied, and he immediately set about organizing the workplace so they could function in an orderly manner.

The Marines doing the tasks studiously avoided Hanson's or Jed's eyes, not knowing how to express their sorrow for the death of the boys. Once the command post was set up, Hanson reviewed the up to the minute reports from Nakamura and Bernstein at the security checkpoints. They seemed to indicate there were no further threats.

"Jed."

"Yes, sir?"

"Send for coffee and sandwiches for the troops and have them take turns eating, so there's always a detail on guard."

"Yes, sir."

"Once that's done, tour all the checkpoints and then we'll decide how long to maintain them."

"Yes, sir."

"Muzi."

"Yes, sir?"

"Make a quick assessment of how many personnel we need here, then send the rest of the troops back to the barracks."

"Yes, sir."

"Mike."

"Yes, Sam?"

"See if you can find out how the bombers got through security."

"I'll try, Sam, but this isn't my jurisdiction. I'll talk to the local precinct commander and the FBI and try to get their cooperation."

"Thanks, Mike. Colonel Warrington."

"Yes, Sam?"

"I think your troops can stand down."

"Yes, Sam. If there's anything we can do, tell us."

"Thanks, Oliver. We'll stay in touch."

Warrington started to say something, then waved goodbye and walked out. Carver had been standing nearby in a daze and the flurry of activity startled him. He looked at Hanson pleadingly.

"What can I do, Sam? Give me something to do, before I go out of my mind."

Hanson thought quickly. "Talk to the mayor and suggest that he immediately form a commission to investigate the attack. Tell him that you and Dr. Van Meer should be on it and recommend that Captain Lonigan be appointed chief investigating officer."

"I'll try. Do you want to be on it?"

"No, Carv. I'll have other things to do."

A flicker of life flitted across Carver's woeful face. "You're going to do something about this, aren't you?"

"I didn't say that," Hanson replied evasively.

"I know you well enough to know you're already planning to get whoever's responsible. Whatever you do, I want to be part of it."

Hanson looked around to see if anyone heard them, then he took Carver aside.

"Anything we do will be illegal and we'll possibly be killed, or end up in prison," Hanson whispered urgently. "You can still have a life as a physician."

Carver shook his head. "My daughter was my life. I'm as entitled as you are to revenge. Let me help."

"Alright, Carv. Just don't say anything to anyone about this."

A hint of life came back to his face and he nodded agreement. Just then, Mei came into the command post and rushed to Carver. She put her arms around him and held him tightly.

"Oh, Carv. I heard about Mavis. I'm so sorry. She was a wonderful girl. We're all poorer without her."

"Take him home, Dr. Yi," Hanson urged. "I'll call him in the morning."

Carver made no objections when Mei took his arm and led him away. A wave of relief swept over Hanson, because Jed and Carver were gone. Now he could pay attention to the business at hand, the only thing keeping him from losing control.

Another part of him, way below the surface, kept wishing that the identification of Kyle was a dreadful mistake and that he was still alive. Every time someone came into the C.P. he looked up quickly, in the hope that it was Kyle. With an exertion of will he concentrated on his duties, while his weaker self wanted to run into the street screaming, "My son is dead! My son is dead! "

He struggled to keep the agony from showing on his face and was able to maintain a stony expression, even though it felt like an alien mask.

Muzzetti reported that there were no further incidents in the area and suggested that they could start sending troops back to the barracks.

Hanson called Lonigan, who told him, "Everyone who had been anywhere near the parade was screened before they could leave the checkpoints, and no one suspicious was detained. We arrested several people wanted for outstanding warrants, but they had nothing to do with the terror attack. We're searching all the stores and the church, but we haven't turned up anything yet."

"There's no chance that it was an accident, is there, Mike?"

"No, Sam. It was a deliberate act. We don't know who did it yet, but we'll do everything in our power to find out where they came from."

"Captain Muzzetti thinks the Marines are no longer needed here."

"He's right," Lonigan said. "The wounded and dead have been removed and the emergency services have left. Everything else that has to be done is either investigative or repair work. You're not a cop and you don't fix streets, so there's nothing more you can do here. Let us do our job now and I'll keep you posted."

"Thanks, Mike."

Hanson quickly considered the situation and concluded that he agreed with Muzzetti's and Lonigan's assessment. He turned to Jed for another opinion, just to get him involved with something more than his son's death.

"What do you think, Jed? Is there anything more we can do here?"

Jed had a haunted look on his face and moved like an automaton.

"I don't think so, sir," he said distantly.

Before he could try to get a further response from Jed, Tico and Le Beau came in, followed by Danowski.

"The package was delivered, Colonel," Le Beau whispered, "and only a few of us know where she is, and I swore everyone to silence. The girl babbled all the way to the barracks and she claims she had to become a suicide bomber, or her entire family would be killed. She seems like a good kid, sir."

"We'll find out what she knows."

"Yes, sir. If there's anything to be done, sir, just tell me, no matter what it is."

Hanson was moved by Le Beau's concern.

"Thanks, Cajun." Then he turned to Danowski.

"What are you doing here, Ski?"

"I thought you might need some help organizing your command post, sir," he answered blandly.

Hanson knew that wasn't the reason, but he let it pass and found some comfort in the support of his fellow Marines.

It was clear that there was nothing more they could accomplish there and he started to give the order to strike the command post, when Agent Royce and Tish rushed in.

Their outraged accusations blared out at the same time, so it was almost impossible to understand them. Royce finally realized that he and Tish were drowning each other out and curtly signaled her to silence. Royce belligerently confronted Hanson and the words poured out in a vehement roar. "Your security arrangements were a failure, Hanson. What a disgrace. Everything is a shambles and the former vice-president of the United States is wounded."

Before Hanson could respond, Jed snarled, "We've got killed and wounded out there and all you can snivel about is a splinter up somebody's ass?"

He grabbed Royce and shoved him against the Wolverine. Royce cowered in the grip of who he thought was a madman and didn't dare resist. It took Hanson a moment to react, then he pulled Jed away.

"Calm down, Jed. Control yourself."

"You heard what he said, Sam. The ass-kissing son of a bitch is more worried about his job than the people who were killed … Our children …"

Hanson turned to Danowski. "Ski. Take Lieutenant Davis back to the barracks and bring him to Captain Kent."

"Yes, sir. Do you want me to escort the FBI anywhere?" he asked menacingly.

"No, Ski. That'll be all." Hanson waited until Jed and Danowski left, then turned to Muzzetti. "Muzi. Strike the command post and let's get ready to move out."

"Yes, sir. What about our troops at the checkpoints?"

Hanson looked quizzically at Lonigan.

"We don't need them any longer, Sam."

"You heard the man, Muzi. Move them out."

"Yes, sir. What about you, sir?" and he glanced significantly at Royce.

"I'll come back with Tico and my bodyguards."

"Yes, sir," Muzzetti said, and he began issuing orders to disassemble the C.P. and return to the barracks.

Royce was badly shaken by Jed's sudden assault and was just beginning to recover his self-possession.

"No wonder we have so much trouble getting you people to respect the law," Tish said. "All you understand is violence."

Hanson forced himself not to smack her.

"His son was just killed by a suicide bomber," he replied in a tightly controlled voice. "You might show some sensitivity for the dead and wounded, before you start blaming anyone."

Tish laughed bitterly. "You're a fine one to talk. Why didn't you protect them better? Then he may not have lost his son."

Hanson gritted his teeth in a monumental effort not to smash her to the ground.

"My son was also killed in the explosion. If you have any more criticisms of my failures, I suggest you save them for another time. I'm running out of patience and there's a limit to how much I'll tolerate."

Tish looked at him in horror and for a moment had an impulse to say something kind, but her festering resentments took over and she just stared at him coldly. During their brief discussion, Royce pulled himself together and offered a token statement of sympathy. Then, although slightly more restrained, he continued his accusations.

"I understand that this may not be the appropriate moment to question your security breakdown, but it's important to start at the top. We had a fiasco here today and you're responsible for it."

Before Hanson could answer, Lonigan held up his hand and cut off any reply.

"First of all, Agent Royce, Colonel Hanson was jointly in charge of security with the New York City Police Department and other agencies, only in the Enclave. In case you've forgotten, that's 23rd Street to 40th Street. His additional efforts were in a volunteer consultant capacity. Since this terrible attack occurred on 50th Street, it was under the jurisdiction of the FBI and I will so testify to the investigative commission.

"On a more personal note, you've got a hell of a nerve accusing a man who has done more for his country than any dozen agents in the Bureau."

Royce was unaccustomed to being spoken to in this manner and his face turned beet red with anger.

"Who do you think you're talking to? You're just a brash flatfoot who's forgetting his rank. My English ancestors knew how to handle your kind."

"My kind?" exclaimed Lonigan, with growing indignation. "My kind? I guess persecution's in your genes. Your exploiting ancestors may have gotten away with it for a while, but their day's over, as yours will be when the investigation examines the facts.

"If you knew anything about law enforcement, you'd never insult a hard-working police officer. And if you were a decent human being, you'd show some concern for the loss of life, rather than try to pick a scapegoat to blame for this tragedy."

Royce dismissed Lonigan's comments without a moment's hesitation.

"Your part in this foul-up will be carefully scrutinized, Captain Lonigan. Come along, Agent Madison," and he stormed out, followed by Tish.

Lonigan looked at Hanson, then said softly, "That man is a menace. He's obviously more concerned with escaping responsibility than dealing with the real problem; we're at war with a relentless enemy. I saw a lot of his type in Iraq II. We called them REMFs ..."

"Rear echelon mother fuckers," Tico blurted without thinking, then he looked at Hanson sheepishly. "Sorry, sir. It just popped out."

"Just make sure you don't say it in front of the wrong people, Tico," Hanson said sternly.

"Yes, sir."

"I didn't know you were in Iraq, Mike."

"Two tours with the 82nd. Airborne all the way."

"Why didn't you mention it before? We may have shared the same sand dune."

"I didn't want to distract us from our problems with a pissing contest."

"Don't worry, sir," Tico said sincerely. "A Marine can outpiss any three Army airheads." Tico put his hand over his mouth. "Sorry, sir."

Lonigan shrugged, trying to suppress a smile and Hanson merely said, "Wait for us in the Humvee, Tico."

"Yes, sir," and he saluted and fled, happy to escape without a dressing down.

"What happens next, Mike?" Hanson asked wearily.

"I'll call in all my favors and get the local precinct detectives and Midtown North detectives on the case, before the FBI has time to cut us out of the investigation and muddy the waters."

"Do you think they'd do that?" Hanson asked, sure that this was a terrorist attack.

"Do you think that Royce is more concerned with covering his ass, or stopping terrorism?" Lonigan demanded.

"I see what you mean."

"The Feebs are as political as any other government agency, Sam. Maybe when Zach Plant takes office, if he's as tough on terrorism as he says he is, the Feebs will change their policy. Right now, it's make-nice to the oil producing countries and play down any terrorist attacks, so they don't shut down the pipelines."

Hanson looked at his friend appraisingly. "That's a very astute analysis. You should have been a Marine."

"Better an airhead than a leatherhead."

"It's leatherneck, Mike."

"Whatever."

They stood there companionably for a minute and Hanson felt the first stirring of hope that he could endure the desolation that possessed him. He also hoped he could control himself sufficiently to effectively avenge the death of his son.

"What do we do next, Mike?"

"I have to subtly help organize the investigation here. Why don't you go back to the barracks and do what you have to do. I'll meet you there, as soon as things are underway here."

"I may be a bit busy, Mike. Why don't you call me and we'll talk."

Lonigan moved away from Hanson's bodyguards and beckoned him to follow.

"I know you have a prisoner, Sam. I'd like to be there when you interrogate her."

"Are you crazy?" Hanson whispered urgently. "If you get involved you could be indicted for war crimes."

"Do you play chess, Sam?"

"Yes. Why?"

"We could have a game, if we're in adjoining cells."

Hanson started to say no, then realized that his friend knew the consequences of what he was getting into.

"Alright, Mike. Ben Franklin said, 'We all hang together, or we hang separately.' Welcome aboard."

"As long as I don't have to become a Marine," Lonigan joked.

Just then a thought flashed through Hanson's mind. "Listen, Mike," he said excitedly. "I made a formal request to Royce to have the FBI sweep the department stores the night before the … The parade. Can you find out if they did it?"

"Why? Is it important?"

"Maybe. If it turns out that the bombers came from a department store, it might keep the feds off our backs for a while."

"I'll see what I can do. Don't count on anything though. My contacts with the Feebs may be reluctant to speak right now."

"The only thing I'm counting on now are my friends. I'll see you at the barracks, Mike."

44

A L WAS WAITING FOR HANSON when he got to the barracks, flanked by Jed and Danowski. They were standing at attention, almost like an honor guard. They saluted slowly and solemnly, and he returned it the same way. Then he walked to his office, followed by his officers.

Everyone they passed snapped to attention and saluted, a formality normally not offered in the workplace. He was touched by the gestures of respect and caring, but wasn't up to saying anything to the men and women of his command.

"Take seats," he said, when the door closed behind them. He knew that Al and Jed were with him all the way, so he addressed Danowski. "We're going to be getting our hands dirty, Ski, and the consequences could be severe. Prison or death are real possibilities. This would be the time to bail out, with no recriminations, if you don't want to get involved."

"I'm with you, sir, for whatever has to be done, unless you don't want me."

"Welcome aboard, Ski."

Al leaned forward and said softly, "I know what you and Jed are going through, Sam. I feel like I lost my younger brothers … Oh God. They were great kids," and she burst into tears.

Jed reached over and put his arm around her and they just sat there, sharing sorrow.

"Our family keeps getting smaller," Hanson murmured.

Al took a deep breath. "I can hold down the fort, while you and Jed take care of … The kids …"

"Thanks, Al," Hanson said. "I know we can rely on you. We'll make the funeral arrangements … later today. We have some serious business ahead of us and I'm sure Jed wants to be part of it."

"Yes, Sam," he said quietly.

"Lonigan and Dr. Carver will be joining us," Hanson added. "Once we identify whoever sent the suicide bombers, we'll plan a retaliation operation against them."

"What if they've left the country?" Jed asked. "Will they get away with it?"

Hanson shook his head. "We'll take a page from the Israeli's book; we'll never forget, until we get them."

The others looked at him and nodded agreement.

Hanson quickly sketched out some ideas for a preliminary operation plan.

"First we'll interrogate the girl. If she can identify anyone, we'll take them into custody and deal with them accordingly. If we have to raid civilian dwellings, we'll use small details, four to six operators. If the targets are more complicated, we'll plan accordingly. It's imperative that we restrict knowledge of the girl to as few people as possible. Once we've finished with her, I'll ask General Griffin to arrange to put her and her family in a witness relocation program for their safety. By the way, General Griffin insists on participating in our operation."

This surprised the others.

•　　　•　　　•

"Is that a good idea, Sam?" Al asked. "He'll be risking a lot."

"So will we. I tried to dissuade him, but he insisted." Hanson produced a weak smile. "What could I do? He's a general."

"When did something like that ever stop you?" Al demanded.

"He's family," Hanson reminded them.

"If we get a firing squad, at least it'll be with a general," Danowski remarked.

"I don't think the Marines do that anymore," Al replied. "Besides, that'll just mean we were dumb enough to get caught."

Hanson listened to the byplay with an air of detachment. It was a constant struggle for him not to give in to the numbness that weighed him down. It was as if he threw a switch that activated functioning that would suddenly click off, leaving him adrift.

Now that he was planning revenge against the murderers, it began to finally sink in that Kyle was dead. A sob burst from his throat, which he immediately disguised as a cough, but he didn't know what to do next. Al felt his distress and offered a suggestion to cover his lapse.

"I think it would be a good idea if I questioned the girl, with Gunny Le Beau. Apparently, she saw the gentle side of him, and a woman's presence would make her feel safe."

Hanson appreciated her help and calmed himself, nodded approval, then issued orders.

"Ski. Check that all our troops and vehicles are back from the parade and have everyone resume their normal duties."

"Yes, sir."

"Al. Bring Gunny Le Beau here. Don't discuss anything with him."

"Yes, sir."

Hanson waited until they left, then turned to Jed.

"It's very unusual for me to know exactly how someone else is feeling …" Jed looked at him and he saw the same shattered universe reflected in his eyes. "If you're not up to functioning professionally, I understand," Hanson said tactfully. "You could take a few days to get used to …"

"I need to do this, Sam. I already swore to myself that I'll get whoever sent them and make them suffer. Tyrone and Kyle require it. I don't care about justice. I want revenge … You can rely on me all the way."

Hanson could see that Jed's struggle for control was overcoming any sorrow that might interfere with his functioning.

"I wouldn't want to do this without you, Jed."

"Thanks, Sam."

"Make a list of personnel and equipment that we'll need for this operation. You know the drill."

"Yes, Sam. What about Muzi?"

"For the time being, let's leave him and his company out of this, except for Le Beau. Pick people who are our old timers and some of the N.C.O.s with families from our building. They won't forget that Kyle and Tyrone saved their families."

"Yes, Sam," and he walked out with a sense of purpose.

For the first time since the explosion had yanked him out of the fog, Hanson was alone with his thoughts and suffering. He put his hands to his head and let his tears flow without restraint. He cried for a minute or so but didn't feel any sense of relief.

He wiped his eyes with a tissue, then focused on clearing his head of the anguish that might prevent him from doing his job. It took a while to exert the necessary control of his raging emotions. When his clerk buzzed and informed him that Captain Lonigan was at the gate, it helped him compose himself. Hanson was glad to see his friend, who had proved to be a trusted partner in the recent crisis.

"How are you holding up, Sam?"

"I'm hanging in there. If I didn't have so many responsibilities, I'd probably dissolve into mush."

"If there's anything I can do, just ask."

Hanson stared at the rugged Irishman, wondering if his friend really understood the risks he was offering to take.

"We're planning some black ops that will put all of us at hazard of our lives. If we survive the operations and are discovered, which we probably will be, we'll be arrested, tried and convicted of war crimes. Valerie will be out of office by then, but Zach wouldn't dare pardon us. We'll be lucky if they don't hand us over to the International Court. You can imagine what they'll do to us if that happens."

"What are you trying to tell me, Sam?"

"There's no need for you to risk everything for us. You're not a Marine."

"I appreciate your concern, but Carver's not a Marine and you told him you'd include him."

"He lost a daughter. He's got a right to join us, but he won't participate in anything compromising."

"I may not have lost anyone close to me, but it happened on my watch, Sam. I share any blame with you for this tragedy. I deserve a chance to make up for my failure."

Lonigan looked so determined that Hanson couldn't refuse him.

"Alright, Mike. You're in. I hope you don't regret it."

"The only thing I regret is the loss of life today. Tell me what to do."

"We have a girl, one of the suicide bombers who didn't detonate herself. Her family may be at risk. I'm preparing a team to go there and catch any Arabs who come to threaten her family. Can you send two plainclothes cops to watch them until my troops get there?"

"Sure. As soon as you give me an address. What else?"

"The next request is personal … I don't know what to do about funeral arrangements for … Kyle and Tyrone … I never expected …"

"I'll take care of it, Sam. I know a funeral home in Brooklyn, owned by veterans. They'll arrange for burial in Greenwood cemetery. It's not that far away and you'll be able to get there easily when you want to visit … Do you have someplace where I can work?"

"I'll have Danowski set up an office for you."

Instead of writing an "I regret to inform you" letter to Nita Vasquez' parents in New Mexico, he called them. He felt a pang of anguish when Mr. Vasquez answered.

"Mr. Vasquez?"

"Yes?"

"This is Colonel Hanson. Your daughter's commanding officer."

"She has written us much about you, senor Colonel. It's an honor to talk to you."

"I have some very bad news for you, sir."

There was a long silence.

"It's my Nita … She's dead, isn't she?"

"I'm sorry to tell you this, but I didn't want strangers telling you."

"Momentito, senor Colonel."

Hanson heard a stream of Spanish, which he mostly understood, then a woman's cries of anguish.

"My wife is heartbroken. Nita was our pride and joy."

"I share your sorrow. I lost my son with her."

"How did it happen?"

"A suicide bomber killed them. I'll write you a letter with more details. For now, if you're up to it, I need to know what you want to do with her remains … I can arrange to have her buried at Arlington National Cemetery, with our other heroes."

"We are illegal immigrants, senor Colonel. That could cause problems. Could you ship her home to us?"

"Yes. I'll let you speak to Lieutenant Danowski, who will make the arrangements."

"Thank you, senor Colonel. I'm sorry for the loss of your son."

"And I for your daughter. She was a special person."

"Si."

The sound of the suffering father's voice lingered long after he disconnected. The fact that others were hurting as much as he was didn't console him. It only made him feel worse.

He thought of the many families who had lost loved ones to suicide bombers in the horrific struggle between Islam and the West, that had been going on for centuries in one form or another. He understood and accepted the ruthlessness necessary to win a limited modern war, but still couldn't comprehend how organized religion could sanction the destruction of innocents. The only conclusion that made any sense was that to radical Islam there were no non-islamic innocents. It was total religious war, pitiless and brutal, nourished by the geographic coincidence of abundant oil to finance jihad against the enemies of Islam. Was it time to consider a different attitude to a remorseless enemy? The ultra-liberal, politically correct sensibility of sympathizing with everyone who hated America because they were exploited or oppressed, always ended up hurting Americans, who were punished for their nationality. It was strictly coincidental that the apologists and appeasers of America's enemies rarely suffered with their fellow citizens when disaster struck.

Al dashed into his office, interrupting his reveries.

"You've got to see this, Sam."

She clicked on the tv and there was the President of the United States, Valerie Beaumont, in all her splendor, speaking at an impromptu news conference.

"We deplore the tragic occurrence in New York City this morning that cost the lives of American citizens, and misguided individuals who may have a grievance against the United States, but have taken the wrong path to express their dissatisfactions. We apologize for our policies that may have contributed to this tragic event and we assure the world community that we will do everything in our power to insure a peaceful and humane solution to all our differences. Thank you."

There were instant clamors from the assembled reporters, but the press secretary announced loudly, "The president will not take any questions."

The reporters instantly called out questions to the president, but she stalked off the stage without responding, and the screen dissolved to the symbol of the United States.

Jed stormed into the office a minute later and he was furious.

"I couldn't believe what I heard. She was apologizing to the very people who sent those bombers to kill us … It's a good thing she's leaving office soon, or I'd seriously consider assassinating her. What a monster. Our sons are dead because of her selling us out and she blames us for causing it …" He took a deep breath and brought his raging emotions under some control. "I know I sound crazy," Jed muttered, "but she just set me off."

Al and Hanson looked at him sympathetically and Hanson said, "We know how you feel, Jed. Just try to ignore her. She's a pestilent disease that we'll recover from. We have enough troubles without letting her add to them."

"Yes, Sam. I was just venting … But I swear that I'll find whoever sent those bombers, however long it takes and kill them slowly."

"I'll do it with you, Jed," Al said and hugged him.

"I'll also do it with you," Hanson added.

Danowski walked in and waited until Hanson gave him his full attention.

"All troops and vehicles have returned from the parade, and they've resumed their regular duties. If I may say so, sir. The entire command shares your and Jed's loss. We'll miss them."

"Thanks, Ski," Hanson murmured and Jed echoed him.

"I arranged to have Nita's remains shipped to New Mexico, sir. I ordered the coffin sealed, so her folks wouldn't have to see her that way."

"Good idea, Ski. Anything else?"

"I set Captain Lonigan up in an office and he said he'd be in to see you in a few minutes. Also, Gunny Le Beau is waiting outside."

"Bring him in, Ski, and stay with us."

"Yes, sir."

Le Beau came in, stood to attention and saluted smartly. "Gunnery Sergeant Le Beau reporting, sir."

"At ease, Gunny. I want you to interrogate the girl with Captain Kent."

"Yes, sir."

"This is strictly volunteer, Cajun."

"Yes, sir. Question, sir?"

"Yes?"

"Are we going to do anything about the rags who sent her?"

"What if we are?"

"I want in, sir."

Hanson smiled. "I think we can use you, Cajun."

"Thank you, sir."

After a careful review of how to handle the girl and what questions to ask, Al and Le Beau left to begin her interrogation. Jed gave Hanson the list he had requested.

"These are the personnel for securing the girl's apartment. I picked three units of six, each led by a senior N.C.O., so they can rotate shifts. Each trooper will carry a sidearm and a light automatic weapon, as well as canteens and MREs. I don't know where the follow-up operation will be, but I assume it won't be big scale, so I selected one of my platoons and put them on alert. I'll prepare their equipment list as soon as you assign a target. We'll be ready."

"Good. Let's get the first unit in place as soon as we have an address. You take them there and place three troops in the apartment and the other three nearby, where they won't be conspicuous, but can respond instantly. I'll ask Captain Lonigan to notify his detectives, who will get there first, that you're coming." And in a feeble effort at humor, he added, "I wouldn't want you to get arrested."

Jed managed a weak smile. "That's all I need … Can we keep the cops there? They'd be real useful if the local cops show up."

"I'll ask Lonigan. Make sure they stay in close touch and you take charge if you're not satisfied with the dispositions."

"Yes, Sam."

Lonigan came in as Jed was leaving and agreed to put his plainclothes detectives on station near the family's house.

"I'll notify the local precinct that we're running a stakeout and they won't interfere with us."

"Thanks, Captain Lonigan."

"Call me Mike, Lieutenant."

"I'll be glad to. I'm Jed," and he saluted and left.

Lonigan sat down with a sigh. "I made arrangements with the funeral home and they'll pick up the boys later this afternoon. They suggest you have the services on Saturday. They need to know if you want open coffins, and also if you have a military chaplain who you want to preside."

Hanson inhaled sharply. "We better have the coffins closed … I don't have a padre, so let's use their minister."

"I know this is a difficult time for you, Sam. Just ask if you need anything … Do you have a list of who should be notified?"

"I'll go over it with Danowski. What you can do is find out anything you can about how the bombers got past our security. That could help determine what we do next."

"I'll see what I can do."

Al called him a few minutes later.

"The girl gave us the address as soon as we told her we would protect her family. It's in Brooklyn, near Atlantic Avenue. It's 754 Bergen Street, Apartment 4. The girl is terrified for her family. Once she knows they're safe, she'll tell us everything she knows. You should see her with Le Beau. I can't tell if she's got a crush on him, or she thinks that she's in a fairy tale and she's been rescued by a gentle giant."

"Well done, Al. Would it help if I talked to her?"

"I don't think so, Sam. I think that would just confuse her. She sits pressed up against Le Beau, with me providing a presence of feminine modesty. The two of us will be the most effective way to gain her trust."

"She's all yours, Al. Get her name, so we can stop calling her she."

Al laughed. "It's weird. We've already become friends, but we don't know her name. I was so concerned with getting her address and she seemed so comfortable with us that it didn't occur to me."

"We'll be sending a detail to her house and we should know her name, so we can tell her family who sent us."

"I'll get back to you with it in a minute, Sam."

Al called back shortly.

"The family's name is al-Fulani and the girls name is Huma."

"That means bird who brings joy …" Hanson said. "She almost brought something else."

He called Lonigan, then gave him the name and address.

"My men are ready, Sam. I'll get them moving right away."

Then he sent for Jed, gave him the name and address and dispatched him with the first unit. Now that everything was underway he had nothing specific to do for the next few minutes, so he concentrated on preparing to make a plan to apprehend the terrorists. He realized that Jed would have no way of knowing who would be a legitimate visitor to the family's building, or who could be a violent terrorist. After considering the problem, he called Jed.

"Once our people are in the apartment, set up a code with the family so they can alert you if the terrorists show up. Pick something that they can use in normal conversation."

"How about 'The cheese is moldy'?" Jed asked, in a brave effort to be humorous.

Hanson laughed dutifully, then said, "This isn't French 101. Pick something that sounds good in Arabic."

"Yes, Sam."

After Jed left with his detail, Hanson realized he had almost forgotten his pain for the last few minutes. It was obvious that the only way he would stay functional was by keeping busy.

He started thinking about a preliminary operations plan to attack either the hideout, training center, homes, or workplaces of whoever sent the bombers. A platoon seemed ample for any of the locations, if it turned out to be a U.N. Mission, or an office in a hi-rise building. A hideout would have to be anonymous, and a training center would have to be isolated, so they would be relatively easy to assault. After proper reconnaissance, two squads would probably be enough.

If it was an office building, that would be more complicated. They'd have to go in civvies, perhaps disguised as a work crew, or painters. An attack on a U.N. Mission would be an act of war. That would require more careful thought. A call from General Griffin interrupted his musing.

"Beverly and I will land at La Guardia in forty minutes. Have a Humvee meet us."

"Aye, aye, sir. I'm glad you're coming, Charlie."

45

T HE ARRIVAL OF GENERAL and Mrs. Griffin took a big burden off Hanson. He knew they would help balance the rage and sorrow he was feeling, so that whatever decisions he made would have a sounding board. Beverly burst into tears when she saw him and held him tightly.

"He was our only grandchild, Sam," she said woefully. "Kyle and you were the children we never had. He'll always be in my prayers."

"I know, Bev. You and Charlie were his family … I never imagined that he would die before me. I always assumed that you would take care of him when I got killed. Now …"

"Kyle first told me he wanted to go to Annapolis just like you and me when he was six years old," Griffin said wistfully. "Ten years later he said the same thing, but by then he knew what the Academy was like. He would have made the Corps better."

"Thanks, Charlie. That's a kind thing to say … I'm glad you're both here."

Beverly, in her usual fashion, immediately took charge.

"Before we do anything else, let's get out of here for a while and have some dinner. Then you can tell us everything that happened and what you're planning."

Hanson looked at Griffin for guidance, but he just shrugged.

"She's the boss, Sam. You should know that by now."

"I do, Charlie. But there are certain things I don't think she should hear."

"And why not?" Beverly demanded belligerently. "Do you think I'm too fragile, or untrustworthy?"

"Not at all, Bev," he said placatingly. "It's just that some of the things we'll be talking about are illegal. I don't want to make you a criminal."

"I'll make up my own mind, if you please, Sam. I've heard that jails are co-ed now and I could probably share a cell with my husband. Besides, you might need an extra gun," and she dramatically took out her pistol and pointed it at the wall. "I'm not too old for a little action," and she took up a shooting stance.

Hanson and Griffin laughed at her flamboyant pose.

Danowski knocked, then walked in and instantly froze when he saw the pistol in Beverly's hand.

"Is everything alright, sir?"

"Yes, Ski. Relax. Mrs. Griffin was just demonstrating her quick draw technique."

"I see," he said nervously.

Beverly put the pistol away, then turned to Danowski.

"You were a sergeant the last time I was here, weren't you?"

"Yes, ma'am."

"There hasn't been time for you to go to O.C.S. How are you doing?"

"Well, I think, ma'am. I'm learning on the job. You should ask Colonel Hanson about that, ma'am."

"I will. And stop calling me ma'am."

"Yes, ma'am."

Hanson rescued him from further discomfort: "His performance since his promotion has been outstanding."

Danowski swelled with pride. "Thank you, sir."

"What do you have to report, Ski?"

Danowski looked at Beverly meaningfully.

"It's alright, Ski. You may speak freely in front of Mrs. Griffin. Report."

"Yes, sir." Danowski took a moment to organize his thoughts. "Captain Lonigan confirmed that two of his plainclothesmen are on station near Atlantic Avenue and Bergen Street, and they've cleared it with the local precinct. Jed and his unit are a few blocks away and they're waiting until it gets dark to move in, so they won't be noticed. He's in communication with the two cops and said to let him know if you want him to move in earlier. I've been checking on the strike platoon that Jed picked and I told them to get some sack time, alternating shifts."

"Good thinking, Ski."

"Thank you, sir. Muzi keeps asking me what's going on and I keep telling him I don't know, but he doesn't believe me."

"I'll talk to him later. Anything else?"

"Yes, sir. Wilkins is creating another fuss at the hospital. He insists on being included if we do anything about the boys, even if he has to crawl."

"Who's Wilkins?" Beverly asked.

"He was in charge of the guard detail at our apartment building when it was attacked," Danowski explained. "The rags killed the other guards and were about to finish him off, when Kyle and Tyrone saved him."

"Sounds like my kind of man," Beverly remarked.

Griffin rolled his eyes at Hanson, then said, "You always liked them bloodthirsty, dear."

"It's a tough world out there, General," she responded. "Pussies don't last long in a combat zone."

Hanson suppressed his grin.

"Tell Wilkins I'll stop by and see him later and he's to stay out of trouble."

"Yes, sir. Will that be all?"

"Yes, Ski."

"Just a minute, Lieutenant."

"Yes, General?"

"Could you hold down the fort here for a bit, while we go out with Colonel Hanson?"

"Yes, sir. As long as I can call him if there's something really urgent."

Griffin nodded to Hanson.

"I won't be gone long, Ski. Call me whenever you need to."

"Yes, sir."

Danowski nodded to them and left.

"He seems like a good kid," Beverly remarked.

"He's not a kid, Bev," Hanson said. "He's a lieutenant in the United States Marine Corps and he fought well the other day when we were attacked."

"You know what I mean, Sam. And don't forget that you're not so big that I can't put you over my knee."

"I surrender, Bev."

"Good. Let's get some dinner."

Hanson took them to an Italian restaurant on Second Avenue and 33rd Street, set off the avenue in a small plaza. He had passed it dozens of times, but never tried it before. It turned out to be a pleasant looking place and the staff didn't freak out when Hanson requested a table near the door for Tico and his bodyguards, who were armed. The waiters were a little nervous at the sight of automatic weapons, but Beverly found this reassuring.

"If this was a mafia joint," she quipped, "they'd be used to seeing machine guns."

Hanson couldn't help smiling at the irrepressible lady's wit and felt the first glimmer of hope that he might endure the loss of his beloved son. The restaurant wasn't crowded, so they had ample privacy and the service was efficient. While they ate, Hanson brought them up to date on everything that happened earlier and what was being planned.

The general considered what he heard carefully.

"Do you think it's practical to order a retaliatory strike at an embassy or U.N. Mission? The consequences could be drastic."

"Jed and I won't let them get away with murdering our children."

"That's not what I meant, Sam. It could embarrass our government if you're caught."

"Does it embarrass the Saudi's when they get caught attacking us?"

"If you survived the attack, the Beaumont administration would turn you over to the International Court."

"I know that. Jed and I no longer have anything to lose. That's why I didn't want you involved."

"I want to be involved. I feel the loss of Kyle almost as much as you do … Would you consider waiting until the Plant administration takes over in January?"

"That's two months away, Charlie. Our targets could be far away by then. Besides, how many more lives will be lost if we don't take action promptly?"

"I just want to be sure you know what you're doing, Sam."

"I'm fully aware of what's involved, sir. We'll plan a well-organized surgical strike."

Beverly changed the subject.

"Did you make funeral arrangements, Sam?" she asked, with a quaver in her voice.

He told them about the plan for the services and burial on Saturday in Brooklyn.

"Is there anything I can help with?" Beverly asked. "Are you planning a reception afterwards?"

"I don't think so. I'm just managing to hold together as it is. I couldn't deal with being polite to people now."

"We should at least notify your friends and the people who knew Kyle," she insisted.

"Danowski's making up a list for me."

"I'll go over it with him … Sam, if you plan to attack a mission or embassy, it won't be hitting the beach. It'll be a covert operation. If you can use an old broad for cover, just ask."

"The last time I hit a beach was when I finished Basic after graduation from the Academy. When I took the required amphibious warfare course I couldn't help thinking about Tarawa and other landings where Marines got slaughtered. I hoped I'd never have to assault a beach."

"You know what I mean."

"Yes, Bev. By the way. You're hardly an old broad."

"Why thank you, Sam."

Griffin observed that Hanson's Marines at the other table were on their second beer.

"Your people are sopping up suds while on duty, Sam."

"They've been going day and night for a while. They earned it, General."

"What about you? Why don't you join me in a beer?"

"I think I will."

"Make it three," Beverly added.

After he ordered, Griffin took out his phone and called the hotel they usually stayed at. Before he could book a room, Beverly said, "Why don't we stay at Sam's house tonight."

Griffin looked surprised. "I don't want to intrude …"

"Don't be silly. He'll be glad to put us up. Besides, you boys can plot and scheme all night without being disturbed."

"You're always welcome," Hanson said. "You can have my room and I'll sleep on the couch."

"If it's alright with you," Beverly said with a catch in her voice, "we'll sleep in Kyle's room."

Tears sprang from Hanson's eyes and it took him a minute to control them, then he nodded assent without speaking. Hanson looked at his watch.

"I've got to get back to HQ. Do you want to come with me, or go to the apartment?"

"We'll go with you," Beverly answered. "I'll go over the list with Danowski, then go to the apartment. You boys can meet me there later."

Hanson called for the check, but Griffin insisted on paying and included the three troopers, who thanked the general for the meal and beer. The brief respite from the gloom at headquarters had helped revive Hanson. When they got back, he quickly resumed an acceptable level of functioning. After taking the latest report from Danowski, he assigned him to Beverly.

"Give her anything she wants, within reason."

And in a sign of his growing confidence, Danowski quipped, "And if it's not within reason?"

Beverly, hands on hips, glared at him fiercely.

"Anything I request is reasonable, Second Lieutenant."

To divert her from Danowski, who didn't know how to deal with her yet, Hanson said, "Whenever Mrs. Griffin finishes, have her escorted to my apartment."

"I don't need an escort, Sam," she snapped.

He ignored her indignation.

"That's an order, Ski."

"Aye, aye, sir."

Al rushed in with an electrifying piece of information.

"The girl told us that the bombers launched their attack from Saks Department store. They went in during the night disguised as part of the cleaning crew. The girl is still freaked out, so we're going slowly and not pressuring her ... Hi, General."

Hanson suppressed a grin at her casualness.

"Hi, Captain," Griffin responded with a straight face.

"May I make a suggestion, sir?" Al asked.

"Go ahead, Al," Hanson said.

"The girl is pretty tired. Unless there's something urgent we have to find out tonight, I recommend we feed her, put her to bed and continue her interrogation in the morning."

"Good idea, Al. Also tell her that we have Marines and police guarding her family and they'll be safe. That should reassure her and make your job easier. Well done, Al."

"Thank you, sir. I'll tell Le Beau."

"Is that Cajun bear doing interrogations?" Griffin asked in surprise.

"He's doing a bang-up job as a gentle giant, General," Al answered. "Will that be all, Colonel?"

"Yes, Al," Hanson said.

"How is Al doing?" Griffin asked, once she left. "I know she was a good small unit combat leader, but how is she doing as an officer?"

"Outstanding, sir. She's my executive officer. With your approval, I'd like to promote her to major when Plant takes over."

"Is she ready for field grade, Sam?"

"Definitely. She's fulfilled all my expectations."

Just then Lonigan knocked on the door, interrupting their discussion of Al. "We have an eyewitness who saw the bombers come out of Saks Department store," he announced.

"Al just told me that the girl told her they came from Saks, Mike. This confirms it if our prisoner told the interrogators the same thing as the eyewitness. The bombers went into Saks during the night with the cleaning crew."

"Why didn't the FBI catch them in the morning security sweep?" Lonigan demanded.

"That's what you have to find out. By the way, this is General Griffin."

"An honor to meet you, sir."

"This is Captain Lonigan, General."

"Sam speaks very highly of you, Captain."

"Call me Mike, sir."

"Mike has committed to helping us in whatever we do, sir."

Griffin looked at him approvingly. "Glad to have you with us, Mike."

"Thank you, sir."

"Do you want to discuss your plan now, Sam?" Griffin asked.

"With your permission, sir. I'd like to wait until Al, Le Beau and Jed get here. They'll be able to contribute to the discussion."

Griffin nodded approval.

"What about Dr. Carver?" Lonigan asked. "He wanted to be involved."

"I don't think that's a good idea, Mike. He's a civilian." Griffin signaled Hanson and looked questioningly at Lonigan.

"Mike's been a big help so far, sir. He's ex-airborne."

"If he's that good why didn't he become a Marine?" Griffin asked gruffly.

"Because I passed the intelligence test at the recruiting office, sir," the feisty Irishman responded.

Griffin looked at him balefully and when he didn't flinch, grinned and said, "Welcome aboard."

"Thank you, sir. I'm glad to be with you. Though I won't be able to hold my head up in front of my old buddies, if I'm hanged with a bunch of jarheads."

"Don't worry, Mike," Griffin said with an evil grin on his face. "We'll let you go first, so you can show us how an airhead jumps."

Jed called and reported that his unit was in place and he would be returning to headquarters shortly.

"While we wait for Jed, why don't we go to the hospital next door, General, and I'll introduce you to Wilkins."

"Lead on, Sam."

"Aye, aye, sir."

•   •   •

Outside, the sky cleared and the earlier rain rinsed away some of the industrial emissions that prevented the viewing of the stars. The moon was three-quarters full and glowed brilliantly. The sad looking Man in the Moon appeared as he always did, since first observed by man, distressed at the human condition. He didn't seem concerned that he had been abandoned after the great human voyages that visited him in the sixties.

He hadn't even blinked at the disaster to the Chinese lunar expedition in 2013, which ended in tragedy when their space vehicle exploded shortly after launch. Venus, the second largest object in the celestial sphere, looked down coldly on lovers and the fools who didn't appreciate them. Hanson could see twenty or thirty stars, many more than usual, out of the five thousand or so that should have been visible but were obscured by urban light and massive air pollution.

"Tell me about Wilkins, Sam."

"He's a real character, Charlie. He comes from upstate New York, some small Appalachian community that's still living in the twentieth century. He's the slowest, sloppiest, slackest Marine in the battalion, until the shooting starts. Then he's a fierce fighter who doesn't fear anything.

"I promoted and busted him several times. It was difficult when I was a Gunnery Sergeant to look out for him because he was always getting into hot water. If I didn't cover up for him, our previous C.O. would probably have drummed him out of the service."

"He doesn't sound like a good example for new recruits."

"He's like the pre-World War II Marines I've read about, who were lazy, shiftless and no account, until war broke out. Then they were the first ones to urge their comrades on when they hit the beach. Wait 'til you meet him and judge for yourself. You always had a soft spot for characters."

When they got to his hospital room, Wilkins was engaged in an eyeball to eyeball confrontation with a short, dark-haired, Hispanic nurse, who wasn't giving an inch.

"I don't care what you think, Sergeant. If I was stupid enough to qualify for the Marines, maybe you could tell me what to do. On this ward, I'm the boss and you take orders."

"Aw, Carmen …"

"That's Nurse Rodriguez to you."

"You said I could call you Carmen earlier," Wilkins said in a plaintive voice.

"That's when you were behaving yourself. Now you're being loco."

"I know what loco means. That's not a nice thing to say," he protested.

"Then don't talk like a loco."

"Aw, Carmen …"

"I told you once already. It's Nurse Rodriguez."

"Aw, Nurse Rodriguez. All I want you to do is help me into a wheelchair, so I can go down the street to Marine headquarters and speak to my Colonel."

"That's why you're loco. You're not going anywhere, until the doctor says you are able to travel. It certainly won't be tonight."

"Then I'll go by myself," he said sullenly.

"Just try it and I'll put you in restraints."

"Aw, Carmen."

"Don't make me tell you again," she warned.

"Yes, Nurse Rodriguez."

Hanson walked into the room, followed by Griffin.

"How is your patient doing, nurse?"

"Colonel," Wilkins yelled. "Get me out of here."

Nurse Rodriguez put her hand over his mouth and hushed him.

"He is recovering from three gunshot wounds, none of them life-threatening, but he requires rest in order for them to heal properly. He'd also be a candidate for a lobotomy, if he was ever eligible in the first place."

"Why don't you let me talk to him," Hanson said.

"Why not," she snapped. "Not that it will do any good. He's as loco as that other one," and she pointed to the next bed, where a large lump was scrunched under the covers and producing basso profundo snores.

"Who's that?" Griffin asked.

"It must be Sergeant Carstairs," Hanson said.

"What's he doing here?"

"He was wounded during the terrorist attack on the barracks, sir."

"You mean that old war horse dropped his pots and pans again and remembered how to use a rifle?"

"Yes, sir. He's living proof that every Marine is a rifleman."

"Knowing him, 80 proof would be more accurate."

"Yes, sir."

Hanson turned to the nurse.

"What has he been doing? Except for breaking the sound barrier, he seems peaceful."

"A lot you know," she replied. "He was pawing every nurse who came near him, until they had to issue us flak jackets." Griffin smiled and she turned to him combatively.

"You think that's funny?"

"No, Miss. I was just appreciating your description."

"What else has he been doing?" Hanson asked.

"He persuaded a ward aide to give him extra morphine and he bribed one of the cleaning staff to buy him whiskey. The only reason he's not making trouble now is because we gave him an extra sedative, so we could get some rest around here."

"He's a hero, Miss," Griffin said.

"He's a pain in the ass, General," she replied tartly. "You ought to lock him up somewhere until you need him, then lock him up again when you don't need him anymore."

Griffin looked at her thoughtfully. "Do you have something against Marines?"

"Yes. My husband was a Marine and I should be used to this gung-ho stuff, but I'm not."

"I'll straighten out both of them," Hanson assured her. "They won't make any more trouble."

"Yeah," she said skeptically and stalked out.

Wilkins had been staring in wonder at Griffin, so Hanson introduced him.

"Wilkie. This is General Griffin."

"How do, sir. I never met a general before. What did nurse Carmen mean that I was a candidate for a lamotabe?"

"It's lobotomy, Sergeant," Griffin explained. "That's when they drill a hole in your head and remove your brain."

"Don't let them do that to me, General. I need it if I'm going to make Gunnery Sergeant. I told Kyle and Tyrone that I'd make gunny by the time they became officers, so I could serve with them … I'm sure sorry about them boys, Colonel. They were my friends. Kyle always stuck up for me when other folks poked fun …

"Those terrorists almost had me and those boys saved my bacon. I was trapped, wounded, running out of ammo and those rags were about to finish me off, when the boys joined the fight, guns blazing, like real Marines … I owe them big time, sir … They were great kids. I'm gonna miss them … We're not gonna let those ragheads get away with it, are we, sir?" and he looked pleadingly at Hanson.

Wilkins was obviously ready to go on all night, so Hanson held up a hand and cut him off.

"If I can get a word in, Wilkie."

"Sorry, sir."

"The boys will be buried Saturday. If the doctor says you're able to travel, I'll arrange to have you join us."

"Thank you, sir. I really 'preciate that … What about getting those rags, sir?"

"I don't want to hear another word about that and I order you to be a good patient and obey your nurse. You can repeat that order to Sergeant Carstairs, whenever he wakes up."

"Aye aye, sir."

"With the general's approval, Wilkie, I'm going to put you in for a silver star."

"Thank you, sir … I wish Kyle and Tyrone could get one. They deserve it."

"Some of us know that, Sergeant Wilkins," Griffin said, "but we're glad that you feel that way. I hope we'll meet again."

"Thank you, General," and he awkwardly saluted them as they turned to leave.

When the door closed behind them, Griffin said, "He certainly is a character, Sam."

"I know, sir. But he's a hard-charger and I can forgive him a lot for that. We can never get enough of them in the Corps."

46

D ANOWSKI MET HANSON and Griffin at the gate and told them that Jed, Al, Lonigan and Le Beau were waiting for them in the conference room. Muzzetti was hovering nearby, sending out signals that he'd like to be included. He snapped to attention and saluted when he saw them.

"Good evening, General. Colonel."

Hanson nodded and Griffin said, "Good to see you, Captain. How are you?"

"Well, thank you, sir. How are you?"

"I'm mourning the loss of my godson."

"I'm very sorry about that, sir. He was a fine boy. We'll all miss him."

"Thank you, Captain."

"If there's anything I can do, sir, anything at all, please let me know."

"You'll have to talk to Colonel Hanson about that."

"Colonel? Can I be of service?"

"I'll let you know, Muzi."

Griffin noticed the look of disappointment on Muzzetti's face. "How is Captain Muzzetti shaping up, Sam?"

"He's an outstanding officer, sir. I'm glad to have him in my command."

The praise was slightly consoling to Muzzetti.

"I'll see you before I leave, Captain."

"Thank you, General."

Le Beau called, "Attention," when he saw the general and he, Jed, and Al snapped to. Even Lonigan stood up.

"As you were, please," Griffin said, then turned to Jed. "I'm sorry about your loss, Jed. Tyrone was a fine boy."

"Thank you, sir. I don't know how I'll go on without him."

Griffin hugged Jed. "Nothing makes up for the loss of a son," he said softly. "We just have to find a way to live with the hurt and go on. There's no choice for some of us who have commitments to others."

"I know, sir. I'll find some way to manage, even though it's tearing me apart."

"Just remember you're not alone, Jed," the general said. "The Corps looks after its own."

"You know that I'll always be with you, Jed." Hanson said. "I'm going through the exact same nightmare that you are. One way or another, we'll survive."

Hanson listened to the latest updates from his staff, then looked at the people he relied on most and saw they were exhausted. He quickly established that there was nothing urgent that had to be done and that everything else could wait for the morning.

He ordered his people to get a good night's sleep, then dismissed them after setting the duty roster for the night. Danowski insisted he wasn't tired and volunteered for the night duty, but Hanson told him to inform Muzzetti that he would have the duty. Danowski was so eager to be useful that Hanson added, "Get some rest, Ski. We all might need it in the next few days."

"Aye, aye, sir," he replied and left to find Muzzetti.

"You were right to promote him, Sam. He's a good man."

"I'm just following your teachings, Charlie."

"Anything in particular?"

"You always told us at the Academy that a good officer recognizes and rewards good performance by his subordinates."

"I wish the rest of my students had listened as well as you did. The Corps would be better off." Griffin looked at his watch. "It's getting late, Sam. Let's find Beverly and get out of here."

"She's in Danowski's office."

"Not if I know her. I bet she's somewhere on the installation talking to the troops, building relationships and assessing morale. She'll tell us about it later."

"I'm always ready to listen to her. She's the smartest lady I know. I wish there was a younger version of her out there."

"What really happened with Tish? I thought you two were getting along so well."

"We were, until the terrorist attacks. When she found out that I didn't inform the FBI that we had a prisoner, she freaked out. Suddenly she became the Robespierre of the justice system, outraged that a tyrant had violated a prisoner's rights. If she found out that I ordered the execution of prisoners, she'd have me before a judge and jury, then hanged without appeal."

"Too bad, but you're still young, Sam. It's not too late to meet someone."

"I don't feel young anymore."

"Are you crazy, Sam Hanson," Beverly yelled, startling both of them. "You haven't reached your prime yet. What kind of nonsense is that? Your whole life is in front of you."

He started to shake his head, but before he could speak she cut him off. "Don't argue with me. I know this is a terrible day for you, but you've had others almost as bad. Charlie and I helped you through them, as we will this time, though it hurts more than ever before. You'll get through it and be stronger and more human after you come to terms with this unspeakable horror ..." and she burst out crying.

Hanson went to her, put his arms around her and held her tight. "He was such a wonderful boy," she whispered through her tears. "I was so proud of him; the fine son of a fine father ... You've got to stay strong, Sam, for after Charlie and I are gone, the Corps will need you as never before. So will your good people ... Now let me fix my face before we go."

They walked the short distance to his apartment building, preceded by a very wary Tico, followed by the two bodyguards, who moved as if they were in Indian country. The night turned cold, but the air was bracing after the crowded headquarters and barracks, and still clean from the earlier rain that had cleared some of the pollution.

The building entrance had been temporarily reinforced with sandbags and wood beams and the guard detail was particularly alert. Hanson dismissed Tico and the two guards and told them to get some sleep and pick him up at 0630.

The building guards all expressed their condolences and reassured him that they were being very watchful. On the way up in the elevator, Hanson began to realize how many friends the boys had made, both with the officers and enlisted personnel. He felt a little better after thinking about how much they impacted so many lives at such a young age.

Beverly immediately went to the kitchen and heated the always necessary pot of coffee. They sat down in the living room, completely at ease with each other, but unsure what to say next. Hanson looked around his quarters as if he had never lived there.

Everything seemed strange and remote, as if it belonged to someone else, in a distant life. He decided that once the current problems were resolved, he'd move into one of the rooms in the barracks. That is if he survived what was to come. Part of him desperately wanted to go into Kyle's room and look at his possessions, touch his clothes, not let the life that held so much promise slip away, as if through tactile contact he could retain Kyle's departed spirit. He felt Beverly staring at him and sensed that she could read his thoughts.

"Let's have a brandy with our coffee and drink to Kyle," she said softly.

A rush of gratitude for her kindness went through him and he went to her, kissed her and said, "Thank you, Bev. Kyle couldn't have had better godparents."

"You're welcome. Now get the bottle."

Beverly made the toast. "To one of the three finest men I know. The other two are here. To Kyle." Hanson and Griffin echoed her and they sat quietly for a few minutes, lost in their separate thoughts. "Perhaps we should have Jed join us," Beverly said.

"Al and Le Beau are staying with him tonight," Hanson replied. "They'll take care of him,"

"Beauty and the beast," Griffin quipped, in an attempt to lighten the atmosphere. "Jed's covered on both fronts."

"Shush, you wicked man," Beverly admonished teasingly. "Though you're not far off the mark … It's too bad in a way that Al's a Marine, Sam. She's smart, tough, capable and an attractive woman. She'd be perfect for you."

"I know how special she is, Bev, but I'd never allow myself to think of her in any other way than as her C.O. Professionally, I'd be taking advantage of my position and betraying her trust if I let a personal relationship develop. You know that."

"Of course I do. I was just thinking aloud."

"I was just remembering when you, Celia, Warren and Kyle stayed with us in Riyadh, in 2001," Griffin murmured. "Kyle was the most curious and active child I had ever seen. He was trying to walk and kept falling down, but he never got upset and he never cried. He had such incredible determination and wouldn't stop until he was able to do it. Then he got this incredible look of satisfaction on his face and immediately started exploring tables and shelves that had previously been out of reach. I was astonished at how carefully he examined things … It was obvious he was meant for engineering school."

"Just before we deployed to Saudi Arabia in 2007," Hanson said, "I took him on a trip to Annapolis. He was excited about going and made lists of what he wanted to see. He kept up a steady barrage of questions all the way there. We got to the gates and they were guarded by sailors for the first time since before the Civil War, because the Marines deployed to Iraq. Kyle took one look at them and asked indignantly, 'Why are squids on guard? Couldn't they afford Marines?' to the embarrassment of the naval detail."

They shared a healing laugh and regaled each other with Kyle stories.

"I remember when Celia brought him to visit us in Riyadh, in 2007," Beverly said with a fond smile. "You had just deployed to Iraq and he decided to visit you. He spoke fluent Arabic, was self-reliant and had no concept that he shouldn't do what he wanted …"

"I'll never forget that," Griffin interjected. "We thought he had been kidnapped and we turned the city upside down. We even issued a plea on Al Jazeera for his safe return."

"If I may continue …" Beverly said.

"Sorry, dear."

"He went to the marketplace, bought a robe and head covering, then bribed a driver on a supply convoy to give him a ride to Baghdad, but we didn't find that out until later."

"I was going out of my mind with worry," Hanson said, "but I couldn't leave my post, even for him. Then, two days later, the Sergeant of the Guard marched him into my headquarters and Kyle was upset that he couldn't surprise me. I was so happy to see him that I forgot to spank him."

"That was quite an adventure for an eight-year-old," Griffin offered.

"He was hardly an ordinary eight year old," Beverly added.

Hanson was about to relate how when Kyle was nine, he read Burton's 'Pilgrimage to Mecca and Medina', which thrilled him and made a plan to emulate it, but a call from Al interrupted him.

"Put on CNN," she said. "Mayor Ramirez has just blamed the Marines for the breakdown in security today. All the media are running the story and now they're going wild. Call me when you've seen enough."

Hanson clicked on the TV in time to see a full repeat of Ramirez' statement, which concluded with a promise to name an investigative commission immediately. His image was inset with various shots of the blood and carnage from the explosion that could only have come from Al Jazeera.

Then the talking heads took over, explaining once again to the American people and the rest of the world that everything bad that happened to America was its own fault, due to oppressive and exploitative policies. Hanson still found it hard to believe that for all practical purposes the American media were anti-American.

"Most of these newspeople sound like they come from the old agitprop crew of the Soviet Union, during the Cold War," he remarked bitterly.

"Why should they be any different than some of our leaders?" Griffin commented.

Hanson called Al. "They're really attacking us on all fronts now and we have to respond. I'll call Carver … No. He may not be able to deal with this yet. I'll ask Dr. Van Meer to call the mayor and remind him that we weren't in charge of security, except in the Enclave. Did you notice the footage of the bombing that CNN was showing?"

"What about it?"

"It came from Al Jazeera. Their camera crew was at the scene before anyone else. They knew there was going to an attack."

"Are you sure?"

"Yes. By the time CNN got there most of the wounded had been evacuated and the dead were being taken away. They couldn't have seen some of the earlier footage."

"I don't think the girl would know anything about that, but I'll ask her in the morning … They shouldn't be allowed to get away with that, Sam."

"We'll see what happens. How's Jed doing?"

"He keeps going up and down, but he's trying to hang in there. Le Beau's been a big help. He and Jed go back a long way."

"Good. I'll talk to you later …" He turned to the general. "You heard what I said about Al Jazeera, Charlie?"

"Yes. We should find out who alerted them. We can assume it was the terrorists."

Hanson nodded, then switched to other news channels while he talked to Van Meer, only pausing long enough at each station to get the gist of the coverage.

The reporting was invariably critical of America, rather than sympathetic for the loss of life, or concerned with the suffering of the wounded. A growing anger at the terrorists and the media slightly dulled the pain he was feeling from the loss of Kyle. He was ready to ignore them for the moment and get back to talking about Kyle when the guard downstairs called him.

"This is Sergeant Morales, sir. There's all sorts of reporters and TV crews in front, demanding to speak to you. They're also attracting a crowd. What should we do about them, sir?"

"Don't fire on them, Julio, unless they fire first."

"Don't worry, sir. Can we at least fix bayonets?"

Hanson managed a laugh. "Don't tempt me. Tell them that our public affairs officer will issue a statement in the morning. Got that?"

"Yes, sir. I'll take care of it. I'm real sorry about Kyle, sir."

"Thanks, Julio. Goodnight."

"I remember Morales from Iraq," Griffin remarked. "He's a good man."

"Yes," Hanson responded. "I'm going to recommend him for O.C.S. as soon as the current situation is resolved."

"Why didn't you promote him with the others?" Griffin asked.

"He needs to build a little more self-esteem before he's ready for command responsibility. Formal officer training will give him a sense of perspective."

"I'm glad to hear you're exercising good judgment about promotions to officer. We're both overstepping our authority in field promotions, which we'll only get away with because Valerie will be leaving soon. It could cause us some problems if these mustangs foul up."

"They won't. They're ready, Charlie. If time ever allows, we'll send them to O.C.S., but you can rely on them … I was going to recommend Nita Vasquez for O.C.S., but she was killed today with the boys."

"Was she another of your Iraq vets?"

"Yes. Good people."

"We've lost too many of them, Sam."

"Yes, sir."

Beverly had been alertly following everything that had been going on. "I have a suggestion." The two men turned to her. "You've been through a lot today, Sam, and tomorrow will probably be difficult. Why don't you organize things for your regular activities and be prepared to deal with whatever develops. Don't go any further tonight with anti-terrorist planning. In fact, wait until after the funeral on Saturday ..."

She started crying again and Griffin put his arm around her consolingly. "I didn't know I had so many tears in me," she muttered.

"I think you're right, Bev. We know what we're going to do. We just need more intel to identify the target, or targets. I just want to be sure that everything's planned very carefully, so no one gets caught or identified."

"That makes sense," Griffin said.

Hanson nodded. "Unless something special comes up, we can have our planning session on Sunday. We should have a lot more intel by then. Now let's get ready for bed."

Hanson got an extra blanket and pillow and gave them to Beverly. He didn't follow her into Kyle's room, not ready to look at his son's things. He waited until both Beverly and Griffin finished in the bathroom to say goodnight, before he began his bathroom chores. He brushed his teeth so vigorously that his gums bled, but he didn't notice until the blood dripped in the sink. He considered taking a shower, but put it off for the morning. He called Al to check on Jed. She told him he was finally relaxing a bit. He asked to speak to Jed and they chatted briefly, both avoiding what was most on their minds. He called Morales who reported that the media were packing up and departing, without taking any casualties.

"That Al Jazeera crew is real obnoxious, sir. They pushed and shoved their way through the crowd, knocking everyone out of their way. Then they demanded to speak to you. When I told them 'No', they tried to get past me, but I didn't butt-stroke them, sir."

"Thanks, Julio. We don't need another media incident. Goodnight."

His last call was to Muzzetti, who reported all quiet, so he finally shut down for the night.

<h1 style="text-align:center">47</h1>

H ANSON SLEPT FITFULLY. He kept waking up every twenty or thirty minutes with an impulse to go to Kyle's room and see if he was home from … somewhere. Then he'd remember that Kyle was … gone, and the Griffins were in there. He sat on the couch for a long time and all he could think about was how many times duty had prevented him from being with Kyle. It seemed that just a short while ago Kyle was a child, then suddenly he was a teenager, mature enough to do things on his own.

He would never see the kind of man that Kyle would have become. He remembered when Kyle first told him that he wanted to go to the Academy and become a Marine officer. It made him so proud. Now it was another treat that he'd never see. Despite all efforts not to, he cried quietly until there were no more tears left. Then he went back to bed, to try to get some rest before the demands of another day.

Beverly had coffee ready at 0545 and Hanson tried to be quiet so he wouldn't wake Kyle, then he remembered. He shook off the paralyzing, depressive thoughts and concentrated on getting ready for the day. He called Tico at 0615, gave instructions to pick him and the Griffins up at 0645, at the service entrance to the building.

"If any media people are hanging around let me know and we'll figure out a way to avoid them."

Beverly and Griffin were ready when it was time to go and they took the freight elevator down to the basement. Hanson surveyed the street very carefully, then signaled Beverly and Griffin to join him in the Humvee. The mood in the vehicle was somber.

Tico remarked softly, "I still can't believe the boys are gone. Just a couple of weeks ago Kyle kicked my ass in karate practice … I'll also miss Nita. I had a crush on her," he added.

The rest of the ride was silent, and Hanson directed Tico to go to the rear entrance of the headquarters building.

Hanson, Griffin and Beverly ate breakfast in the mess hall. A constant stream of Marines stopped at their table to offer their condolences. Except for occasional voices raised in anger at the terrorists, the mood was like a funeral.

Jed, Al and Le Beau came in a few minutes later and Jed and Al sat at the officer's table. Le Beau went to the senior N.C.O. table, where the talk was how the boys had saved their families from the terrorists, only to become victims themselves. The most popular subject throughout the mess hall was payback, especially from the N.C.O.'s, who were outraged at the attacks on their families and wanted revenge. Several of the officers drifted in, but they were careful to sit at some distance from the general. Only Danowski joined 'the brass' and he ate as silently as the others.

When they finished eating, Hanson gave Danowski his orders, "Have Jed, Al and Le Beau come to my office at 0800. Tell Nakamura to take over as officer of the day from Muzzetti and instruct him to call you with any problem. Join us as soon as you have the morning report."

"Aye, aye, sir."

Hanson led Griffin and Beverly to his office, sent for a pot of coffee, then turned to Griffin.

"This is your last chance to pack your bags, take your beautiful wife and get out of here before you become a war criminal."

"We already settled that, Sam … Unless there's something specific I can contribute, it's your show and I'll just lend authority."

"You mean like the use of your gun moll?"

This produced a weak laugh, but the quip reduced the tension in the room. Hanson called Lonigan and asked him to join them at 0800 for a planning session.

"I'll be there, Sam. I've also got some news that won't make you happy."

"Happiness has become an alien quality lately. Do you want to tell me now?"

"If it's alright with you I'd only like to tell it once."

"I'll see you in a few, Mike."

"Are you sure he should be included in whatever we do, Sam?" Griffin asked. "After all, he's not a Marine."

"He's been a trusted colleague and he's become a good friend. He also has access to resources through the police department that we can use. We can rely on him."

Hanson finally called Carver, a call he had dreaded making.

"How are you, Carv?"

"If it wasn't for Mei, I'd go out of my mind. I don't know what I'm doing … I haven't even made arrangements for … Mavis …" Then he broke down and cried. Hanson waited patiently while Carver collected himself. "Sorry about that, Sam."

"Don't be. I've been doing the same thing … We're burying the boys tomorrow at Greenwood Cemetery, in Brooklyn. It'll pretty much be a formal Marine ceremony. Captain Lonigan arranged it. He can do the same for you, if you like."

Hanson heard Carver talking to Mei for a minute.

"Ask him for me, will you, Sam?"

"Of course. I'll have him call you and you can discuss the details. I hope you know I'm heartbroken about our loss."

"Why did it have to be our kids?"

"We'll never be able to answer that. I only know these terrible crimes will keep happening in a violent, insane world."

"What are we going to do about it, Sam? We can't let them get away with murdering our kids."

"I'll call you this afternoon and we'll get together soon and talk about it."

"Thanks, Sam."

When he disconnected, Hanson turned to Griffin.

"He won't be involved in anything we do, no matter what. He's too distressed to be reliable."

The meeting started promptly at 0800 and Hanson had everyone review the situation up to the moment. Al outlined the information they hoped to get from the interrogation of the girl. Jed updated the status of his reaction platoon and commended Danowski for his thorough preparations in getting them ready for possible action.

"I'm monitoring the teams at the girl's house in Brooklyn and I'd like to station another squad nearby, in case they're needed."

"Good idea," Hanson approved. "Before we go further, Captain Lonigan has some information for us. Mike?"

"I don't know an easy way to say this, so I'll read a memo I got early this morning from our FBI liaison. 'The FBI didn't make the security sweeps of the department stores that Colonel Hanson requested'."

It took a few moments for the impact to sink in, then Jed sprang to his feet, cursing furiously.

"Those fucking Feebs. If they did their job, our sons would still be alive." Then he remembered who was present and turned to Beverly. "Sorry, ma'am. My temper got the best of me. I'm having trouble dealing with this."

"That's alright, Jed," she said. "I feel the same way and so does everyone else here."

Hanson gave everyone a minute to cool down and at the same time brought the killing rage he was feeling under control.

"Is your information confirmed, Mike?" he forced himself to ask calmly.

"Nothing official yet, but I think it will turn out to be accurate. The source is reliable."

Hanson's knees wobbled for a moment and he silently ordered them to stand fast. He looked at his comrades-in-arms, who he knew shared his suffering.

"What do we do about this, people?"

"What are our options?" Beverly asked.

He nodded in appreciation at her rational response. "First we have to confirm the report. If it's true, we can explore a legal process to punish the guilty parties, or we can deal with it ourselves and take justice into our own hands."

"We should take care of them ourselves," Jed blurted.

"Would you murder FBI agents?" Lonigan asked.

"It would be execution, not murder," Al replied.

"What are our chances of getting justice in the legal system, sir?" Hanson asked Griffin.

"It's hard to say, Sam. In all honesty, I can't assure you that we'll get satisfaction."

Beverly said, "I think we should wait until the boys' funerals are over, out of respect for them, before planning violence."

Griffin nodded agreement and Hanson knew they were right. "We'll meet here Sunday, at 0900, and continue the discussion."

Jed, Al, Le Beau and Danowski left for their assignments and Lonigan went to make funeral arrangements for Carver, leaving Hanson, Griffin and Beverly staring at each other.

"Once we start, there's no turning back," Griffin mused. "It will be the end of our careers and probably prison, if we're not killed."

"Do you think we should let the legal system handle this, Charlie? You know they'll get nowhere."

"I agree with you, Sam. I was just speculating aloud."

"It's still not too late to back out, Charlie. You have a lot more to lose than I have. You can leave after the funeral and give me a written order instructing me not to take any retaliatory action."

"I don't want to hear that again," Beverly snapped. "We're with you all the way. Charlie just wants to be sure you understand all the implications of what we're intending to do."

"I understand, Bev. I won't bring this up again."

"Good. You also better come up with a master plan, so that we don't get caught, or I'll pop a cap in your ass."

They all laughed at her phrasing.

"You're too much, Bev."

"That's what Charlie says," she replied smugly.

Danowski knocked, then came in. "The media are gathering at the gate, boss. They're demanding to speak to you and threatening to camp outside until you make an appearance."

"Let them wait," Griffin ordered, "Maybe it'll snow and bury them."

"Aye, aye, sir."

Before Danowski could leave, Beverly said, "Wait. Let's give them a statement that will satisfy them for the moment. Then get business cards from them and promise a press conference following the mourning period. Is that alright, Sam?"

"Good idea, Bev. Do you want to write it?"

"Give me a minute." She sat down, started writing and when she finished, read, "The Veterans Parade Day organizers deeply regret the tragic events that took place and offer their heartfelt condolences to those who lost loved ones and those who were injured. We are confident that law enforcement agencies will bring the perpetrators of this inhuman attack to justice."

"Well done, Bev. Go read it to them, Ski."

"I'm not much for making speeches, boss."

"Good. You'll sound more convincing."

"Aye, aye, sir."

"What's next on the agenda, Sam?" Griffin asked.

"Mostly waiting, unless something specific happens. The troops are staked out in Brooklyn, the interrogation is underway and Lonigan will get confirmation about whether the FBI failed to check Saks."

"Is Tish involved in that?" Beverly asked.

A look of mixed anger and pain flashed across his face. "She was with Royce when I requested the check. Unless it turns out that they were ordered not to by higher authority, I hold them both accountable."

"That's unfortunate," Beverly mused. "We hoped you found someone, not to take Celia's place, but so you'd have a fuller life … What will you do to her if she's part of it?"

He had a harsh, unforgiving look. "The same thing we'll do to Royce, if we establish that she's also responsible. This isn't just personal, Bev, though heaven knows that's reason enough for me. Our country has to wake up to the fact that we're losing a war, before it's too late. Maybe shock treatment will make people realize that we're in a life and death struggle for survival against a pitiless enemy."

"I'm glad to hear you say that, Sam," Griffin said. "It's reassuring that you're not a loose cannon, only reacting to a personal tragedy."

"You know me better than that, Charlie. The best teacher I ever had taught me to never deny my passion, but to act with reason. That was in my second year at the Academy … I was dating a girl at the time who had just discovered Taoism. She was always quoting Lao Tse's lofty words of wisdom. When I quoted your aphorism to her, she said it was typically western and the kind of attitude that proved the superior wisdom of China. We broke up shortly after that."

"I hope it wasn't my fault," Griffin said.

Hanson managed a weak grin. "No. She was already tired of the uniform. When I tried to explain that China was ruled by the Communist Party, not enlightened sages, and was fiercely militaristic, she had enough of my insensitivity."

"Aren't you glad that Celia made up for ten like her?" Beverly offered.

"I was lucky to find her … After her and Warren's death, all I had was Kyle. Now they're all gone."

Danowski interrupted and reported that the media had dispersed, except for a few die-hards.

"You better use the rear entrance until things calm down, sir."

"Thanks, Ski."

"Any orders, sir?"

"Yes. Resume your regular duties."

"Aye, aye, sir."

Hanson turned to Griffin and Beverly. "I think we should give the appearance that the situation is relatively calm now and after the funerals we'll go back to condition normal. This will give our enemies the impression that we're too paralyzed to react with any kind of force. It'll also reassure our authorities that we're not going off half-cocked and retaliating for the loss of our sons."

"That's an great thought, Sam," Griffin commented. "There's no reason to alert our enemies that we're planning to target them for a violent response. If there's any choice, I'd rather not spend my declining years in a cell at Leavenworth."

"Belay that talk, bud. You're not declining yet," Beverly asserted.

"That's Navy talk, Bev," he protested weakly.

She glared. "You know what I mean, General Jarhead."

Then things began to happen quickly. Lonigan called and confirmed that the FBI didn't check the department stores, because they didn't get orders from Agent-In-Charge Royce, or his assistant, Agent Madison, and that they'll be issuing a press release blaming the police department for the oversight. A blaze of fury coursed through Hanson, but again he maintained control.

Griffin and Beverly were as upset as he was at the news and they exchanged angry, sympathetic looks. Carver called and told him that Lonigan had made the funeral arrangements for Mavis.

"I'm grateful to him. I'd like to meet you this afternoon to discuss what we're going to do about the murderers."

"First we have to bury our children, Carv. We'll get together after the funerals."

Then Al called. "All we've learned from the girl is that the recruiters said they were Al Qaeda. She's being completely cooperative, but that's all she seems to know. I believe her."

"The terrorists will visit her family to find out what happened," Hanson said. "If we bag them, we'll find out who sent them. Make sure the girl is comfortable, then you and Le Beau return to your regular duties."

"Aye, aye, sir."

Hanson looked at Griffin and Beverly. "Now it's time for our least favorite activity, waiting."

48

A HEAVY RAIN SWEPT IN Saturday morning, setting a dismal scene for the funerals of loved ones. To add to the pall, Al Jazeera released a video tape of the leader of Hezbollah, Prime Minister of Lebanon, extolling the martyrs, calling them righteous defenders of the faith who killed the crusader enemies of Islam and were now enjoying the rewards of paradise.

The Marines who watched in the barracks and spoke Arabic translated for their comrades, which further provoked outrage and calls for reprisals. Danowski called Hanson and told him to turn on the TV. Hanson watched the outrageous statement with Griffin and Beverly.

"He's gone too far this time, Charlie," Hanson growled, as they got ready to leave for headquarters. "He's a Head of State now. He can't go on the air praising suicide bombers and expect us to ignore the provocation. That's approving an act of war."

Griffin shook his head. "There's nothing we can do about him now. When the Plant administration takes over, we may be allowed to react differently. Maybe we can send him cruise missiles, instead of apologies."

He stared at Hanson suggestively, who got the message: *the day might come, but it wasn't today.*

Spouses of the Marines and their children who lived in the building were waiting in the lobby when Hanson and the Griffins came downstairs. Esther Morales, wife of Sergeant Morales, stepped forward.

"We want you to know how sorry we are for the loss of your son. Many of us would have been killed if it wasn't for the bravery of Kyle and Tyrone. It's a terrible day for all of us when we have to say goodbye to such fine boys. If there's anything we can do, Colonel, just ask. We can never repay our debt to them for saving us. We just want you to know how much we care."

Other men and women offered their commiserating comments.

Many of them cried. Hanson was touched.

"Thank you, Esther, and the rest of you. Your concern means a lot to me."

Then he got too choked up to say anything else. Beverly thanked everyone and led him out the door. The guards had alerted them that the media were in front and in back, so there was no point in ducking out the rear door.

Before they could get into the waiting Humvee, the reporters, who had been camped outside for hours, rushed at them. They thrust microphones in Hanson's face and bombarded him with questions, while the cameras recorded his reaction.

"Are you responsible for the breakdown in security?" "Do you know who the terrorists were?" "Is there a final count of the dead and wounded?" Hanson resolutely ignored them and with the help of his bodyguards, who were running interference, made his way towards the Humvee. The rabid journalists yelled louder and louder and vigorously objected when the Marines shoved them out of the way. One obnoxious reporter bellowed, "How does it feel to get what you deserve, warmonger?"

Hanson froze in his tracks, then whirled around, intent on identifying the offender and dismembering him. Beverly grabbed him by the arm and pulled him away.

"There may be worse to come today, Sam. Don't let them get to you."

The reporters followed them to headquarters in mobile broadcasting vans and other vehicles, prepared to wait as long as necessary for a hot story of violence, death and sorrow, a combination guaranteed to appeal to a world-wide viewing audience.

Tico dropped them at the front gate, since the media was watching both entrances and there was no way to avoid them. They rushed into the building, shoving the reporters aside and ignoring their clamor. Danowski met him at the door and asked if he wanted to inspect the formation, which was mustered in the barracks because of the rain.

"It would mean a lot to the troops, sir."

Hanson nodded and Danowski led the way, followed by Hanson, Griffin and Beverly. When Gunny Le Beau saw them, he called, "Ten-hut," and the men and women snapped to.

Hanson moved slowly down the line, once again noticing how threadbare and mended many of the dress-blue uniforms were. Even General Griffin's uniform was worn and shiny in places. He also noted with pride that everyone's brass and decorations sparkled.

There wasn't enough room in the barracks for all the troops to assemble at once, so Hanson and the Griffins waited while the platoons moved in and out, then repeated the inspection. Le Beau led the last platoon in that included Wilkins, looking pale as a ghost, unable to close his blouse because of his wounds, trying to sit at attention in his wheelchair.

"At ease, Wilkie," Hanson said.

"Sorry I can't be of more use to you at a time like this, sir. I swear I'll find a way to avenge them."

Tears almost sprang from Hanson's eyes but he forced himself to remain calm. "Thank you, Wilkie. That's not our concern right now. Lieutenant Danowski."

"Yes, sir?"

"Thank our people for me and express my regrets that not everyone can be with us today."

"Aye, aye, sir. We're planning to leave at 0930. It'll be a big convoy. I'd like to review final preparations with you, sir."

"Come to my office in fifteen minutes, Ski."

"Aye, aye, sir," and he saluted and did a precise about-face that would have made his drill instructor in boot camp proud.

Al met Hanson at his office with a request.

"Jed and I should go ahead to the funeral home, so we can check the police security that Lonigan has arranged and let you know if it's satisfactory."

"Good idea, Al. Go to the cemetery first. Take Jed's reaction platoon and establish a perimeter around the place in cooperation with the police. The cemetery's big, with local streets running around it and it has lots of easy access points."

"I'll take care of it, sir. I'd also like to send two more squads to the funeral home, just to be sure."

"Do it, Al. We don't want any disruptions today. We'll probably be here for another hour. Call me if you need anything."

"Can we accidentally mistake some reporters for terrorists, sir?"

"Tempt me not. How's Jed doing?"

"He got some sleep last night and he's starting to accept what happened. He'll be alright. What about you, Sam?"

"I'll get through this. Now get moving."

"Aye, aye, sir."

Lonigan came in a few minutes later, still shaking off raindrops.

"I won't be able to join you at the funeral home, Sam. I have to go to the funeral for the police officer who died trying to stop the bombers, but I'll meet you at the cemetery."

"Thanks for all your help, Mike. We'd be in a real mess without you."

"I wish I could do more … Let's go over the schedule. The service for Mavis will be at a different funeral home, so you won't have to deal with that. She will be buried at Greenwood, near your son, so a lot of V.I.P.s will be there. I've requested extra security and we'll have a S.W.A.T. team on standby. You might consider sending a detachment of your troops."

"We've already sent a platoon to the cemetery and we'll send two extra squads to the funeral home."

"Good. I'll appoint liaisons for both sites. I've got to go. I'll see you later, Sam. General. Mrs. Griffin."

Danowski appeared as ordered and gave his report.

"We might run a few minutes late in starting, sir, because we had to arrange transport for the additional security troops. Al and Jed just left with their platoon for the cemetery and the two squads for the funeral home are just about ready to mount up. The trucks and private vehicles with the families from your building will be here in a few minutes and our troops here are ready to go. I took the liberty of ordering a traditional Marine ceremony for the boys at the cemetery, sir. I know it's not exactly regulation …" and he looked at the General expectantly.

"That's very thoughtful of you, Ski," Griffin said. "The boys earned it."

"Thank you, General," Danowski replied. "I think it's appropriate, sir. There's one more problem, Colonel."

"What?"

"The media have been watching our preparations and they're getting ready to follow us."

"There's nothing we can do about it, Ski. We still have freedom of the press."

The convoy was ready to roll at 0945 and Hanson, Griffin and Beverly, preceded by his bodyguards, forced their way through the crowd of reporters, who once again shoved microphones and cameras at them and yelled questions. The Al Jazeera crew was pushiest, elbowing colleagues aside and their arrogant demands for answers were infuriating. Hanson recognized them as the same crew who had arrived so early at the bombing of the parade. He indulged in a brief fantasy of drawing his pistol and shooting them for all the world to see, live and in color, on CNN.

He dismissed the idle thought, helped Beverly into the Humvee, followed by Griffin. He shook off some of the more aggressive reporters who were yanking at his sleeve for his attention. He took a final look at the convoy and noted with approval that Danowski had placed civilian vehicles between military vehicles for additional security.

He got into the Humvee, told Tico to radio everyone that they were starting, then sat back for the ride that would lay his son to rest.

A police car led the convoy down 30th Street and another police car stopped traffic at the entrance to the East River Drive. They proceeded south on the highway at thirty miles per hour and police escorts made sure that no one cut in on the forty or so military and civilian vehicles.

Because of the steady rain, the machine guns on the Humvees and Strykers weren't manned and the hatches were closed, but after the recent attacks, the troops were watchful and alert. Many of the cars speeding by slowed and their drivers gaped at the military convoy, an infrequent sight in Manhattan, unsure whether it was an indicator of war or peace.

In a pleasant surprise, when they passed a public housing complex below 14th Street, the residents, mostly Hispanic, opened their windows and waved in friendly greetings. Some of them even held signs, saying, 'Our prayers are with you', 'We love America'. 'We support the Marines'. The spontaneous outpouring was touching and made the troops feel connected to the people they were sworn to defend.

The police car led the column onto the entrance ramp to the Brooklyn Bridge. As they crossed the river, some passengers looked at the South Street Seaport and the old sailing ships, a link with a more secure past, when it took more time to receive news of disaster. Others stared at

Miss Liberty, a vague shape in the harbor that they could barely make out in the rain, a slightly battered symbol of the besieged republic, still presiding over the hope of freedom.

They exited the bridge and got onto the Brooklyn-Queens Expressway, an elevated highway overlooking the harbor on one side and the city of churches on the other. They passed the decayed Brooklyn waterfront, once a teeming dock area of the great port of New York, now mostly crumbling piers and deserted warehouses. Even the last effort to revivify the dying commercial waterfront, the plan for cruise ship piers, had become a lost cause in the recession of '09. The abandoned buildings sat like jagged skeletons, awaiting final dismemberment.

The convoy turned onto Fourth Avenue and drove through changing ethnic neighborhoods of mostly small residential buildings and retail shops, punctuated by the occasional hi-rise and condo building. There was an impression of fading vitality, as if the struggle for prosperity had overcome the local dwellers when their country suffered a devastating series of afflictions. The few people on the street stared at the ominous procession as it passed, not reacting in any way to the sight of armed vehicles. They were possibly used to seeing military convoys from Fort Hamilton, a government installation that was not too far away. Hanson wasn't familiar with Brooklyn and hadn't realized how large it was. The ride past almost identical street after street seemed interminable and it took a great effort not to fidget. Beverly held his arm, sensing his impatience and tried to make conversation, but he didn't feel like talking and she was sensitive enough to perceive that. Instead he thought about the different ethnic communities they passed and wondered what kind of future they would have.

The funeral home was on a narrow side street, so the drivers let everyone off at the entrance, then double parked around the corner, on Third Avenue. Only Hanson's Humvee remained in front, in case of emergency. The funeral home had been converted from an old, two story residential building and was much too small to hold all the mourners. The building didn't have an elevator, so they used the coffin lift to bring Wilkins up in his wheelchair, an eerie sight to see him suddenly rising through the floor. The Marines and their families took turns paying their respects, then waited in the vehicles.

The funeral home's staff let everyone know that the home was owned by veterans, as if they expected this to be some sort of consolation.

Griffin, who had attended many funerals all over the world, commented to Beverly, "At least they're not as unctuous as most funeral homes."

She nodded agreement, never taking her eyes off Hanson. She knew that at Hanson's instructions Al would not leave Jed's side. Then she heard a loud noise from another room and instinctively reached for her pistol. She relaxed when she realized that it was only a door slamming and let out a sigh of relief that she didn't pull a gun and panic the crowd.

When everyone who was remaining for the service was seated, the minister took his place behind the lectern, welcomed them, then recited a psalm in a solemn, soothing voice. He briefly talked about the boys, praising them in words that Hanson knew could only have been provided by Beverly. Then he invited family and loved ones to speak. Hanson gestured to Jed to go first, but Jed shook his head and muttered, "I'm not ready yet."

Hanson stood up and deliberately avoided looking at the coffins.

"A father never expects to bury his son. When it happens we have to find a way to go on, because our responsibilities are still there and the causes we dedicated ourselves to still require our services …

"Kyle was an exceptional boy who never ceased to delight me with his accomplishments. He and his best friend Tyrone did everything together. Unlike many troubled or confused youth, they had a sense of purpose and a concept of duty and honor. They proved that during the terrorist attack …

"They're gone now and all the promise of the future is tarnished. This is the most painful farewell of my life … Only my duty to my country permits me to continue what has become a hollow existence without Kyle … I do not know if there is an afterlife, so I do not know if I will be reunited with the son I loved so dearly. I only hope that someday the world will be a better place, so fathers will not lose their sons as we did."

The crowd was silent as he went back to his seat and everyone he passed touched him sympathetically. Griffin spoke briefly, followed by Beverly, who recollected incidents from her godson's life. She brought many of them to tears when she said, "I never had a child of my own, so Sam Hanson became my son. It was a blessing when Kyle was born because he became the grandchild I would otherwise never have. Now I won't be able to buy him presents anymore … When he was six, he confided in me that he wanted a pocketknife. I took him to an expensive department store and showed him the collection of Swiss knives. He said, 'I don't need all those blades, Aunt Bev. The Marine knife will do. Let's go to the PX." Then she burst into tears and sat down.

No one spoke for a while, then, as the minister urged someone to speak, Al stood up.

"I knew Kyle and Tyrone since they were little kids, when we were in Iraq. They were the finest boys I ever met. They were always up to something new and they made enough mischief for five boys … I loved them and I'll miss them, and I'll never forget them."

Le Beau, Morales and Wilkins spoke next, each praising the boys and saying how much they'd miss them.

The minister recited another psalm, then turned to Jed and beckoned him to come to the lectern. Jed moved slowly and like Hanson, he didn't look at the coffins.

"When I was growing up a lot of black fathers had abandoned their kids. I vowed I would never be like that. My reward was a wonderful son. The more I got to know Tyrone, the more I loved him … It never occurred to me that I'd have to get along without him. Like Colonel Hanson said, I have to find a way to go on. Sam Hanson is the best friend I ever had. We've been through a lot together. We lost our wives and our other children at the same time, in the great flu pandemic of 2013. We lost our boys at the same time to a terrorist's bomb. Tyrone and Kyle were all we had left of our families. Now they're gone. Sam. My brother in arms. My brother in suffering. I would have given my life for my son, as you would have for yours. I know you'll help me to go on."

The two men embraced, fighting back tears and sat down together. The minister recited the Lord's Prayer.

With that, the ceremony ended.

49

T HE RAIN CAME DOWN HARDER and it took more time to load the vehicles then it had in Manhattan. Al was glad the extra security squads hadn't been needed at the funeral home. The police were able to easily contain the reporters and camera crews, even nabbing several reporters who tried to sneak inside.

A police car led the convoy up Fourth Avenue and this time Hanson noticed individual shops, bakeries, pizza parlors, bodegas and lots of other small businesses that nourished a neighborhood. Somehow, despite the anguish he was feeling for the final separation to come, he couldn't help noticing a more vital pulse on the street. On one corner, a man in civilian clothes stood at attention and saluted as they passed.

The CNN helicopter was still trailing the procession and Hanson called Lonigan and asked him to try to keep it from hovering over the cemetery.

The ride was over too quickly and they turned into the forbidding gothic entrance of the cemetery that awaited with open mouth the expected dead, soon to be swallowed by the implacable earth. The structure was massive, made of turgid brown stone, capped by eerie spires that proclaimed only the dead would be welcome. The bathroom at the funeral home had been out of order, so the first priority at the cemetery for many of the mourners was a visit to the toilet. Al and Le Beau organized the large group into orderly lines that would take turns. Then Al left Morales in charge and she and Le Beau inspected the security arrangements.

Carver's funeral procession arrived a few minutes later and the bereaved fathers greeted each other. The V.I.P.s came next, including Mayor Ramirez, Ambassador to the U.N. Blunt, city and state elected and appointed officials, as well as a legion of doctors, friends, and families. Mei, Dr. Van Meer and Jennifer Van Meer stayed close to Carver, sustaining him in this time of terrible loss.

When everyone was ready to proceed to the burial site, they got back into their vehicles and the convoy snaked its way through the narrow roads to the final resting place for the children. The graves were adjacent and it took a while for the large crowd to assemble. The minister had arrived first and he also presided over Mavis' funeral. He recited a psalm, then offered a blessing as Mavis' coffin was lowered into the rain-slick, muddy ground. Jennifer, elegantly dressed in black, including a veil, dropped a rose on the coffin, bid her friend farewell.

She turned to Hanson and said, "My friend would still be alive if it wasn't for your son. She died because she went to meet him just as the bombers got there. If she stayed with me on the grandstand she'd only have gotten a few scratches, just like I did. If only she never met him."

Then she stalked off dramatically, leaving a stunned group behind. Van Meer looked at Hanson apologetically, shrugged, then followed his daughter.

Hanson experienced a kaleidoscope of emotions that ended in sorrow for the terrible loss of their children, so he dismissed Jennifer's shocking tirade.

"My son wouldn't have wanted any harm to come to Mavis. Eye-witnesses told us that he tried to warn her in his last moments …"

Carver came to him, hugged him and said loudly, "The only cause of our childrens' deaths was the relentless hatred of savage terrorists. Sam, Jed and I lost the persons most precious to us, our only children. The blame for this senseless tragedy is not on Kyle because my daughter loved him. The enemies of civilization, who have no regard for the innocent are responsible … I know the three of us share the same pain and the same feelings of bereavement … I could never have imagined us here, burying our children …"

He fell silent and stumbled towards his limo, immediately assisted by Mei.

The minister, obviously used to all kinds of emotional outpourings, uttered soothing words and tried to reassure them that they were there to say goodbye to loved ones, and that recriminations were inappropriate. Mavis' mourners nodded agreement, made their individual farewells to her, then headed for their waiting vehicles without saying anything to Hanson or Jed.

Some of the Marines began to mutter angrily at the disrespect shown by the mayor and Ambassador Blunt in ignoring Kyle and Tyrone, but Griffin silenced them with a scathing glance. Lonigan rushed up to Hanson and Jed and offered his apology.

"Sorry I'm late. The service for the police officer attracted hundreds and hundreds of cops from all over the country. It took a long time for them to pay their respects and I was part of the official organizing committee, so I couldn't leave until the funeral was over. I got here just as that Van Meer girl flipped out. I hope you didn't take her seriously."

"Even if what she said was true, it's just one more burden that I have to live with," Hanson replied sadly.

Before Lonigan could reply, Al presented herself formally, stood at attention and saluted.

"We are ready to proceed with the ceremony, sir."

Hanson nodded. "Carry on, Captain."

She went to Le Beau, who saluted her, then gave him the order to begin. He about-faced and went to the honor guard, who were waiting to carry the coffins. He led them to the hearse, where they lifted the coffins and in a slow, solemn march, brought them to the graves and placed them on the supports.

The coffins were covered by American flags and the honor guard painstakingly saluted them. Le Beau led them off, then returned with a firing squad. They took positions and on Le Beau's command, presented arms and fired twice in an eight-gun salute. As Le Beau led them off, many of the women and some of the men were weeping.

Le Beau came back with the bugler, who played 'Taps', the heartbreaking hymn of the dead, that frequently brought tears to the eyes of the most hardened soldiers. The honor guard returned and folded the flags, which they presented to Hanson and Jed.

Hanson turned and gave his to Beverly. She took it, pressed it against her chest, then finally broke down crying. Hanson put his arm around her and they watched as Marine after Marine went to each grave, took off medals or ribbons and laid them reverently on the coffins.

The wives or husbands went next, placing earrings, rings or other personal items on the coffins. Two small children dressed in white came last, a black girl and a white girl. They each carried a sprig of flowers and a Ken doll, one white, one black. The black girl put the white Ken doll on Kyle's coffin. The white girl put the black Ken doll on Tyrone's coffin.

Jed burst into tears and Al led him off. The minister recited a prayer and the ceremony ended. Griffin led Hanson and Beverly to the Humvee and the rest of the mourners straggled to the vehicles for the doleful ride back to Manhattan.

The media, who hadn't been allowed to enter the cemetery grounds, were hovering just outside the gates, lusting for a spectacle of grief they could show the world. The police brusquely moved them aside as the convoy passed and only the hard-core video crews followed, in the faint hope of an accident, a suicide, anything that would allow them to broadcast the anguished feelings of death for their viewers to feast on.

Once again the Al Jazeera crew was the most aggressive, driving right next to Hanson's Humvee, trying to get a picture of one of the most hated enemies of Islam, while he was suffering his well-earned retribution. Lonigan saw they were all getting tired of the harassment and called one of the police escorts, who pulled the Al Jazeera van to the side of the road, then started writing a summons.

The last glimpse Hanson had of them was the crew springing angrily out of the van and arguing with the police officers, who spread-eagled them against the vehicle.

"That's one less annoyance," Griffin remarked to no one in particular.

Hanson collected his distracted thoughts and called Danowski.

"What's happening, Ski?"

"Everything's secure here, boss. Muzi just went off duty and I'm keeping an eye on Nakamura. How are you and Jed?"

"We're coping. Anything new to report?"

"Not really. Nothing that can't wait until later."

Hanson sensed something in his voice. "What is it?" he asked listlessly.

"I'd prefer to wait until you get here, boss. I know we're securely encrypted, but you never know."

Hanson decided not to push for an answer. "Alright. We just left the cemetery, and we should be there in less than an hour. Until we get there, post extra security at headquarters, our residential building, and the V.A. hospital. Have additional Humvee patrols sweep the Enclave and instruct them to report anything suspicious. Keep two Strykers on five-minute alert."

"Yes, boss. Is there anything else I can do right now?"

"No. We'll review security arrangements with our people and Captain Lonigan when we get back. Call me if anything develops."

"Aye, aye, sir."

Although they left most of the media behind at the cemetery, several video vans persisted in following the convoy, obviously not having a hotter story at the moment. The CNN helicopter was still pacing them overhead and broadcasting live. One of their reporters had just learned of Kyle and Tyrones' recent heroic battle with the terrorists and kept repeating the details, as the camera recorded the progress of the boys' procession.

When the convoy turned onto Fourth Avenue it was lined with people, despite the rain, waving small American flags and holding up homemade signs expressing regret for the death of the boys. 'Farewell brave boys', 'we mourn two heroes', 'we share your loss'. Some of the men and women, probably ex-service personnel, saluted.

Hanson, the Marines and their families were deeply moved by this spontaneous demonstration. At Hanson's order, they slowed the convoy and waved to the kind-hearted supporters, who in an unusual response bowed their heads in respect.

Lonigan suggested they continue on the avenue, rather than get on the Expressway, so they'd give local residents the opportunity to share their sorrow. They stayed on Fourth Avenue up to Flatbush Avenue, which they took to the Brooklyn Bridge. More and more people were on the streets in a public outpouring of grief.

It was completely unexpected and deeply reassuring to Hanson and the other Marines that their country still cared. By this time, the Al Jazeera van had caught up with the convoy and was broadcasting crowd shots live, accompanied by insulting remarks about government-controlled crowds who had been forced to demonstrate their support of the enemies of Islam by the American secret police.

CNN decided it was a developing story and brought in one of their big guns, Lamb Dasher, who wasn't quite as anti-American as Al Jazeera, but still snidely disparaged the patriotic spectacle in his monotonous, self-righteous, droning voice.

The traffic on the bridge stopped as the convoy passed and the drivers honked their horns in greeting. When the convoy got off the bridge, Hanson opted for local streets instead of the East River Drive and they took Park Row past the center of municipal government, onto East Broadway, then Allen Street, which turned into First Avenue at Houston Street.

Mixed crowds of ethnic Hispanic and Chinese from the ungentrified buildings, as well as middle class residents of upscale condos, waved flags, saluted, or bowed their heads reverently as the convoy slowly drove by. The most stirring moment was when the convoy reached the V.A. hospital on 23rd Street. The vets, on stretchers or in wheelchairs, wearing black armbands in mourning for the comrades killed in the bombing at the parade, sat or lay at attention. Those who had arms saluted. Hanson turned to Beverly, struggling to maintain his composure.

"I can't take much more of this. I had no idea how many people cared."

"It's almost over, Sam," she responded. "We'll get through this."

"Then what?" he asked woefully.

"We'll take it one day at a time."

By this time the event had become a huge media circus and every reporter who could walk or crawl was waiting for them at headquarters. The police cleared a lane for the convoy that turned onto 30th Street and entered the motor pool area at the back of the building. They were pursued by media hordes outraged by the lack of response to their presence and frustrated in their efforts to present emotional reactions that would divert their viewers from their own problems. Danowski met Hanson at the rear entrance.

"At the suggestion of Mrs. Griffin we prepared a meal for everyone that we'll serve in the mess hall. She thought we'd have more privacy than in a restaurant, where the media would harass us. With your permission, sir, I'd like to request that General and Mrs. Griffin preside."

"Permission granted, Ski."

"General. ma'am," Danowski asked formally. "We'd be honored if you would say a few words to the troops and their families."

Griffin nodded agreement and Beverly said, "It will be our honor."

"Thank you, sir. ma'am."

"Ski."

"Yes, ma'am?"

"Don't call me ma'am."

"Yes, Ma ... Mrs. Griffin."

The first thing Hanson noticed when he entered the mess hall was the black bunting draped on the walls. As the Marines filed in, he saw they were all wearing black armbands, a practice not allowed in regulations. The civilians who weren't dressed in black also wore black armbands. Danowski escorted General and Mrs. Griffin to the head of the officers' table, then called the gathering to silence.

"Ladies and Gentlemen, please be seated." He waited until everyone had settled down, then said, "General Griffin will address us."

Griffin slowly stood up and faced his audience.

"I will be brief. Nothing I say can bring back two boys who brought honor to the Corps. They were not supposed to fight for their country until they were older. As Marines always have, they answered the call. They will not be forgotten. It is up to all of us to remember that we must always be ready to answer the call to duty and place our bodies between our enemies and our loved ones. God bless the United States of America."

There was a hushed silence as he sat down, and Beverly waited a minute before she stood to speak.

"We lost two of our precious children and some of us will never get over their absence. In these difficult times for our nation, too many men and women of the Corps have been killed in the performance of their duty. Now two young boys have joined our hallowed dead. I need not remind our Marines that they are always at risk. We all know that too well.

"Instead, I want to talk for a moment to the spouses of our Marines, the men and women whose fears and sufferings are unknown in the civilian world. Without your love and support, our Marines might lose their sense of belonging to the country they protect with their lives. I have known your fears and loneliness longer than all of you. It is the price we pay for marriage to our dedicated men and women. The Corps has been my extended family, as it has been yours. We share the same hopes and dreams for our loved ones. We must never falter in our duty."

Some of the most hardened veterans were weeping when she finished. It took a while for many of them to regain control of their emotions. In the aftermath of Beverly's feelings they all felt uplifted.

Danowski announced that wine would be served with lunch and he invited everyone to join in a toast to the two boys and the Corps.

"With your permission, sir," he asked Hanson. "Wilkins would like to offer the toast."

Hanson nodded. "Granted."

With Le Beau's assistance, Wilkins, still looking pale, wobbled to his feet.

"To the two finest boys I ever knew, and the Corps."

He drained his glass and flopped down in his wheelchair, completely exhausted by the exertions of the day. One of his wounds had opened and the bandages on his chest were turning red. Hanson told Le Beau, "Have Wilkins taken back to the hospital, gunny."

"Aye, aye, sir."

"I'd like to stay, sir," Wilkins said.

"I'm not up to another funeral, Wilkie. I'll see you when you've recuperated."

"Yes, sir."

The cooks had outdone themselves and the menu offered a choice of steak, roast chicken, or salmon, accompanied by red or white wine. Despite the good quality of the food, everyone ate mechanically. There was almost no conversation, except for the occasional child's voice, immediately shushed by a parent. Although there was no real enjoyment of the food, they lingered over the meal, reluctant to part from the communion shared with the brotherhood and sisterhood of the Corps. When everyone had finished and the children were getting restless, Al stood up.

"On behalf of Colonel Hanson and Lieutenant Davis, I'd like to thank all of you for attending. All Marines can resume their regular assignments. To their husbands, wives and children, we will see you soon, hopefully on a happier occasion."

Al nodded to Le Beau, who called, "Ten-hut," and the Marines snapped to, as she led Griffin, Beverly, Hanson, Jed, Danowski and Lonigan from the mess hall. Mrs. Morales touched Hanson's sleeve as he passed.

"God bless you, Colonel. You saved our men and women in Saudi Arabia. The boys saved our families. Our prayers are with you."

He clasped her hand and nodded, then walked out. Danowski moved to his side.

"Let me know when you're ready for a sitrep, sir."

"When we get to my office, Ski. What were you hinting at earlier?"

Danowski moved closer so he wouldn't be overheard. "We got a notice from the Pentagon. An investigatory commission will be here Monday morning, at 0900. They require your presence and will inform you if they require anyone else to answer questions regarding the bombing at the parade."

Hanson mumbled a curse or two under his breath.

Danowski said, "I could lose the email, boss, and you could be away Monday on a training mission."

"Thanks, Ski. I better see them."

"We could have a terrorist attack Monday morning and they could be unfortunate casualties."

Hanson grinned. "You have a criminal mind, Ski."

"Yes, sir. You're making me all I can be."

They both smiled, provoking Al's curiosity.

"What's up, guys?"

"The boss is ignoring my recommendations, Al."

When no further explanation was forthcoming, she shrugged.

"Jed has a request, Sam."

"Let's hear it."

"Unless you need him here, he wants to wait at the girl's house for the terrorists to show up."

"What do you think, Al?"

"I can take over his company for a few days and Ski can cover my administrative duties."

"Is he in sufficient control not to kill them?"

"Yes, Sam. He understands how important they could be."

"We'll review it in a few minutes at our meeting."

"Yes, sir. We won't let them get away with murdering our children, will we, Sam?"

"Not this time, Al."

50

W HEN THEY REACHED Hanson's office, Beverly took him aside, while the others went in.

"It might be better to wait until tomorrow before making any important decisions, Sam. We're still involved with the extreme emotions from the funeral."

"Thanks, Bev," he said gently. "Events may not want to wait for us."

She concluded he was ready for the responsibility of command, patted him fondly, went in and sat down. Hanson gave them a moment to get settled.

"Ski. Bring us up to date on the situation here and any new developments."

"Yes, sir. Everything at headquarters is running smoothly. Except for several messages from the Pentagon for General Griffin there's nothing new."

Hanson verified that the reaction platoon was back from the cemetery and standing down but was on ten-minute alert status. Hanson turned to Griffin.

"When the Green Machine is at its best, it's a model of efficiency. Would you like to say anything to our fellow conspirators, sir?"

Griffin grinned. "It's your show, Sam. Carry on."

"Aye, aye, sir."

Hanson looked at them and realized that these people in the room were his closest friends in the entire world. He smiled to himself when he couldn't decide whether it was an indication of wealth or poverty.

"It's still not too late for any of you to withdraw without recrimination," he said, for what felt like the tenth time. Everyone stared at him, confident and determined, so he didn't bother to wait for a response. "I've been considering the problem that occurs when we capture the terrorists at the girl's house. If they don't return or communicate with whoever sent them, their masters will know they've been caught. If they have an observer on the street, he'll have to be dealt with for the same reason.

"You all understand the necessity of news of their capture not getting back to the terrorists. We also have to provide an acceptable explanation why they haven't returned."

Everyone nodded.

"Tell us your plan, Sam," Griffin urged.

Hanson smiled grimly. "The operation will take place in three phases. One. When we catch the terrorists in the apartment we'll evacuate everyone, then set off flash-bangs with lots of noise and smoke, which will simulate an explosion. That will later explain what killed the residents and their guests.

"Two. Captain Lonigan will arrange to apprehend their observer, who it will be announced later was killed in a shoot-out with the police while fleeing the scene of a crime. Mike. The police will have to cordon off the apartment for an official investigation of the explosion. You'll have to maintain the integrity of the crime scene, so the terrorists can't check it.

"Three. Press releases and unofficial news leaks will be given to the media, hopefully from the appropriate police officials, that will deal with the two events as separate incidents. Questions?"

"Do you expect a cop to execute the terrorist?" Lonigan asked.

"No, Mike. If it happens accidentally, fine. We'll take care of the individual once he's in our custody. Can you arrange the media contacts?"

"I think so. If there's any problem I'll let you know."

"Good."

There didn't seem to be any more questions.

"Jed. You and Le Beau review the evacuation procedure so the neighbors will think there are no survivors. Ski. Make sure they get everything they need."

"Yes, sir."

"I'd like to go to the apartment as soon as we're finished here, Sam," Jed requested. "I have a feeling they'll be nosing around soon. When we catch them we can evacuate everyone out the back way, then set off the flash-bangs."

"Alright. If there's anything you need, let me or Ski know. See me for a minute before you leave."

"Yes, sir."

"General. Is there anything you'd like to add before we get under way?"

"No, Sam. The plan seems simple enough, but we should all be prepared when things go wrong."

"What could go wrong, sir?" Hanson quipped, and they all smiled at the absurdity of a perfect plan.

"One thing more," Griffin added. "If anyone thinks of any improvements or unforeseen problems, tell Colonel Hanson immediately. I think we're finished, Sam."

"Thank you, sir. Mike. Stay for a minute please. Al. You and Ski work out a liberty schedule for everyone you can spare until 0700 Monday. Give priority to the men and women with families."

"Yes, sir."

"Carry on."

Hanson talked to Lonigan first, wanting a more private word with Jed without the policeman who was a good friend, but not family.

"Mike. The success of this plan is in your capable hands. If we don't secure the crime scene and apprehend the observer, the terrorist planners will know we're on to them. They'll either send the planners home, or surround them with enough security so we won't be able to get at them without triggering an international incident."

"I understand, Sam. I'll arrange for teams of my undercover tactical officers to blanket the area. They and my superiors will be informed that they're setting a trap for an international drug dealer with high government connections. That'll explain why we bypassed D.E.A. and other feds. They'll understand the importance of keeping his capture a secret."

"Good. Stay in close touch and let me know immediately if there are any problems."

Jed was looking at him apprehensively, afraid that he wouldn't be allowed to go on the operation. He waited until Lonigan left, then blurted,

"I'm really fit, Sam. I can handle anything that comes up. You've got to let me go. I'll go out of my mind if I have to wait here, eating away at myself, wondering if they'll show. Give me this chance. I owe it to Tyrone."

His last statement caused Hanson to suppress any sign of amusement at Jed's urgency.

"Don't worry, Jed. You're going. I just want to review a few things with you." The relief on Jed's face was almost painful to see. "Some of your troops may get restless after hours and hours of waiting," Hanson explained. "They've got to understand that any careless behavior might spook the terrorists. The family has to go about its normal business as if you're not there. The neighbors can't know you're there."

"I'll take care of it."

"Bring back some live ones, Jed."

"Aye, aye, sir. General. Ma'a … Mrs. Griffin."

They watched him march out, straight-backed and resolute, containing his tormented feelings with an iron grip.

"A good officer," Griffin offered.

"A good man," Beverly added.

"The people you promoted to officers have worked out really well," Griffin said. "Hopefully, Zach Plant will find a way to reopen the Academies and restore the R.O.T.C. program. We've got to be able to tap our young, elite population to fill out the officer corps. I'm glad we can promote from the ranks, but we'll never get enough quality officers that way … But enough wishful thinking. The plan seems sound. How sure are you that Al Qaeda will visit the family?"

"You know them as well as I do, Charlie. They have to find out what happened. They know the suicide bombing took place, but they're not sure if it was one man or two and they don't know what happened to the girl. By now they know she didn't detonate herself and that's a loose end."

"I agree. Once again, we wait."

Beverly, a glint in her eye, said, "Samuel Hanson. I am obliged to observe that you have become a master criminal."

"I had an excellent teacher," he replied innocently, staring at Griffin.

"Hold on a minute," Griffin protested. "You're not going to get away with blaming me for your illicit tendencies."

"Why not? I was just a callow midshipman when you took me under your wing and taught me all sorts of devious means of breaking the law."

"That's gratitude for you," Griffin told Beverly in a mock-aggrieved voice. "I nurtured a lost sheep who had strayed and brought him back to the fold and this is the thanks I get."

"He worried about you more than any other middie, Sam, and so did I," Beverly said.

"You're a fine one to talk," Hanson replied. "You taught me to shoot first and say something witty afterwards."

By this time, they were laughing so loudly that an alarmed Danowski knocked on the door.

"Everything alright in there, sir?"

Hanson took a deep breath. "Yes, Ski. The general and I were discussing the battle of Balaclava."

"Yes, sir," a puzzled Danowski replied, while the three of them looked at each other as if they were caught with their hands in the cookie jar.

"The real decision," Griffin said somberly, "will come if we apprehend terrorists at the girl's apartment. Information from them will determine what course of action we choose to follow. Once we have them in custody, we don't necessarily have to do anything else."

"I'm afraid we do, Charlie. If we don't deal with Al Qaeda now, we'll just have to deal with them later, after they kill more of our people."

"Alright, Sam. Don't get on your high horse. I was just playing devil's advocate."

"You know what has to be done as well as I do." Griffin just nodded.

"Where will it all end?" Beverly asked.

"I don't know, Bev," Hanson answered. "One lesson I learned the hard way in Iraq and Saudi Arabia was that the terrorists won't go away if we don't retaliate. They take that as a sign of weakness. Whether we like it or not, we're in a clash of civilizations that is not resolvable by reason and negotiation. The radical Islamists oppose our way of life because it threatens them. They despise our multiculturalism and our values. And most of all, they do not believe in live and let live."

They sat silently for a minute, thinking about what Hanson said.

"So what's the answer, Sam," Beverly asked. "Do we have to kill them all?"

"No, Bev. Only the ones who want to kill us. It no longer matters how it reached this point. The disaffected liberals spend their energies blaming Plant junior, or the Pentagon, or the oil companies, or hateful foreign policies. They don't understand current reality.

"Extreme Islam has declared war on the West. Traditional Islamists accept this, perhaps they even approve of it. They certainly make no effort to stop it. That limits our options to enduring their attacks or fighting them. I will never stop resisting the enemies of our country who mean us harm."

"We're with you all the way, Sam," Griffin said.

"We'll all hang together," Beverly added.

"We don't hang people anymore, Bev," Hanson said. "Not even traitors. It's considered cruel and unusual punishment. They'll probably slip something in our coffee."

"Stop quibbling, Sam. You know what I mean."

"Yes, ma'am."

Hanson and Griffin grinned at her look of exasperation, until she grinned back.

The three friends sat quietly for a few minutes, each preoccupied with their own thoughts.

Beverly finally broke the silence.

"Is there any reason you can't get away from here for a while? You've been under a terrible strain and right now things seem relatively calm."

"What do we do with your husband, baby?"

She rolled her eyes at Griffin and put a finger to her lips, which brought a chuckle to all of them.

"Come to our hotel for the rest of the night. We'll upgrade to a suite, spend some time together and just relax."

"How?"

"The hotel has a great spa, with a swimming pool, steam room, massage …"

"Sounds tempting, Bev. How can I resist you?"

"Good. Next time we're in, or on a happier occasion, we'll go to a Broadway show. When was the last time you saw a play?"

"It was so long ago I don't remember … I thought they only put on musicals these days?"

"A musical is still a play, Sam. Do you have something against musicals?"

"Tell you the truth, the ones I saw all sounded alike."

"We'll see if there's a revival of 'West Side Story'. It's an update of Romeo and Juliet."

Hanson stared at her strangely, then shrugged.

Beverly turned to Griffin for help, but he elaborately looked away. She glared at him, then looked at Hanson.

"I just want to get you away from everything here long enough so you'll feel human again. Now will you come quietly, or …?"

He held up his hands. "I surrender. I'm at your orders, ma'am."

"Don't provoke me, Sam. Now make whatever arrangements are necessary and let's get out of here. One rule for the weekend. You wear civvies and pretend to be a normal person."

"Yes, ma'am."

"I'm going to talk to Al," she said frostily. "I'll be back in fifteen minutes. Be ready."

"Aye, aye, ma'am."

She walked out mumbling about impertinent pups who should be paper-trained.

"She is a force to be reckoned with," Griffin said admiringly.

"That she is," Hanson agreed. "She's also the finest woman I ever met."

"She knows you feel that way, Sam. I'm going to drop in on Le Beau. We haven't had a chance to talk since I caught him stealing my cigars one time in Baghdad. I'll also be back in fifteen."

Hanson quickly scanned the duty roster and operations plans and discovered that he really could get away for a day or so. He felt a brief glow of satisfaction, realizing his people were so capable that they could function without him for a while. He knew that Jed, Al and Danowski would contact him instantly if there were any developments and he wouldn't be far away, so he concluded that he could leave the installation in good hands. He buzzed Danowski and told him that he would be leaving shortly and might not be in tomorrow.

It was further reassuring when Danowski said, "I'll let you know immediately if something warrants your attention."

"Thanks, Ski."

The Griffins returned a few minutes later and Beverly urged him out the door.

"After we thoroughly indulge in the spa, we can order room service and watch old movies on cable."

"That sounds like fun," Griffin said. "We can watch *The Sands of Iwo Jima*."

"How about *Battle Cry*?" Hanson asked.

"No gung-ho movies, jarheads," Beverly ordered.

• • •

After they upgraded the room at the hotel, at Beverly's insistence, they swam, steamed until they were well done, then submitted to powerful hands that kneaded the aches from their overstressed bodies. They were too tired to go through the formality of dressing to go to a restaurant, so they ordered a luxurious meal of lobster and steak, as well as a nice Échézeaux from room service.

The food and wine were delicious, further adding to their lethargy. They watched a recent hit movie, a dreadful comedy about mate swapping by a gay and straight couple. Except for the hackneyed sex references, it would have made an awful sit-com. Beverly finally relented and surprised them by ordering 'Wake Island', a World War II film about the heroic Marine resistance to an overwhelming Japanese invasion force that was not as Hollywoodized as many of the gung-ho flics. Hanson was dozing off even before the Japanese hit the beach, so Beverly sent him to bed.

He barely had the energy to get undressed and flopped on the bed like a k.o.'d boxer, all thought driven from his head by exhaustion. He snapped wide awake just before dawn and his first impulse was to go to Kyle's room and make sure he was safe in bed.

Then he remembered. He cried for several minutes, the agony of missing Kyle sending shooting pains through his body. He finally calmed down and silently made a vow that he would avenge his murdered son, no matter what it cost. A rational part of his mind noted that he should take extra care not to risk his friends' lives or careers by hasty or ill-considered action.

He understood that Jed was feeling a burning need for revenge that might outweigh caution, so he resolved to be extremely careful in his decision making. He fell back into a deep sleep and didn't stir until late Sunday morning.

Beverly had ordered a large breakfast from room service, and it was waiting when Hanson finished shaving and showering. Fresh orange juice, waffles, bacon and eggs, croissants and jam, and coffee continued the program to restore their battered spirits.

"It's raining heavily again," Beverly remarked. "Unless you really want to go somewhere, Sam, I suggest we spend another day lolling in luxury at the hotel."

"I think I can survive that, Bev."

"I only require two things," she said.

"What's that?" Griffin dutifully asked.

"One. We have dinner tonight at one of the hotel restaurants." Both men nodded agreement. "Two. No more gung-ho movies."

"Killjoy," Griffin said.

"How about an anti-war film?" Hanson suggested.

"Like what?" she asked.

"Kubrick's 'Full Metal Jacket'."

Beverly looked at him suspiciously. "Isn't that another gung-ho Marine film?"

"No, Bev," Hanson said. "It shows the grotesque effects of war during the Vietnam War. My favorite scene has a lunatic helicopter gunner cackling to himself while machine gunning civilians. Then he brags about his kills and claims they are all certified, including fifty water buffalo. He laughs like a madman when he describes how he shoots women and children. It's an incredible scene … If you don't like it we'll pick something else."

"You're being entirely too accommodating, Sam. Are you sure you're alright?"

"Yes, Bev. I'm just trying to take it easy and come to terms with …"

"I understand and I won't push you."

And for the rest of the day Beverly was so considerate that Hanson really began to relax. The only disruption of the routine of swim, steam, massage, was a call from Carver, who still sounded completely distraught.

"I need to talk to you about getting the terrorists. Can we get together tonight?"

"I can't, Carv. I'm preparing for a meeting at 0900 tomorrow with an official commission investigating the security failings in the bombing that killed … Our children … They've already tried to blame me and I have to make sure I'm ready for whatever they accuse me of. Once that's resolved, I'll call you and we'll arrange to get together."

"Can I help in any way?"

"I don't think so, Carv. Thanks for asking."

When he disconnected, Griffin said, "We were planning to return to Washington in the morning, but if you don't mind, I think we'll stay a bit later and I'll sit in on your meeting."

"That'll freak out those armchair commandos and it may buy you some trouble."

"I can handle it."

"I know you can. Thanks for your help, Charlie."

"That's what mentors are for."

51

BATTALION MUSTER at 0700 Monday morning signaled the first return to normalcy in days. Al and Danowski, with some adept juggling, had arranged liberty for most of the troops and the effects of the time off were reflected in their faces. The married personnel looked calm and relaxed after two nights with their families. The singles wore various looks from fatigue to satisfaction, a result of the usual enlisted Marine's efforts to procure sex, drugs, drink, gambling, or other forms of temporary relief from the demands of duty.

Yet despite their slightly shopworn condition, they all stood at rigid attention when Hanson and General Griffin inspected them, confident in their ability to carry out their mission. Griffin nodded to old acquaintances who were proud to be singled out by the popular general. Hanson was pleased with their turnout and complimented Le Beau.

"The troops look good, Gunny. Perhaps they earned a two-week furlough in Cuba now that they finally shut off Castro's respirator."

Le Beau allowed the troops to laugh and merely said, "Thank you, sir."

Hanson spent some extra time with Muzzetti, Nakamura and Bernstein, concerned that they might be feeling a bit neglected by him in the last few days. They were slightly nervous in the presence of General

Griffin, so he went out of his way to praise their recent performance of their duties. Griffin understood his purpose and audibly murmured, "Well done," to them, which delighted the dedicated officers.

With Al and Danowski once again concentrating most of their efforts on running headquarters, he assigned Muzzetti's company to mobile patrols of the Enclave. After cautioning them to be particularly alert, he called Al and told her to work out a patrol schedule with Muzzetti. This was Griffin's first opportunity in years to spend time with a field battalion for more than a short ceremony or inspection. He was impressed with what Hanson had accomplished in such a short time, with what had been one poorly led company and another new, inexperienced company.

"You've done an outstanding job here, Sam."

"Thank you, sir. I really appreciate that coming from you."

He went over the plans and schedules for the day with Al and Danowski, and was relieved that there were no crises. Jed had reported that there was no contact with the terrorists and they managed a smooth change of shifts, so all they could do was await developments. Danowski had organized the procedures of reordering supplies and equipment, so all Hanson had to do was sign off on requisitions. He silently congratulated himself once again for promoting him. Al informed him with a grin that no one had fallen out for sick call, an unusual occurrence on a Monday morning.

"Wilkins is requesting to be returned to duty," she said with a twinkle in her eye.

"Let him know that it's up to the doctor to release him."

"Yes, sir. One other problem. Carstairs is acting up again and the nurses are going ballistic. When you get a moment, go over there and straighten out that beached whale. When he's not cooking or shooting terrorists he's the biggest pain in the ass in the battalion."

"I bet every battalion in the history of the Corps had someone like that," Hanson said, and he looked to Griffin for confirmation.

Griffin pretended not to notice, so Hanson dismissed Al and Danowski to go about their duties.

Lonigan called at 0800 and brought him up to date.

"I have a surveillance team assigned 24/7 for two weeks or longer. They'll blanket the area and most of them will blend in. We'll release a rumor in the neighborhood that detectives are hunting a child molester and that should cover their presence. I arranged for the public relations department to contact the media when we're ready. Everything seems to be falling into place."

"So far, so good. Well done, Mike. I'll talk to you later."

He filled Griffin in on Lonigan's side of the conversation and both men agreed that the initial stages of the plan were going well.

"Where do you perceive possible problems?" Griffin asked.

"My biggest concern is that neighbors will notice the shift changes of the Marines in the girl's apartment, but I don't see an alternative."

Before he could go further, Danowski buzzed and announced, "Sir. There's a delegation outside of naval officers and the FBI A Captain Evans says they're the official investigating commission."

"Have them brought in, Ski."

Captain Evans led the way in, followed by Commander Hooper, a female lieutenant commander and Royce and Madison of the FBI, looking more hostile, but less aggressive.

Hooper said sarcastically, "So we meet again, Sergeant … I mean Colonel. I knew we'd have another chance at you …" Then he saw General Griffin and his face collapsed in confusion, shattering his brief moment of triumphalism over Hanson. "I'm sorry, sir," he stuttered. "I didn't see you sitting there. I meant no disrespect …"

Griffin stared at him coldly. "I should hope you don't need instruction in how to address a field grade officer."

"Yes, sir. I mean no, sir."

Griffin turned to Evans. "I'm Colonel Hanson's commanding officer. I'm here on a general inspection. I'd like to sit in on this meeting, if there are no objections."

"Of course not, sir," Evans said. "We're honored to have you with us, sir."

Griffin felt he had sufficiently established his presence and said formally, "I think introductions are in order. I'm General Griffin."

"I'm Captain Evans, sir, of the Naval Investigative Service. This is Commander Hooper, also from N.I.S." Hooper fidgeted at Griffin's appraising look and Evans continued, "This is Lieutenant Commander Brattle from the Judge-Advocate's office."

"Any relation to Admiral Brattle, Commander?" Griffin asked.

"He's my father, sir," she replied.

"He was a senior when I entered the Academy. How is he?"

"He retired on a disability a few months ago, sir."

"I'm sorry to hear that. He was a fine officer. The service will miss him. Please give him my regards when you talk to him."

"I will, sir."

Griffin sensed the animosity towards Hanson from the remaining two members of the commission and slowly turned to them.

"Who are these civilians?" he asked Evans.

Before Evans could respond, Royce blurted, "I'm Special Agent-In-Charge Royce and this is Special Agent Madison."

Griffin didn't indicate that he knew Madison and said quietly, "Don't let me interfere with your procedures. I'll just sit here quietly and observe."

The unexpected presence of a general officer who also happened to be Hanson's C.O., complicated things for Evans. He was trying to figure out how to proceed when he got another unpleasant surprise. Danowski buzzed Hanson and announced, "Captain Lonigan of the New York City Police Department is here and would like to join you."

Before Evans could react, Hanson said, "Send him in," and they went through another round of introductions.

Evans was making a strenuous effort to adjust to the circumstances when he got the final shock. Danowski buzzed again.

"Doctor Carver is here, sir."

"Ask him to join us, Ski."

Hanson introduced Carver to everyone.

Griffin stood and shook his hand.

"Colonel Hanson speaks very highly of you, Doctor Carver. I'm sorry we have to meet again like this. Please accept my condolences for your loss."

"Thank you, sir," Carver said sadly.

Evans realized that he could no longer proceed as planned and gestured to Royce to take over. Royce's usual bluster deserted him, and he was apprehensive of what Lonigan might reveal, so he tried to downplay the original purpose of their visit, which had obviously been to scapegoat Hanson for the parade disaster.

"As you all know, any incident involving terrorism has to be thoroughly investigated." He glanced at Evans and saw no support there, so he hurried on. "In this case, we're just here to tie up a few loose ends regarding the security failure."

He cast a desperate look at Evans hoping for assistance, but Evans, an experienced Pentagon bureaucrat, had decided to cut his losses and wouldn't meet his gaze. Royce mumbled on for a few minutes about the need to establish better interagency cooperation for increased security, and expressed the hope that with improved communication they could prevent future terrorist attacks.

Carver had been fuming during the rambling monologue and suddenly yelled at Royce, "You're to blame for the death of my daughter. You were asked to check the department stores and you didn't."

He leaped at Royce, who cowered in fear at the sudden assault by the outraged physician. Only the prompt action of Hanson and Lonigan in restraining him prevented Carver from throttling Royce.

"That's an unfounded rumor," Royce protested. "There was a breakdown in communications. I requested the stores be checked."

"Who did you assign?" Lonigan asked.

"I'll have to check my files and see."

"I'd like to see the written order," Lonigan said, then asked quietly, "Are you acknowledging that you received Colonel Hanson's request for a security sweep of the stores?"

Royce couldn't think of any way to evade the facts and reluctantly admitted, "Yes."

Carver stood up and yelled furiously, "I'll see that you pay for this," and stormed out the door. Hanson felt the same murderous rage but forced himself to remain calm.

Evans assumed that the navy was no longer on the hot seat and stood up to go.

"Thank you for your time, Colonel Hanson …"

Griffin shot down his attempted escape. "One moment please, Captain Evans. Why did you bring a representative from the Judge-Advocate's office to a security inquiry?"

"Since this was a multi-agency operation, we brought Lieutenant Commander Brattle along in case there were any legal questions that required clarification."

"Like what?" Griffin demanded.

"We'd only know that after we finished all the interviews, sir," Evans replied vaguely.

"I see. Then there was no intention of bringing charges against Colonel Hanson, was there?"

"That was not the purpose of this commission, sir."

"I should hope not, Captain Evans. Colonel Hanson has received numerous awards and medals for his bravery and fine leadership. He was awarded the Navy Cross for his heroic conduct in rescuing his troops from Al Qaeda, during the retreat from Riyadh. His superiors have recommended him for the Medal of Honor, which I endorsed. I would assume you wouldn't embarrass our service with any unfounded charges."

"No, sir."

"Good. Do you have any further business here this morning?"

"No, sir."

"Then you are dismissed."

The Navy beat a hasty retreat and Griffin turned his attention to Royce.

"Now there have been various versions in the last few days of how the bombers got through our security. I'd like to hear yours."

Royce tried to evade answering. "The incident is still under investigation and I'll have to check with headquarters for the latest information."

"I thought you said you were the agent in charge. Are you telling me you don't know what happened?"

"It's not that simple, sir."

"Why not? You admitted that the FBI was requested to make a security check of the department stores, didn't you?"

"Yes, sir."

"And it was Colonel Hanson who made the request to you personally, didn't he?"

"Yes, sir."

"Then who did you order to do it?"

"I'll have to check my notes. There was a lot going on that day."

"You did order someone to make the security check, didn't you?"

"I'm sure I did. I'll have to get back to you."

Hanson realized at that moment that Royce could get away with causing the deaths of Kyle and Tyrone, since the system would protect him. With cold certainty he resolved, no matter what the cost, not to let that happen. One way or another, legal or not, Royce would be held accountable for his crime.

A calm acceptance possessed him, and he was able to look at Royce without revealing the loathing he was feeling. Royce had been watching him nervously since he came into the office. Now he began to think he was going to have an opportunity to dismiss the incident in the maze of bureaucracy that among other functions was designed to shelter its servants from the consequences of their mistakes. Tish might also have had similar thoughts. She kept looking at him strangely, as if surprised that he wasn't foaming at the mouth like Carver. Hanson had strong feelings about the way she had treated him, but he knew she wasn't really guilty of Kyle's death, except by association, so he chose to ignore her.

Griffin said, "Is there anything further we should review, Agent Royce?"

"No, General."

"Then this meeting is over. We'll expect a copy of your report when it's completed. Good day Agent Royce. Agent Madison."

The two agents scurried out like mice urgent to escape the cat. In other circumstances their undignified departure might have amused Hanson, but he could never forget that Royce was responsible for Kyle's death and that precluded any possibility of finding humor in their flight. Griffin stared at Hanson for a minute, then finally broke the silence.

"Do you think I let them off the hook too easily?"

"No, Charlie. Royce thinks he got away with it. As far as he's concerned it's a closed case. Tish doesn't count. She didn't have any authority, so she's not responsible. Whatever happened between us was personal and it's over now."

"What do you intend to do about Royce?"

A stony expression crossed Hanson's face. "He will be held accountable, after we deal with the terrorists."

Beverly and Griffin ate lunch in the mess hall and just before they finished Griffin stood up.

"Ladies and gentlemen. May I have your attention for a minute, please. I just want to tell you that I think you're doing an exemplary job, under difficult conditions, in the best tradition of the Corps. I consider your commanding officer, Colonel Hanson, to be the finest officer who ever served with me. He has my complete support. Thank you."

Griffin offered his hand to Beverly and they started to leave. Le Beau stood and called, "Battalion. Ten-hut." Everyone snapped to attention.

Le Beau saluted smartly. "Semper fi, sir. ma'am."

All the troops, including Hanson, saluted and held position until the Griffins left. Then Le Beau called, "At ease. Resume your meal," and everyone settled down again.

Al, who hadn't sat near Hanson and the Griffins, moved next to him.

"That was quite an endorsement, Sam. It's great when your boss is in your corner all the way."

"That's the same way I am towards you, Al."

It took her a moment to regain her composure.

"Thanks, Sam. That's the nicest thing anyone ever said to me."

"You earned it."

Hanson accompanied the Griffins to LaGuardia Airport, where they would catch a flight to Washington, D.C. He and Griffin were in uniform, so Tico insisted that the bodyguards accompany them into the terminal. The airport security staff began to worry about invasion when they saw the heavily armed Marines approach the security checkpoint. They only relaxed when the Marines stopped a short distance away. Hanson kissed Beverly goodbye and she held him tightly.

"Now don't do anything gung-ho without inviting us," she admonished.

"Yes, ma'am."

"You're messing with the wrong woman, Sam," she warned, but smiled affectionately.

Hanson saluted Griffin.

"Thanks for everything, sir. I'll keep you informed about developments."

Griffin hugged him. "I want to be there when you go operational."

"I wish you'd reconsider, sir."

"Why? Do you think I'm too old for it?"

"There's nobody I'd rather have next to me in a firefight, Charlie. It's just that …"

"We both know all the reasons, Sam. Don't make me issue an order."

"It would be illegal, sir, but I'll be honored to have you with us. Have a good flight."

They drove back to Manhattan on the Long Island Expressway. It didn't have as many potholes as the Baghdad Highway and it was still safe from improvised explosive devices, at least for the time being. It was a grey, overcast afternoon and the trees had shed their leaves, a stark contrast to some of the brightly painted homes they passed that were making a futile effort to cheer drab, fretful lives. The closer they came to Manhattan the seedier the houses became, except for the occasional large condo building, still striving to convince its tenants that their upscale illusions were real. As the residential area turned industrial, the film of soot that covered buildings and streets became denser, a gritty coat that would not wash away, however hard it rained.

The tired look of a defeated city was alarming. Hanson idly thought, *How do you stop the decline and fall of the country you love and serve?* He understood how Roman legionnaires must have felt during the long decline of the Empire.

Tico stopped in front of headquarters, ending Hanson's reverie. The bodyguards rushed him past the remaining journalists who were still lingering in the hope of an interview, or most desirable, another terrorist attack that they could broadcast live and in color, as long as it didn't harm the dedicated reporters.

Al and Danowski met him at the entrance and escorted him to his office.

"I just spoke to Jed a few minutes ago and there are no new developments," Al said, then added, "The girl is getting restless and she wants to speak to her mom."

"No communication between them until we nab the terrorists."

"Yes, sir."

Hanson looked at Danowski.

"Nothing new to report, sir. The reaction platoon is on ten-minute alert and Muzi is still unhappy at being left out of the loop."

"He'll learn to live with it, Ski."

"Yes, sir."

"Anything else?"

"Not really, sir. Everything is proceeding in a proficient manner."

"You're starting to sound like a staff weenie."

"We need some normality around here, boss," Danowski responded.

A call from Lonigan brought Hanson fully alert.

"The plainclothes men near the girl's house just reported that a car with three men of apparent Mid-Eastern extraction has been cruising the neighborhood. It's too early to tell, but it may be them. My people will let me know instantly if there's any kind of development."

"That's good news, Mike. Remind your men to take extra precautions not to be noticed. I'll call Jed and alert him. Maybe we'll get lucky and they'll make a move on the house."

"I'll let you know as soon as I hear something."

Al and Danowski were also excited at the news.

"If it's only three men, do we still need the reaction platoon on ten-minute standby?" Al asked.

"Let's maintain them like that for a while, until we know for certain that there are only three."

"Yes, Sam. That's great news. I hope it's them."

"Me too, Al. We may not have to wait much longer to find out. Just keep in mind that they could be three locals, cruising the hood, looking for chicks."

"I don't think that's the right word for Arab girls, boss," Danowski said with a straight face.

Hanson winked at Al. "I'm glad someone around here is politically correct."

52

T HE EXPECTATION OF ACTION kept Hanson focused for the rest of the day. Late that night he went back to his apartment and despite the strange feeling of aloneness managed to sleep soundly. Tuesday morning he awoke completely refreshed and ready for what the day might bring, although he studiously avoided looking at Kyle's room.

He called Jed before he went to headquarters and was satisfied that he was highly functional, despite the terrible loss he had suffered. They had both learned patience in Iraq, waiting long hours in ambush for insurgents planting bombs next to the roads. They knew what it was like to wait and wait and in the end see no one.

This time it was different. The terrorists had to find out what happened to the girl and the only way was for them to go to her house and see for themselves. The three men in the car might have nothing to do with the terrorists, but Hanson's combat honed instincts told him they weren't innocent joyriders.

When he left the apartment building, his purpose showed in every step and the guards responded to his confidence and were bolstered by their leader's jaunty air of command.

Hanson walked the few blocks to headquarters, ignoring Tico's disapproval, who paced him in the Humvee, while the two bodyguards kept scanning non-stop for possible threats. He made a mental note to resume running as soon as the current situation was resolved, as well as karate practice and to get to the firing range.

It was a brisk, chilly morning. The distant, late fall sun was barely able to warm the struggling urban life forms. But the days of rain had partially cleared the air of various pollutants and he could almost breathe through his nose, the way nature intended. He paused to look at the weeping willow tree on the corner of 30th Street that retained green tendrils sobbing for the sorrows of winter to come. For a few moments the summons to destruction was neglected and he felt a fleeting ease that comforted him before the return to duty.

For the first time in days the media weren't lurking in front of headquarters and he was able to assess security at the entrance without being besieged by cameras. He chatted with the guards for a few moments and they were pleased at his attention. For a brief interlude life almost seemed normal.

Everyone was expecting him and he idly wondered for the thousandth time how word of his arrival always preceded him, whether by means electronic or ESP. Danowski was waiting at his office and they quickly reviewed the orders of the day before going to breakfast.

By 0640 the troops were straggling into the mess hall, exchanging the usual banter and insults that indicated high morale. The mess hall was full by 0700 and the hum of conversation was punctuated by the thunk and clank of plates and utensils in a familiar morning serenade. Hanson couldn't put his finger on something that was out of place, then realized that he missed the grumbling presence of Carstairs, often a pain in the ass, but a Marine who always answered the call when the shooting started. He made a mental note to visit him in the hospital and try to get him to settle down and be a good patient.

Then he smiled at what would surely be the futility of that effort. He made another note to talk to Wilkins' doctor about when he could be released and return to duty and decided that he would promote him to gunnery sergeant.

During breakfast his officers had been eyeing him covertly, trying to assess his mood. When he finished eating, he announced, "I will meet with all of you in the conference room at 0800. Plan to bring any requests or problems to my attention." He stood up to leave and the officers started to get up. "As you were," he said. "Please finish your breakfast."

Al and Danowski went with him and he observed that they were both looking eager for action.

"Anything you want to tell us before the meeting, sir?" Al asked.

"I spoke to Jed earlier and he and his team are alert and ready. I'll call Mike Lonigan shortly and we'll see how things are developing. Remember. No mention of anything related to our Brooklyn operation to anyone."

"It's no secret that Jed and some of the troops are off on a mission somewhere, boss. Some of the troops are wondering ..."

"Let them wonder, Ski. Anything else?"

Al nodded. "I think it's time you promoted Le Beau to master sergeant."

"Good idea. Recommend it in front of the other officers. It might encourage them to consider who else deserves promotion."

He wanted a few minutes alone before the meeting, so he dismissed them at his office, pointedly closed the door behind him, then called Lonigan.

"Morning, Sam. I was just about to call you. Two of the suspects have been wandering around the neighborhood for the last hour or so, trying to be casual while asking all kinds of questions."

"Like what?"

"Has anyone seen the girl and her family? Have they heard anything about the suicide bombing at the parade? Are there more police than usual in the neighborhood? One of our informers told them that the police are looking for a child molester who groped one girl, then tried to lure another girl into a green van. They seemed to accept the explanation as being reasonable. They're our guys, Sam. Only the terrorists would be asking those questions."

"Agreed. Make sure your officers know that we don't move on them until they go to the girl's apartment. Then they must get the driver before he can call anyone or get away."

"I've gone over that with them, Sam."

"Do it again, Mike. I'll alert Jed. Stay in close touch."

Jed was raring to go when he heard the latest report.

"I posted a sniper team on the roof, Sam. They can monitor the street and come downstairs in a minute, if we need them."

"Good. Make sure you identify the terrorist's car for them. Once the trap is sprung, if it looks like the car is getting away from the cops, have them take the driver out. Can we rely on your team leader's judgment?"

"Yes, Sam. Lance Corporal Williams is in charge. She's real steady."

"Good choice. If there's any way to take them quietly, that would be optimum."

"Yes, Sam. What if we can't take them alive?"

"Then we're back to square one, except they'll know we're on to them and they'll probably go underground."

"We'll do our best, Sam."

"That's never in doubt. Are you ready for the explosion, once you capture them?"

"All set."

"What about bringing them here?"

"If we capture them in daylight, we'll take them and the family through the backyard onto Dean Street, where we have a civilian car waiting. If it's nighttime, we'll go out the front door. I just hope they don't get suspicious and take off."

"Inshallah, Jed."

Hanson quickly reviewed the options if the terrorists suddenly took off and concluded it just wasn't practical to pursue them.

"Let's assume you'll get visitors soon. I'll have Lonigan communicate directly with you until your team on the roof confirms the target's entrance. Unless something urgent occurs, once they're on their way into the building, I won't talk to you until the action is over. Call me as soon as you can. I'll be waiting to hear from you. Good luck."

"Thanks, Sam."

Hanson set up the direct connection between Lonigan and Jed, made sure there was no confusion, then sat back to wait. He tried to do some paperwork, but gave it up as a lost cause, instead opting for a light physical workout that definitely didn't relieve the tension, but at least prevented him from pacing or fidgeting. Images of Kyle kept flashing through his mind and he resolutely pushed them away.

He made a final check on the alert status of the reaction platoon, ordered Danowski not to disturb him unless war was declared on Venezuela, then sat staring at his phone, waiting for it to ring.

After what seemed like hours, but was only forty minutes, Lonigan called and said in a rush, "Sam. Two of the men went into the building.

The third is in the car parked across the street. I alerted Jed and my officers are ready to block both ends of the street, so the car can't get away. It's up to Jed now. I'll get back to you," and he disconnected.

Hanson sent out a silent wish that nothing would go wrong, then called Danowski on the intercom.

"Ski. It's a go. Get Al and come to my office."

They must have both been waiting right outside, for a moment later the door opened and they came in, looking as excited and expectant as he felt.

"What's the situation, Sam?" Al asked.

"Two of them just went into the building and the cops are going to block the street so the third one can't get away in the car. We should hear from Jed very soon, unless something goes wrong."

"What could go wrong?" Al asked with a wry smile.

He smiled back, remembering how many combat situations they had been through where something always went wrong. A few minutes later his cell rang and an elated Jed said breathlessly, "We got 'em, Sam. They knocked on the door claiming to be from the local mosque, concerned about the rumors of the girl's disappearance. We had the mother let them in and we took them completely by surprise, without a struggle. I immediately called Lonigan, who ordered his cops to get the driver. I watched from the window as they took him down without firing a shot."

"Did he have time to call anyone?"

"No, Sam."

"Are you sure?"

"Yes, Sam. I'm sure. I saw the whole thing. So did the sniper team who were ready to take him out."

"That's great. Did anyone on the street see the cops take him?"

"I don't think so. They grabbed him and hustled him into the building without a fuss. Lonigan will be able to tell you more. Right now I've got to set the flash bangs and get everyone out of here. I'll call you as soon as we're on our way."

"Well done, Jed."

Lonigan called and reported jubilantly, "No one seemed to notice us make the arrest. As soon as I hear that Jed's people have left the building, I'll have one of my officer's drive the terrorist's car to where we planned to stage the crash and fake shootout. It's only a few blocks away near the Brooklyn-Queens Expressway."

"Make it look good, Mike."

"Trust the N.Y.P.D … Hold on a sec."

Hanson updated Al and Danowski while he waited. Mike came back with more good news.

"The explosion just went off and the neighbors are pouring out of their houses. You're going to love this. One of the neighbors saw the car drive off with my man in pursuit and asked an officer on the scene if that had anything to do with the explosion. The officer told him they were in pursuit of a suspected child molester and the guy bought it and spread the word … I hear emergency services approaching. Once they get to work I'll have my men spread the rumor that the explosion was caused by a gas leak. I'll talk to you soon."

Hanson turned to Al and Danowski.

"Jed's on his way with the three terrorists. When they get here, bring them in the back entrance and clear the corridors so no one sees them. Put the prisoners in the basement like last time. Set up the girl's family in a sergeant's room temporarily …"

"I've got a better idea, Sam," Al said.

"What is it?"

"Let's move the family into our apartment building."

Hanson nodded approval. "Have them moved before they get out of the vehicle, with as few people as possible seeing them. Have the girl ready to go with them. Let Le Beau escort them and put a guard on their door."

"Yes, sir."

The next call was from Jed.

"We're heading for the Brooklyn Bridge. We should get to HQ in about twenty minutes."

"Don't get stopped for speeding," Hanson quipped.

Jed laughed for the first time since that terrible day.

"Don't worry, Dad. We're law-abiding citizens."

Then Lonigan called again.

"We staged the crash, fired a few shots and our officers will report that the suspect died while trying to escape. I turned him over to Jed. Everything's going according to plan."

"Unusual, isn't it? Come here as soon as you can."

"Yes, Sam."

Hanson began to relax. "Phase one has been completed without a hitch," he told Al and Danowski.

"Stranger things have happened," Al replied.

Hanson ordered the reaction platoon to stand down and commended them for their good response to the readiness drill. He sent Al and Danowski to make a final check on the basement rooms they'd use for interrogation of the prisoners. Then he reviewed the duty roster to insure that only a trusted few troops would be stationed in the corridors when they brought the prisoners in. Danowski opened the door and stuck his head in.

"Captain Muzzetti is here, sir, and he requested permission to speak to you."

"Ask him to come back later, Ski."

"He says it's urgent, sir."

Hanson sighed in resignation. "Send him in, Ski."

"Aye, aye, sir."

Muzzetti came in, stood at attention and saluted formally. Hanson returned the salute.

"At ease, Muzi. What's so urgent?"

"Permission to speak frankly, sir?"

"Go ahead."

"I'm not happy about being left out of the loop, sir. I have a pretty good idea of what's been going on since the bombing at the parade. I don't think it's fair that I'm being left out of the action."

Hanson didn't want to deal with ego or job dissatisfaction problems right now and was about to send him packing, then he reconsidered. Muzzetti had been sent to a career-ending posting and had performed optimally and cheerfully from the moment he arrived. He deserved a few words of approval, even if an explanation wasn't possible.

"You've done an outstanding job since you got here, in especially difficult circumstances. If you have any complaints, write them up and submit them to me through Lieutenant Danowski."

"I'm not here to complain, sir. I think I've earned your trust. I want to participate in whatever covert operations are taking place."

"I'm sorry, Muzi. That's just not practical right now."

"Why not, sir. Don't you think I'm capable?"

"That's not the issue."

"Then what is it, sir?"

"I don't have time to go into it now. I'll meet with you tomorrow morning, at 0930, and we can talk then."

He was about to dismiss him when he saw the frustration on his face.

"I'm sorry you have a problem with your current assignment. You're a good officer, Muzi. I intend to promote you to major once the Plant administration takes office in January."

"I don't want to be placated with a promotion, sir," he said angrily.

Hanson suppressed his annoyance and said patiently, "I don't promote anyone to placate them, Captain Muzzetti. Certainly not to field grade. Only first-rate officers will have that privilege. You should be intelligent enough to know that."

Muzzetti was abashed at the rebuke. "Sorry, sir. I know I'm out of line, but I hope you can understand my frustration."

"Yes, I can. But right now you have to carry out your orders and assume that I'm aware of your problems. I will talk to you in the morning. Dismissed."

"Aye, aye, sir … Sir?"

"Yes?"

"I apologize for anything I said that might have offended you."

"You're not on the shit list. Now get out of here."

"Aye, aye, sir."

On his way out, Muzzetti closed the door a little harder than necessary to express his frustration. Hanson had to smile, thinking about how he might have reacted in Muzzetti's situation. He would certainly have been much more outspoken and probably a lot less respectful to his superior. His musings were interrupted by Danowski rushing in.

"They're here, boss."

"Are the corridors cleared of all non-essential personnel?"

"Yes, sir."

"Good. Let's go."

Jed was waiting for him next to the vehicles.

"There they are," he said, pointing to the three captives who were bound and gagged, lying on the floor of the SUV.

"Let's get them inside and have a look at them," Hanson ordered.

Jed's team picked them up, carried them inside, then downstairs, where they locked each one in a separate room.

"We'd like to get information as soon as possible, before their masters decide that the disappearance of all three isn't a coincidence," Hanson said.

"Any restrictions on the methods we use?" Jed asked.

"By any means necessary," Hanson replied.

Just before they went into the first room, Hanson called Griffin.

"The packages have arrived, sir. Their contents may suffer damage in the handling. Is that a problem?"

"No, Sam. Do what you have to."

"Thank you, sir."

He pointed to the first room and Jed opened the door. The prisoner had been left on the floor and he had managed to prop himself up against the wall. He glared at them defiantly and mumbled indecipherable curses.

"This one will sing for me," Jed said in Arabic, "once I take him on the road of pain."

The prisoner cursed more rabidly and would have spit if he was ungagged. The second prisoner had detached himself from his captors and lay there muttering what were probably verses from the Koran, preparing for martyrdom. Al shook her head at the dubious prospect.

"Let's look at the last one," she suggested.

They met Le Beau in the corridor.

"I installed the family in our building, sir. Now I'm going to bring the girl there. I didn't want them getting any attention here with a big reunion."

"Well done, Gunny," Hanson said.

"I'll explain that they have to stay indoors for the time being, until we can make arrangements for their long-term safety. I'll be back as soon as they're set."

Hanson, Al and Jed waited until Le Beau brought out the girl. When she saw Al, she ran to her, kissed her hand and said in Arabic, "Thank you for saving me, warrior sister. My family and I are in your debt."

"Repay me by serving Allah righteously, Huma," Al replied, then added, "Now the kind giant will take you to your family."

The girl burst into tears. "Thank you. Thank you."

"Thank Allah and the mercy of the Desert Serpent," pointing to Hanson.

The girl's eyes widened at the name that Al Qaeda had given their hated enemy. She bowed respectfully.

"You will always be in my prayers, great warrior."

"Go to your family, little one," he said kindly.

The human interlude was forgotten as soon as they entered the third room. The prisoner tried to maintain a look of bravado, but they could see him trembling.

"I hope I don't have to hurt this one too much, before he cooperates," Jed said in Arabic.

"Once he knows that his friends have talked, I'm sure he will not want to suffer needlessly," Al said, automatically falling into the good Marine–bad Marine routine. She reached out and took off the duct tape holding his gag, without removing any skin. "What is your name?" she asked gently.

"Bashshar."

"If you tell us what we want to know, we won't hurt you and we'll send you where you'll be safe."

His resistance instantly dissolved. "I'll tell you anything you want to know."

Al turned on a tape recorder and within a few minutes they had the names of two major terrorist planners based in the Saudi Mission to the U.N., Abdul Qadir al-Mihdar and Dhul Fiqar al-Hazmi, as well as their descriptions. Abdul was big, fat and talkative. Dhul was short, thin and quiet. Then Bashshar told them about the Al Qaeda safe house on Baltic Street, in the Court Street section of Brooklyn, and gave them the address.

When the prisoner fell silent, Jed asked, "Is there anything more you can tell us? Names? Contacts? Plans?"

"I've told you everything I know," the man answered brokenly.

Jed looked at Hanson, who nodded and Jed drew his pistol and shot the man in the heart. Bashshar was dead before he realized what happened to him. Hanson stared at the body for a moment, then said softly, "It's ironic that these terrorists take the names of the 9/11 suiciders."

He shook his head to disperse unwanted memories, then said, "This is a real break. Now we have to launch an operation against them before they have time to get suspicious. Finish off the other two using plastic bags over their heads. We'll have to blow up their bodies so they look like they died in an explosion. I'll ask Lonigan to take the bodies to the Brooklyn morgue in case Al Qaeda comes snooping around. Let's meet in the conference room in thirty minutes and plan the assault on the safe house. We should set the attack for 2000 hours. That way it'll be dark and if we're lucky, we'll catch them while they're still trying to figure out what's going on. We'll have to discuss how we'll get their people at the Mission to the U.N. I've got to talk to General Griffin now."

53

G ENERAL GRIFFIN WAS DELIGHTED that they had captured the terrorists so easily, and that they got the necessary information to plan a strike quickly.

"I'm glad phase one went so well, Sam. But I'm not happy that I won't be participating."

"Sorry about that, Charlie. We can't wait for you to get here. If we don't move immediately our birds may fly away."

"I understand. You better have a good excuse ready for Beverly. She was looking forward to some action. She's been practicing her fast draw from under her *jalaba*."

They both laughed at the description.

"She's a real fireater," Hanson said admiringly. "Please explain to her that speed is of the essence. I'm sure she'll understand. I've got to go now, Charlie. I have a planning session in twenty minutes and I'd like to hit the safe house at 2000 hours. I'll call you as soon as I have news."

"Good luck, Sam."

"Thank you, sir."

He made some notes in his computer about attacking a safe house that would have defenders with automatic weapons and multiple escape routes. He remembered the Iraqi insurgent's penchant for getting away through interconnecting houses and called up an area map of the neighborhood, as well as a close-up satellite photo of Baltic Street and Court Street. He was just getting absorbed in the problem of street control when Danowski knocked and entered.

"Captain Lonigan just arrived, boss, and everyone is assembled."

"Thanks, Ski. I'll be there in a minute."

"Yes, sir."

He waited until Danowski closed the door, quickly reviewed his notes, then wiped them from the hard drive. He reminded himself to stress the urgency to everyone involved not to leave any kind of paper or electronic trail that could provide evidence against them in the event of discovery of what would be considered criminal actions. He smiled to himself at the fantasy of being indicted at the International Court in the Hague, because he had never been anywhere in Europe, except for Germany, when staging to the Mid-East.

When he entered the conference room, Le Beau called, "Ten-hut," and everyone stood, including Lonigan.

"Be seated. Before we go any further, anyone who wants out should leave now." As expected, no one moved, so he continued. "Please make sure that nothing about this operation is written down anywhere, or on your computers. There is to be no record for obvious reasons." Everyone nodded that they understood.

"We have identified the terrorist's safe house. It's in Brooklyn on Baltic Street, off Court Street. I intend to hit it at 2000 hours. We also know that two of the master planners are from the Saudi Mission to the U.N., located on U.N. Plaza. According to our informant, they leave the Mission together every day at the same time, 1800 hours. If we can devise a functional plan, I'd like to get them too."

"Alive?" Jed asked.

"They'd be a treasure trove of information," Hanson mused, "but they'll be right across the street from the U.N., in full public view. It may not even be feasible to hit them, let alone abduct them. It's 1420. We'll start considering the target at U.N. Plaza, followed by the safe house, then we'll review everything else that must be done. Let's see what we can come up with."

Al spoke first.

"The options for the Mission targets are limited. If it's a hit, it'll have to be done on foot, up close, with a quick, unobtrusive departure to a waiting vehicle. First Avenue will be much too crowded for a drive by shooting and escape, so that's out. A snatch is complicated and risky. We'd have to seize them and get them into a vehicle without being noticed, and the avenue should still be busy at that time. I conclude that a hit on foot is the only practical option."

"Other opinions or comments?" Hanson asked.

"I think Al summed it up pretty well," Jed offered.

Danowski nodded agreement.

"What if I have some of my police officers arrest them?" Lonigan offered.

Hanson immediately ruled that out. "We don't have any legal evidence against them and we don't dare involve any outsiders, Mike. It would put us at great risk. Anyone else?" No one responded, so Hanson continued. "I agree with Al's assessment. If we go after them, it will have to be on foot."

"I'll get Penn and Teller with Le Beau," Al said.

"Why call them Penn and Teller?" Lonigan asked.

"They fit the description," Al replied.

Hanson reluctantly concluded that Al would be the best choice, since she had the sense to properly evaluate the situation and know whether to go ahead with the hit or not.

"The only problem is that Le Beau is too noticeable," Hanson said. "We need someone else."

Le Beau reluctantly nodded agreement.

"How about Sergeant Blakney?" Al asked. "She's capable and we can look like tourists."

"If she volunteers."

They went over the details until Hanson was satisfied that there was a good chance for success.

"Just keep in mind at all times, Al, that if you can't do it and manage a clean getaway, you abort the mission. No pun intended." This brought the tension relieving laugh. "Select someone reliable for your driver who has a personal vehicle."

"I'll ask Sergeant Morales."

"Good choice, Al, but let him know it's strictly volunteer."

"Aye, aye, sir."

"One other thing. Don't use your official sidearms. Draw pistols from Ski's concealed stash. Perhaps he has silencers. Dispose of them safely if you use them."

"You're not supposed to know about them, boss," Danowski protested.

"You'll learn that our commander is all-seeing," Al joked.

Hanson gave them a minute to relax.

"Alright, Al. You're authorized to try for the hit. I'll talk to you and Blakney, if she volunteers. Now let's make the plan to take the safe house.

"Unlike our previous experiences in Iraq and Afghanistan, we have no legitimate authority to do this. That means it's more important to get away unidentified than to take out our objective. We'll go in wearing civvies.

"Our target is a two story, unattached house, with an attic and basement. They may have surveillance cameras and the doors and windows might be booby-trapped. There'll be four to six bad guys, maybe more and they'll have automatic weapons, possibly heavier stuff. We don't want to take anyone alive, but we want any documents and computers that we can find in a quick search. They may have escape tunnels to next door houses in the basement, so securing the basement quickly is a vital objective. When we're through we'll blow the place. Questions? Comments?"

"It sounds like you're planning to go," Danowski said hesitantly. "Is that a good idea?"

"That's not open for discussion, Ski. Jed will lead the assault. I'll tag along."

They were silent for a minute, considering the problems. Jed spoke first.

"I'd like to use the stake out teams from the girl's house. With you, me and Le Beau that makes fifteen. That should be enough."

"What about me?" Danowski protested.

"Sorry, Ski. You'll have to guard the fort here and lead the reaction platoon, if we need them."

"Aw, boss. That's not fair."

"It can't be helped. Go on, Jed."

"We hit the front and back doors with those old LAWS that aren't any good for armor any more, followed by flash-bangs. You and I will go in the front with four of our people. Le Beau will go in the back with four. Two will go in on each side through a window, once they hear us go in the front and back. The window entrants will use flash-bangs. My team will go in the front first and hose anything that moves.

"Le Beau's team comes in as soon as our small arms fire slackens. The window entrants will take out anyone they see. If for any reason they can't get in the windows, they should go in the back door. We'll all be wearing night vision goggles, but we need to take extra care not to shoot our own people."

Jed paused to let his first thoughts sink in, then continued at Hanson's nod.

"Once the ground floor is secure, my team will hit the basement, Le Beau's team will take the second floor and the attic, and the window people will hold the front and back door. As soon as we're finished, we exit the back door and go to our vehicles waiting on Warren Street. I think that covers everything," he concluded with a straight face, which brought chuckles from all of them.

"A good plan," Hanson commended.

"They may have a reinforced basement door," Al offered.

"Good point. What do you think, Jed? C4, or another LAWS?"

"LAWS. It'll save time. We don't care whose brains we scramble down there."

"Alright. Let's look at the map … One last thought. Remember our Iraq motto?"

"Move quick, shoot straight and get ass out intact," Al and Jed recited in unison.

After careful study of the map they finalized any details that Jed hadn't covered in his general briefing. Hanson asked Lonigan to arrange for emergency services to arrive after they evacuated the building.

"If the Fire Marshal declares the fire suspicious, we can keep everyone out long enough so we might be able to use any information that we find before Al Qaeda knows what happened."

"Sure. Which group will I be with?"

"You can't go in with us, Mike. I'd like you to be in a support vehicle. If we run into any unexpected glitches, especially with the police, you can take care of it."

"I'm a combat vet, Sam. I can be useful."

"You'll be more useful outside. If there's nothing else, Al, recruit your volunteers and bring them back here."

"There is one thing, boss."

"What, Ski?"

"Doctor Carver. He keeps calling."

Hanson thought fast. "If it's alright with you, Mike, I'll have him go with you, so he can treat any wounded immediately."

"Sure."

"I rely on you to make certain he stays in the vehicle, with no heroics or other foolishness from either of you."

"Don't worry, Sam."

"When have I heard that before?"

Al went to get her volunteers, Jed went to assemble the assault force and Danowski left to prepare equipment and alert the reaction platoon to stand by. Lonigan brought him up to date on the media plan.

"The Police Department press office notified the media about the explosion on Bergen Street. They'll leak news items about the pursuit and shooting of a child molester. We should be covered. How do you want to handle today's news?"

"However it plays out, Mike. Al Qaeda will know they've been attacked. They just won't know who did it, unless we get caught. One other problem. We have to get the three bodies from Bergen Street to the morgue in Brooklyn. That's where anyone would expect to find them. Can you handle that?"

"Sure. I'll arrange to have them taken to the Kings County Hospital Morgue."

"Thanks. I've got to call Carver."

He expected all sorts of objections from the overwrought doctor for being left out of the action, but Carver was grateful just to be going along.

"Thanks, Sam. This means a lot to me."

"I know Carv. I just need your word that you'll obey orders."

"You've got it."

"Good. Come to headquarters in thirty minutes. I'll notify the guard post to admit you."

Hanson studied the map with Lonigan until Al came back with her volunteers. He carefully assessed Sergeant Blakney, another Saudi veteran. She was a tall, dark-skinned black woman, whose posture revealed her self-confidence. He remembered her from the desert crossing as being one of the leadership types, constantly helping her comrades.

"Did Captain Kent explain the mission to you?"

"Yes, sir."

"Do you understand what's involved?"

"Yes, sir."

"You realize that you will be performing an assassination?"

"Yes, sir."

"Does that bother you?"

"Not if it's Al Qaeda, sir. We should get all of them."

"What about you, Sergeant Morales?"

"I wish I could pull the trigger, sir."

He nodded to them approvingly, then showed them a street map.

"The targets will be on the west side of First Avenue, going north. Hit them right away then walk at an average pace to 47th Street, where Julio will be waiting, between First and Second Avenues. Al. Alert me on your headset if there are any problems. Call me as soon as you get away safely. Do not. I repeat. Do not discuss this operation with anyone. Ever. Understood?"

"Yes, sir," they responded.

"Al. Take your team and finish your preparations. Let me know when you're ready to leave."

"Aye, aye, sir."

"Good luck."

"Thank you, sir."

Jed came in with his troops and Hanson listened attentively while Jed outlined the operation and pointed out the attack routes and the backyard exit to Warren Street, where the escape vehicles would be waiting. Jed was painstakingly thorough and turned to Hanson when he finished.

"Anything to add, sir?"

"Good briefing, Jed. Something I just learned. Doctor Carver will be with us and he will immediately treat any wounded. You will all oblige me by not getting wounded." This brought a laugh.

"In the event that anything goes wrong and you get separated and cannot withdraw as planned, go north on Court Street to Atlantic Avenue and call for pick-up on your personal communicators. If that's not possible, take a taxi or car service back to Manhattan. I'll have a detail waiting at First Avenue and 23rd Street, and they'll pay your fare and bring you back here. Questions?"

There were none, so Hanson concluded, "Study the map and check your gear thoroughly. Lieutenant Davis will alert you when it's time to move out. Jed. One more chore. We have to make the two bodies from the girl's house look like they died in the explosion. As soon as it's dark enough, take them out back, cover them with old armor vests and blow them up with a concussion grenade and an incendiary grenade. Captain Lonigan will have them brought to the morgue later."

"Aye, aye, sir."

Danowski rushed in.

"Good news, boss. It's raining. That'll make it harder for them to see our troops at the safe house."

"It also might mean that the Mission targets won't go out in the rain," Hanson mused.

"Then we'll get them another time, boss."

Hanson smiled at his confidence and was about to praise him when the Sergeant of the Guard called and told him that Doctor Carver was at the gate.

"Thank you, Sergeant. Have him escorted to my office and tell him I'll join him there shortly. Ski. When Al's team gets back, put her and Blakney in my office. They are to wait there until I get back. Make sure they're fed."

"I'll take care of it, boss."

"If for any reason you have to bring the reaction platoon to our aid in Brooklyn, Al is not to come with you under any circumstances. Muzi will take command here until I return."

"Yes, boss."

"A lot could go wrong this evening. If Al gets caught, call Captain Lonigan immediately. He'll be more useful with the police than we would."

Danowski looked around to be sure no one could overhear them. "What are her chances, boss?"

"If our info is solid and there are no unexpected glitches her chances are good. She'll call it off if the risk is too great. I've got to see Carver for a few minutes. Keep an eye on things 'til I get back."

"Yes, boss."

Carver had aged since the death of Mavis. His customary ebullience had been replaced by a solemn expression and a tentative manner. He perked up considerably when he saw Hanson, anticipating that he would finally be able to do something to pay back the terrorists for his daughter's tragic death.

"Hi, Sam," he said softly, offering his hand.

Hanson ignored the hand and hugged Carver. "Hi, Carv. I'm glad you'll be with us."

"I'll never forget this, Sam. If there's ever anything you want, just ask."

"It's only fair that you go with us. There are conditions, however."

"Whatever you say."

"One. You are not to get out of the vehicle under any circumstances."

"Yes, Sam."

"Two. You will never talk to anyone about this operation, ever, no matter what."

"Yes, Sam."

"Three. Even if we don't need your professional skills this evening, your presence is important to all of us and I hope it gives you some closure."

"Thanks, Sam. You can rely on me."

"Good. Can you put a basic medical bag together quickly?"

"I could be back with one in ten or fifteen minutes."

"Then go get it. When you get back, you can wait in the mess hall. Danowski will come for you when it's time to leave."

"I'll be ready. Thanks again, Sam."

The tempo of activity throughout the building had picked up enough so that those not included knew that something was going on. The rumor mill was working at top speed. As Hanson walked back to the conference room everyone he passed looked at him speculatively, but no one dared question him. Al and Blakney were waiting for him, dressed in slacks and bright colored sweaters. It was hard to believe that they were going out to commit murder.

He looked at Al and for a moment the mask that she always wore to conceal her feelings slipped. He plainly saw what she had hidden from him for years, that she loved him. He tried desperately to control his swirling thoughts that he was about to send the woman closest to him to possible death. A look of serenity lit her face and she said softly, "Don't worry, Sam. We'll be fine."

"Is everything ready?" he asked gruffly.

"Yes, Sam."

"Then shove off. Call me as soon as you're back in the car."

"Yes, Sam."

"Come back to me, Al."

"Aye, aye, sir." She turned to Blakney with a jaunty air. "Let's move out."

"Aye, aye, sir. I mean ma'am … Aw, shit. I'm ready, Al."

Al winked broadly at Hanson, slipped her arm through Blakney's and said, "Then let's go see the U.N."

He watched them leave with a combination of admiration and apprehension. He couldn't help thinking about the service that women were performing in the military, at least in the Marine Corps. For the first time he could easily imagine them in a Roman legion, Napoleon's Imperial Guard, or leading a rifle platoon in a Vietnam jungle. They were true warriors. Before he could imagine other historical scenarios, Jed interrupted his musing.

"We took care of the bodies. Sam. The troops are ready and we're just waiting for your orders, sir."

"You and I will go in one SUV with your team and one window team. Le Beau, his team and the second window team will go in the other SUV, along with Captain Lonigan and Doctor Carver."

"Carv and I can keep the motors running, so you don't have to leave a driver," Lonigan offered.

"Thanks, Mike. That'll help. This may sound paranoid, Cajun, but just in case anyone is observing us, we should leave separately." Le Beau nodded that he understood.

"Take local streets and be sure no one is following you and rejoin us at Canal Street and The Bowery for the rest of the trip. Use the encrypted cell phone if there are any problems. If there are no questions, let's move out."

54

W HEN HANSON GOT to the motor pool the vehicles were loaded. Tico was dressed in civvies, sitting in the driver's seat of the SUV, elaborately studying the map and refusing to meet Hanson's eyes. He briefly debated refusing to let him go with them, then accepted that he would be useful. He got into the vehicle and Tico instantly knew that he was included in the operation.

"Where to, sir?"

"Canal Street and the Bowery. Take side streets and make sure we're not being followed."

"Aye, aye, sir," he said happily.

The rain was coming down harder and Hanson welcomed it, because it would cut down visibility at the target house. He looked at his watch and it was 1655 and he knew that Al should just be getting to U.N. Plaza. Right on schedule, she called a few minutes later.

"We're doing a slow drive-by to check the route, then we'll circle around on Second Avenue and get off and walk from 42nd Street. If they don't show by 1830, do we wait?"

"No. You might be too conspicuous by then. How's Blakney doing?"

"She'll be fine, Sam."

"Don't take any unnecessary chances, Al. They're not worth it."

"Yes, Sam."

The atmosphere in the SUV was tense with anticipation. Everyone knew they might be killed or wounded and were even risking prison, but they were eager for the rare opportunity to take down an Al Qaeda safe house. Tico had been constantly monitoring the mirror and made several abrupt stops to see if anyone behind them reacted.

"I'm pretty sure we're not being followed, sir, but I'd like to take a roundabout route, just to be certain."

"Good idea. We've got time."

Traffic was surprisingly light considering that rush hour was starting, and Hanson decided to advance the attack by one hour, to 1900. This would narrow the time frame after Al hit the Mission targets and would give Al Qaeda much less time to figure out what happened, let alone react. He called Le Beau in the other SUV.

"I've moved the attack up an hour earlier, to 1900. Does this cause you any problems?"

"No, sir. We're ready."

"Where are you now?"

"Broadway and 14th Street, and we're not being followed."

"Good. I'll see you at the rendezvous."

When Hanson got to Canal Street he called Le Beau, who had gotten there before him.

"We're going to turn on the Bowery and circle around towards the Brooklyn Bridge. Let me know if you spot a tail. After a few blocks you pass me, and I'll check if you're being followed."

It turned out that no one was following them, but the precaution helped everyone prepare the mindset for the assault to come. They crossed the bridge and stopped just off Cadman Plaza, on Tillary Street, to wait until it was time for the final approach to Baltic Street. Al called him in 1745.

"We're in position on the corner of 46th Street and we'll play tourist until Penn and Teller show up. How are you doing, Sam?"

"Good. We're in Brooklyn, about ten minutes from Baltic Street. I moved the attack up to 1900. Depending on what happens with you, we might even go a little earlier."

"I'll call you as soon as something happens. Don't get hurt, Sam."

Jed's troops were all Saudi veterans and they settled down to wait with typical behavior. Some of them dozed, others talked quietly, and a few moved into a space of their own, but they were all getting ready. Tico was humming a tune and softly beating out a rhythm on the steering wheel. Rather than finding it irritating, Hanson was soothed by it.

He went over the plan in his mind and could find no apparent flaws, though he knew that everything would change when they hit the house. He resisted the impulse to look at his watch and sent fervent ESP messages that all would go well with Al.

He felt a lot better having Tico at the wheel, because Lonigan would now stay with Carver, the only unpredictable participant. He carefully checked his equipment, making sure the grenades were securely attached to his vest, and checked the action of his sidearm, verifying that a round was in the chamber and the safety was off. He knew from experience that in the excitement of combat mistakes happened, so painstaking preparation was an ally.

After waiting for what felt like hours, but was less than fifteen minutes, Al called excitedly.

"We got 'em, Sam. We got 'em. Penn, Teller and their bodyguard. It was easier than a practice run."

"Are you alright?"

"Yes, Sam. No problems."

"Report."

"We're in the car, just turning onto Second Avenue. This is how it went down. We saw them about 1805. A big guy came out of the Mission with a big umbrella, followed by Penn and Teller. They looked exactly like Bashshar described them. The bodyguard held the umbrella over them, and they started towards 47th Street. People were hurrying along to get out of the rain, but these guys sauntered along as if they had forever … Joke.

"We moved behind them and I shot the bodyguard twice in the back of the head. Shin shot Teller and as the bodyguard fell, Penn turned, and I shot him twice in the face. We were turning the corner before anyone reacted to the bodies. Nobody followed us."

"Well done. Go back to headquarters."

"Can we go with you?"

"No way. In fact, I think we'll hit them now. I'll see you later."

He passed the word to Le Beau, nodded to Tico and they headed for Baltic Street.

"From now on we use our headset communicators," Hanson ordered. Jed and Le Beau did a system check and everyone responded properly.

Traffic had become a little heavier around Borough Hall, but in a few minutes, they crossed Fulton Street and cut over to Court Street. Le Beau turned onto Warren Street and Hanson waited until he saw him stop, then nodded to Tico, who went to Baltic.

"Saddle up," Jed ordered. "We go in fifteen seconds."

Tico pulled up in front of the house, the troops piled out and they took out the front door with the LAWS. A few seconds later Le Beau's team hit the back door with a LAWS. Jed's team tossed in flash-bangs, then went in through a cloud of smoke and sprayed the house with their M16s.

Screams and the sounds of falling bodies let them know they hit people. As soon as they stopped firing, Le Beau's team entered through the back door, while at the same time the window teams went in at each side of the house. They killed everyone on the ground floor in a few moments and Le Beau's team went upstairs, while Jed's team headed for the basement.

Jed signaled for the LAWS, and they blew in the basement door. They charged through the smoke and debris, firing as they went and took some return fire. Jed was hit in the armpit, where the vest didn't cover a vulnerable spot, but he was so pumped up that he kept moving and urging the troops on.

They killed everyone in the big room, then came to a small room in the back. The door was open, and Jed saw a man with a box trying to escape into a tunnel. He rushed in, shot him in the head and when the man fell with a thud, said with satisfaction, "No rats are escaping into the sewers tonight."

Then a wave of dizziness overcame him, and he slumped down on the floor. He had trouble focusing and as he looked around the room everything seemed far away. He saw a man who was gagged and tied to a chair, but he couldn't comprehend what he was doing there and didn't have the energy to ask.

Hanson came in a moment later. When he saw Jed, he cried, "Oh, no." He knelt down, checked him and saw that he was seriously wounded and going into shock. "Jed. Jed. Look at me. I'll get you to Doc Carver. Hang in there."

Jed summoned his last reserves of strength. "I'm hit bad, Sam. I don't know if I'm going to make it … The rat in the tunnel was trying to get away with a box … It might be important. I got to know what it is."

"Sure. As soon as we take care of your wound."

"It can wait. I gotta know. Please, Sam."

Hanson realized that Jed was insistent and there was nothing he could do about it. He picked up the box which was unusually heavy and brought it to him.

"What are those markings, Sam?"

"Radioactive material symbols. They may have been making a nuclear bomb."

"And we stopped them, right?"

"Yes, Jed. You may have saved New York City."

"Then it was worth it …"

"Oh, Jed. I'm sorry."

"Don't be. I'm not passing on yet. If I do I have only one regret."

"What?"

"Promise me …"

"What?"

"Promise me you'll get Royce."

Hanson hesitated, then gave in to the pleading look from his good friend.

"I'll get Royce," he whispered, then watched his friend pass out.

He hadn't been aware that the troops had gathered around him and with a tremendous effort snapped back to awareness of their situation. He tossed a cloth over the box so no one would see what it was, then told some of them to carry Jed and others to bring the box. Then he finally noticed the man tied to the chair. He started to approach him cautiously, then realized that the terrorists didn't have time to rig a booby trap. He took off the gag and demanded, "Who are you?"

"Water," the man croaked.

"Talk, or I'll shoot you and leave you with the others."

"Am Russian scientist, but am physics teacher, not nuclear expert. Russian Mafia sell me to Al Qaeda for debt I owe. Deliver me to Arabs in Mexico. They smuggle me across border and bring me to Brooklyn, U.S.A. Not believe when I tell can't make bomb. Beat and torture me. You save. Take with. Please."

The man looked like they had really worked him over and if his story was true, he could be a valuable source of information. There didn't seem to be any risk, so he decided to take him. "Untie him and bring him along," he ordered.

They had been in the building for almost two minutes, and it was time to get out of there. He called Le Beau on his communicator.

"Cajun. Sitrep."

"We're on the ground floor. We swept the second floor and attic and killed everyone. Lance Moskowitz has a flesh wound, but she's mobile. We took a computer and a bunch of papers, and I collected their cellphones."

"Good work. Listen up. We found something big. The situation's changed and all of us are going out the front door. I'll have Lonigan drive around and stop behind Tico. As soon as he's there, we go. I want everyone on high alert.

"The neighbors will be coming out to see what happened. There could be Al Qaeda among them. No one is to be allowed to interfere with our departure. If necessary, fire warning shots in the air. If that doesn't work, shoot to kill. Your team will cover us, and you'll follow as soon as we reach the corner safely. Questions?"

"Where's Jed?"

"He's wounded."

"Oh."

"We're coming upstairs. Are you ready to go?"

"Yes, sir."

Hanson called Lonigan.

"We changed the plan. Come around the corner and stop behind Tico. As soon as you stop, we're coming out. Be alert."

"I'm moving. What happened?"

"Later."

Hanson followed Jed's team up the stairs, and he saw Le Beau's troops staring at Jed, the box and the prisoner.

Le Beau had sent someone to the front door, who reported, "Lonigan's here with the SUV."

Le Beau looked at Hanson.

"We're ready, sir."

"Take Jed with you. Have doc Carver take care of him. I'll take the box and the prisoner. Stay close together and be alert for any kind of resistance. Let's move out."

Hanson led Jed's team out first. He saw people straggling out of their houses, but they didn't appear to pose a threat. They piled into the SUV and Hanson yelled, "Drive."

Tico took off, scattering some people on the street who were in the way. The neighbors were more interested in the fire than the SUV speeding off.

When they reached the corner, someone in the back said, "Le Beau's moving, sir."

"Good. Tico. Don't wait for them. They'll catch up to us. Get us home as quick as you can, without being stopped."

He called Lonigan. "Keep an eye on us, Mike. If anyone stops us, get us out fast."

"Yes, Sam."

Tico took Clinton Street to Atlantic Avenue, turned west to the Brooklyn-Queens Expressway, which led to the Brooklyn Bridge. Le Beau was right behind them, and he had two of his troops watching for anyone following them.

"We seem to be clear, sir." he reported.

Hanson heard the troops quietly falling into the after-action easing of tension, but the usual bragging and teasing was muted by Jed's condition. Hanson forced himself to compartmentalize the fear of the loss of his friend so it wouldn't distract him from assessing the new problem. He began to consider the implications that they might have actually captured nuclear material and concluded that this was now way beyond a basic anti-terrorist strike.

They crossed the bridge with no one following them and Hanson began to think they may have gotten away without being identified. The one thing he knew for sure was that the parameters of the punitive raid had changed drastically. What had been a relatively simple, well-executed assault mission had now become a highly complex situation with far reaching consequences. Though they could get rid of the prisoner without too much trouble, there was no easy way to resolve how to deal with the captured nuclear material.

He wracked his brain but couldn't come up with a practical solution, so it was time to consult higher authority. He called General Griffin.

"Charlie. We're on our way back to HQ. Something's come up and I need you here."

"What is it?"

"I can't tell you even on this line, but it's big. Can you get on a plane right away?"

"If it's that urgent, I'll take a chopper to the east side heliport."

"Call me when you're ten minutes out and I'll have a Humvee waiting."

"I should be there in ninety minutes."

"Thanks, Charlie."

Hanson called Danowski next.

"We'll be there soon, Ski. We have a prisoner and a box. Have a detail waiting for us to bring them to my office. Post a guard at the door and no one in or out without my say so."

"Yes, sir."

A few minutes later they reached the guard post at the motor pool and pulled into the parking lot. Danowski was waiting with a detail, and they took the box and prisoner inside. Hanson dismissed Jed's team after praising them for their exceptional performance. Then he went to Le Beau's SUV.

"Well done. All of you. How's your patient, doctor?"

"It's a severe wound. I've got to get him to the E.R."

"Cajun. Bring Jed to the hospital, I'll dismiss your team. Carv. Keep me posted about Jed."

"Yes, Sam."

He watched them leave, then turned to the team. "You all did an outstanding job."

"Thank you, sir," they answered.

"Remember. Not a word about this to anyone."

"Aye, aye, sir."

"Dismissed."

Hanson turned to Lonigan. "Come with me, Mike."

"It went pretty well, didn't it?"

"Yes. But there are some new developments."

"I saw you come out with a prisoner."

"That's the smallest part of it."

"What happened?"

"Wait 'til we get to my office."

"Sure. Thanks for taking me with you. I'm feeling a little better about things now."

"Thanks for all your help. We're going to need more of it."

"Just ask."

Word had obviously spread among the troops that Jed was seriously wounded, because everyone they passed nodded solemnly, or expressed a few words of condolence. The possible loss of Jed was finally sinking in, and Hanson knew the future would be bleaker without him. Another part of him was consoled because at least Jed knew he avenged Tyrone, took some of his enemies with him and may have saved his country from a nuclear disaster.

The guard at his office door snapped to attention when he saw Hanson.

"Stand at ease, but remain here until relieved. Except for General Griffin, no one in without orders."

"Aye, aye, sir."

Lonigan was beginning to get the idea that whatever was going on was really big and he followed Hanson into the office burning with curiosity. Danowski called, "Attention," and everyone snapped to.

"As you were," Hanson said and looked at Blakney. "Sergeant Blakney."

"Yes, sir?"

"You carried out your mission with exemplary ability, as I expected, You are promoted to Gunnery Sergeant. Congratulations."

"Thank you, sir."

"I don't have time to take your report right now because something urgent has come up. You are to remain in your quarters until we can review everything in detail. If you have to go out to use the head or mess hall, you are not to discuss anything with anyone regarding this operation."

"Aye, aye, sir."

"You did a great job, Shin. I'm sorry for the inconvenience."

"Semper fi, sir."

Hanson waited until she left, then turned to Al. "I'll talk to you privately as soon as I can."

"Yes, sir. Where's Jed?"

He didn't answer right away, then said gently, "He's seriously wounded, Al."

"What are his chances?" Hanson shrugged. She tried to conceal the stab of pain and struggled to maintain control. "There aren't many of us left, Sam."

"I know. Hopefully, there'll be other good Marines to take our place."

Danowski had a faraway look. "He's a good guy and a great Marine," he muttered.

"I don't mean to sound harsh, but we don't have time for brooding now," Hanson said. "We found what might be radioactive material at the safe house. The prisoner is a Russian scientist who was sold to Al Qaeda by the Russian mafia to help construct some kind of nuclear device." Their stunned expressions told him all he needed to know. He gave them a minute to digest the bombshell, then added, "General Griffin is on his way and should be here in about two hours, when we'll have a full discussion of the problem. If you have any bright ideas, be ready with them later."

Hanson began to question the prisoner. "What is your name?"

"Dmitry Goncharov."

"Tell us what you know."

"Yes, sir. Al Qaeda got uranium 235 from Iran to make bomb. Want Russian scientist so blame not go to Iran ..."

"How do you know it was from Iran?" Al asked.

"Heard men speaking, lady soldier. I not tell them was in Afghanistan during war and speak Pashtun and Arabic."

"Go on," Hanson urged.

"When I tell that I high school physics teacher, not bomb maker, Arabs get angry, beat and torture me. Ask if I make bomb with help from books. Get angry when tell I not know. Tell I of no use if can't make bomb and threaten kill me. No want die, so tell maybe can do if have books. They say get soon. Then you come kill Arabs. Save life. I help. You no kill?"

"We won't kill you, Dmitry, but you've got to tell us all you know," Hanson said.

"Will tell. Want help."

"Good. Ski. Put Dmitry in one of the sergeant's rooms, get him something to eat and drink and place a guard at the door. No one in or out without an order from me."

"Aye, aye, sir. Come along, Dmitry," Danowski said.

"No hurt?"

"No hurt."

"Let's take a break and get something to eat," Hanson suggested. "We'll continue in an hour."

55

D ANOWSKI HAD ALERTED the mess sergeant earlier that they might need to feed some of the troops, so platters of sandwiches and jugs of coffee were waiting for them in the mess hall. On the way, Hanson stopped for Blakney and brought her along.

Hanson couldn't relax with the burden of nuclear material weighing on him, but it was comforting to sit with old comrades and new friends who had paid their dues. Unlike other after-action let-downs, they could neither sleep nor babble away, but they all felt secure in the bond between them, built with blood and caring.

Everyone who wasn't on duty, officers and enlisted personnel, casually drifted in at various times. They were hoping for some news, some morsel of information that would let them know what was going on, because they all knew that an operation had taken place. Even Muzzetti couldn't resist an appearance. He nodded to Hanson, who nodded back, then lingered over a cup of coffee, until he accepted that he wasn't included in the inner circle. He left with a reproachful look.

Hanson wasn't annoyed, because he knew the man was craving action. How could he fault a Marine for that?

Hanson leisurely led the group back to his office, dropping Blakney on the way. He took Al aside while Lonigan made phone calls and Danowski checked the duty stations.

"Are you alright, Al? Any qualms? Concerns?"

"I wouldn't want to be a full-time assassin, but I did the right thing for Kyle, Tyrone and all the others … Do you want my report now?"

"I'd like you to make it when General Griffin gets here, unless there's something you wouldn't want to say in front of the others."

"I may leave out some of the gory details and how good it felt to see them go down. I wouldn't want to give the impression that I'm a bloodthirsty wench."

He had to smile at her unquenchable spirit. "I'm sorry, Al. That's not the kind of service I intended for you."

"There was no other choice this time. I know the enemy as well as you do. This is not an honorable war. If we want our country to survive, we'll have to get our hands dirty. I just never want to be like them and carry out indiscriminate killing and senseless slaughter."

He nodded agreement. "That's not our way."

Lonigan noticed that Hanson and Al had fallen silent. "Sam?"

"Yes, Mike?"

"The three bodies have been taken to the morgue in Brooklyn. There's been no news about the shootings at the Saudi Mission. The police press spokesman will issue a release later tonight speculating that the incident on Baltic Street may have been a drug deal gone bad. If you don't like that, we can say something else."

"Let's wait on that until we talk to General Griffin."

Le Beau came in, but just shrugged when they asked about Jed. "Doc Carver said he'd call as soon as he knows something."

Danowski informed him that the guard posts and Enclave patrols reported all quiet. "This might give you a laugh, boss. The guards at the V.A. hospital are having some problems with the vets."

"I don't feel much like laughing. What kind of problems?"

"The vets keep coming to the guard posts carrying weapons and insisting on taking turns at guard duty."

This did bring a flicker of a smile. "We'll deal with them tomorrow."

A moment later Griffin called. "I'm ten minutes out, Sam."

"Yes, sir. Your driver will be waiting."

Hanson sent Tico to pick up the general, then sat down to collect his thoughts for the upcoming meeting.

When the general arrived, the sergeant of the guard paged Hanson to tell him.

They stood when the general came in and he shook hands with all of them.

"Be seated. Colonel, I'm eager to hear your report."

"Yes, sir. I'll give you the short version to bring you up to speed. We attacked an Al Qaeda safe house in Brooklyn, killed everyone and rescued a prisoner."

"Casualties?"

"Lance Corporal Moskowitz got a flesh wound and … Lieutenant Davis was seriously wounded."

"Jed."

"Yes, sir."

"Let's hope he makes it, Sam. He's a good Marine."

"Yes, sir … We also captured a box of what may be radioactive material."

"What?"

"To be more precise, sir. The box supposedly contains uranium 235, provided to Al Qaeda by Iran. I got this information from the prisoner we rescued, a Russian physics teacher who claims he was sold to Al Qaeda by the Russian Mafia."

Griffin stared at Hanson, his mind a jumble of racing thoughts, but foremost was the hope, however premature, that they may have prevented a nuclear disaster. "Now I understand the urgency of your call. Who knows about this?"

"Everyone in this room and the prisoner."

"What about the troops who were there?"

"Only Jed saw the box before he passed out. He understood what it meant."

"I'm glad."

"No one else knows what it is, sir."

"Good. That'll give us some time to consider our course of action."

Danowski said, "Excuse me, sir."

"Yes, Ski?" Hanson asked.

"Some Al Qaeda people probably know."

"You're right," Hanson said. "Mike."

"Yes, Sam?"

"Make sure the police and fire department keep everyone out of the building. This will buy us some time."

"Yes, Sam. I'll make a quick call right now."

"I don't see how we can contain this, Sam," Griffin stated.

"I know, sir. That's why I need you here … We really lucked out tonight, but what if they have more nuclear material in other cities?"

"A terrifying thought," General Griffin said.

Hanson nodded. "Hopefully the prisoner might have some information about that."

Griffin shook off the ominous feeling that was growing.

"Let's hear what your people think, Sam."

"Yes, sir. Ski?"

"I think it depends on whether or not this is the only nuclear material. I'd like to consider it longer before saying anything else."

"Mike?"

"Well we can't just dump the stuff somewhere and it's essential that we find out if there's more of it."

"Al?"

"We have to answer all sorts of questions first. For example, since it was an illegal raid, how did we get the material? We don't want to go to jail for the rest of our lives. Once that's resolved, we can bring in appropriate help, Homeland Security, Intelligence agencies, etc."

"Good point, Al," Hanson said. "We should deal with how we got the material before talking to anyone else. Also, just so we don't lose track of the big picture while worrying about saving our asses, be clear that Iran's giving nuclear material to Al Qaeda is an act of war."

Griffin nodded. "Whatever happens, there are more important concerns then our going to jail."

"I may have an explanation we can use for this situation," Hanson said.

"Tell us," Griffin replied.

"Men of apparent Middle East extraction fired shots from their car at one of our patrols in the Enclave, wounding one Marine. Then they drove off and the patrol pursued them. I was nearby in my vehicle with Captain Lonigan. When the patrol radioed us we joined the chase and followed them into Brooklyn.

"When they got to Baltic Street, the men got out and ran into a house. Captain Lonigan and I knocked on the door, but they didn't answer. We were about to call for police reinforcements, when they fired at us from a window, wounding one of my officers. We kicked in the door and demanded their surrender, but they kept shooting. We shot back and killed all of them.

"When we checked the house, we found nuclear material and a prisoner in the basement. We didn't want knowledge of discovering a possible nuclear weapon to become public without first consulting higher authority, so we brought the material and prisoner back to my headquarters. I immediately informed my commanding officer, General Griffin, of the situation … Comments?"

There was a minute of silence while they considered the story.

"Why didn't Captain Lonigan call for assistance right away?" Danowski asked.

Griffin nodded to Lonigan to respond. "I didn't want to risk a shootout in the streets that might put civilians at risk."

"Why did you go into the house without backup?" Al asked.

"To avoid a siege that might cost more casualties," Hanson replied.

"There are a few weak spots to be ironed out," Griffin said. "You could be accused of rash, or even faulty judgment, but you might get away with it."

"After all," Hanson explained, "we're heroes. We may have saved New York City from a nuclear disaster. The powers that be might cut us some slack …"

"Only if they believe you," Griffin said.

"What do you think, sir? Does it sound plausible?"

"I hope so. Unless someone comes up with a better idea, this at least covers the basics."

"I'm sorry, Sam. It won't work," Al said.

"Why not?"

"You and Mike may manage the explanation, but what about the troops? Even if you prepare them thoroughly, I don't think they'll be able to deal with an investigation."

"She's right, sir," Hanson confirmed. "Maybe we can come up with something better."

They tried to think of a better story for fifteen or twenty minutes without coming up with anything that sounded credible.

"We should give it a rest, sir," Hanson suggested, "and try again later." Griffin nodded agreement. "What do we do next, sir?"

"I'm working on it, Sam. Give me a few minutes."

"Yes, sir."

Hanson took everyone else aside and focused on the main problem. "The big questions are why we went there in the first place and why we didn't request assistance from various government agencies, especially the police department. We don't have to worry about what happened once we went into the house, because that course of action is clear. If we find good enough answers, we can be heroes and we won't face jail. I suggest we all wrack our brains until we have a good explanation ... By the way. It has to be soon, because we can't sit on the discovery of nuclear material for much longer."

"What if we can't come up with anything, boss?" Danowski asked.

"Then our next posting will be at exotic Fort Leavenworth," Hanson answered with a sardonic grin.

Griffin called them back to the table. "Regardless of how we got the material, I must notify the Commandant of the Corps immediately and inform him that we have a crisis situation. I won't go into details, but I'll tell him that we got the material in a raid on an Al Qaeda safe house. He will be obligated to immediately inform the appropriate civilian and military authorities, as well as Homeland Security and the intelligence community. This will panic the Beaumont administration and Valerie will probably wet her panties in the White House."

He paused a moment for the expected snicker, then continued. "The usual turf struggle will start, but Homeland Security will probably take primary responsibility and assign tasks to the FBI and CIA Once they stop blaming each other for what might have been a catastrophic intelligence failure, they'll look for a scapegoat. That's us, unless we have a damn good explanation for our involvement ... I heard your reference to Fort Leavenworth, Sam. Frankly, I'd rather not spend my remaining years there ... I'm going to call the commandant now. Get some answers fast."

"Alright," Hanson said. "You heard the man. Let's get to it. Does anyone have an idea?"

"Nothing yet," Al replied.

Danowski shook his head. "No, boss."

"What about you, Mike?"

"I may have something. I haven't worked it out completely ..."

"Let's hear it."

"Okay. This is how it started. I was in the Enclave with Colonel Hanson when I got an anonymous call informing me of a possible Al Qaeda safe house in Brooklyn. The caller was very excited and warned me that they might be evacuating the house within the next hour. He gave me the address and disconnected. There wasn't time to go through police channels and organize a raid, so I asked Colonel Hanson to assist me in checking it out ..."

"Hold on, Mike," Hanson interrupted. "That's taking the brunt of responsibility on yourself."

"What's the difference, Sam? We're either heroes, or we're going to the clink."

"But we don't have to involve you. You didn't go into the house."

"It doesn't matter. Too many people saw me go there with you."

Hanson considered the alternatives and couldn't come up with anything else.

"It might work, Sam," Al said. "It explains why you went to the house. At least it sounds quasi-legal."

"What does that mean?"

"It means we may have a chance."

"Al's right, boss," Danowski added. "We don't have anything better."

After weighing their options, Hanson decided that it was their best choice. "Alright. We'll try it. Al. You and Ski don't have to know it, because you weren't there ..."

"We're as involved as you are, Sam," Al objected.

Danowski supported her. "I agree with Al, boss."

"You're both missing the point. If only Mike and I knew about the confidential tip and we were the only ones who made the decision to go to the safe house, no one else can contradict our story. The worst that higher authority could do would be to accuse us of overly aggressive decision making. But how could they fault success?"

The explanation seemed reasonable and they felt the beginning of a sense of ease, since the story might be acceptable. Some of their tension dissipated and they sat back and tried to relax while they waited for General Griffin to finish his round of calls.

Hanson mused aloud about something preying on his mind.

"I haven't really worried about nuclear issues since Mahmoud Ahmadinejad of Iran threatened to nuke the Saudi oil fields in 2012. If it wasn't for that rogue scientist, A.Q. Khan of Pakistan, who created a nuclear weapons black market and supplied any country that could afford his services, especially enemies of America, nuclear proliferation wouldn't be such a threat. Now it's come to our shores and we have no idea what else is out there … We were lucky tonight. Let's hope we'll be lucky next time."

"Did you look in the box, boss?" Danowski asked.

"No. I don't know how to handle nuclear material."

"What if there's nothing in there?"

"Then we have a big problem and Mike and I will be in real trouble."

Before he could go further, Griffin finished his calls and rejoined them. "I informed the Commandant and stayed on the line while he made emergency calls. The National Security Advisor briefed Valerie, who ordered Homeland Security to take charge, assisted by the FBI and the CIA

"The finger pointing has already begun and the FBI is blaming Homeland Security and the CIA for allowing nuclear material to be smuggled into the country. The FBI also accused you of exceeding your authority by not requesting them to come to the site immediately."

"That's ridiculous, sir," Hanson said. "If we stayed there, Al Qaeda would have known what happened right away and they might have sent suicide bombers to destroy the evidence."

"I know, Sam. I'm just trying to give you an idea of what we're in for. I only told the commandant the basic details, so you better have your story ready when the suits get here."

Hanson quickly outlined the explanation that only involved him and Lonigan.

"That sounds much more functional," Griffin said. "In this case, the powers-that-be may decide that the ends justify the means, although this administration is dangerously lacking in moral conviction. One more item: I have been ordered to turn the prisoner over to the FBI who will lead the investigation."

"That's a big mistake, sir," Al protested. "This is too important to leave to them. We should do the interrogation. We'll get everything he knows from him."

"I understand your thinking, Al, and I agree with you. However, orders are orders and these come from the top."

"He thinks Colonel Hanson saved his life. Can we at least keep him for a few days?"

"No, Al. From now on we have to cooperate completely with higher authority, regardless of how we feel … We have to be realistic and accept the obvious. We're not qualified or equipped to take this investigation any further. We'll have to rely on the FBI"

The emergency alert circuits on Griffin's phone went off, a rasping buzz rarely heard outside of readiness drills. Griffin turned aside and all Hanson could hear was "Yes, sir. Yes, sir," repeated over and over. Griffin's face was taut with suppressed anger when he disconnected.

"These are our orders," he said tersely. "I am to return to Washington immediately and report to the commandant. Colonel Hanson. You will isolate anyone who may have knowledge of the presumed nuclear material and provide suitable facilities for the FBI to question them. You will cease any military operations that go beyond the parameters of your mission in the Enclave. You and your staff will cooperate fully with the official investigation. You will confirm to the investigators that you called me and requested permission to assist Captain Lonigan in investigating a suspected Al Qaeda safe house, which I approved …"

"That's not right, Charlie," Hanson protested. "That will leave you holding the bag."

"Don't worry. It was the commandant's suggestion, Sam."

"Oh."

"The Corps looks after its own. I've got to go. Good luck."

They watched General Griffin stride out the door, back straight, head high, ready to face the brewing storm on the Potomac.

"You heard the man," Hanson said. "Let's get organized. You may as well stay here with us, Mike. The FBI will expect it."

"Fine, Sam."

"I have a suggestion, Sam," Al said.

"Go ahead, Al."

"Everyone who was with you on the raid saw the box, right?"

"Yes. But they didn't know what was in it."

"That doesn't matter. You ordered them not to discuss anything with anyone. They're not stupid. They know it was something important …"

"Make your point."

"If only five of us know about the box they could easily disappear us. It's more complicated to dispose of us if there are twenty-five of us who know."

"Your suspicions of your government might be considered unfounded by some … But not by me. It's a good idea. Now there's nothing more we can do right now, except wait for the inquisition to arrive."

Carver called just then. "Jed is still critical and in intensive care, but I think he'll pull through."

"That's great news, Carv. Thanks."

"I wish I could do more. We got some of them, didn't we, Sam?"

"Yes. We got the planners and their nest. Thanks for all your help."

"Mavis will rest easier now."

"So will Kyle and Tyrone. Go home. We'll talk tomorrow."

"Thanks, Sam. I might be able to sleep tonight."

<h1 style="text-align:center">56</h1>

I T DIDN'T TAKE LONG before the FBI arrived, always eager to take the credit whenever opportunity allowed. Agents Royce and Madison were at the guard post demanding admittance in record setting time. He told the Sergeant of the Guard, "Have them escorted to the conference room and place a guard at the door."

A moment later the sergeant called. "They're objecting to being confined, sir."

"They can wait on the street if they prefer."

"I'll tell them, sir."

There was no call back, so he assumed the FBI had accepted the confinement. He reminded himself not to reveal his murderous thoughts about Royce. As for Tish, she just didn't exist for him anymore.

About ten minutes later a convoy arrived out front and the guard alerted him that it was Homeland Security and a FEMA hazardous material team in full protective gear, with haz-mat trucks. The haz-mat team milled around their vehicles, then rushed to the door, protesting vigorously when they were stopped by the guards.

Hanson ordered them escorted to the conference room, where they immediately began arguing with the FBI The Homeland Security honcho demanded to see the commanding officer and the guard relayed the message. Hanson instructed Danowski to tell them that he was on a conference call at the highest levels and would join them as soon as possible. The invocation of 'the highest levels' partially mollified the rank conscious group, who were seething at being told to wait by a junior officer.

"They're not very happy being confined together in there, boss." Danowski reported.

"That's alright, Ski. This way they may be more upset with each other than with us."

The CIA agents showed up next and made no objection to waiting in the conference room. Their belief in their inherent ivy-league superiority to the less well-bred members of the government insured that their condescending attitude would rile their colleagues, already agitated by what they perceived as insufficient respect for their positions.

Hanson knew he was sitting on a time bomb by making them wait, but he thought it was the best way to keep from struggling with each agency, one at a time. The arrival of an admiral sent by the Secretary of Defense, along with his aide, forced him to face the lions' den.

Hanson greeted Admiral Porter, who made a distinguished first impression with his military bearing, voluminous gold braid, and chest full of ribbons. Hanson saw that none of the ribbons were for combat, indicating that Porter was a political admiral. His aide, Captain Rutherford, also had not seen combat. Hanson knew from bitter experience that armchair warriors were the most officious, so he prepared himself for a difficult session, and said, "Follow me, please, Admiral."

They could hear voices raised in angry dispute before they got to the conference room. The guard at the door snapped to attention when he saw Hanson and stiffened even more at the sight of the dazzling gold braid. The guard opened the door smartly and Hanson stepped aside to let the Admiral enter first. The arguers fell silent at the approach of another service that would further complicate jurisdiction. Their baleful glances turned to Hanson, but before they could launch a frontal assault on him, Admiral Porter saved the day by diverting their attention.

"I am Admiral Porter and I'm here at the request of the SecDef to take charge of the situation."

There was a moment of stunned disbelief at the admiral's unexpected broadside. It didn't last long and the veteran bureaucratic infighters focused their ire on the pushy sailor who presumed to blithely sail in and take control.

The CIA haughtily sat back and observed the squabbling of lesser mortals. Hanson, for once in his outspoken career, resolved to stand mute until questioned.

The confrontation had the fuel to go on until exhaustion rendered the combatants senseless. Only Hanson and the CIA noticed the entrance of a civilian, who paused in the doorway and observed the raucous confrontation. Several aides and Secret Service agents hovered around her with arrogant amusement.

Hanson recognized the Special Assistant to the President, Jessica Hatcher, known in political circles as 'The Hatchet', for her fierce assault on anyone who distressed her master, Valerie. She was tall, thin and pale-skinned, as if she never got out of doors. She wore her dark hair in a tight bun and her dark blue power suit was the only concession to social convention. She had a scornful look on her face and emitted an aura of relentless opposition to anyone who threatened her. The quarrelers gradually became aware of her presence and subsided into an uneasy silence. When she had everyone's complete attention, she announced coldly, "I am Ms. Hatcher. I am here to take charge at the request of the President. I will read her written order.

"'November 16, 2015. The White House. I authorize Jessica Hatcher, Special Assistant to the President, to lead the investigation of the discovery of a possible nuclear threat to New York City. All concerned agencies and individuals will give Ms. Hatcher their complete cooperation and her requests will have the highest priority. Signed. The President of the United States. Valerie Beaumont'."

Hatcher coolly surveyed the room, allowed the message to sink in, then asked, "Any questions? Ladies? Gentlemen?" She obviously expected no response and looked at Hanson.

"Colonel Hanson?"

"Yes, ma'am."

"Ms. Hatcher will do."

"Yes, Ms. Hatcher."

"If everyone will be seated, Colonel Hanson will brief us." Even the CIA quickly sat. "Colonel."

Hanson proceeded to relate the Lonigan version of the raid, carefully omitting several details that might lend another interpretation to the action. Hatcher wouldn't allow any interruptions and listened attentively, without showing any reaction to the story.

When he finished, she asked, "Is there anything more, Colonel Hanson?"

"That's the gist of it, Ms. Hatcher. I think that should be enough for us to consider a suitable response."

"Thank you, Colonel Hanson. Questions? Ladies? Gentlemen?"

Everyone started yammering at once and Royce, glaring at Hanson, out-shouted the others. "How dare you attack a private residence? The military has no right to wage war without authorization. You should have notified the FBI immediately and let us deal with …"

Hatcher held up her hand, cutting him off.

"The only thing that concerns us right now is do we or do we not face a nuclear threat. I require constructive suggestions."

There was no quick response and she looked at Hanson. "Do you have anything to say?"

"Yes, Ms. Hatcher. Our first task should be for the experts to verify that we captured genuine nuclear material. Once that's determined, we can explore an action plan."

"I concur, Colonel. Does anyone disagree with that suggestion?" Again there was no response. "I see there is a haz-mat team here. Can you tell us if we have nuclear material?"

"Yes, Ms. Hatcher," the team leader replied, relieved at the possibility of not having to sit around much longer in their haz-mat suits. "We should move the material to our containment vehicle, where we can properly assess it."

"How long before you can tell us what we have?"

"Barring the unforeseen, twenty to thirty minutes, Ms. Hatcher."

"Please get started at once. Where is the material, Colonel?"

"In my office."

"Let's go then. Everyone else remain here and prepare written suggestions as to what we should do if the material is confirmed to be nuclear. Lead the way, Colonel."

Everyone stood respectfully while she exited, followed by the haz-mat team, a grotesque contrast in their bulky white protective suits to her trim appearance.

The team checked the box with their equipment for radiation emissions, then checked the room and its occupants who were pronounced contamination free. Hatcher ordered them to test the material and bring the results to Colonel Hanson's office, where she would be waiting.

They rushed off to their containment vehicle to examine the prize, as eager as science hounds with their first experiment. Hanson introduced Lonigan, Al and Danowski and Hatcher asked them to wait in the corridor. Hatcher waited until the door closed behind them.

"I heard of you before this episode, Colonel Hanson. You caused this administration and the President herself considerable public embarrassment."

"That was not my intention, Ms. Hatcher."

"I was under the impression that you had been reduced to the rank of sergeant."

"Actually, it was gunnery sergeant."

"Well?"

"Well what, Ms. Hatcher?"

"How do you explain your current rank?"

"I don't, Ms. Hatcher. You'll have to ask my superiors."

"You don't intimidate easily, do you Colonel?"

"Is that what you're trying to do, Ms. Hatcher?"

She looked at him appraisingly, then let out a brief snort of laughter. "Did you really think that your bullshit story would be believed?"

"I think that the facts speak for themselves, Ms. Hatcher," he answered calmly. "We captured nuclear material ..."

"That's not confirmed."

"And a prisoner who revealed the machinations of a nuclear plot, presumably targeting New York City. I didn't go into specific details about the firefight at the house because it's of minor importance compared to what we found."

"I don't doubt that there was a raid that led to violence. The real questions will be about the alleged confidential tip and how you responded to it ... You better hope that the material you captured is nuclear, otherwise you're in big trouble."

"We acted in what we believe were the best interests of the country."

"Then I'm sure you'll understand that one of the major issues we'll consider will be whether or not you used good judgment ... Do Captain Kent and Lieutenant Danowski have any involvement in this situation?"

"No, Ms. Hatcher."

"Then dismiss them and bring in this Captain Lonigan of the Police Department. I'd like to hear his version of the story."

Lonigan substantially related the same story, with more details about the tipster's information and the decision-making process once they were faced with a possible nuclear threat that had to be responded to immediately. He concluded, "I didn't go into the house with the Marines, so Colonel Hanson will have to tell you about that."

She eyed both of them skeptically. "So you decided on your own to attack a house in Brooklyn that might have been inhabited by innocent civilians."

"Not exactly on our own, Ms. Hatcher," Hanson said. "I consulted my commanding officer, General Griffin, who decided on the basis of the possible nuclear threat to approve our investigating the suspect's house."

"Do you think a Marine general has the authority to order the invasion of civilian property?"

"We all agreed that the situation warranted immediate action."

"Those could be your last words when you face a firing squad."

"We don't use firing squads anymore, Ms. Hatcher."

She smiled and he smiled back, a mutual respect forming.

The Sergeant of the Guard called. "One of those guys in the spacesuits is back, sir."

"Have him escorted to my office." Hanson turned to Hatcher. "The haz-mat team leader will be here in a minute."

"Then we'll know what we're dealing with. As I said earlier, you better hope it's nuclear."

"I hope it isn't," he replied.

"Why? That's the only thing that will save your ass."

"I'd prefer that there wasn't a nuclear threat to my country. The implications are terrifying."

The haz-mat team leader entered, then paused dramatically.

Hatcher impatiently demanded, "Well? Is it or isn't it?"

He was slightly miffed at being deflated in his big moment, but understood the importance of his announcement and stopped pouting. "We have positively identified the material as enriched uranium 235. Our preliminary assessment is that it has the signature of a P2 centrifuge, which indicates it was produced at the giant Iranian nuclear facility at Natanz. We concluded that there is enough material to make a low yield, nuclear device."

"That tears it," she muttered. "We have a genuine event to deal with … What will you do with this material?"

"We'll take it to our laboratory for further inspection and wait for disposition instructions."

"Alright." She handed him a card. "Call me immediately when you have more information."

The team leader started to go.

"One moment, please," Hanson said. "I'd like a receipt that confirms I transferred possession of the nuclear material captured in an Al Qaeda safehouse to FEMA."

She eyed him calculatingly. "Why do you want a receipt?"

"To make sure that there's an official record of captured nuclear material, in case anyone decides to cover up this event."

"Are you trying to cover your ass, Colonel Hanson?"

"This is a lot bigger than my ass, Ms. Hatcher."

"I think you can trust your government to handle this properly."

"I trust my government, Ms. Hatcher. It's certain individuals that I doubt."

"What if I refuse your request?"

"Then I'll just have to retake possession of the material and turn it over to the U.N."

"Are you threatening me?"

"No, ma'am. I'm trying to convince you of the importance of not letting this event disappear into the limbo of bureaucracy."

She nodded to the team leader. "Give him a receipt."

"I'd like it on a copy of your presidential order, if you please," he said softly.

She grinned. "You have balls of brass, Colonel."

"Thank you, Ms. Hatcher."

"Call me Jess," and she stuck out her hand.

He was not surprised by her firm grip. "Sam."

Hatcher went to the copier, made a copy and handed it to the team leader.

"Write the receipt," she ordered. When he finished, she took it and turned to Hanson. "Can he go about his business now?"

"Yes, Jess." Hanson waited until he left, then said, "I'd like you to sign it, Jess."

She laughed loudly. "I'm starting to believe the things I heard about you, Sam." She signed the document, which he folded and put in his pocket, Lonigan watching every movement with wide-eyed amazement. "Before we rejoin the others, Sam, is there anything you'd like to tell me that you wouldn't say in front of them?"

"I hope that everyone agrees that our highest priority is to find out if there is any more nuclear material in the country."

"What about retaliation if we prove that this was sponsored by Iran and the Saudis?"

"Our first need is to protect the homeland, then we can consider other issues."

"It's a pleasure to meet a military man who's not eager for war."

"Some of us know how to think, Jess."

"Not many. Do you think your prisoner can be helpful?"

"Possibly."

"Does he speak English?"

"Enough."

"Then I want to talk to him."

Dmitry was as eager to please as a puppy. "I thank again for saving me, General, sir."

"I'm a Lieutenant Colonel, Dmitry. Are you comfortable here?"

"Much. Is better than with nasty Arabs."

"Good. This is Ms. Hatcher. She is the Special Assistant to the President."

"Of all U.S.A.?"

"Yes."

Dmitry bowed. "My honor to meet boss lady."

"What is your name?" she asked.

"Dmitry Goncharov."

"Tell me about yourself."

"What want know? Where from? How old?"

"Tell me how you became involved with Al Qaeda."

"Was physics teacher in high school. Not enough money make for family to live, so borrow from Russian mafia. When not repay, they give choice. They take daughter, or I work off what owe. Not say how, but love daughter, so choose work off. They say work as science advisor in foreign country and while gone they help family.

"They take me to Denmark, then Mexico, where meet Arabs who smuggle across border. We walk in little river, then desert, where we meet SUV. Then long ride to New York Brooklyn, where they say work with uranium 235. Arabs angry when tell cannot make bomb. Hurt me. Say kill if not make. Then ask if I make with book help. Not want them kill, so say yes. Then colonel sir save me. I'm glad. Will help. Just worry family not safe."

Hatcher studied Dmitry without revealing her thoughts. "Is that what he told you, Sam?"

"Basically. He added a few more details."

"Do you believe him?"

"I need to know a lot more before I answer that. I have an interrogation team that can find out everything he knows."

"I'm afraid that won't be possible. The Justice Department has insisted that they are the only agency with jurisdiction over terrorists captured in the U.S."

"Can't Homeland Security override that?"

"Not in this case. The Director of the FBI made the arrangements with the National Security Advisor."

"That's too bad."

"Why?"

"They've been intimidated by the A.C.L.U. They place terrorist's rights above the safety of the nation."

"I think you're exaggerating."

"You'll find out the hard way, Jess."

"You sound like one of those right-wing reactionaries who are ready to suspend the constitution."

"The constitution wasn't carved out of stone. I think due process has to be negotiable when terrorists plan to nuke our country."

She stared at him appraisingly. "I'm beginning to get an idea where you're coming from. I'll see what I can do about interrogation, but don't count on it. Now it's time to hear what our colleagues have to say."

"What do with me, boss lady?" Dmitry asked.

"You help us. We'll help you," she said bluntly.

"I help."

57

THE JURISDICTIONAL DISPUTE was going full blast when Hanson and Hatcher reached the conference room. Hanson had to force himself not to react to Royce's grating voice. The volume of disagreement was sufficiently loud so that Marines passing in the hall deliberately slowed to overhear a few choice morsels.

The guard opened the door for them and whispered, "Semper fi, sir." Hatcher heard the comment and glared at him, but the guard just nodded politely to her and resumed his neutral duty countenance.

Hatcher murmured softly to Hanson. "I've never been able to make up my mind whether loyalty to a military leader is good or bad for the nation."

"True loyalty is a two-way street," he replied. "And in that case it's good and a military organization can't function well without it. One of the unfortunate failings of our system of government is the frequent lack of loyalty both ways."

"Who has your loyalty, Sam?"

"The troops who serve well. My trusted superiors. The Corps. The constitution."

"You didn't include the president."

"I'm loyal to the office, not necessarily the temporary occupant."

"You're not the cave man warrior who was described to me … I noticed that you omitted God."

"That's personal and we have padres in the Corps for that."

She wasn't sure if he was being impudent or sincere. Before she could question him further her secret service detail rushed to her like pet dogs urgent to greet the returning master and formed a protective phalanx, ready to ward off any threats, real or imagined. The angry voices trailed off and everyone looked at Hatcher expectantly. She paused for a moment to get their full attention.

"Ladies and gentlemen. This is an official statement. The material in question that we are concerned about has been confirmed by the FEMA experts to be enriched uranium 235 …" Everyone spewed out questions trying to outshout the others, except the CIA, who sat back smugly as if they knew it all along. Royce was the loudest of all.

Hatcher held up her hand for silence. "Before I left you earlier, I asked you to write down your suggestions as to our course of action if the material turned out to be nuclear. Who wants to go first?" Suddenly the aggressive representatives of their agencies were hesitant to participate in what they suspected might turn into a career threatening situation.

Hatcher waited for a minute and when no one responded, said, "Admiral?"

Looking more like a flustered midshipman, he reluctantly got to his feet and consulted what might have been a shopping list his wife had entrusted to him for an upcoming cocktail party. He hemmed for a moment, then read slowly, stumbling over half-formed thoughts. "We need to discover where the material came from. Then the civilian authorities must decide how to deal with the situation … We must explore every option before we consider resorting to military force."

A snicker, probably from the CIA, caused the Admiral's face to turn red.

"Do you have anything else to add, Admiral?"

"No, Ms. Hatcher."

"Then thank you."

He was grateful to escape being singled out so easily and sat down, wiping his sweating forehead with a large handkerchief, letting out a slightly audible sigh of relief. Royce held up his hand to be recognized, but Hatcher ignored his urgent waving and selected the CIA

"Let's hear from your agency next, gentlemen."

Their spokesperson slowly stood up, almost insolent with his casual attitude.

"I'll have to consult my superiors first, then verify the level of security clearance for anyone receiving privileged information."

Hatcher looked at him coldly. "That's not very helpful."

"We're restricted by certain parameters from discussing foreign operations," he replied, without the slightest hint of apology.

Hatcher realized that a power struggle was purposeless and turned to her aide, a young, competent looking black man, and instructed him to get the CIA agent's name, so she could deal with him another time. Then, once again ignoring Royce's now frantic waving, she pointed to Homeland Security.

A trim, attractive blonde in her early thirties, who looked as if she could jump right into a beach volleyball game, said crisply, "I'm Sandra Palfrey, regional director of the tri-state area. Our first requirement is to get additional verification that the material is in fact uranium 235. Once that is confirmed, we must establish the origins of the material, how it got to the purported terrorists, how they got it into the country and what their intentions were. If this indeed proves to be a valid threat, we must present our findings to the National Security Council, who will then determine the appropriate response. Homeland Security will do everything it possibly can to facilitate the investigation into this most serious situation. Thank you."

Now that Royce knew he would speak next, he composed himself so that he would be fully prepared to uphold the honor of the FBI in front of their rival agencies. When Hatcher finally signaled him, he rose pontifically and raised his arms so that in anyone but a bureaucrat it would be a benediction. That elicited snickers from the CIA, who smirked at his impotent glare. He quickly forgot the assault on his dignity in the pleasure of once again occupying the spotlight.

"As you all know, the FBI has jurisdiction over all investigations of domestic terrorism. My director has entrusted me with the responsibility of carrying out that task in this case ..."

"I'm not sure that it's purely a domestic issue if the terrorists are foreigners," Palfrey commented.

"I don't have time for jurisdictional disputes, Ms. Palfrey. If you have a problem with the allocation of authority, take it up with my director."

Palfrey was ready to argue the point, but Hatcher cut her off. "We can discuss that later. Right now I want to hear from the FBI Please continue, Agent Royce."

"Our preliminary inquiry indicates that an illegal military operation was carried out, resulting in the loss of civilian life, damage to property and the unlawful detainment of an individual." He glanced at Hatcher to assess her response, but she was watching Hanson for a reaction. He was aware of her gaze and maintained a polite and slightly distant expression.

Royce took out his notepad and read, "We will thoroughly investigate this incident and present our findings to the U.S. Attorney for further action. We request the immediate transfer of the detainee to our custody. We require Colonel Hanson and Captain Lonigan to give us a list of the names of all personnel who participated in the incident. We will question everyone involved and determine whether or not they violated the law. If it is determined that violations of the law took place, we will obtain warrants from the U.S. Attorney for the arrest of any violators, who will be held for trial in a federal court. Thank you."

Hatcher was annoyed that Hanson was right when he suggested that none of the agencies would give the highest priority to the search for possible additional nuclear material. She was also dismayed that she hadn't thought of that herself and that she might have casually dismissed Hanson as a troublemaker and an ongoing problem for the administration, rather than a capable individual. She was appalled that the sophisticated, professional anti-terror agencies were oblivious to the most important problem they faced, while a controversial Marine saw things so clearly. She knew that the President would accept the FBI's agenda as a practical solution to a difficult problem, but she also knew that Hanson was right. She briefly considered allowing a coverup to avoid a crisis, and throwing Hanson to the jackals to appease the various agencies. The image of a nuclear fireball consuming an American city deterred her and she immediately rejected that option, however much it might have benefited Valerie to complete her lame-duck term without a major crisis and let Zach Plant inherit the problem.

Hatcher gave her full attention to her expectant audience. "Ladies and gentlemen. I want to thank you and your respective agencies for your prompt response to a federal emergency. This group will convene tomorrow morning at 9:00 a.m., at the Federal Building, in the main FBI conference room. Please bring anyone from your agencies who can be of direct help in further developing our objectives. Please clarify the initial suggestions that you presented today and prepare a priority action plan to search for possible additional nuclear material in our country. I will see all of you in the morning."

Each group was startled at their dismissal while they were still trying to assess the implications of her statement for their agencies.

Only Royce was obtuse enough to question her. "What about our legal investigations? Should we postpone them?"

"I believe I specifically said I wanted a written proposal in the morning."

"What about the prisoner? I want custody of him right now. The director arranged it with the national security advisor …" He trailed off weakly at the look on her face.

"We'll consider your request in the morning," she said coldly. "Thank you for coming." Everyone quickly left, eager to avoid her well-known temper.

Hanson stood calmly while Hatcher conferred with her aides, and her secret service detail eyed him warily. He finally got tired of her gamesmanship.

"Is there anything further I can do for you, Ms. Hatcher?"

"I'll be with you in a moment, Colonel."

"Yes, ma'am," he replied.

She glared, finished what she was saying to her aides, then said, "We haven't eaten for a while, Colonel, so that's next on our agenda."

"We'd be pleased to have you and your staff dine with us in the mess hall," he offered.

"That's very courteous of you, Colonel. We're staying at the Waldorf, in the Presidential Suite. Would you care to have dinner with us there?"

He quickly considered the risks of facing them alone.

"Thank you, Ms. Hatcher. May I bring my staff?"

"I wasn't thinking of anything so formal. Perhaps we can talk here for a few minutes instead."

"Certainly, Ms. Hatcher. Shall we go to my office?"

"Yes." She told her aides to wait in the car and squelched the objections of the Secret Service to leaving first without her. "I think I'll be safe with the Marines."

Hanson held the door for her, but not her chair. When she was seated, she said, "It appears that you are the only one who thinks our highest priority is searching for possible nuclear threats."

"My staff and superiors agree with me."

"I'm afraid that your rogue operation has disturbed a lot of influential people."

"I resent that description, Ms. Hatcher," he said quietly.

"What would you call it?" she asked.

"Necessary and appropriate. We produced results."

"Are you claiming that the ends justify the means?"

"In this case, yes."

"The FBI thinks you broke the law and should be prosecuted. The other agencies think you over-stepped your authority."

"I did my duty, Ms. Hatcher, and I will do it again, if I have the opportunity."

"Regardless of consequences?"

"That will be determined by what's at stake. If there's a nuclear threat to my country, I'll do whatever is necessary to avert it."

"You may be surprised to learn that I agree with you completely, Colonel," and she observed him closely, looking for a reaction.

He replied without a change of expression. "I'm glad that someone in our government has the common sense to see the obvious."

"There are still a few of us," she replied.

She paused thoughtfully for a moment and he studied her, beginning to understand that she had such an imposing reputation because in the land of the uncertain the decisive were feared. His admiration for her was growing, but he didn't know her well enough to reveal it and just watched her patiently.

"I will advise the president that we must urgently launch an immediate search for nuclear material throughout the country."

"Will she believe you?" he asked skeptically.

"Yes. We will involve every possible agency that can help; federal, state and city, and we'll use every resource available to the best of our ability."

"If I can help, just let me know."

"I don't think we'll need the Marines, but I'll keep you in mind. Can you get any useful information from your prisoner by tomorrow morning?"

"I don't know, but we'll try our best."

"Royce will have complained to the director by now and he'll be complaining to the national security advisor. You'll probably have to give up the prisoner in the morning."

"We'll do what we can. I'll tell you what we find out at the meeting."

"No, Colonel. Your presence will not be required. I'll call you at eight a.m. for the information. Now, on behalf of President Beaumont, we thank you and your troops for your exemplary service. Goodnight."

He was taken aback by the abruptness of her departure and realized that he would have no further participation in the nuclear crisis. The only contribution he might still make would be if he gleaned useful information from Dmitry. He had no idea if he, Lonigan and the troops who went on the raid would be prosecuted for their actions. The thought of possibly going to prison was depressing and for a moment he gave into despair, then forced himself to pull out of that negative state of mind and focus on other things. He buzzed Danowski, who had been waiting nearby.

"Send in Captain Lonigan, please, Ski."

Lonigan was a refreshing change from the people he had just met with.

"Thanks for all your help, Mike. Ms. Hatcher is going to recommend to the president that the search for nuclear material in the country be given the highest priority. We'll see what happens."

"What about our version of the raid?"

"That's a wait and see. You've done a great job. Go home and we'll talk in the morning."

"Thanks, Sam. I'll work with you anytime." They clasped hands, then said goodnight.

Danowski poked his head in. "How did it go tonight, boss?"

"They may not hang us."

"That's reassuring. Did they buy your story?"

"We'll find out in the next few days. In the morning I want you to prepare the paperwork for promoting Le Beau to master sergeant. Also, put a letter of commendation in everyone's file who was involved in today's action, including yourself."

"Thanks, boss. What do I say it was for?"

Hanson thought for a moment. "Make it for exemplary conduct in a firefight with Al Qaeda."

Danowski nodded. "That'll work."

"Find out how Moskowitz is and let me know before you go off duty."

"She's fine, boss. I checked on her a little while ago. Doc Carver gave her some pain pills after he treated her and as the saying goes, 'she's feeling no pain'."

"Good. Thanks, Ski."

"You look beat, boss. Why don't you call it a night? I'll hold the fort."

"I need to talk to Al first. Ask her to come to my office."

Al looked as tired as he felt and she slumped in a chair in a decidedly unmilitary posture. "You look exhausted, Al. Why don't you go home and get some sleep?"

"Look who's talking."

"Do I have to make it an order?"

She grinned impishly. "Don't be my C.O., Sam. I want to know what happened tonight."

"I'll tell you in the morning."

"I can't wait until then," she snapped impatiently.

"You're being insubordinate."

"Yes, Sam. But I don't do it often."

He finally grinned back. "Alright." He outlined what each agency rep had said, going into particular detail about Admiral Porter, the ineffectual representative of the Navy. He avoided any personal comment about Royce, confining himself to relating his accusations of criminal wrongdoing and his demand for the prisoner.

"He sounds like he's out for blood," she said.

"He won't rest until he hangs us high."

"What are we going to do about him?" she asked.

"I'll get to that. Fortunately for us, he's just a bureaucrat who's only a threat because he knows how to use the system."

Fatigue caught up with him and he paused for a moment.

"I'm sorry, Sam. I didn't mean to pressure you."

"You have a right to know."

"Then correct me if I'm wrong, but I bet no one said how urgent it was to look for more nuclear material."

"I regret to say yes. But there's a surprise. Hatcher agreed with me and said she would recommend to Valerie that they give the highest priority to the search for nuclear material."

"I thought she was Valerie's pit bull? She should hate you."

"Apparently she has a mind of her own and understands the danger. Whether Valerie will let her do anything about it is another question."

"You've got to be kidding, Sam. Even Valerie should recognize a nuclear threat."

"She may not want to deal with it and prefer to leave it for Zach."

"That's scary."

"Yes."

"What can we do to help the search?"

"Nothing. Our participation is no longer required."

"You mean that's it for us?"

"Yes, Al."

"That's crazy. We discovered the threat. We captured the nuclear material. We've accomplished more than all the security agencies combined."

"You're right. But it's out of our hands now and there's nothing we can do about it."

"That sucks. They need us."

"That's the way it is, Al. We have to stand down."

Al muttered curses softly and he gave her a minute to get used to the situation. "There is one thing we can do."

"What?" she asked hopefully.

"We have to turn Dmitry over to the FBI in the morning, but we can question him until then. Maybe we can learn something that will be helpful."

"Good. I'll get Le Beau."

"Not this time, Al. He knows I saved his life, so I think he'll cooperate. You and I will question him."

"Sure, Sam. Do you think he knows anything about additional nuclear material?"

"If he does, we'll find out."

She looked at him pensively. "Now that we're officially no longer participating in the nuclear crisis, what will they do to us?"

He considered her question carefully. "If we're lucky, they'll buy our story and treat us like heroes."

"And if they don't?"

"Then the story won't hold up when they question the troops. There are too many contradictions."

"Like what?"

"I said we were on patrol, but we left from the barracks. Why were we dressed in civvies? There are too many other loose ends, but at least they won't find out about you and Blakney."

"I'm not worried about myself," she said indignantly.

"I know. But you won't to be able to help me if you're in the cell next to mine."

She nodded begrudgingly, sat there brooding for a while, then asked quietly, "What about Royce? I know that you and Jed hold him responsible for the deaths of Kyle and Tyrone. You aren't going to let him get away with it."

He took a deep breath. "As Jed was lying in my arms, he made me promise to kill Royce. I intend to keep that promise."

"I knew it. I'll help you."

He shook his head. "I don't want you involved in this. What you did earlier tonight was in the service of your country. Killing Royce will be murder."

"I know that, Sam, but Kyle and Tyrone were also my family. I couldn't live with myself if I didn't avenge them. Besides, you need my help. You can't do it alone. How would you do it? Walk right up to him on Federal Plaza and whack him? I'm an experienced hit woman now. I'll guide you until you make your bones."

He finally managed a weak grin as he gave in. "Alright."

"Thanks, Sam. You can always rely on me."

He hesitated for a moment, searching for the right words. "This is not what I meant for you, Al. I planned a long, honorable career for you that would let you use your considerable abilities to serve your country. Now I'm recruiting you for murder."

"I don't see it that way. First of all, I'm volunteering. Even insisting. Others may not see it the way I do, but I know I'm serving my country honorably. In the last few days I've lost most of my family. I'm running out of tears for my country and my loved ones." She took his hand. "I can't afford to lose you."

"You're all I have left, Al," he said softly. "I don't want anything bad to happen to you."

She grinned jauntily. "Why didn't you tell me that before I joined the Corps?"

He smiled back. "I didn't know it would come to this. We might even be dismissed from the Corps."

"Then I guess we could do hits for hire," she said lightly.

"I'm glad you can joke about it."

"It's either that or tears and I'm tired of crying."

"Then we'll go to the firing squad with a smile."

"I'll follow you anywhere, Sam. Even there."

"Let's hope it doesn't come to that."

"Will I be able to request a last cigarette?"

"You know that smoking kills, Al."

"So now my exalted leader is a comedian?"

"Not really. But I'm also running out of tears. Everything's so uncertain that the only way to endure may be to laugh at our suffering."

ABOUT THE AUTHOR

Gary Beck has worked as a theater director and an art dealer, when he couldn't earn a living in the theater. He has also been a tennis pro, a ditch digger, and a salvage diver. His original plays and translations of Moliere, Aristophanes and Sophocles have been produced off-Broadway. His poetry, fiction, and essays have appeared in hundreds of literary magazines, and his published books include 37 poetry collections, 14 novels, 4 short story collections, 1 collection of essays, and 7 books of plays.

YOU MIGHT ALSO ENJOY

SEA OF BETRAYAL

Mitchell Sam Rossi

Two men. A father and a son. Their destinies separated by forty years, yet secretly bound by the most daring covert operation ever undertaken by America's silent service.

Available from Paper Angel Press in
hardcover, trade paperback, and digital editions

paperangelpress.com